Beyond the Cattle Arch

Beyond the Cattle Arch

John David Harris M.Ed

Matador
9 Priory Business Park,
Wistow Road, Kibworth Beauchamp,
Leicestershire. LE8 0RX
Tel: 0116 279 2299
Email: books@troubador.co.uk
Web: www.troubador.co.uk/matador
Twitter: @matadorbooks

ISBN: 978 1788035 705

British Library Cataloguing in Publication Data.
A catalogue record for this book is available from the British Library.

Printed and bound in the UK by TJ International, Padstow, Cornwall
Typeset in 11pt Georgia by Troubador Publishing Ltd, Leicester, UK

Matador is an imprint of Troubador Publishing Ltd

In loving memory of my mother and father,
John & Violet, who faithfully served the people of
Portslade between 1918 and 1952.

Chapter 1

THE BEAUTIFUL SUMMER of 1947 had slowly matured into an early golden autumn and the first rays of a new morning sun heralded yet another glorious day. As it slowly rose above the neighbourhood rooftops, the last shades of night fled away towards the east while the low sunlight sent long fingers of shadow across the narrow little streets. It was about 7.30am and the small terraced properties stood quiet yet expectantly as their windows reflected the early morning brilliance. Local pigeons resting high up among the chimney stacks remained hushed and, somehow, subdued, oblivious to the radiance that was creeping up on them. Only the slight movement and gentle cooing of a few indicated any sign of life in the whole neighbourhood.

It was Tuesday 7th October and at this early hour not even a gentle breeze disturbed the stillness but inevitably the tiny streets gradually became more active, with the first real sign of life being the local milkman as he went about his rounds. Always on

1

time, his faithful customers appreciated his reliability with many of them having been with him for longer than they would care to remember. His real name was Jack Harper but he was sometimes affectionately referred to as 'Bottles'. The local people saw him as almost a permanent part of their environment.

Being a First World War veteran sergeant, he was perhaps more appreciative than most of the tranquillity afforded by early morning daybreak. In fact, he would even sometimes stop in the middle of his work and gaze up at the blue untroubled skies and compare them with those that had looked down on the Somme area in France on that first fateful day of July 1916. Although almost an unbelievable forty years ago, he still remembered it as the start of a battle unprecedented in human history for its ferocity and loss of life. On that occasion, the heavens were suddenly rent with exploding artillery shells which had defaced the blue with great drifting black clouds of cordite.

By now, however, he had been at work since well before dawn and paused for a moment to rest on the handlebars of his old delivery bike. Strapped to the front of this ancient contraption was a metal crate which, when fully loaded, could make for heavy going.

Jack had been a local tradesman in the area since his army discharge in 1917 and was familiar with virtually every street and alleyway for miles around. Although, at the moment, he was moving along

Gordon Road towards his little general store and dairy yard, which were situated at the corner and where he lived with his beloved wife Violet and their two children, John and Margaret. Almost certainly named after General Gordon of Khartoum, this particular road was very much his home patch.

In addition to the delivery of milk to virtually every front door in the vicinity, he could also recite the names and occupations of the residents, together with a lot more if he chose to do so, for gossip constituted common currency across the counter of his shop. Scandal, however, held little interest for him although he tolerated it knowing it went with the business.

Deep in thought, he suddenly found himself interrupted by a cheery voice:

"You'll never get the job done like that, young Jack!"

The milkman turned to recognise the familiar figure of one of his neighbours. Unheard, Mr Grimshaw, the local glazier, had just emerged from number 11 and was obviously on his way to start another day's work.

"Jim!" retorted the roundsman good-humouredly. "If I were to exchange this old boneshaker for your little van, then I'd get my work finished in half the time."

"Sorry Jack," grinned his neighbour. "That might sound an attractive idea, but I think I'll just stick with the status quo thanks."

Then, with a wry smile, he climbed into his little black trades van and pulled away. But it left a perplexed Jack wondering how on earth he could afford such a luxury in the austerity of post-war Britain.

After the brief encounter, he allowed his gaze to wander over the familiar street, which, he had to admit, was far from inspiring. Bright sunlight failed to conceal the prevailing drabness. If anything, it served to highlight the dreariness. Grey slate roofs and monotonous grimy brickwork were relieved only in part by the odd late summer rose. Even the narrow pavement was a dark, dull tarmac colour and held together with numerous patches and repairs which bore stark testimony to a lack of public money or the local district council's indifference.

In fact, many residents had long been thoroughly dissatisfied with the shabbiness and were acutely aware of living in what they considered to be the deprived part of town. In a sense, theirs was a justifiable grievance, for Portslade was an urban area effectively divided in two by a steep east-to-west railway embankment. Unquestionably, the area above the line enjoyed the higher standard of living, with housing which far surpassed the cramped conditions of Jack's vicinity. Why such a division of prosperity existed seemed an open question, and was a frequent topic of discontent in his little shop.

However the embankment constituted more than just a social partition, for it physically restricted residents' movements and had an adverse effect on trade. Although, with customers located everywhere, Jack had overcome the problem by making use of a small dark tunnel which passed directly under the railway. Situated close to his business premises, it allowed for the access of his trades bike but very little else. Larger vehicles had no alternative but to skirt their way round the edge of the town.

Known locally as the 'Cattle Arch', it was also a well-recognised landmark while, at the same time, enjoying a rather unsavoury reputation. Gloomy and forbidding even in broad daylight, its dank, cave-like interior could only be accessed down a long narrow twitten. Over the years, its very isolation had made it a haunt for latter-day spivs and other undesirables. Worse, it seemed completely off-limits to the local sanitation department; an inhibition not shared by the local dog population. Jack had never been quite sure why it was located in its current position but he did know it long predated the present town and assumed it had been built to comply with the dictates of some ancient right of way.

The tradesman, however, lived with a very real sadness, for although he thoroughly enjoyed his work and the interaction it afforded with his customers, he nevertheless wrestled with an insoluble emotional problem over his wife's unhappiness with having to live in such a run-down locality and her desire to live in the countryside among the fields and the trees. Unfortunately his hands were financially tied and there was little he could do. Sometimes he would bitterly recall her words, "We do not live as we'd like to, Jack, do we? But as we must." Every time he thought of the sadness in her voice, it turned the screw just that little bit tighter. Their living, however, depended on the location of his business, and with tens of thousands of young men returning to the job market at the end of World War Two, he knew that any other form of employment at his age would be out of the question.

The agonising dilemma was all the more painful because his wife was not only the great love of his life, but also his loyal and best friend who had stood by him through all the hardships of the war years. Moreover, while away on his rounds, she would hold the fort behind the counter of his little shop for hours on end. It was with these sombre thoughts that he endeavoured to pull himself together and return to base. There was, however, just one last call at number 6 to collect Mrs Miller's empties. Then his round would be complete.

Jack had often thought of this particular customer as being somewhat eccentric, for her sole purpose in life seemed to revolve around the welfare of the local pigeon population. Over a period, flocks of these birds had gravitated towards Gordon Road and Jack reckoned that, by now, they would probably number in their hundreds. Most of the time they spent just squatting high up on the rooftops among the chimney stacks, both of which bore mute witness to the whiteness of their droppings. However, when the occupant of number 6 appeared with their feed, they would rise in the air with a great flurry of wings and swoop down to monopolise the road in a frantic mass of feathered and flapping activity. Croaking and pecking, they would jostle and fight for every morsel.

Unquestionably, similar roads existed in the area but Jack knew they would be hard put to boast a single bird. The local benefactor's reputation, it seemed, had spread far and wide. Nevertheless, the pigeons formed part of the local scene and Jack often felt the road wouldn't be quite the same without them.

By 8am Jack had wheeled his trades bike round the bend in Gordon Road to draw level with his shop where his wife was already attending to customers. As always, she smiled and waved with a warmth that never failed to raise his spirits and somehow make all his efforts seem worthwhile.

Pleased as he was to see his shop so busy, he did occasionally question the volume of talk that often accompanied the most trivial of purchases – much of which was only questionable gossip anyway. While he would be the first to recognise the need for social interaction – particularly for the elderly and lonely – he did feel it could sometimes waste a lot of his wife's valuable time. However, his thoughts again became interrupted as his wife appeared in the shop doorway.

"Jack, love. Be an angel and fetch a fresh crate of milk from round the back. We've had an extra run on it this morning and I've sold out already."

So, waving in compliance, he made his way to the rear yard.

After opening the large iron gates, he propped his trades bike up against one of the outbuildings before proceeding to the main dairy block; a place stacked high with milk crates and where, as a one-man band, he worked long hours.

Meanwhile, back in the shop, his wife was greeting yet another early customer.

"Good morning Gwen," she said brightly. "What can we do for you today?"

Gwen, who lived three doors away, was a diminutive but sometimes fractious soul. Permanently dressed in a crossover floral pinafore, she tended to suffer from chronic arthritis in her fingers which had distorted both her hands: a feature which Violet found quite distressing. In her late forties, she could occasionally be quite tactless, and after casting a doleful eye at the empty milk crates, she observed testily:

"Well, I had hoped for a pint of milk but by the look of it I'm a bit late."

"Oh, don't worry." Violet hastened to assure her. "If you can hang on for a minute Jack will be back shortly with a fresh crate."

"Ah good," she sighed. "I really didn't want the hassle of traipsing up to the main shopping centre for just one item." Then, with an almost unbelievable insensitivity, she added, "It's different, isn't it, when you are up there for a proper shop." And then, not content with this barb, she glanced around the shop shelves. "Of course, you don't carry a very wide range of stock, do you? Pity."

Although by now quite familiar with her customer's inappropriate remarks, Jack's wife, nevertheless, began to feel it was a pity she had come into the shop in the first place. Hers was an understandable reaction because, during the war, and even in the following decade, commodities had been either severely rationed or unobtainable and, despite the shortages, Violet had always tried to make the little shop appear attractive; where there should have been groceries she had placed a graceful potted palm and even resorted to dummy cartons to fill out the gaps in her shelves, while such items that were available she'd always arranged with care and thought.

"You must realise, Gwen," she protested with a patience she didn't really feel, "that everything is in very short supply and my wholesalers are limited in what they can offer. Surely you must understand that's why the black market is still flourishing so well."

"I suppose," she replied, in her unmistakable Hartlepool accent. But then, looking through the shop window and seemingly oblivious to her tactless remarks, she observed brightly, "I do like your tree.

It's so beautiful at this time of the year with its white blossom and lovely fragrance."

Still miffed at her rudeness, however, Violet just about managed to nod.

"Yes, it's lovely, isn't it? Although, to be honest, it's in desperate need of pruning – isn't it, Jack? Jack...!"

But Jack had heard enough and made himself scarce while Gwen had moved on to the subject of the weather.

"I sometimes think, you know, that this is the loveliest autumn I can ever remember. It just seems to go on and on."

Her remark appeared to trigger Violet's memory.

"It's certainly been exceptional," agreed the shopkeeper. "Well, it has been up until now, that is, but I'm not sure how long we can expect it to last. Did you happen to hear the *Six O'Clock News* and forecast this morning?" Gwen, who obviously hadn't, raised her hands in a mock gesture of horror at even the suggestion of such an unearthly hour. "Well," continued Violet, "I might have got it wrong but there appears to be an unusual area of low pressure over the mid-Atlantic with large build-ups of black cloud and that," she winced, "means there's plenty of rain and it's probably coming our way."

However, before Violet could say any more there came an interruption in the form of a new arrival who had obviously overheard her last remarks. Bent by the toll of advancing years, his age somehow seemed accentuated by a perpetual droplet attached to the end of his nose – a feature poor Violet found quite repugnant and she often wondered why on earth he didn't use a handkerchief. She'd known him as Mr Baker from their earliest days in the shop and he'd been far from young then. Constantly out of breath and suffering from a weak heart, he would insist on smoking, which always made Violet feel guilty for selling him cigarettes.

"Ah, Violet my dear," he enthused. "I don't think you can have heard the whole bulletin."

"Well," she objected, "you didn't give me the chance to finish but – no – to be fair, that's quite true."

The old boy apologised but then stressed:

"It's really quite exciting because, from what I heard, Iceland has become so concerned over the scale and appearance of this build-up that they despatched an observation plane to investigate just what's going on." Pausing to catch his breath he then continued, "Apparently, the edges of this cloud are quite close to their shores. Anyway, it appears that, contrary to his instructions, the pilot actually flew directly into the cloud bank and hasn't been heard of since."

"Well," objected Violet, "I fail to see what's exciting about any of that. It's the pilot's family I feel sorry for."

But the 'excitement' suddenly appeared too much for the old boy and, wheezing and coughing, he gradually sank down onto the chair that Violet had thoughtfully provided for her more elderly customers.

"When you get to my age," he smiled through the wheezing, "you don't sit down. You just stand in front of the seat and let go."

"When you get to your age, Mr Baker," objected Violet, "you should know better than to smoke so much."

"Ah well," smiled Gwen waving her 'pinta', "I must be on my way before that nasty black cloud catches up with me."

With good-humour restored, the little group dispersed.

By midday, Mrs Grimshaw, the local glazier's wife whom Jack had encountered earlier, arrived to take over the shop until closing time. Violet was always grateful to see her because it allowed for time to catch up on household chores and, occasionally, help her husband with the deliveries. However, on this occasion, Mr Baker had aroused her curiosity and she decided instead to listen to the *One O'Clock News*.

One of Violet's attributes that had first captivated Jack had been her sensitivity, but it could be a dubious quality and one that often caused her a great deal of anxiety. In fact, as the latest News unfolded, she began to wish she hadn't listened in the first place because, for the remainder of the afternoon, she fretted desperately over what she had heard. Determined, however, to keep it to herself, she decided to concentrate on her chores until her husband returned.

By 8.30pm Mrs Grimshaw had closed the shop and, while her daughter Margaret was busy doing homework, Violet settled down to prepare the evening meal. Then, with a few minutes to spare, she relaxed in the small lounge behind the shop and reached for her current copy of *Woman's Own*. Jack usually got back around the same time as her son, John, who studied at Brighton Art College and, sure enough, right on the dot she heard the sound of her husband coming in through the back door. Dropping her magazine and in time-honoured tradition she rushed to welcome him with a kiss and a lingering hug, for theirs was a true and enduring love. Today, however, as he held her close, he sensed something was wrong.

"What's up love?" he asked gently – knowing only too well how easily she could become distressed.

"Am I that obvious?" she smiled. "Oh, it's just something Mr Baker said in the shop earlier."

"You mean the old boy with the dripping nose?" he grinned.

"Jack – that's not nice!"

But, all unrepentant, he replied:

"You know, one day, gravity is going to get the better of that drip."

Violet, however, refused to rise to the bait.

"Anyway," she persisted, "he was discussing something about a strange cloud that appears to be hanging over the mid-Atlantic."

She then went on to describe the loss of the meteorological plane.

"Well that's nothing to get upset about," he muttered. "I mean, so what? It was probably a navigational error. These things do happen. I'm sure there's nothing sinister about it. Flying has come a long way, but it's far from perfect."

But Violet was not placated so easily.

"But Jack, that's not all," she insisted. "The *One O'Clock News* really frightened me because now it appears that an American troop ship has also disappeared in the same region. That's nearly three thousand young men, Jack..." she stressed, "... just gone!"

At this, her husband's expression became more serious, but, nevertheless, he tried to remain positive.

"If that's true then it's tragic I must admit," he observed slowly. "But, at the same time, it's no good us fretting over something that's going on some two thousand miles away – I mean, there's nothing we can do about it anyway, is there? So," he added as he put his arm around her, "try not to worry over it too much. Remember it's a problem for the likes of President Truman and our Mr Attlee and not for the likes of Violet of a little corner shop."

"But, Jack," she protested tearfully, "we've barely come through the last horrific war and we're still existing on ration books – and, what about our son, John? He'll be among the first to be called up if there's another war. You don't think we're faced with some new threat from Russia, do you?" she added desperately. "I just couldn't face any more of it."

At this outburst, Jack drew her close again while at the same time acknowledging to himself that her fears had a certain justification, for when World War Two ended with the Germans' capitulation in 1945, it had left Stalin's divisions controlling most of Eastern Europe. In fact, many believed he'd only halted their further advances due to fear of the American atomic deterrent. Jack was also mindful that any expansionist hopes the dictator might still cherish would very much depend on his swift annihilation of American airfields in Western Europe in order to prevent any nuclear retaliation. It would further make a great deal of sense for the Russians to deploy some kind of Atlantic barrier to block any U.S. reinforcements. However, his wife was his immediate concern and he again did his best to reassure her.

"I think, you know," he answered brightly, "we really do need to keep this in some sort of perspective because the news media always tends to hype up the facts just to get your attention. So," he smiled, "why don't we put it on the back burner until tomorrow, but," he quipped, "let's not do the same thing with the evening meal."

And, with his arms around her shoulders, he led the way towards their little kitchen which also served as a their eating area. However, this part of the house tended to be dreary and far from inviting. It had little or no outlook and even on a bright day there was a constant need for electric light while the dilapidated late 19th century fitments were nothing short of an eyesore. It was an additional worry for Jack for he knew only too well how desperately his wife hated its claustrophobic atmosphere.

"Where's everybody?" he asked suddenly as he noticed that only two places had been laid.

"Well," she replied slowly, "Margaret's gone to bed early after a heavy day at school with her midterm exams; and John," she paused momentarily, "I'm not absolutely sure. He just said something about not waiting up for him so, at a guess, I'd say he's probably out with that Jill again." She hesitated reflectively. "Personally, I think he's getting far too involved. It's not that I don't like her, I do; but our John's barely twenty and for him to even contemplate taking on the responsibility of a girl with a young child is just too much... I don't know, I just think he's too young, that's all."

"Hey, wait a minute," observed Jack mischievously. "Aren't you forgetting something? Weren't you supposed to be too young for me? Well, at least you were according to your father and a fat lot of difference that made!"

"Mr Harper!" retorted his wife. "You're talking about an entirely different matter and well you know it."

The exact nature of the difference, however, eluded Jack and he changed the subject.

"As a matter of interest, have you ever stopped to think how that girl resembles you at the same age?"

"Oh, rubbish Jack. It's just the way she does her hair – that's all."

"I think there's a bit more to it than that," he smiled. "But, in any case, if our John feels anything like I did about you then our opinions will count for nothing."

"Well, let's be quite honest Jack," she protested bluntly, "you were just a silly old romantic who wouldn't take no for an answer."

Shepherd's pie was on the menu that evening and only after dishing up did she finally manage to sit down. Noticing her weariness, he leaned across the table and gently took hold of both her hands.

"Have I ever told you how much I love you?" he murmured.

"Well, for what it's worth Jack Harper, you have. Many times over! In fact," she added starting her meal, "you have my full permission to remind me as often as you like."

Their environment might have been dreary but they never allowed it to detract from their mutual happiness and, upon clearing the table and washing up, they headed for the foot of the stairs, hand in hand.

Chapter 2

THE FOLLOWING MORNING fell on Wednesday 8th October and daylight was still a long way off as Jack struggled out of bed around 3.20am. In doing so he took great care not to disturb his wife, whose working day did not start for another three hours.

Duly rising at 6.30am, Violet followed her normal routine with a leisurely bath before reaching for her dressing gown which, she knew only too well, had seen better days. Then, crossing the tiny landing, she tapped sharply on her son's bedroom door but only to draw the expected lack of response. Finally, peering inside, she was greeted by the usual incomprehensible grunt; a sound which came from an inert lump in the bedcovers and signalled the start of yet another long struggle to get him up.

"John!" she exclaimed. "Can you hear me? You know you have to be in college early this morning in order to catch up with your work. It's no good relying on that dreadful old car of yours because if it won't start you'll have left it too late for the bus to get you there on time." Doubtful if any of this had registered, she resorted to a final threat. "If you don't get up now John, I'm not going to call you again – I have far too much to do. You can just lie there and rot as far as I'm concerned."

But, as she turned to descend the stairs, she heard a faint plea.

"Mum, give me another five minutes then call me again."

However, his mother had had enough of his laziness and proceeded down the stairs while wishing her son could be a little bit more like her daughter, Margaret, who would, even now, be in the kitchen waiting for breakfast.

By 7.30am she had the shop open and breakfast prepared ready for Jack when he returned from the first of his deliveries while, half an hour later, Margaret was well on her way to school. But, with still no sign of John or her husband, their breakfast was just left to get cold. Feeling her efforts had been wasted, Violet crossed the hallway towards the shop where customers were already beginning to arrive. Her dual role of housewife and shopkeeper was well underway for yet another day. Entering the little store, she suddenly found herself unexpectedly face to face with Jill who, despite her reservations the previous evening, had to admit was an extremely attractive and stylish young woman; although Violet knew some uncharitable people in the local ossified community would only see her as provocatively glamorous. Violet, on the other hand, saw her as a fashion-conscious young lady who presented herself with imagination and taste.

Older than John by several years, Jill had emphasised her slim figure with close-fitting black trouser slacks together with a spotless long-sleeved white blouse tied in at the cuffs; while her thick shoulder-length blonde hair was offset by a black neckband. In addition, her flawless skin contrasted with the depths of her sparkling blue eyes. So, Violet could well appreciate her son's interest in such a feminine vision while at the same time feeling a twinge of remorse at the thought of her own fading youth.

Smiling, 'the vision' asked after John's whereabouts but, when informed he was not yet up, it drew a quick expression of frustration.

"Oh, that's just not good enough!" she exclaimed irritably. "He absolutely promised me last night that he would drive us both to college by 8.30am. We'll never make it now if he's still in bed," she added disgustedly.

Violet looked sympathetic.

"Don't tell me. I have the problem every morning and, to be quite frank, I'm browned off with it, but," she stressed raising the counter flap, "why don't you have a go – come on through and see if you can drag him out of his pit."

Then, as Jill made her way through the rear shop door, Gwen arrived and reached for her morning 'pinta'.

"Well, that nasty black cloud didn't get you after all then, Gwen?" quipped Violet.

Her diminutive customer frowned.

"Well, not yet anyway." But looking past Violet she nodded towards the rear door. "Was that Rita Bower's eldest daughter? You know, the one from 62 Norway Street."

Violet looked slightly askance.

"Yes, as it happens," she replied, somewhat disconcerted by her customer's tone. "John's taking her to college. Well – at least he will be if he deigns to get out of bed."

"Eeeh!" exclaimed Gwen in her high-pitched northern accent. "I know it's none of my business, but I'm surprised your boy has anything to do with her." She leaned forward on the counter with a conspiratorial air. "I suppose you realise that both she and her mother are the scandal of their street?"

"I did have some idea to that effect, Gwen," retorted Violet. "Unfortunately, there's little that escapes me in this business, but it's something I choose not to dwell on."

However, undeterred, her customer refused to pass up the opportunity for further scandalmongering.

"Well," she continued, "I'm not one to gossip, but the way that mother of hers cavorted about with the Canadian soldiers while her husband was fighting abroad was nothing less than a public disgrace. Such a fine man too; tall and handsome. Did you know he was parachuted behind enemy lines at Arnhem and was lucky to get back alive? Such a shame. Eventually, of course," she added almost gleefully. "Mrs Bower got pregnant and produced a baby girl." Gwen shook her head. "But when her husband was demobbed he was absolutely furious. Well, you can understand it, can't you? Anyway, he walked out but only after the most terrible scene. I can't say I blame him. But then," stressed her customer, "if that wasn't enough, that daughter of hers goes and does the self-same thing with another complete stranger; so now there are two illegitimate children in that household. I ask you, what sort of morality is that? I don't know, but if I were your John..."

"Well," countered Violet with a touch of irritation, "you're not my son and, in any case, he's quite capable of making his own decisions about such matters. But I will say this – I have never found that family to be anything but pleasant and, what's more, those two girls are always immaculately dressed and spotlessly clean."

"Huh!" grunted her customer. "It's moral cleanliness that counts. Mark my words, no amount of scrubbing can wash away that kind of dirt." Despite herself, Violet began to feel her hackles rise at Gwen's uncharitable onslaught but she still persisted. "Rita's one of Jack's customers, isn't she?" Gwen shook her head again. "I tell you, I wouldn't let any husband of mine within a hundred miles of that woman."

"Well," retorted Violet, "it's not your husband so

you've nothing to worry about but I can tell you this – my Jack and I have something so special that no other woman could ever hope to get near it."

Still full of negatives, Gwen wagged a warning finger as she went to take her leave.

"I tell you, you can never be sure with a woman like Rita Bower."

Then, with her 'pinta' in hand and much to Violet's relief, she was gone.

Meanwhile, Jill had finally managed to prise John out of bed and get him downstairs, but it was far too late for any thoughts of breakfast. Looking dishevelled and disaffected, he led a quick dash to his little old pre-war Ford parked beyond the side gate. The ancient car had originally surfaced in one of Jack's rented garages, where the landlord had been only too glad to offload it on to his new tenant. Finally, after years of neglect, the car ended up in the backyard of his dairy where John had come to the rescue and gradually nursed it back to life. However, the vehicle had always remained notoriously difficult to start and today was no exception, which proved the last straw for John, who, muttering unmentionables, hauled himself out from behind the steering wheel.

"It's no good, Jill," he exclaimed irritably. "I'll have to crank the wretched thing. If we're late, we're late – it's just too bad."

She smiled for she had long come to realise that John was far from his best first thing in the morning. She'd also found that, despite his naturally protective disposition and the generally easy way he had with people, patience was not among his virtues.

Strangely enough, although they were virtually neighbours and attending the same college, that was not, in fact, how they had first met.

After the euphoria and street parties marking V.E. day in 1945, England had settled down to a continued period of austerity; a situation exacerbated when America suddenly withdrew its financial aid. Things were destined to remain bleak for some time with the rationing of many items extending well into the early fifties. Indeed, the stagnated economy and shortage of most commodities combined to make the post-war period a depressing experience.

Gradually, however, as people regained their 'breath', cracks began to appear in the monotony and among the first of these was a much trumpeted and anticipated reopening of the Regent Ballroom in Brighton. With a new swing band reflecting the American trend, its first dance was scheduled for the Christmas Eve of 1946 and it attracted the younger generation in droves.

By 9pm the dance floor had become a seething mass of revellers swaying excitedly in an atmosphere of dim lights, perfume and cigarette smoke. It was among them that John first caught sight of Jill – a graceful fair-haired girl who was dancing with what appeared to be a young army officer. In fact, as she glided past with her long silky blonde hair and black sheath dress, he found it difficult to avoid staring.

Moreover, after glancing around the floor, he realised just how outstandingly attractive she was compared to the other girls and, like his father before him, he experienced the same instinctive reaction. However, he knew that to act on it might prove a daunting proposition for, although well over six feet and no mean performer on the dance floor, he was nevertheless very conscious of not sharing his father's good looks. And that was without the additional problem of her partner.

Even so, the current dance offered an excellent opportunity for such a move because it allowed existing couples to be approached with a request to exchange partners. Basically, it was a good idea and designed to encourage social interaction, but it also carried the risk of a humiliating refusal. So, even though this might be his only chance, he hesitated. Finally, biological temptation became too great and he found himself edging across the crowded floor to tap the girl's uniformed partner on the shoulder. Fortunately, the brief but painful uncertainty that followed was quickly relieved by her smiling acceptance of his offer, although what he failed to see was the malevolent expression that crossed the face of her deposed partner.

The reward proved well worth the risk as he slipped his arm around her slender waist just above the fullness of her hips, for only then did he fully appreciate the extent of her allure. Barely five and a half feet tall, she glanced up at him with wide and seductive eyes.

"That was very courageous of you."

Overawed by her sudden closeness he found himself struggling.

"I almost didn't make it," he admitted lamely.

"Well," she smiled with a suppressed giggle, "you're tall enough and my partner didn't raise any objections, did he?"

John paused, still uncertain of himself.

"To be honest with you, it wasn't him that really worried me."

"You mean you weren't sure if I'd accept?" she teased.

John pulled a tight-lipped smile.

"Something like that, I guess."

"Well, I did – didn't I?" she insisted with the same mischievous look.

But then, before he could reply, the music suddenly came to an end and, to his dismay, she quietly thanked him before slipping away across the crowded floor.

Disappointed, he could only watch her elegant figure disappearing among the mass of noisy revellers. Reluctantly he turned to make for the bar and the consolation of a cigarette and a drink. Leaning on the counter he drew in a deep draught of smoke as he nursed feelings of rejection while acknowledging the probability that he had overestimated his chances in the first place. As he aimlessly contemplated the rows of bottles lining the rear of the bar, his misery was suddenly interrupted.

"Nice looking girl you were dancing with there, John, if I may say so."

Exhaling a thin stream of cigarette smoke, he turned to see an old friend.

"Hello, Doug. How are you doing?" Then, without waiting for a reply he quickly added, "Yes, I thought for a moment..." he shrugged. "But she just didn't seem interested enough to stay around." He looked out over the dance floor. "She was something special Doug. Something very special. You don't often see a girl like that, but, if I'm honest, I'm afraid she was out of my league."

"Well," answered his friend, "she danced with you once. I'd at least give it another try."

John shook his head and drew on his cigarette again.

"No point, Doug. She's with some army bloke – a lieutenant by the look of it. I can't just go over there and butt in."

"If you look across towards the entrance," observed his friend, "I think at the moment she's sitting there on her own. This could be your chance. Honestly, if I were you, I'd give it a go. I mean, what have you got to lose?"

"My front teeth for a start!" smiled John.

"You mean that army bloke? You've gotta be kidding. You'd flatten him!"

"You've got me all wrong, Doug."

His friend shook his head knowingly. "I don't think so, John."

So, taking his friend's advice and although feeling very far from confident, John once again weaved his way across the floor while knowing only too well he could face outright rejection or some sort of violent confrontation with her companion. However, to his immense relief, as he approached the girl's table she looked up and smiled.

"May I?" he asked, indicating the chair opposite.

"Please," she invited. "Be my guest."

Unable to believe the warmth of her reception, he reached nervously for his faithful Woodbines and placed one between his lips.

"I'm afraid," he began hesitantly, "I didn't even get the chance to say hello."

"No thanks," she declined as he offered her a cigarette, "but please do feel free yourself – and yes, I'm sorry I rushed off, which was silly really because I was actually quite glad to see you." She leaned forward for a moment as if to share a confidence which allowed her long hair to brush seductively against the tabletop. Unlike current fashion, she had emulated the movie star Veronica Lake and allowed it to grow down past her shoulders. Blonde and luxurious, it had been brushed to a high sheen and enhanced her already sensual appeal. "You see," she explained, "I really only came here this evening with my friend Jenny to have a little fun, but this lieutenant has tried to monopolise me and I'm just not interested." She paused. "But I mean, how do you tell a person something like that without hurting their feelings?" Again, she paused before adding despondently, "I don't even know what's happened to my friend. She's probably just given up and gone home on her own – which makes me feel awful."

"I'm afraid," observed John bluntly, "you sometimes have to say these things outright or risk getting lumbered!" He turned in his chair to look around. "Anyway, where is this guy?"

But then, seeing her expression, quickly realised he hadn't turned quite far enough, because immediately behind him came the sound of a belligerent but cultured voice.

"Excuse me, but you're in my seat." Moving around in his chair, John suddenly found himself confronted by the man in question. Immaculate in his tailored military uniform and carrying two glasses of wine, he was obviously very irritated. "I'm sorry," he continued in the same exasperated tone, "but I happen to be with this young lady so would you please be good enough to move?"

Like his father before him, John found this sort of confrontation difficult to handle without being either aggressive or outright violent. He glanced enquiringly across at his new acquaintance, but she just looked embarrassed and shrugged. Hooking his elbow over the back of his chair, he dragged slowly and deliberately on his cigarette before exhaling the smoke in a gradual provocative stream.

"I think, soldier," he murmured quietly and without getting up, "it's time you were somewhere else." But, seeing the furious expression on the officer's face, he added pointedly, "If, however, you want something different...!"

In the tense atmosphere that followed, John held himself ready for trouble while people at nearby tables were beginning to pick up on the unpleasantness. However, observing John's demeanour, the lieutenant decided on probably the wiser of two options and handed the young lady her drink before turning to walk away. As John turned his attention back to the girl, he became shocked to see how pale and shaken she appeared.

"I'm sorry," he apologised while slowly getting to his feet. "The last thing I wanted to do was to cause you any distress – it's just that – well, I didn't quite know what to do and I'm afraid I got it wrong."

And, with that, he reluctantly made to leave.

"Oh, there's no need to rush off," she assured him. "He needed to be told and I hadn't got the courage – but I hate scenes like that and the possibility of violence. Oh, I know how some women admire aggressive men but," she observed wearily, "I'm afraid it frightens me." It was only later that John would discover just why she was so averse to discord, but in the meantime, his world exploded into a new dimension as she rose to join him. "I think this is the last waltz," she smiled holding out her hand. "So, shall we make the most of it?"

Unable to believe it could be happening, he drew her close as they glided their way across the dance floor. Moving gently to this softer music and the closing magic of the evening, he suddenly heard her gently murmur:

"Jill."

Puzzled, he looked down into her shining eyes.

"Jill," she repeated softly. "That's my name. I just thought you might like to know for future reference."

The Sunday following Christmas had found them strolling hand in hand through the local recreation park. It was 10am and a mild, beautiful day for the time of year with a pale morning sun that still hung low in the eastern sky. The area was deserted and quiet apart from distant chiming church bells and the mellow twittering of various birds, both of which added to a prevailing sense of tranquillity. Even the air seemed clear and a joy to breathe. Finally, coming to a bench, they sat down in a companionable silence as Jill looked out over the park.

"It's so beautiful and quiet," she murmured softly. "I love it here. We must come again." Then, as if to heighten the experience, several sparrows flew in to land close by with one actually hopping onto the metal armrest where it perched expectantly. "Oh, John!" she exclaimed. "We should have brought them something."

"Well," he smiled diving into his pocket, "as it happens, I did think about it before I left home." And with that, he produced a rather tired-looking piece of bread. "I'm afraid it's not much," he observed proffering the crust, "but, as they say, it's better than nothing."

"Oh, I'm glad!" she exclaimed breaking it into small pieces. Then, with a slight tilt of her head, which he had first found so appealing, she added: "You know, I'm really quite fond of you."

Scattering the bread on the ground, she leaned across to put her arms around his neck and kiss him full on the lips.

This was, in fact, the first time they had been together since their Christmas Eve encounter at the Regent. In part, this had been due to the normal seasonal festivities but also because John had succumbed to a particularly virulent form of flu. Although quite ill, he had remained consumed with excitement over their meeting and had been frustrated at not being able to see her. Still not fully recovered, he feared that he might be contagious and instinctively drew back from her embrace. His action, however, conveyed completely the wrong message and, feeling repulsed, she quickly moved away.

"I'm sorry," she murmured quietly. "I didn't mean to be pushy. It's only that I got the impression – oh, it doesn't matter what I thought." She shrugged. "I obviously got it wrong."

Her sense of humiliation was painfully obvious and he quickly reached to take her hand.

"Jill," he hastened to assure her, "it does matter

what you thought, believe me. Please, please believe me. It's just that I'd hate you to catch this vicious bug because it virtually ruined my Christmas." He shook his head and smiled. "I'm not the best with words, but do you realise I can hardly believe you're even here with me? I see everything about you as beautiful and lovely." He drew a breath. "I just can't begin to describe how I feel... I mean," he confessed, "the fact you're even interested."

At this she began to look slightly embarrassed.

"I do suppose you realise that I won't always be lovely and beautiful as you put it," she observed soberly. "One day I'll be old and far from lovely and probably sooner than you might think. I'm twenty-seven next birthday so I'm quite a bit older than you." She shrugged before continuing, "I don't know if that makes any difference, but all I can say is, yes, I am interested – very interested. I mean, for heaven's sake, why shouldn't I be? You're far too modest."

But, deep down, she recognised his problem for, conscious of her appeal, she realised only too well the uncertainty and insecurity it could generate within a relationship. Her face suddenly clouded over.

"I know you might think I'm attractive, John, and who am I to argue? But, in all honesty, you know very little about me and there are things in my life that I wouldn't want you to hear from elsewhere."

"If you feel you need to tell me something," he responded gently, "then of course I'll listen. But I can assure you, nothing you might say could ever change how I feel."

"You, John," she teased, "are just wandering around in a love fog. But seriously, do you even know where I live?"

"Norway Street, I think, isn't it?" he replied, suddenly puzzled by the question. "At least, that's where I dropped you off after the dance."

At this, she seemed to become hesitant and paused for a moment to glance down at the birds by her feet as they scrambled over their frugal meal.

"But do you know which number?" she insisted without looking up.

"I don't," he admitted. "You were adamant that I left you on the corner, remember?"

She looked up with a slightly challenging expression.

"Well, as it happens, I live at number 62. Does that ring any bells?"

He shook his head.

"No – should it?"

"You surprise me!" she exclaimed. "Living in this gossip-ridden locality – especially as your parents run the local shop – I mean that must be an emporium of scandal in its own right."

But again he shook his head.

"The fact is, Jill," he replied, "I have very little to do with the business and next to never go into the shop."

"Well, anyway," she persisted, "I think you should know that I have a little half-sister called Julia. She was born to my mother early in the war as a result of a liaison with a Canadian soldier. As you know, there were thousands of them over here at the time waiting to join the war in Europe. Worse, it was while my father was abroad. I begged her not to cheat on Dad," she stressed bitterly, "especially as he was away doing his duty." Her eyes misted over as she continued, "But my mother refused to listen." A brief silence ensued. "I don't know why the Canadian, whatever his name was, never got called to active service – I think he must have been involved in some kind of administrative work. Anyway," she sighed, "he gradually became more and more part of our everyday life. It was all so wrong because, effectively, he had taken Dad's place – and I hated it. While the self-righteous neighbours... well, you can imagine, can't you?"

At this, John again reached to take her hand.

"Then, one day, quite unexpectedly," she added sadly, "my father returned home. Unbeknown to us he had been demobbed shortly after the end of the war." John noticed a tear overflow from her eye and gradually creep down her cheek.

"My poor Dad. He walked right into the middle of a discussion between Mum and this man about Julia's future." For a moment, she broke off and stooped to move the last scrap of bread within reach of one of the sparrows. "Do you know," she said bitterly, "when he first arrived home he was so happy. I heard him call out, 'Hello everybody, I'm back' – some homecoming. I was upstairs at the time and rushed down to try and warn him, but it was too late. He'd already gone into the room where they were talking. Dad had brought Mum some flowers – although I can't imagine from where because you know how difficult it's been to get anything. But anyway, when he realised the situation he threw them violently onto the floor and – do you know – even to this day I can still see their bright colours as they lay on our old brown carpet. A sort of symbol of broken trust I suppose. Strange how you remember things like that, isn't it?" As if lost for words, she just gazed down at the sparrows before adding, "It was all so sad and unnecessary."

"Jill, how awful for you," John gently murmured. "I'm so sorry."

She smiled a brief response.

"I was sitting at the foot of the stairs at the time and watching through the banisters. There was a lot of sudden terrible shouting as my father ordered the Canadian out of the house. Funny," she added vacantly, "I remember his name now – it was William. But Mum always referred to him as 'my Will' and it used to make me feel sick. Anyway," she sighed, "he refused to go and stupidly insisted that my mother was now 'his woman'. Well, when my father heard that, all hell broke loose. You see, Dad had been trained as a Paratrooper and the man stood no chance at all. He was just grabbed by the front of his tunic and hurled against the back window. There was the most terrible sound of smashing glass and it obviously alerted the neighbours. But then," she shuddered, "my father dragged him back through the splintered glass which cut his face and hands to ribbons.

"John, it was just awful. There was blood everywhere. My little sister was crying and my mum was screaming at my father to stop, but he was beyond control. And who could blame him? This William creature did his best to defend himself, but it was hopeless in such a small room. The furniture was being smashed to pieces, but my father didn't care. He had the man on the floor and was beating him about the head with both fists. I'm sure he intended to kill him and I honestly believe he would have succeeded had it not been for the intervention of several neighbours. Two of them finally managed to drag him clear. Them," she added disgustedly, "and their professed piety. They loved every minute of it and the prospect of condemning my parents for months to come."

John had listened quietly to every word and not let go of her hand for a moment.

"But what happened to your Dad?"

"He just left without a word," she sighed. "And the flowers he had brought lay trampled out of existence and to this day I've never seen him again. I don't even know if he's still alive – and, I love my

Dad," she added. "He was such a good man and I still miss him terribly."

At these revelations, John found himself virtually at a loss for words. Finally, however, he observed gently:

"I do sympathise because I know only too well how I feel about my own parents – and you say you've never heard anything from him since?" But she shook her head sadly. "You know," he observed reflectively, "now you've told me all this, I can well understand why you got so upset over my confrontation with the lieutenant on Christmas Eve."

"It just surprises me," she shrugged, "that you've never heard anything about it."

"Well," he replied, "now I come to think about it, I do seem to remember my parents discussing some kind of ruckus in your street but I had no real cause to be interested. Anyway, tell me, how did it all end up and what became of this William person? Presumably he didn't die or there would have been a murder investigation."

She watched the last sparrow spread its wings before flying away.

"No, he didn't," she continued in a tired voice. "Although sometimes I wish he had. The hurt and damage he caused to my family. Anyway, soon after my father left, the police arrived. Some 'kind' neighbours had obviously made it their business to report the disturbance. After that a Canadian military policeman turned up accompanied by an

English officer. It was absolute chaos. Everything seemed to be happening at once – the ambulance bell was ringing, then two stretcher-bearers barged their way into our home before lifting William onto the stretcher but he was unconscious and looked terrible. It was even difficult for them to get past the gate because it was blocked by nosey neighbours anxious to know all the sordid details. People can be so unkind. I heard one of them say she wasn't at all surprised after the way my mother had flaunted herself about with the foreign troops – neighbours, John!" she stressed bitterly. "They don't even know the meaning of the word." But then, suddenly changing the subject, she observed brightly, "Look, all the sparrows have gone. We really must bring them some more food next time."

"I'll try and do better in future," John promised playfully while at the same time indicating a small tea room across the park. "Let's have a coffee and we can continue our conversation over there... er..." he smiled, "that's if you want to continue talking about it?"

Still holding his hand, Jill murmured wistfully:

"I really do hope we can come here again – it's such a lovely place to be together."

Although unable to put his finger on it at the time, the reflective tone in her voice gave him a vague feeling of unease. However, once sitting in the tea house and with their coffee ordered, he leaned across the table to again take her hand.

"What?" she asked as if sensing his thoughts.

"You see," he replied, looking into her eyes, "I'm an artist and I love all things beautiful. Do I need to say any more?"

Again she looked embarrassed.

"I wonder if you'll be so keen when you've heard the rest of my story."

"Is there enough room for any more?" he cried with a certain mock horror as their coffee arrived.

"The fact is, John," she said quietly gazing down at her cup, "you've yet to hear how it all affected me. You see, both Mum and I were traumatised by what had happened and the sympathy of the military people was particularly welcome, especially after the neighbours' unkindness." She paused for a moment before continuing, "Well, anyway, after about a week, the English officer called again. Apparently, it seemed, just to check if we were all right." She stopped again and stirred her coffee. "I should have seen it coming, but naively I accepted his invitation to the local cinema." She shrugged. "He was kind and seemed nice enough looking. He was certainly very smart in his officer's uniform, so you see really I had no reason to refuse." She gazed briefly through the window towards the parkland beyond. "Oh, I know it's no excuse," she added falteringly, "but the fact is I allowed him to take advantage of me. It was only the once, but it was enough because shortly afterwards I found I was pregnant – even more fuel for the Norway Street gossips." She again idly stirred her coffee and watched the dark liquid as it continued to rotate. "So... you see, like my mother, I also have an illegitimate daughter; my little Anna. But," she added suddenly and with a certain assertiveness, "I'm not a bit ashamed and I love her dearly." She sat back and looked him straight in the eye. "So there. What do you think of me now? Not quite the attractive proposition you might have first imagined."

"Do you really suppose," he said adamantly, "that any of that changes how I feel?" he smiled. "You won't get rid of me that easily."

"Do you mean that, John?" she said suddenly smiling. "Because you really would love my little daughter – she's such a darling and Mum's been so good about looking after her when I'm at college. You must come round one day and see her. I know she'd take to you straight away – the same as I have."

Prising his lean six-feet-two frame from the chair, he grinned in response.

"The question is: would you have been so keen if I'd just been a mere five foot something?"

"Well, that," she smiled mischievously, "is something we'll never know, will we?"

But despite the humour, John felt a certain chill of unease over the identity of Anna's father and the complications he might cause. He even wondered if he was the same officer he'd encountered at the Christmas dance. However, suppressing these uncertainties, he slipped his arm around her waist as they stepped back out into the sunlight. By now it was virtually midday and the church bells had fallen silent to leave a perceptible hush as they slowly made their way back towards the bench they had occupied earlier.

"I think," teased John, "we should call this the 'confessional seat'."

"Oh, don't be so horrible John," she retorted happily. "Let's just sit here again for a few minutes before we go home."

Sitting close and gazing out over the sunlit park he observed:

"No sparrows."

"No food," she smiled back. "What do you expect?"

"Jill," he said gently after several minutes of a companionable quiet, "we ought to think of this bench as our special place and when we are apart and thinking of each other we should remember it and our Sunday morning here together – then it will be forever a private meeting place in our hearts."

She didn't reply immediately but hugged his neck and gently replied:

"Now you know, John, why I love you a hundred times."

Chapter 3

THE DAY AFTER John's early morning car problems found his mother enjoying a peaceful five minutes between customers. It was Thursday 9th October, but she had no means of knowing that this particular Thursday would mark the beginning of a trauma destined to haunt her in one form or another for the rest of her life. Still only about 9.30am and comfortably seated in the small lounge behind the shop, she was deeply engrossed in the current copy of *Woman's Own*. Among other articles, the magazine featured weekly episodes of a romantic novel by the popular author Barbara Cartland, and Violet thrilled to the clandestine affairs of rich predatory men and beautiful but gullible young women.

However, mundane reality was suddenly about to wrench her away from these book-bound fantasies, and it came in the form of three noisy customers who arrived simultaneously. So, with her curiosity aroused by their animated chatter, Violet put her magazine aside and got up to cross the hallway into her shop. But, even before reaching the counter, she saw that one of them, old Mr Baker, had already commandeered the shop chair and, with his nasal drip gleaming, was in full verbal flow. However, despite any distaste she might have felt over his appearance, it was what he had to say that really distressed her.

Always the first with any news, local or otherwise, he constituted the gossips' dream; although Violet had long since realised it was not just tittle-tattle for its own sake but, rather something that helped him cope with an otherwise lonely existence. With his wife having been dead for some twenty years and his mobility now greatly reduced, she knew only too well that his visits to her shop were a social lifeline. On this occasion, however, unlike the other two customers, he had apparently listened to the early morning News bulletin and, in his rather breathless, incoherent way, was struggling to describe what he'd heard.

Finally, it became clear that certain scientists now thought the strange dark formation straddling the North Atlantic was the result of a total absence of light. Puzzled and anxious, Violet pressed the old boy for more details.

"How on earth can there be no light during daytime?"

"That you might well ask," he asserted, "but all I can tell you is what I heard and that is there is no traceable evidence of light in the affected area – the newscaster didn't give any more information, only to say that the shadow is getting bigger by the hour and is now estimated to be nearly a thousand miles across at its widest point."

Upon hearing this, Violet felt her nerves begin to tingle and the blood drain from her face.

"And no further news of that American troopship?" she asked anxiously.

But the old boy just shook his head.

"None that I've heard of."

At this juncture, Mrs Walker from next door chimed in.

"It does make you wonder though, doesn't it?" she observed with a touch of uncertainty. "I mean – what with the Americans dropping that 'atanomic' bomb, or whatever it was called, on Hiroshima. Mind you, I don't think they should mess about with nature and the things they don't understand. They've probably gone and started something they can't control and now we'll have to live with the consequences. It's all so wrong if you ask me," she concluded with a touch of finality.

It was, of course, the voice of ignorance, but nevertheless reflective of the prevailing uncertainties of the time. However, their discussion suddenly became interrupted by the arrival of Gwen, who reached for her morning 'pinta'.

"And if you could just let me have ten Woodbines please, Violet, then I'll be off to my old air-raid shelter. From the sound of this lot, it looks as though I'm going to need it!"

Then, with a dismissive wave of her hand, she was gone.

But Violet was far less able to absorb such news and her fears were made far worse towards the late afternoon by the arrival of the rather unsavoury Mr Dean. Never one of her favourites, she'd always viewed him as an intermittent and miserable customer at the best of times. Today proved no exception for all he wanted was the one item he'd forgotten in the high street. Obviously, he just used her shop for convenience and it thoroughly irritated her.

Apart from her husband, Violet was not a lover of men in general and she found this rather portly and aging specimen particularly repulsive. With his ancient Russian-style fur hat and his grimy old brown suit, he exuded a noxious air which could only be attributed to a gross lack of personal hygiene, while the rubbed-in food adhering to his waistcoat only added to her sense of revulsion. She had never seen him in any other outfit and it made her seriously doubt whether any of his clothes had ever seen the inside of a washtub.

However, suppressing her natural feelings, she managed the semblance of a smile while at the same time asking if she could be of help.

"Ah… good afternoon, Violet," he replied in his usual offhand manner. "Just give me half a dozen eggs please." And so saying, he proceeded to place a rather soiled and dog-eared-looking ration book on the counter. But it was what he said next that shook poor Violet. "I suppose you must have heard about the goings-on in the high street earlier today?"

The shopkeeper shook her head.

"No, I've heard nothing... why? What *has* been happening?"

But then she almost immediately regretted asking for she had no desire to protract his visit.

"Well," he began, tantalisingly slowly, "I must have arrived up there around 10.30am and the first thing I noticed was a group of people standing outside Sainsbury's. But, as I got closer, I suddenly realised they were all getting excited by something down towards the coast."

But, at this point, he broke off suddenly to eye up the iced buns which Violet had displayed on the counter. "I must say, they look rather nice – do you mind?"

And, with that, he removed their glass cover and helped himself. Then, as if this liberty wasn't bad enough, Violet was forced to watch while he noisily consumed one of the buns on the spot; although seeing her expression, he lost no time in wiping his mouth with the back of his hand and offering to pay, but the whole procedure had left Violet feeling physically sick.

"Anyway," he continued with a sheepish expression, "I asked one of the women just what was going on – she didn't actually say anything but just pointed south at the sky. Frankly, at first, I couldn't see what she was on about, but then she nudged my arm and pointed again at something just above the horizon. The clouds had begun to lift and I could see what appeared to be some sort of black stain in the sky. Mind you, it was a fair old distance so I couldn't swear to its actual size. It was probably not much bigger than a full moon but with ragged-looking edges."

On hearing this, Violet's hands tightened on the counter till her knuckles showed white.

"Did you happen to get any idea of what it might have been?"

"None at all." he replied flatly, apparently oblivious to her distress. "Some of the people there seemed to think it could be connected with the problem over the Atlantic. Although, from what I've heard, this thing seemed tiny by comparison." He shrugged casually. "So, I just don't know – and, in any case, they were only guessing. I tell you what though," he added idly, "it rather reminded me of black ink spreading out on a sheet of blotting paper." Then, having reduced Violet's mind to a state of turmoil, he prepared to take his leave with a casual parting shot, "Do give my kind regards to your Jack. He never forgets my milk and it's always on time."

With that, he stooped to snap on his cycle clips before reaching for his ancient old boneshaker propped up against one of the pillars outside. The last the shopkeeper saw of him was as he pedalled unsteadily away towards the end of Gordon Road.

Life had never been particularly kind to Violet. The experiences of two World Wars had taken their toll. A teenager during the first conflict, she had been faced with the death of two soldiers who had been billeted with her parents. Moreover, during the recent hostilities, she had lived in daily dread of German paratroopers actually landing in the streets outside. On top of all this, there had been the long nights of terror spent on her own with young Margaret and her older child John because, during the Blitz, Jack had been away doing his duty as an air-raid warden.

Violet didn't mention her new fears to Margaret when she returned from school, but later, when Jack got home and her daughter was safely in bed, she gave vent to her feelings.

"What is it?" he asked gently, guiding her towards their little settee.

"Oh, Jack." she cried brokenly. "I'm becoming so worried about everything. I had old Mr Dean in the shop this afternoon and from what he was saying it seems that the trouble over the Atlantic has now reached the Channel – it's right on our doorstep, Jack," she sobbed frantically.

Hating to see his wife so distraught, he put his arms around her shoulders and drew her close.

"What gave the old fool that idea?" Then once acquainted with the afternoon's events, he observed quietly, "Look – does it really matter if there's some sort of smudge in the sky? And that," he added "is supposing it even exists. In all probability, it's just a figment of the old fool's imagination. He's always been a bit – well, you know – funny, which I know sounds uncharitable, but I'm afraid it's the truth.

In fact, I sometimes wonder if anyone who comes through that shop door isn't a bit strange in one way or the other." He paused and gave her an extra squeeze. "Anyway," he stressed, "whatever happens, we've got each other and we'll see it through as we've always done. Remember, nothing has ever stopped us before has it?" he grinned. He deliberately paused. "Now, I know you don't like listening to the news, but I think we should if we're ever to get any idea of the true situation – because it's possible that you may be fretting over nothing."

She tried a wan smile.

"That's the difference between you and me Jack," she managed. "Nothing ever phases you, does it? Whereas, I worry about everything. I just wish I could be a bit more like you."

"Well," he asserted, "you're not and I'm grateful for it. Now are we going to listen to the news or what? You never know, it could be good." Violet took a deep breath before nodding reluctantly. "That's my girl," he said brightly, giving her a peck as he got up to turn on their old wireless set.

The ancient machine crackled into life just in time to catch the final strains of a symphony concert before the booming chime of Big Ben struck 9pm. Echoing across their little room, it was immediately followed by the announcer's solemn cultured voice.

"This is the BBC Home Service broadcasting on 330 and 202 mega-cycles. Here is the *Nine O'Clock News* for today – Thursday the 9th of October 1947.

This evening the American Ambassador in London announced that President Truman has, with deep regret, accepted the total loss of the troopship *The Detroit* and that a national day of mourning will be announced later this week. It is believed the vessel passed either close to, or actually through, the huge shadow now stretching from Iceland to The Azores. However, whether that was responsible for its disappearance has yet to be established. In the meantime," he continued, "Congress has decreed that no American shipping or transatlantic flights are to pass within 200 miles of its outer limits. This exclusion zone is to remain in force until any threat the shadow might pose has been fully determined. It still remains to be seen if the British Government will follow suit."

Although unseen by his wife, Jack felt his expression change and he began to wonder if he should switch the set off, but the announcer was continuing.

"It is understood that, earlier today, Congressman Abraham Jackson expressed extreme concern over the 'ever-widening curtain', as he described it, that is now threatening to partition the Atlantic. He went on to liken the barrier's effect to that of the German U-Boat menace. 'Both in their time,' he stressed, 'held the potential to seperate the Americas from Europe'."

"Oh, Jack!" exclaimed Violet. "It's just what I feared."

"Hang on a minute, love," he insisted. "Let's at least hear the rest of it."

"Early this morning," continued the announcer, "I recorded an interview with the eminent Professor Sinclair of Cambridge University who specialises in physics and meteorological studies, and this is what he had to say:"

"It is with deep regret," observed the lecturer, "that I have heard about the loss of these fine young servicemen, some of whom, I understand, were returning home from Germany for the first time since the end of the war. It's very tragic. At this point in time, however, I can only speculate about what might have caused the disaster and whether there is any connection between their loss and the current difficulties being experienced in the mid-Atlantic. I have no direct knowledge of these problems, but I am given to understand from unofficial reports that this huge area of darkness may, in fact, be caused by a complete absence of any light rather than a normal cloud formation of moisture-laden air. Should this prove to be the case, there is a strong possibility that whatever force is absorbing the light may also be responsible for consuming the troop ship."

At this point, the lecturer was interrupted by the announcer:

"I also asked the Professor about today's alleged sightings off the south coast near Portsmouth and even as far east as Brighton, but having no information about these developments, he declined to comment. Now, here is the rest of today's news. Two small boys have been found dead in the Coventry area and it is believed they died while playing with an undetected wartime bomb..."

However, Jack had heard enough and reached to switch it off. His wife, looked devastated.

"I think," he said slowly, "although all that sounded pretty dramatic, we have, in fact, heard nothing that's really new." But his was an uphill struggle, for in reality, there was little in the way of anything positive he could offer, but he determined to do his best. "I know it's only a guess," he tried to assure her, "but I suspect it's all to do with some unknown natural phenomenon. I don't think for a moment that it's any sort of new super-weapon being deployed by the Soviet Union – because that's what you're afraid of, isn't it?"

Violet nodded in silent misery.

"But Jack," she cried tearfully, "what's going to happen if this shadow, or whatever it is, just keeps on growing? Where is it going to end? Will it gradually cover everything and kill us all? And what about our poor Margaret and John? They've barely started their lives – what about their futures?"

Recognising her approaching hysteria, he did the only thing possible and held her close.

"Please love, try not to let your imagination get out of control. I'm still here and we have no reason to think that anything like that is going to happen. I've spoken to dozens of customers today and none of them showed more than a passing interest in what's going on. In any case," he stressed, "as I've said before, it's all taking place thousands of miles away."

"But it's not, Jack," she insisted between the tears. "Remember what old Dean was saying?"

"Well!" shrugged Jack. "I put as much credence on that as..."

But mention of the reprobate customer momentarily diverted Violet's thoughts and she gave an involuntary shudder.

"Ugh, that man gives me the horrors, Jack. He's so repulsive."

Her husband grinned.

"Men aren't exactly your favourite animals, are they? I guess I must have just got lucky."

"Luck had nothing to do with it, Jack Harper, as well you know. In any case, it's not men I hate – it's their disgusting habits. Have you ever noticed the front of old Dean's waistcoat? There's egg and..." she shuddered again. "Really, Jack, it makes me feel absolutely ill. No wonder he never got married. No self-respecting woman would ever get near him." Jack was fleetingly relieved at this change in their conversation, but it was to prove a brief respite. "... And," continued Violet, "I suspect he's suffering from a touch of religious mania. He's forever going on about living in the last days, and now," she added miserably, "it looks as though he's probably right."

Chapter 4

FRIDAY 10th OCTOBER, the day after the 'Mr Dean' episode, witnessed a contrite John drawing up outside the notorious number 62 Norway Street in his ancient old Ford. Unbelievably, it was something just short of 8am, but he was desperate to make amends for his failings the previous day. It was his first visit to Jill's home and, understandably perhaps, he felt a little uncertain of quite what to expect. When the front door finally opened, however, he momentarily thought it was Jill herself, but then almost immediately realised that the lady must be her mother. Slim and very attractive, she could easily have been mistaken for her elder sister. Close-fitting dark slacks accentuated her full hips while long, well-brushed, blonde hair extended down to her shoulders. This, and the hint of exotic perfume, combined to create a very sensual impact; an impact that left him briefly lost for words.

"Hello John," she smiled. "I've heard all about you. Please – do come in. Jill's expecting you and won't be a minute. Oh, and by the way, my name's

Rita." Following her through the narrow hallway to the rear living room, he couldn't help but appreciate the lithe and provocative way she moved. In fact, everything about her seemed to epitomise the current popular concept of a glamour girl. But then, as if sensing his thoughts, she half turned with a seductive smile. "Do have a seat," she invited while waving towards one of the armchairs by the fireplace. "Jill's just upstairs attending to little Anna. She won't be long – could I perhaps offer you a cup of coffee or something?"

He nodded appreciatively.

"Yes, coffee please. Black but no sugar."

And then, with a lingering smile, she disappeared in the direction of the kitchen leaving John with his emotions in overdrive. Glancing idly around the room, he was forced to admire the immaculate way she kept her home and it had obviously all been done on a very limited budget. Thin pink distemper struggled to cover the original wallpaper yet it made the living room look fresh and light, which was aided by the spotless white lace napkins protecting the heads and armrests of the two faded floral armchairs. In addition, the solemn ticking of an ornate china clock on the marble mantelpiece further enhanced the almost timeless air of serenity.

But then his attention drifted to the window, where the fine net curtain showed evidence of careful repair. He assumed it was here that violence had erupted when the Canadian had been sent crashing through the glass. It seemed hard to imagine that this peaceful atmosphere had once witnessed a man being virtually beaten to death. He gazed briefly at the floor and tried to imagine the flowers being trodden into the threadbare carpet and how sad it must all have been at the time.

Displayed on a small dining table against the far wall, he noticed a framed monochrome photograph of a soldier. Curious as to the man's identity, he crossed the room and picked it up, whereupon he found himself gazing at the handsome features of a man in his early thirties; a man who's dark trim moustache and paratrooper's beret gave him an undeniably striking appearence.

"My husband – he was with the First Airborne."

Unheard, Jill's mother had re-entered the room with their coffee and caused John to look up as he replaced the picture.

"A fine-looking man," he observed.

She nodded.

"Yes, someone very special. He was in the Arnhem drop, you know. But I suppose you've heard all about what happened?"

John looked diplomatically vague.

"Only," he replied carefully, "that he left home several years ago and that Jill still misses him very much."

"She's not alone in that," sighed her mother quietly with an almost detectable note of sadness. However, John refrained from comment as she offered him his cup. "Your coffee. I hope it's how you like it. But, please do sit down." She smiled as she took a seat in one of the armchairs. "Wasn't it strange you both being at the same college and yet not knowing each other?"

"Well," he explained, conscious of her nearness, "that's because we are based on separate campuses. Jill's involved with fashion design and I'm studying sculpture."

"Actually, John," she said unexpectedly and quietly while glancing towards the door as if to ensure she was not being overheard, "I've wanted to thank you for some time and, when I say that, I presume you know all about little Anna's father. Well," she continued, "ever since her birth he's made an absolute nuisance of himself and, really, Jill doesn't want any more to do with him." Her words captured his immediate attention for the subject had caused him a certain amount of concern. "It's not that we want to deny him access to his daughter, you understand," she emphasised. "Far from it. But really, that's where it's got to end."

"I see," he nodded, reaching for his cigarettes. "But I'm not quite sure why you think it necessary to thank me."

"Because," she replied in her lilting voice, "we haven't seen him since the Christmas Eve dance."

At this, the penny finally dropped, as his earlier suspicions suddenly became a reality.

"You mean," he stressed, "the officer I saw off

at the dance is, in fact, Anna's father?" He shook his head and shrugged. "I must admit, I suspected as much but I wasn't sure. Not that it matters, I suppose. Although, for little Anna's sake, I would have thought it better to remain on good terms." But, as Rita made to reply, he caught sight of a small face, complete with pigtails, peering at him around the edge of the door. "Hello!" he exclaimed warmly. "You must be Anna. I've heard so much about you." Then, supported by her mother, the little girl proceeded to make her way unsteadily into the room. "Jill, you were so right," he enthused. "She's absolutely adorable and so tiny." Still guided by her mother, the little girl gradually approached him with a mischievous grin. "Now," encouraged John, "why don't you come and tell me all about the things you will be doing today. You see, I'd just love to know what you'll be up to."

With that, he reached down to lift her onto his knee. Obviously delighted, the small child responded with a broken speech which John found difficult to follow, but this in no way detracted from the obvious pleasure of each other's company. However, in the middle of it all, Jill interrupted brightly,

"That sounds very nice, John, but if we stay here and listen to all her goings-on we won't get to college until this afternoon and we can't afford a repetition of yesterday's fiasco. So, come on," she urged, "you know what your old car can be like."

Surprisingly, however, the temperamental old Ford

obliged first time, but, as John eased off the handbrake, Jill's mother suddenly arrived unexpectedly at the passenger's window.

"Here," she gasped, passing a small bottle to her daughter. "You forgot your aspirins. You know how you need them about this time." Then, turning to John, she added, "By the way, if you take the coast road it might be worth keeping an eye out for this shadow that's been in the news lately – apparently, there are reports of it being seen close to Portsmouth."

"Thanks," he replied. "I'll certainly bear it in mind."

And with that, he finally managed to pull away while the last thing Jill remembered was seeing her mother standing by the kerb waving and holding little Anna's hand.

As it was another beautiful autumn morning, John turned due south after deciding to take the coast road. He knew Jill enjoyed the views and it also provided the most direct route to their college. By the time they reached the sea front, it was barely 8.45am and everything seemed very quiet apart from the occasional pedestrian and one solitary cyclist. But, as Jill lay idly back in the passenger seat to gaze out at the calm, sparkling blue sea, something at the edge of her vision caught her attention. Swivelling round for a better look she suddenly felt herself take a sharp breath.

"John," she whispered urgently. "I think we need to stop."

"Why?" he protested. "What's the matter? We don't want to make ourselves late again."

"Look, John!" she then almost shouted. "Just stop, will you!" Reluctantly he pulled over and followed the direction of her gaze. "There," she pointed almost hysterically. "Look out there – just to the right and virtually on the horizon. Can you see it? There's a funny-looking black area. It's a bit like a cloud but I'm sure it's not. The edges are too sharp and ragged and it's moving too quickly." She gripped his arm until it almost hurt. "You don't suppose it's anything to do with the darkness that's been hanging about over the Atlantic, do you?" she asked fearfully.

Squinting out to sea he could now clearly make out what appeared to be an extensive black stain against the dawn-like sky and, fascinated, he could only watch as it continued to expand over an ever-increasing area above the sea. Edged by long salient fingers, the fearful mass seemed to first contract and then extend itself in a pulse-like rhythm.

"John," she cried frantically. "What is it?"

"I'm not sure," he muttered slowly and cautiously, "but I certainly don't like the look of it."

"John," she shuddered. "It looks absolutely evil."

As they continued to watch, the early morning sun gradually became overcast, which caused a deep gloom to set in as the daylight began to fade.

Between the coast road and the sea a deep canal ran due east towards Brighton and John suddenly noticed that the trees lining its banks were beginning to bend and strain at their roots as if under the influence of some attractive force. In the meantime, the deepening murk had drawn a number of curious householders out onto the road, although many of them, having seen seeing the deteriorating situation, rapidly withdrew indoors. Less easily intimidated, however, John made to get out of the car.

"And where do you think you're going?" protested his companion agitatedly. "For heaven's sake, don't leave me!"

"I'm not," he assured her. "I just want a closer look at what's going on out there – that's all."

"You can see what's going on perfectly well from here!" she almost screamed. "Haven't you seen enough? Let's just get the hell out of here!"

Despite her entreaties, however, he had his own way, although, once outside the car, he suddenly found himself fighting to even remain upright. An unbelievably powerful magnetic pull threatened to drag him towards the canal. Frantically, he tried to brace himself against the car door while, at the same time, struggling desperately to get back behind the steering wheel. But, even as he did so, he suddenly heard her scream almost uncontrollably.

"John! John! By your leg!"

With his mind in a whirl, he looked down to see a small spiky black sphere hovering desperately close to his left knee. No bigger than a tennis ball, the alien-looking entity hung there with its irregular circumference emitting the same pulsations as its huge counterpart out at sea. His first instinct was to try to brush the thing away, but fear of releasing his grip on the car caused him to hesitate. If this wasn't frightening enough, he caught sight of a smaller sphere further to his left behaving in exactly the same way. At this stage, he realised more and more of these entities were springing into being all around him, some of which were barely the size of a child's marble.

"John!" she screamed again with an ever-greater urgency. "For God's sake, get back in the car!"

But, even as he struggled to comply, he saw the black enigmas suddenly rush together as if in response to some unseen signal. Then, having coalesced into one throbbing mass, the whole thing suddenly raced out to sea towards its giant parent.

Once inside the car, he glanced across the road at the fence lining the upper reaches of the canal bank. Normally acting as a protective barrier from the two hundred feet drop, today its wire mesh was fast becoming clogged with debris being sucked towards the threat. It was then, much to his horror, that he caught sight of a man who had been desperately clinging to the fence suddenly lose his grip and disappear to certain death in the filthy canal waters far below.

Peering up at what little blue sky now remained, John could make out vast flocks of seagulls trying to break free from the relentless pull, but many were losing the struggle and being sucked back out to sea where the furious flapping of their white plumage stood in stark contrast to the advancing wall of darkness. However, even this brief delay had proved costly, because the whole situation had deteriorated at a horrifying rate as the pulsing threat advanced in all directions with its extremities fast encroaching the coast road and, seeing the danger, Jill was quick to react.

"John, will you please..." she almost screamed. But she need not have bothered for he had already seen enough and realised the danger of them actually becoming enveloped. But, reaching to start the car, he suddenly found himself inexplicably short of breath and, turning sideways to his passenger, he could see that Jill was now also struggling for air. "John," she gasped in desperation. "I can hardly get my breath."

And then it dawned upon him.

"It's that dammed darkness!" he managed hoarsely. "It's dragging at everything – even the light and the very air we breathe. Quick, close your window or we'll have no air left at all."

Starved of oxygen and becoming weaker by the moment, he attempted to start the car. However, true to form, the ancient engine coughed but then fell stubbornly silent. With rising panic, he glimpsed up at the rear-view mirror to discover that the expanding shadow had now swung in behind them which not only blocked any thought of retreat but was also now threatening to engulf them completely. Worse, if that were possible, the car itself was beginning to lurch violently in response to the huge gravitational force now being exerted on it.

Fearful that the vehicle would be dragged to the bottom of the canal, John frantically summoned up his remaining strength for one final attempt. This time, and with his foot hard down on the throttle, the engine reluctantly spluttered into life but, as he thankfully released the clutch, the car failed to move forward. Furiously pumping the accelerator, he desperately willed it to move but, for several nerve-wrenching moments, it seemed unable to break free from the force field. Not daring to look at the effect this was having on Jill, he finally felt the vehicle leap forward and, caught off guard by the fierce jolt, his companion was violently thrown against the back of her seat in a whiplash movement.

"Are you all right?" he managed to gasp.

But by now she had insufficient breath to reply and, frighteningly, he noticed a bluish tinge creeping into her cheeks. With his own lungs feeling on fire, he became ever more frantic to escape the danger zone. The pain in his chest was reducing his thinking to a bare survival instinct and he was only vaguely aware that any real safety probably lay north of the South Downs. However, the hills he had in mind were well beyond the range of his meagre petrol supply and the only alternative his befuddled mind could think of was to seek protective shelter such as the massive Victorian Hove Town Hall. This was a public building about half a mile inland and situated along Church Road, which ran parallel to the coast.

Driving as fast as the diminishing visibility would allow, he took the first turning north, but in doing so narrowly avoided colliding with an oncoming police car as it raced out onto the sea front road at high speed. With its headlights on full-beam, the driver had his loudhailer blaring at a deafening pitch.

"This is an emergency. This is an emergency. All people must vacate the streets immediately and seek shelter – this is an emergency..."

But, loud though it was, it failed to drown a sudden and long-drawn-out roar as several coastal buildings collapsed onto the pavement and spread their debris far across the road. Unable to withstand the huge gravitational strain on their structures, they had finally given way, although John would only discover all this at a much later date. At the moment he was fully occupied attempting to peer through the ever-intensifying darkness. He had kept his main headlights full on, but they did little to penetrate the artificial gloom and tended to reflect back into his eyes, which further diminished his vision and forced him to reduce speed to a crawl. However, even as he did so, he heard a horrifying choking sound and, frantically glancing sideways, saw Jill suddenly collapse against the dashboard wheezing and fighting for life. Fearing she would die, he desperately strained ahead for any sign of the traffic lights he knew would mark the junction with Church Road, but visibility was now so poor that he could barely see beyond the end of his bonnet and, in complete despair, he pulled the vehicle to a halt.

Reaching across, he gently eased Jill back into her seat, but she was barely conscious and just sagged lifelessly. Desperately short of breath himself and with no first aid experience, he was at a loss as to what to do and only gut instinct finally impelled him to wind down his side window. But it proved the right thing to do because the relief was immediate as air flowed into the car which, until then, had effectively become a vacuum. Gulping in the oxygen, he frantically begged the girl he loved to try and breathe. Terrified it was too late, he urged her again and again but the influx of air was already beginning to work its magic because she suddenly murmured faintly,

"John – where are we?" Indescribably relieved, he held her close and that's the way they remained for some time. The headlights were still on, the engine was still running, and he couldn't begin to comprehend what had happened, but he didn't care. It only mattered that Jill was still alive. Then, as her mind began to clear, she moved her head to look up at him. "You know, John," she whispered, "I really do love you a hundred times."

He nodded while feeling the warmth of her hair against his face.

"I know," he murmured. "I remember."

"John," she breathed finally. "What on earth are we going to do?"

"I only wish I could tell you," he replied gently, glancing about at the encircling darkness. "We can breathe again – but the question is, for how long? And there's something else. It's either my imagination or the darkness out there doesn't seem quite so impenetrable as it was along the coast – hang on a minute, I'm going to try something." And with that, he got out of the car. "Well," he observed after a minute or two, "there's nothing pulling at me now. Perhaps we finally managed to get out of range."

He'd actually travelled about two hundred yards since leaving the sea front and now, standing by the car with his arms resting idly on its roof, he suddenly noticed that his headlights were picking out the road ahead, although, glancing back he could see the coast road itself was still enshrouded with the same impenetrable blackness. Suddenly, acting on impulse, he looked up, but only to be confronted by deep, drifting, patches of mist. However, above this, incredibly, he could just make out a star-studded sky. Totally mystified, he turned to get back in the car.

"Believe it or not," he exclaimed as he settled behind the steering wheel, "but the darkness out there now seems more like normal night-time – I know, I know! It sounds incredible but there's an actual night sky overhead. Have a look for yourself," he shrugged. "Because I'm damned if I know what's going on."

"Night-time? How can it be?" she gasped looking down at her wristwatch. "It's barely 10.45am. It's simply not possible."

He slumped wearily back in the driving seat with a sigh.

"I know it's not possible," he murmured resignedly, "but that's how it is. And I'm beginning to wonder if that thing along the coast has affected time in some way." For a moment, he sat in silence before straightening up. "Look, I had it in mind to try and reach the Hove Town Hall and I still think it's a good idea because I just don't know what to do – the police station forms part of the main building and if they don't know what the situation is, no one will." Releasing the clutch to move forward, he indicated a right-hand turning just ahead. "I'm sure that's the junction we're looking for. It should lead straight into Church Road. But," he added in a puzzled voice, "it looks very different to how I remember it. I mean, where the hell are the traffic lights and the buildings? Where on earth are the buildings?"

"I'm afraid I can't help you there, John." she replied. "I've never been very familiar with this part of Hove." But, as he completed the turn, she suddenly screamed at the top of her voice, "Look out! Look out! Mind those horses – oh no!" she agonised. "You've hit one."

Realising fatigue and anxiety might have affected his reactions, John stopped abruptly to peer through the passenger side window where he could just make out two animals harnessed to a four-wheeled wagon. Facing the wrong way and parked dangerously close to the junction, it had effectively been an accident waiting to happen. However, although he looked carefully, neither horse appeared injured in any way and he'd certainly felt no impact.

"Well, they look okay to me," he said slowly. "I don't think I can have hit them."

"But you did, John," she insisted. "I saw the wing of your car go straight into the nearest grey horse."

"Well, I can't see any damage – but, much more to the point, how's your breathing?"

"It's fine, thanks," she replied gratefully, "although, honestly, I thought back there for a minute I was going to die. I imagine it must feel a bit like that if you were drowning."

He reached across and squeezed her hand.

"Right then, let's get down to the police station." But, as he turned to look straight ahead, he found himself faced with an ever-thickening wall of haze. It seemed that the heavy patches of mist he encountered earlier had descended to form an almost impregnable fog and he immediately stamped on the brakes. "Stuck again!" he muttered, and then, with a typical outburst of impatience, irritably reversed back towards the kerb. "What are we going to do now?" he exclaimed in response to her questioning look. "You tell me, because, as far as I'm concerned, all we can do is sit and wait it out until this lot decides to lift. I tell you what though – you can forget all about college." So, with nothing better to do, John reached for his Woodbines. "Bloody pea soup," he muttered under his breath, peering through the windscreen as he inhaled the smoke. "First we nearly get dragged into the canal and now this." Jill sank resignedly back in her seat, closed her eyes and let him get on with it but, as John's cigarette burned low and he leaned forward to stub it out in the ashtray, he thought he could detect a slight thinning of the fog and a glimpse of the street ahead – but it was still insufficient to allow for any driving, so he again settled down to wait. "How's the time now, Jill?" he asked idly.

"Well," she replied slowly, "by my watch – that's if I can see it in this murk – it's about 11.10am."

"But that's just in here," he grunted disconcertedly. "What it is out there is anybody's guess."

He reached for another cigarette, but only to discover he'd smoked the last one, so he again wound down his side window and tossed the empty packet outside.

"John!" she protested. "And you smoke far too much."

"Well, I haven't got any more," he grinned, "so you won't have to worry." Over the next hour, the mist continued to thin until, eventually, it became possible to see the dim silhouettes of people and various items of traffic. "At last!" he exclaimed. "I think we can make a move."

But then, as he carefully edged his way forward in the direction of the Town Hall, he felt Jill desperately clutch at his arm.

"John, what on earth's going on?"

Too mesmerised to answer, John stopped the car to stare incredulously at the vague and insubstantial scene that now lay ahead. To the left loomed the outline of what he knew to be St Andrew's Church. However, emerging through the lingering haze, dim street lights revealed a busy thoroughfare of people moving about between the shops and traversing the road amidst a melee of horse-drawn vehicles and handcarts. It was indistinct but nevertheless unmistakable and, although not entirely unfamiliar with horse transport, John had never seen anything like it. As visibility improved, Jill began to point out how strangely some of the people appeared to be dressed.

"It's like a scene from a film. I mean look at the outfits some of those women are wearing – and their huge hats! Oh John!" she sobbed. "I feel so confused." And with that, she buried her face in her hands.

"It's like a different age," he muttered, unable to wrench his gaze from the surreal spectacle. "Somehow, in some way, we're looking at a scene from the past. If you ask me, it all looks a bit like a mirage of the Victorian era. There's no way it can be anything else. It's just possible that thing along the coast has affected us in some way."

"John – I'm so frightened. I'm so frightened,"

she repeated fearfully. "It's becoming an endless nightmare that keeps changing from one horror to the next. It just goes on and on. I want to wake up but I can't. It's not real, is it? Please tell me it's not real."

"It's only real," he assured her, "in the sense that we are still sitting here together... and remember that we are together. You're not alone. We're both having this experience – although what it is that's going on out there," he shook his head, "is another matter altogether... I can only think... no, I don't know what to think... I just don't know. It's something way beyond my understanding."

Faced with the apparently inexplicable, John began to wonder privately whether just his own mind had been affected and if the whole episode was an illusionary spasm of his imagination. But, even as he dismissed the idea, his attention became drawn to the side window where, passing dangerously close, he could see two horses straining to pull a high-sided vehicle. Unbelievably, the whole contraption came so near that, for a moment, he wondered how the driver had avoided a collision. Winding down his window he was stunned to realise that he was looking at a horse-drawn bus. But, far stranger, was the persistent lack of any sound.

"That," he exclaimed, pointing through the windscreen, "is, or was, a horse-drawn bus. But then," he added almost to himself, "it can't be. The last one must have run some forty years ago!"

Momentarily overcoming her fear, Jill seemed fascinated by a couple as they walked past her side of the car and, leaning across from his driving seat, John could immediately see why – because, as they passed under what he now took to be a street lamp, they looked every inch like characters from a Dickensian novel. The woman gazed fixedly at her companion from beneath the wide brim of a floral hat, while her narrow-waisted, dress flowed to the ground. He could make out less of the gentleman, but from what he could see, her companion appeared to be wearing a low-crowned top hat and a dark cutaway frock coat. John also couldn't help noticing there was a certain panache in the way he carried his walking stick. Incredibly, although they walked within inches of the car, there was no hint of their voices, even though they were obviously engaged in an animated conversation.

"Did you notice how there's no sound?" whispered John, almost as if afraid they might hear him. "You can see them but you can't hear a word. In fact," he added as he cocked his head attentively, "if you listen, there's absolutely no sound anywhere."

"No sound!" his companion almost screamed. "Is that all you can think of? The whole thing's insane." Then, lowering her voice, she pleaded, "Oh, John let's get out of here. I'm terrified. Please take me home."

Nothing would have given him more pleasure

but he knew it would be impossible to get back along the coast road, although whether it would be safer further inland he had no means of knowing. In any case, he was not about to find out because the engine of his old car finally cut out and refused to go any further. Even worse – no amount of effort with the cranking handle made any difference. Resignedly, he got back into the car and again reached for his cigarettes, but only to remember there were none left.

"I'm afraid," he admitted in disgust, "the old girl's had it. If we're going anywhere, it'll have to be on foot." He then indicated the Victorian nightmare through the windscreen. "The problem is," he added, "when you talk about going home you don't know how far that thing out there extends."

In the dim light of the car's interior he could see her worried reaction.

"What do you mean, John?" she asked anxiously. He hesitated not wishing to add to her distress. "John," she insisted desperately. "For heaven's sake, tell me, what are you trying to say?"

"If," he answered reluctantly, "although it's pure speculation – if what appears to be going on out there is affecting the whole coastal region, then all we might find back home could be nothing more than open fields."

"You mean," she said tearfully, "that our houses won't even be there anymore?"

He nodded mutely.

"I think it's a distinct possibility. But of course, on the other hand, all this might be a localised illusion which could be gone by the morning."

The outline of Hove Town Hall with its soaring clock tower loomed ahead in the distance, but now its existence seemed virtually irrelevant. However, squinting with difficulty, he could just make out the hands pointing to 8.30pm from which he estimated daybreak to be about nine or ten hours away. Glancing across the street, he saw what appeared to be a post office or newsagent. Various posters adorned its windows and the entrance was festooned with newspapers.

"I don't think there's any point in going to the town hall now," he observed. "Our best bet would be to wait for daybreak and then try to make our way back on foot. I tell you what, though," he added, pointing across the road, "it might be an idea to look at some of those newspapers. I bet they could tell us a thing or two and you never know, I might also be able to get some tobacco."

At this suggestion, Jill shrank frantically into her seat.

"John," she protested desperately. "We're not going out there. Not among all those... those ghosts or whatever they are. Please," she begged. "Please. We don't know what we might be getting into. Can't we just stay here until tomorrow? Please, I feel safer in the car."

"You've got me with you," he grinned. "Surely

you're not afraid with me around?"

Then, to her utter dismay, he proceeded to climb out of the car. However, as he moved round the vehicle to open her side door, he noticed one of the 'pedestrians' approaching along the pavement and, had it not been for his swift evasive action, there would have been a collision.

"Hey, look out where you're going mate!" he shouted irritably, although he almost immediately sensed the man couldn't hear him. "Did you see that?" he exclaimed as he finally opened Jill's door. "That idiot nearly walked right into me." In her present distraught state, idiots of any kind did not come as a high priority and in an emotional outburst she threw her arms around his neck and began to sob hysterically. "Hey, hey, what's all this?" he exclaimed. "We'll be okay, I promise."

For a long time, she clung to him before finally looking up through tear-dimmed eyes.

"I know but I just want to go home," she whispered pathetically.

The newsagent proved a dimly lit experience with what appeared to be oil lamps. Of the variety of newspapers on display, John immediately gravitated to a copy of *The Times* significantly dated Monday 10th October 1887.

"Let's see – that's some sixty years ago to the day," he murmured to himself. "God knows how," he added turning to Jill, "but, somehow, we've either slipped back to or we're witnessing events that took place here some sixty years previously – look at those headlines: 'The Failed Mafeking Relief Column'."

Then, straining to make out the smaller print, he continued to read the account out loud:

'It's now six months to the day that the British Relief Column failed to reach Khartoum in time to save General Gordon. Besieged by overwhelming numbers he finally succumbed to the rebel forces and died an agonising death it is understood...' But the paper was folded, preventing further reading.

"Serves him right," John muttered. "What the hell's he doing in the Sudan anyway? Should have stayed in his own country."

"John!" exclaimed an exasperated Jill. "For heaven's sake!"

"I know, I know" he retorted. "We've got other things to think about – funny though, isn't it, how I live in Gordon Road and there's even a place called Mafeking Street just behind our college?"

However, events were about to take an even more bizarre turn because, as he reached to unfold the paper, his hand passed straight through it. With a terrible suspicion forming in his mind, he pushed against the shop window but, likewise, it offered no resistance. Seeing his expression, Jill tried for herself but with the same result.

"John – what on earth's going on? It's as though the window's not even there."

"It's not," he asserted, pushing his hand in and out of the 'glass'. "As I said before, I think that what we're seeing is some sort of illusion. In fact, I suspected as much right from the start. There's nothing physically here at all."

His assessment of the situation was almost immediately vindicated by a customer who had emerged from the shop. Immaculately dressed in Victorian style, the woman seemed completely oblivious to their presence and appeared to cannon straight into Jill but, unbelievably, there was no impact and, undeterred, she just passed on her way out into the street.

"That's it!" John almost shouted. "We're witnessing some sort of rerun of events that happened here long ago. These people are not actually here – they're just images or impressions that were somehow left imprinted on the atmosphere. It's a bit like watching a silent movie only it's three-dimensional and happening all around us. We can see it, but there's no way we can interact with it – and, you know, I can't help but think the whole thing might have been triggered by that hell over the coast – like some sort of chain reaction."

"And," exclaimed Jill, "when you first turned into Church Road and I thought you'd struck one of the horses, it wasn't hurt because it wasn't actually there."

John nodded.

"And remember, those traffic lights I couldn't find?" he murmured. "Of course they weren't there

– because they weren't even invented until 1912. I think these people keep bumping into us," he explained, "because we were not part of their lives at that time – and I'm certain they have no awareness of our being here now or, for that matter, any means of contacting us."

"Oh John," she whispered. "It's too horrible to think about, but I suppose it happens to us all in the end. We're here for a time and then..."

"There's nothing to be gained by dwelling on misery," he stressed. "So let's get back in the car and wait for morning."

The town hall clock showed the time to be approaching 9pm, although the area still remained comparatively busy. Strangely, despite their new understanding of the situation, they nevertheless took care to avoid any heavy vehicles as they crossed the road. Nearing the car, Jill suddenly stopped, thinking she could detect the odd clip of a horse's hoof and the occasional shout of the drivers.

"John!" she exclaimed. "I think I'm beginning to pick up on some of the sounds."

He stopped for a moment and listened carefully but shook his head.

"Well, I can't hear anything. Are you sure you're not imagining it?"

Back in the car she began to express a new fear.

'I've suddenly realised, if we can't take hold of anything, how are we going to eat or drink? I've got the lunchbox Mum packed but what's going to happen after that? The little money we have would obviously be quite useless in this phantom existence."

He took her hand reassuringly.

"By this time tomorrow, we'll probably be back home so it won't matter anyway, will it?"

But she was not to be so easily placated.

"We don't know that John," she stressed. "We don't even know how far this thing extends. You said so yourself, remember? Supposing... supposing..." she added brokenly, "it goes on forever?"

"Look, I've already said that's not very likely but, if it happens, it happens. At least we'll be in it together."

Even while he was trying to reassure her, he was suddenly struck by an unimaginable horror for, as his arm closed round her shoulders, he realised the usual sensual firmness of her body no longer existed. Swamped by a freezing terror, he frantically tried with the other hand, but the result was the same. There was nothing of her that remained tangible – only the passenger seat itself offered any resistance. He could still see her but, she had suddenly and inexplicably become as insubstantial as the rest of their illusory surroundings.

Not immediately aware of this horrific transition and again thinking she had heard something, she turned to John.

"Listen. I think I can hear virtually all the sounds now."

But John could only hear her voice and, frighteningly, even that was now gradually becoming less audible and intermittent – like a poor radio reception. Finally, although he strained to listen and could see her still speaking, it faded away altogether. Unfortunately Jill had descended into a far greater hell, because John and the interior of the car were, effectively, dematerialising around her as she slipped ever further into the limbo of a phantom existence. Caught off guard amid this harrowing transformation, John saw her suddenly lunge at him with her face distorted in a silent scream of terror.

Grabbing and tearing in his direction like a demented animal, it suddenly dawned on him that she could no longer see or touch him. It was the ultimate horror. Although he could watch, he knew she would be totally alone in this ghostly existence. She was now rapidly becoming part of this other world and would, therefore, be forever beyond his reach.

In a state of pure mental anguish, John was reduced to being a spectator of her torment as she frantically grabbed at the interior of the car, which, for her, now no longer existed. Beside himself with grief and utter frustration, he was forced to watch as the girl he loved staggered towards the pavement with both hands clutching at the sides of her shaking head. He could see her silently screaming, "John, John!" It was an unbearable torture but there was nothing he could do. Her face was tear-stained and terrified, as she desperately looked back to where she knew the car ought to be. It was too excruciating to watch and, unable to stand it any longer, he felt his head sink slowly down onto the steering wheel in abject despair.

Chapter 5

THE EARLY MORNING of Friday 10th October, the same day that John had collected Jill from the infamous number 62, turned out to be a relatively quiet one for Violet – quiet at least until the sudden arrival of old Mr Baker who, at about 9.45am, burst into the shop frantic to impart the latest news.

"It's here, it's here!" he gasped, struggling to regain his breath. "You can see it at the bottom of the road. It's just moving up above the rooftops." And to emphasise the point, he indicated the shop door. "Go and look for yourself if you don't believe me. I tell you, it's absolutely pitch-black and everybody's out there looking at it."

"What do you mean 'it's here'?" repeated Violet, irritated by his behaviour. "What's here? What on earth are you on about?"

Lifting the counter flap, she made her way outside to see what had set the old boy off. Once in the street, however, the cause of his excitement became only too clear. The first thing she noticed was a group of neighbours in the middle of the road. Talking animatedly, they were busily pointing south and, following their gaze, she felt an icy chill of fear as she stared unbelievingly at a great black stain soiling the distant sky. Situated above the distant rooftops and just as John had experienced, its constant convulsions seemed to push its long extremities ever higher into the atmosphere. At first the little knot of observers continued to watch in fascination, but, finally, panic prevailed as, one by one, they fled to the sanctuary of their homes.

Again, as John had experienced along the coastal road, the daylight also slowly began to fade as an ever-increasing area of the sky became affected. In the threatening gloom, his mother felt herself bite deep into the knuckles of her clenched hands.

"Come on Violet," came a sudden and unexpected voice. "Let's get back into the shop." Unnoticed, her assistant Mrs Grimshaw had emerged from number 11 and taken in the position at a glance. Born in the Welsh valleys, her dour mentality was quite different from that of Violet and, although alarmed, she was better equipped to handle the situation. "Come on," she urged. "There's nothing to be gained by watching the problem, so let's get back inside."

Unfortunately a return to the shop only found old Mr Baker still ensconced on the shop chair and in full flow between bouts of heavy wheezing.

"There you are!" he exclaimed with an almost inordinate exuberance. "What did I tell you? We've got it on our own doorstep now. If that thing out there is anything like the trouble they've got off Iceland, then I dread to think what's going to happen to us. We'll probably all end up the same as that troopship."

What dumbstruck Mrs Grimshaw was the man's macabre excitement over the problem.

"Look, Mr Baker," she replied, acutely aware of Violet's distress. "I think it would be a lot better for all of us if you just managed to keep quiet for a bit because it really does nothing to help. Now I don't know what you actually came in for but first I'm taking Mrs Harper through to the house so you'll just have to wait until I get back. And when I do, I can tell you I don't want to waste any time with idle chatter." Then, leaving the old boy muttering under his breath, she guided her employer to the rear room. "You could do well without all that," she emphasised, pointing back the way they'd come. "But never mind. Leave it to me. I'll get rid of the old fool." Then, changing the subject, she added, "It might be an idea, you know, if we listen to the *Ten O'Clock News*. Perhaps then we might be able to find out what's actually going on."

The suggestion held a familiar ring – that to know the facts would somehow make them more tolerable. Fear of what she might hear, however, made Violet hesitate and it was a fear thoroughly justified when they switched on the old wireless set.

"... Earlier this morning," announced the newscaster, "our southern reporter spoke to one of the first eyewitnesses of the strange developments seen off the Plymouth coast. The man in question described how at about 8am this morning he had been alarmed to see the dawn sky over the sea suddenly erupt in a series of dark but silent explosions. He went on to describe how they had gradually converged before drifting east up the English Channel. Details of further sightings," he continued, "have also come in from the coastal towns of Portsmouth and Littlehampton while further, although unconfirmed, reports, suggest that an actual inland incursion may have occurred in the Brighton area."

Hearing this, Violet caught her breath knowing in all probability that her son would have taken the coastal road on his way to college. Frantic with fear, she desperately listened for further information as the news broadcast continued.

"... Speculative parallels are being drawn between these sightings and the drama which has been unfolding over the Atlantic. So, we again approached Professor Sinclair for his observations. This is what he had to say:"

"It is still extremely difficult," explained the university man, "to determine exactly what we are dealing with – either over the Atlantic or over the south coast. So anything I say should be treated as purely speculative. However, as I stressed on the previous occasion, there does seem some evidence for the existence of strong localised gravitational disturbances. However, I don't think for a moment that these dark areas of the sky are caused by physical explosions; quite the opposite in fact. I suspect they are probably the result of intense points of gravity which have suddenly materialised and are even capable of extracting light from their immediate vicinity. The cause of all this is very much an open question, but I would cautiously add that our present knowledge of the subatomic world is extremely limited, and it's possible we may have meddled with physics at a level beyond our present understanding. I hope I'm wrong, but, if a process has been set in motion that arbitrarily generates these vortexes, then I'm not quite sure where that leaves us. If this is a limited reaction then I don't think there's much to worry about. But if, on the other hand..."

Ominously, the Professor failed to finish, which caused the newscaster to observe superciliously,

"All very uplifting I'm sure – now here is the remainder of the News. Today the Prime Minister, Mr Attlee, called an emergency meeting of the cabinet at Number 10 to discuss..."

But Violet had heard enough and reached to switch it off. Then, with her fears in overdrive, she sank slowly back onto the old settee to gaze, stupefied, around the small living room with its threadbare lino, shabby furniture and tired curtains – all of which spoke of the careful conservation of money. Immediately after the broadcast, Mrs Grimshaw dutifully returned to the shop to deal with old Mr Baker, which was a relief for Violet because she felt totally unable to face anybody. She was also grateful to know that her loyal assistant would take all responsibility for the business until closing time.

Jack was really the only person who could comfort her at such times, but he wouldn't be back for several hours, which left a lot of time to be prey to her fears. However, over the years Violet had learnt that physical activity often helped so she threw herself energetically into the housework. Unfortunately, even this failed to completely ease the trauma she'd just experienced. The newscaster's voice still rang chillingly in her ears and she felt constantly drawn to the bathroom window with its uninterrupted southerly view of the advancing menace from the sea. She prayed that her daughter would be safe in school and wondered briefly whether the situation would warrant her being sent home early.

As twelve noon approached, most of the chores appeared complete, but then Violet remembered the perpetual chaotic state of her son's room. However, upon entering, she was dumbfounded to find him apparently still asleep in bed. This was totally inexplicable for he had left home about 7.30am earlier that morning and there was no way in which he could have returned without her knowledge.

"John!" she exclaimed in sudden exasperation. "What on earth are you doing back here? I thought you were at college. Do you realise it's approaching one o'clock in the afternoon?" However, the figure in the bed remained inert and, weary of the thankless task of constantly trying to keep him up to scratch, she decided to just let him lay there. Switching on the Hoover, she began to steer it across the debris-strewn floor. however, when even this failed to arouse him, she became concerned and, approaching the bed, noticed for the first time how desperately pale he appeared. "John – are you all right?" she enquired urgently, shaking him by the shoulder. But her efforts were to no avail. "John! John!" she then almost screamed in desperation. "Wake up! Wake up!"

To her increasing horror, there was still no reaction and, worse, as she looked more closely there seemed no sign of him breathing.

Gripped by blind panic, she raced from his room across the landing to the rear window that overlooked the yard. Although she didn't expect her husband back for some time, she frantically hoped that he might have returned unexpectedly. Desperately she searched the area below for any sign of him but then, to her immense relief, she heard the rear gate click as Jack pushed his old trades bike in towards the main dairy building.

"Jack! Jack!" she cried out. "Thank God you're back. Come up and look at John – there's something terribly wrong with him."

Seeing his wife's distress, Jack raced for the house and, belying his sixty years, bounded up the stairs two at a time to join her in their son's room.

"What's going on?" he exclaimed breathlessly. "I thought John was at college today." But then, catching sight of the still figure, he immediately realised from experience that their son needed urgent medical attention and, striving to conceal his anxiety, he spoke quietly. "Tell Mrs Grimshaw to close the shop and stay up here with you while I fetch the doctor. She's a good sort. I know she'll help – I'll be back as soon as I can."

Residential phones were all but unheard of in 1947, and it left Jack with no alternative but to race to the local surgery on his trades bike. However, hard as he cycled, it was well past 2.30pm before he finally arrived to find the place closed. Completely undeterred, however, he pounded on the front door, which, after several such sessions, was finally answered by the doctor's irate wife. Ignoring the agitated Jack, she took an inordinate time to examine the door.

"Really," she protested. "There's no need to bring the door down. Can't you see we're closed? The doctor's unavailable until evening surgery which doesn't start before 5.30pm and, in any case, you'll need an appointment."

Her condescending attitude to the old sergeant would have been inappropriate at the best of times.

"Look, whoever you are, my son may be dying so, believe you me, I'm not here to waste my breath on the likes of you. Just get the doctor," he demanded. "Or I'll come in and get him myself! Do you understand me?"

Before the poor woman could respond, the doctor appeared in the hallway behind her and demanded to know what was going on. He had not met Jack previously, but nevertheless recognised trouble when he saw it and immediately advised his wife to go back indoors.

"I do hope you understand," he stressed turning to Jack, "that I don't take kindly to people speaking to my wife in such a manner." However, in his present state of mind, Jack was in no mood to listen, but bluntly stated the plight of his son and, recognising the urgency in his visitor's voice, the doctor came straight to the point. "Tell me, is there anybody at home with your wife?" When assured this was the case he added, "I'll phone for an ambulance immediately. In the meantime, the best thing you can do is to get back home and I'll come and examine your son while we wait for it to arrive."

It was a time of intense anguish at John's bedside as the doctor conducted a thorough examination. Seeing his wife's distraught state, Jack put his arms around her shoulders.

"Oh, Jack," she sobbed. "He'll be all right, won't he?" But, lost for words, all he could do was give her a reassuring squeeze.

Finally, after what seemed an eternity, the doctor straightened up and folded his stethoscope.

"I'd like to offer you some reassurance," he said slowly. "But the fact is, I can't." Obviously perplexed, he shook his head. "As far as I can tell there are no external injuries. The life functions seem normal to a degree, although the body temperature is low and his heart rate is extremely slow." He paused for a moment as if unsure quite what to say next, but then added, with a certain hesitancy, "It's almost as though he were in some kind of hibernation. Certainly I can't rouse him. All we can do at the moment is to await the results of hospital tests – I suppose you don't happen to know how long he's been in this condition?" he asked turning to Violet.

But Jack's distraught wife could only tell him what little she knew.

"I just don't know, doctor. In fact, I didn't even realise he was here. He left for college around 7.30am this morning and I hadn't expected him back until this evening. It's a total mystery to me how he got in without my knowledge."

At this point, the doctor's attention was drawn to a slight movement of John's lips and he leaned forward to place his ear close to the patient's mouth. However, although he listened carefully, the faint murmurings remained unintelligible and he waved for silence as he urged John to try again. After several agonising moments, the lips moved briefly once more.

"What did he say? What did he say?" begged his distraught mother.

But, despite her pleas, the doctor remained firmly focussed on his patient.

"I'm not sure," he muttered finally. "It was

difficult to make out, but it sounded something like, 'Can't teach Jill,' or it might have been, 'I can't reach Jill.'" He looked up suddenly. "Does that mean anything to you?"

Before Violet could reply, there came a knock at the bedroom door, which heralded the arrival of the faithful Mrs Grimshaw who had come to announce that the ambulance was waiting outside. Once, the orderlies came in, they moved back the bedcovers and lifted John onto the stretcher, which caused his mother to cry out in anguish at the sight of her son's emaciated appearance and the translucency of his skin.

"Oh Jack – whatever's happened to him?" she sobbed.

Equally appalled, her husband was lost for words.

"Tell me, Doctor," he finally managed, "which hospital will my son be taken to?"

The answer was short and to the point.

"Brighton General. He will be in St Catherine's Ward. You'll find it located at the top of Elm Grove. You can't miss it," he grimaced. "It used to be the old workhouse and, if I'm quite honest, there hasn't been much improvement since. But I can say, the staff there are all excellent."

Once outside in the gathering gloom, John was quickly loaded into the ambulance, but as the doors clanged shut, his mother burst into tears. Standing close to his wife, Jack glanced south at the threat that had so upset her earlier. The strange darkness now covered virtually half the sky and it prompted a pessimistic observation from the ambulance driver.

"Doesn't look too good, does it? Bloody terrifying if you ask me. I'm beginning to wonder what sort of hell we've brought on ourselves. In fact, after I heard the news this morning, it makes me wonder if we've even got a future. Certainly, I'm not going to use the coast road and risk getting caught up in that lot."

This kind of talk was the last thing Violet needed and, mindful of his wife, Jack lost no time in telling the driver curtly to keep his thoughts to himself.

Brighton General Hospital in the late 1940s proved a far from inspiring experience and differed little in appearance from the days of its original function in the 1880s. Liberal coats of whitewash applied to its internal walls did virtually nothing to silence the echoes of its unsavoury past and there seemed little in the way of comfort as John was finally wheeled into an examination room. After what felt like an inordinate wait, the house doctor arrived accompanied by two nurses, whereupon his first action was to ask Jack and Violet to take a seat outside while he conducted his examination. The 'seats outside', however, proved little more than hard, narrow, wooden benches lining the corridor.

"Hmm. Hardly home from home, is it?" observed Jack wearily as he slumped down with a sigh. It was, however, only the start of a lengthy vigil during which he never once removed his protective arm from his wife's shoulders. And, leaning against him, she murmured brokenly:

"What I still don't understand, Jack, is how on earth John got back into the house without my seeing him – I mean, for a start – where's his car? He always leaves it by the front gate and he's never once come home without first giving me a hug."

Her husband was at a loss himself and could only shake his head.

"I don't know, love, any more than you do. It's a complete mystery."

Time dragged slowly, and after about an hour he restlessly determined to find out just what was going on. But even as he got to his feet, the examination door suddenly swung back to reveal a grim-faced house doctor who, ignoring Jack, crossed the corridor to sit beside Violet. Immaculate in his white housecoat and with a stethoscope still round his neck, he leaned forward.

"There's nothing actually wrong with your son that I can immediately detect. He is, of course, desperately thin. But, apart from that, for whatever reason, all his physical functions seem to have slowed right down. It's almost as though he were comatose. But again, that's not quite the right description because he's able to respond at a superficial level to various stimuli." He paused. "What I don't understand is his extreme lack of... well, for want of a better expression... his lack of internal vitality. I have ordered a number of tests which may throw some light on the situation, but, at present, I must admit I've never seen anything quite like it before."

"But he will be all right?" asked his mother desperately.

"I'm afraid only time will give us an answer to that," he replied quietly, but then hesitated before adding, almost to himself, "The only case I can ever recall which even remotely resembles his condition is one I encountered as an intern, but I mustn't burden you with the realms of metaphysics and speculation so, in the meantime, I think it better that we just wait for the test results."

He got up to make his way down the corridor, but after a few steps he turned and looked back. "By the way, does the name Jill mean anything to you? Because your son certainly seemed very agitated about someone of that name." But then, without even waiting for a reply, he continued on his way.

As far as Jack was concerned, the whole situation was totally unsatisfactory and, striding after the doctor, he called out abruptly:

"And what's supposed to happen from here on out?"

Being unused to this sort of rudeness, the house doctor looked round with an expression of disdain.

"If you're addressing me, Mr Harper, then I would suggest that you use a more moderated tone. I realise this is a distressing time for you both but please remember you are in a hospital and not an ale house... however, I've arranged for your son to remain in the examination room for the time being because, at present, he is too frail to be moved. He will be monitored regularly and if you and your wife wish to remain overnight you are welcome. But as you can see, the accommodation is very limited."

"You mean, these wooden benches," retorted Jack. But the doctor had heard enough and was already retreating round the bend in the corridor. "Lovely. Very helpful," muttered Violet's husband under his breath.

"Jack!" protested his wife. "Don't be so rude. It makes me ashamed to be with you sometimes."

"Well these doctors..." he retorted derisively, "all white coats and posh talk. I don't think half the time they know what they're on about."

"That's still no reason to be rude, Jack," she insisted.

"No," he nodded absently. "I suppose you're right. But then again," he added with a sudden smile, "you always tend to be right, don't you?"

The next hour witnessed a succession of visiting doctors and nurses. Jack assumed they were conducting the promised tests so, leaning back wearily with folded arms, he sighed in resignation.

"And all you can do is wait... and wait."

Finally, getting up to stretch his legs, he wandered across to one of the opposite windows, which faced due south and normally afforded extensive views over the English Channel. Today, however, was a very different story and he became appalled at what met his gaze. The situation had obviously deteriorated rapidly from earlier in the morning and now, in the prevailing twilight and dusk, the usually busy road in front of the Palace Pier was barely visible. Worse, from what little he could see, the whole area seemed completely deserted and conveyed a sense of utter desolation.

Although hovering just off the shoreline, he could still barely discern the pulsating and impenetrable darkness that had so terrified his wife. It was now past 6:30pm and the hospital authorities had already deemed it necessary to switch on the lights.

Being a war veteran, Jack was, of course, no stranger to impending danger, but his experience had been limited to well-established possibilities, whereas now he felt nothing but the sharp chill of something unknown. Feeling almost sick, he turned away while determining to say nothing to his wife. However, Violet was a perceptive woman and not easily fooled.

"What is it Jack? What's going on out there?" she asked anxiously.

He gave her an honest look.

"Nothing new, love. Nothing we don't know about already." He patted her arm. "So try not to worry."

"But Jack, I am worried, I'm desperately worried about John. What do you think the doctor meant when he talked about metaphysics?"

"I'm afraid, love, subjects like that never appeared on my old school curriculum so I've no idea what he was on about – I do know, however, that it's now well past six thirty and I'm famished so if we're to be stuck here all night then I suggest that the hospital canteen might be a good idea."

When Jill failed to arrive home that evening, consternation set in at number 62. Her mother usually expected her back around 6pm and when 7.30pm came and went with still no sign of her, Rita became extremely worried. Frequent glances at the mantelpiece clock did little to help. She tried desperately reassuring herself that perhaps Anna's mother had deliberately stayed on late at college in order to complete some project. She even considered the possibility that the delay might be due to John's unreliable car. However, nothing really helped and by 8.30pm she was almost frantic.

Adding to her distress, as she glanced at the clock for the umpteenth time, was the plaintive sound of little Anna calling for her mother. Racing upstairs to the toddler's tiny bedroom, she found the child sitting up in her cot and obviously very distraught. It was an unenviable situation, for Jill had never once failed to settle her little daughter for the night and the break in routine was obviously causing the youngster a great deal of distress.

"Shush, it's alright darling," she assured the child gently. "Mummy will be back soon and Grandma is here, so why don't you try and go to sleep. Then

Mummy will be surprised and pleased when she gets home."

Although too young to understand the actual words, her grandmother's soothing tone seemed to have the desired effect. Anna lay back quietly, but Rita knew all too well that it was but a temporary solution and, in the long term, Anna would naturally want her mother. It was only later that Rita would discover just how 'long' the 'long term' would be.

Confined to the house by two young children and with the nearest public phone box several streets away, there was little she could do to alleviate her anxiety. Finally, however, in desperation she asked a reluctant neighbour to keep an eye on the girls while she visited John's parents to see if they had any news. Knowing their shop's late hours, she was surprised to find it in complete darkness and with no apparent sign of life. Even after repeatedly knocking on the side door there was still no response and she wondered frantically what to do next. Finally, it occurred to her that Mrs Grimshaw might know something although she felt reluctant to disturb her so late in the evening. Moreover, her personal reputation among the local women alone was always a disincentive. However, with no option she tentatively approached number 11.

When the front door finally opened, it was to reveal a picture of complete opposites because the two women could not have been more dissimilar. While about the same age, Mrs Grimshaw was the archetypal housewife: prim, domesticated and essentially loyal to her husband. With her short, permed hair and floral crossover housecoat, she stood in stark contrast to Jill's glamorous mother. Rita was arguably a precursor of the morally lapsed sixties generation yet to come. Recognising her visitor, Mrs Grimshaw felt an instant reticence.

"Oh, it's Mrs Bower... isn't it? Can I help you?"

The reserve was all too familiar and did nothing to strengthen Rita's resolve.

"I'm so sorry to trouble you, Mrs Grimshaw," she apologised, "but I'm beside myself with worry over my daughter. You see, John collected her this morning, but now she's over three hours late home and I've no means of contacting either of them. There's no one at the shop, so I don't know who to turn to – I just wondered if perhaps you might know anything."

Faced with the mother's desperation, Mrs Grimshaw felt her natural disdain give way to a limited sympathy.

"I think perhaps you better come in," she offered coolly, "and I'll tell you what I know."

'Come in' meant an invitation to the front room 'museum'. Only friends and 'acceptable' neighbours ever saw the inside of the actual living area. Front rooms in the post-war era could afford an icy experience. They were often places where time stood still and nothing was ever touched; places where the ready-laid fire was never lit and the gleaming open-topped piano never played.

With Rita comfortably seated, her host managed a slightly less frosty attitude.

"I don't know if you're aware of it, but John's mother found him unconscious in his room sometime around midday. I closed the shop to stay with her until the ambulance arrived and the last I saw of her and Jack was as they left for the hospital." She paused. "It's a complete mystery how he got home in the first place. There was no sign of his car and I certainly saw nothing of your daughter – which," she observed, "seems strange because, if he had been taken ill at college, I would have expected her to come back with him – even if it was just to see he was all right."

"So, the question is," broke in the sudden sound of a male voice, "what's happened to her?"

Unnoticed, Mr Grimshaw had entered the room to pick up on the discussion and, although their visitor's allure was not wasted on him, he nevertheless demonstrated a genuine concern as he took a seat on the corner of the piano stool.

"I think, at the very least," he observed guardedly, "we should notify the police because there's been a lot of real problems in Brighton today due to the offshore threat. I was working in Hove and the southern parts of the town were in complete chaos. In fact, the whole of the coastal road as far as Brighton Pier was cordoned off and even some of the streets further inland were inaccessible. I assume, the ambulance got through all right but, there were certainly no buses running and I found it extremely difficult to get back home – even in the van. So, it's possible," he added addressing Rita, "that your daughter might have experienced the same sort of problem."

The light of law enforcement in the Portslade district had never burned particularly brightly, although, admittedly, it was an inefficiency due in part to a shortage of manpower – there being only one elderly sergeant and two part-time constables to service the entire area. However, that night Rita felt nothing but relief at the sight of the blue lamp glowing dimly above the station entrance. Although now well past 10pm, the old sergeant was still on duty – albeit deeply engrossed in a mug of tea. But, seeing her enter, he immediately placed his drink on the counter and asked if he could be of assistance. So, there in the station's drearily lit interior, Rita poured out her anxiety concerning her daughter, after which Mrs Grimshaw, who had kindly accompanied her, described John's inexplicable return home and his hospitalisation later that afternoon. Despite the lateness of the hour, the officer listened attentively and took a detailed statement. Then, in a move which emphasised the deep furrows in his forehead, he looked up.

"I suppose you don't happen to know the registration of this young man's vehicle because that would give us a lead."

"I'm afraid I don't," Rita apologised. "But I can tell you it was black and an old pre-war Ford. It was also very dilapidated and, really, I didn't like my daughter travelling in it."

"Well if you can find out the registration number, it would be helpful," the officer observed. "However, I do appreciate your anxiety Mrs Bower and we will do all we can, but I am sure you must understand that it's been an extraordinarily difficult day in the whole Brighton area with a number of people being reported missing. The problem out at sea has caused a lot of panic and as it moved inland, everything came to a virtual standstill."

He paused for a moment to drink from his mug. Upon hearing this, Rita drew a sharp breath and raised a hand to her face in horror.

"Oh, I didn't know that. You see, John probably took the coast road to college."

"Well, let's not read too much into it at the moment," reassured the officer. "It's quite possible your daughter got caught up in the mayhem and decided to stay overnight with a college friend. Let's also not forget that when this young man recovers consciousness, he should be able to shed some light on her whereabouts." Then, emptying the dregs of his tea down a nearby sink, he added reflectively, "I've known Jack Harper for some twenty years – right from the time, in fact, when he set up his milk business after the first war. He's always been a hard worker and they're a good family. I'm sure your daughter won't go far wrong with their boy so I shouldn't worry too much."

"Thank you, Sergeant," she replied graciously. "I do appreciate it."

"Now," he added more formally, "I'll contact the local hospitals and forward a description of your daughter to our Brighton branches – although heaven only knows they've got enough on their hands already." Again, he paused. "I'd like to do more, but as you can see I'm here on my own. I promise you though, the moment there's any news, we'll be in touch. Oh, and there's one other thing – please don't forget to contact your daughter's college first thing tomorrow morning to find out if they arrived safely."

The first thing Jack noticed when he awoke the following morning was the early, but subdued cold light radiating through from the opposite windows. It was Saturday 11th October, and almost immediately the grim realities of his circumstances flooded back making him wonder how it could be so light after his experience the previous day. He tried to sit up but realised it would disturb his wife who was slumped asleep against his shoulder and he had no wish to shorten her brief respite from anxiety. Glancing to the right he saw the hands on the corridor clock standing at 7am but there was little he could do except wait.

Promptly at 7.30am, the house doctor appeared

with the night nurse and it was his early morning greeting that finally brought Violet back to reality. However, as they entered the examination room, Jack became alarmed to hear their voices suddenly raised in heated debate. Jumping up, he raced towards the still open door to find the doctor by his son's bed agitatedly talking to the nurse. However, hearing the newcomer, the physician immediately broke off what he was saying.

"Mr Harper," he said, with a touch of exasperation. "Can you kindly tell me what's happened to your son?"

As the doctor moved aside, Jack could see to his horror that the bed was completely empty while at the same time becoming aware of his wife's hysterical voice.

"What's happened? Where's John?" she almost screamed.

"That, Mrs Harper, is the problem," stated the doctor shortly. "He's not here. Which begs the question, just where is he?"

He irritably turned back to Jack. "You were here all night, Mr Harper – did you notice anyone enter or leave apart from the night nurse?"

Jack shook his head.

"The only people I saw were medical personnel, although I must admit I dropped off around 5am so what happened after that..." he shrugged. "I just don't know."

At this point the night duty nurse intervened.

"I feel it necessary to say that when I first came on duty I was horrified at the patient's frail appearance. I visited him on a number of subsequent occasions and, unbelievably, each time he seemed paler and more emaciated." She paused to look directly at the house doctor. "I registered my concern with the duty doctor, although I was a little surprised when he decided to leave the matter until you arrived this morning. But, I can assure you, there was no way the patient could have left here on his own. He wouldn't even have had the strength to get out of bed."

On hearing this, Violet looked absolutely devastated and clung tearfully to her husband while the doctor, who carefully avoided any reference to his colleague's questionable behaviour, directed the nurse to immediately report the situation to the hospital security department. Although, even as he spoke, his eyes had remained trained on the vacant bed.

"I'm no detective," he said slowly, "but there's something odd about the position of those bed covers. It seems to me that if your son got up and just walked away – which admittedly is highly improbable – then you would have expected them to be thrown back in disarray. On the other hand, if he'd stayed to make the bed. Which is even more unlikely, you would have expected them to be straight."

"What are you getting at?" demanded Jack abruptly.

"I'm not sure," mused the medic. "But if you

look, the pillow is depressed and the covers are just rumpled down the middle."

"So?"

The surgeon chose to ignore his borderline rudeness and instead looked directly at Violet.

"I don't want to speculate, but for me, the facts don't add up. Anyway," he stressed with a sudden objectiveness, "there'll be an internal enquiry and, if necessary, the police will have to be informed because, effectively, your son is a missing person."

Violet's nightmare finally seemed to have peaked with her son's disappearance and the subsequent failure to find him anywhere on the hospital campus. After a fruitless search, the authorities were notified and within an hour the police arrived in the formidable form of Detective Sergeant Hobbs and his somewhat less impressive assistant Detective Constable Imms. Addressing the hospital security staff, the sergeant wasted no time in pointedly emphasising how lucky they were to have his services while a large part of Brighton wallowed in virtual chaos.

Having established the sequence of events from John's strange appearance at home to the empty hospital bed, the senior detective studied his notes as though somehow expecting an answer to leap out of the pad itself. For a long time, he didn't speak but finally observed abruptly:

"We know the patient spoke briefly about somebody called Jill. Now, does anyone happen to know who she might be?" As Jack filled in the details, the officer merely nodded while casting his eyes slowly and carefully over the room. "Jim," he said suddenly turning to his assistant. "Go down to the reception area and contact our Portslade branch. Before we left the station, I thought I heard something come through about a missing girl called Jill and I want to know if we're talking about the same person. I suspect, Mr Harper," he then observed turning back to Jack, "that we are in fact faced with two missing people and their disappearances may be linked in some way... but how?" he shrugged, "I've no idea."

Again reverting his attention to the hospital security officer, he asked what floor they were on.

"This is the fourth floor, Sergeant."

"And fire escapes?"

"None on this side of the building," replied the security officer.

Well, the patient couldn't simply have flown away," was the officer's immediate response. "And that's even supposing he managed to exit that air vent you call a window."

The detective fell silent while running his fingers curiously down the middle of the bed covers.

"Are you sure," he asked emphatically, "and I mean, absolutely sure, that no one left this room last night?" He'd not looked up but was clearly addressing Jack.

"Absolutely not," answered the old soldier flatly. "I was sitting outside that door all night and saw no one except medical personnel."

At this point, the night nurse, who had dutifully stayed on after her shift, reinforced his observations.

"Well!" exclaimed the detective in exasperation. "If he didn't get out of that window and he didn't go out via the door, it begs the question how the hell did he get out? Logic dictates a vanishing act."

"Logical or not, sir, I have a theory," voiced his assistant who had just re-entered the room.

"Never mind the theories, Constable. I deal in facts. So, what actual facts have you managed to unearth?"

The sergeant's charm seemed inexhaustible.

"Apparently, sir," he answered, "the girl in question is known as Jill Bower and she was reported missing by her mother at Portslade Police Station around 10pm last night. It seems she was picked up by," and he indicated Jack, "this gentleman's son at around 8am that morning and hasn't been seen or heard of since."

"And that's it?" exclaimed his superior, sounding more exasperated than ever.

"I'm afraid so, sir," replied his subdued assistant.

"Two missing people and nothing to go on," muttered the sergeant under his breath. At which, his assistant again tried to make his point.

"I think, sir," he ventured, "that taking all the

facts as we know them we might be dealing with a case of doppelgänger."

"And what is that supposed to mean to the uninitiated, Detective Constable?"

"Well, if I might explain," replied his assistant, "on very rare occasions, it has been known for people in dire distress, or even at the point of death, to project an image of themselves in order to warn their loved ones. A number of such cases are known to have happened during the last war. Remember, comatose as this young man appeared to be, he still struggled to mention his girlfriend's name as if she were in some sort of danger. I do believe it's possible that the figure we've been dealing with is nothing more than an insubstantial projection of his real self."

"Pure conjecture," snapped his superior.

"Does that mean," asked Violet frantically, "that John could have died in some sort of disaster and tried to tell us of Jill's involvement?"

"There's nothing to substantiate any of that. It's pure theatre," replied the detective sergeant acidly.

When Jack really looked at the speaker, he saw a certain shrewdness but precious little else to admire. In some ways, he felt the sergeant was not dissimilar to himself, except this man obviously took wanton pleasure in belittling other people. However, the old milkman had other things to think about – not least being his wife who was standing quietly sobbing by his side, and that, more than anything else, was the real agony. She had been a beautiful teenage girl whose vision had sustained him through the horrors of the trenches and with a protective arm he pulled her close.

"Oh, Jack," she whispered brokenly. "We've lost him, haven't we?"

"Hey, come on, love," he said gently. "He's not dead yet you know – only missing. In the meantime, remember, we have our little Margaret to think of. Mrs Grimshaw has been very kind to look after her so far, especially during last night, but we mustn't take advantage of her goodwill."

"Before you both leave," interrupted the detective, "I shall need a description of your son to enable me to circulate his details to all units – although the service is already grossly overstretched so I don't anticipate any quick results."

Turning to his wife, Jack whispered:

"Where the hell on earth did the police manage to get that lovely specimen from?"

Chapter 6

WHILE JOHN WAS being officially declared missing from Brighton General Hospital, the night-duty sergeant turned south into George Street. He realised that, not only would this be another hot day, but also that he was close to exhaustion. Thirty-six hours of almost continuous duty had taken their toll; a fact reflected in his whole posture. Originally, he had been scheduled for patrol during the night of Thursday 9th October, which meant he should have spent most of Friday in bed, but even before he got to sleep, his wife had called him with an urgent message from the station.

Together with other off-duty officers, his assistance had been needed to help combat any possible dangers posed by the approaching offshore threat. And the result had been a long and demanding day with hospital, police and fire services stretched to breaking point as the mysterious darkness suddenly swept in over the coastal road around mid-morning. His responsibility had been to keep the sea front between Brighton and Hove clear of all pedestrians and traffic. It had been while looking south that he had first caught sight of the darkness as it writhed above the sea and he had become mesmerised to see it encroach ever-closer in great pulsating waves as if it had a life of its own.

The stupefying spectacle filled him with dread and it had taken all his courage just to stand his ground. Fellow officers were also similarly affected and as the advancing danger reached the beach area, several had requested permission to withdraw further inland. But this was not before a number of his fellow colleagues had been virtually dragged off their feet by the enormous gravitational pull.

However, as the expansion began to envelope the coastal road itself, the officers had finally retreated back into the town. In most cases, this was as far north as Church Road, where John's car had refused to go any further. Meanwhile, as the darkness continued to advance and contract, it seemed to absorb everything in its path. Sadly, this included a young woman and her child who had strayed unwittingly into the danger-zone where a sudden surge had engulfed them both.

The situation only seemed to stabilise after the whole area between Church Road and the coast had become affected. At which point, he had been recalled to the station. Unfortunately, the unexpected emergency had been such a drain on manpower that it had left no alternative but for him to continue duties right through the night. Therefore, after a brief rest and a mug of hot tea in the staff canteen, he had returned to the streets. Fortunately, his next patrol turned out to be well north of the affected areas and virtually incident-free – although his involvement with the sea threat was to prove far from over.

Glancing wearily down George Street, he idly noticed that some of the shop blinds still remained drawn from the previous day. He assumed this was in anticipation of continued fine weather. In fact, although still quite early, the western half of the road already basked in a watery sunlight. The commercial life in the area was also showing signs of life, which, he knew, by midday would have swollen into an array of shoppers from the surrounding district. Although what the effect of yesterday's upheaval would have was probably an open question. However, by then, he hoped to be home and catching up on some desperately needed rest.

The local coffee shop was situated about halfway down the street and, in the past, its aromatic attractions had often tempted him to drop in, but fear for his job and what people might think had always been a deterrent. Today, however, feeling bone-weary, he gave in and took a seat.

"Good morning, sergeant. This is an unexpected pleasure. It's not often we have the privilege of serving one of His Majesty's police officers."

The Sergeant looked up slowly to find himself faced with the proprietor who seemed genuinely pleased to see him.

"No," he admitted wearily. "I must admit I don't

make a habit of it but, the fact is, I've been on duty for some thirty-six hours without a break and I'm almost out on my feet. That threat along the coast's got a lot to answer for – not least being the amount of my lost sleep."

The shopkeeper nodded sympathetically.

"I think it's caused a great deal of worry all round," he shrugged. "The trouble is you just don't know what's going to happen next. There was virtually no trade here all day yesterday – but never mind that – you really do look exhausted. Let me get you one of our 'specials'." And giving the officer a knowing look, he added, "You obviously need something a bit stronger than just coffee."

And with that, the proprietor lost no time in disappearing behind the counter. He emerged several minutes later with a steaming cup, which he placed in front of his customer.

"Now, don't ask any questions, Sergeant. Just get that down you." The officer responded to the gesture with a dubious look, but nevertheless swallowed the contents in virtually one go. "You know," admitted his host, "we were getting quite desperate yesterday. Especially when we heard the darkness had reached Church Road. Now, if you ask me, that was a bit too close for comfort. In fact, at one point we seriously considered abandoning the premises altogether."

"Well, I think the worst might be over now," observed the officer reassuringly. "Because from what I could see from the higher ground further inland, it seems to be retreating back towards the coast and getting much higher in the sky." He stopped for a moment to look at his empty cup and then back at his host as if to convey a certain disapproval, although he refrained from actually making any comment. "Thanks," he managed finally. "How much?"

The proprietor shook his head.

"Just take care of yourself Sergeant – we appreciate all that you do."

The officer never found out exactly what had gone into his drink, but by the time he stepped outside he felt distinctly better.

The busy shopping centre of George Street ran due south to a junction with the eastbound Church Road. Upon reaching the intersection the sergeant's first instinct was to check the sky above its rooftops. To his immense relief, there was only the pale blue harbinger of a fine day ahead. With barely a quarter of an hour left before the end of his shift, he felt no compunction in losing a few minutes by taking up a vigil on the corner. It had now been light for some time and as he gazed idly west along Church Road he happened to notice someone peering over the wall of St Andrew's graveyard. Initially he took no notice, but finally overcome with curiosity, he decided to enquire what the man was up to.

"Good morning, Sir," he greeted the stranger formally. "Nothing much going on in there I would imagine."

The overture drew a wry smile.

"Ironically officer, it's the lack of movement that's worrying me. If you stand here for a moment and look at the tombstone on the right – about halfway up the path – can you see him? He's been like that for the past half hour to my certain knowledge. I first noticed him on my way to the newsagent and he was in exactly the same position when I came back. He hadn't moved a muscle as far as I could see. I just hope he's all right."

Thanking the man for his civic-mindedness, the sergeant opened the lychgate and made his way towards the crouched figure lying against one of the memorial slabs. His first impression was that of a young man somewhere in his early twenties, well over six feet and with a shock of dark blond hair. However, he was quite motionless and lay in an almost foetal-like position with his arms tightly grasping his drawn-up legs and with his head sunk deep into his chest. The blue tinge of his pale skin sent a shiver down the patrolman's spine. It spoke of death and for a moment he wondered if the man was not already beyond help.

Totally ill clad in thin cotton trousers and an open necked shirt, the figure presented a pathetic sight in the early morning chill that still pervaded the graveyard. Greatly concerned, the officer bent down to touch the man's hand but then only to recoil at its icy feel. Whereupon, shelving any thoughts of his own weariness, he gently shook the man's shoulder.

"Sir, sir?" he asked urgently. "Can you hear me?"

The man's body felt stiff with cold and initially there was no response. Eventually to the officer's relief, he slowly raised his head with bleary eyes that looked blank and stupefied as he attempted to focus on the officer. Greatly encouraged, the sergeant quickly removed his cape and proceeded to wrap it round the man's upper body in an attempt to prevent further hypothermia. Even while he did so, a great shiver passed through the victim as he tried to speak.

"Constable," he faltered, "I'm so thankful to see you... a real tangible person." The enigmatic remark was lost on the officer, but, in any case, the man's speech faltered and it was several minutes before he finally managed to gasp through chattering teeth. "I've been through hell... I don't even know what day it is or even what year it is." It sounded as though the man's brain had been affected but there was worse to come as he desperately clutched his rescuer's arm. "You must help me... please... help me find my friend."

Before he could say any more though, he became convulsed by violent shivering as his head sank slowly back down towards his chest. Alarmed, the officer's chief concern was to get the man on his feet and to a safe refuge. Regulations dictated, in the 1940s, that recruits should be six feet or over in order to qualify for the constabulary and the duty sergeant was no exception. Although powerfully built, he knew all his strength would be needed for he suspected the man would be a dead weight.

"Sir," he said gently. "It's essential that we try to get you up." He squatted down to place the man's left arm around his shoulders while positioning his own right arm around the victim's waist. "Now, Sir," he continued, "I'm going to try and stand up slowly and pull you with me." Still very weak, the man could offer little assistance and, for a moment, it seemed touch and go. However, after drawing on the last of his reserves, the weary officer finally managed to get him upright. "Sir," he said after regaining his breath, "I want you to lean your weight on me and we'll try and make it to the church gate. Do you think you could do that?"

The man managed a silent nod.

By the time the oddly assorted pair reached the exit, the rising sun had gained sufficient strength to make itself felt and, after the struggle to get thus far, the officer was only too glad to offload his burden at the lychgate seat. Initially, the rescued man who was none other than the tragic John Harper, remained slumped and dejected but gradually, benefitting from the sun's warmth, he began to take an increasing interest in his surroundings. From where he sat, the familiar shape of Hove Town Hall with its elegant clock tower was clearly visible. It was ironic that, even as he looked, it struck 9am, which completed the twelve-hour cycle exactly since he'd last seen it. But then, the world had been very different, whereas now everything looked desperately normal. Approaching on the far side of the road, a familiar red corporation bus announced its destination as Portslade Station. In fact, the scattering of cars and pedestrians made him wonder whether the whole fearful episode had been nothing more than a mental aberration.

Glancing in the opposite direction, he caught sight of his faithful old car still parked by the roadside where he had last seen his terrified Jill. He knew then that it had been all too real and he buried his face in his hands at the reminder of her torment.

"Are you all right, sir?" enquired the officer, concerned at the man's behaviour.

The question sparked a release of all John's pent-up anguish.

"It was that darkness off the coast," he almost sobbed. "It nearly swamped us... but even when we managed to escape, it was into an unbelievable nightmare."

His own experience the previous day made the duty officer sympathetic.

"Do you feel able to tell me a bit about it?"

John shook his lowered head and his response became emotionally disjointed.

"You wouldn't believe me even if I told you... You wouldn't believe me... You can't lose someone in a nightmare, can you? I mean, not really lose them, because a nightmare is insubstantial and only exists in the mind... but that's what happened to me. I actually lost the most precious person in my life because, you see, my nightmare was real."

John's apparent ranting made absolutely no sense, although the officer was just glad to see him regaining his strength. It was only later that he would fully appreciate the implications of what he'd heard.

"I think, sir," he replied encouragingly, "that a number of people involved in yesterday's difficulties have gone missing, but I'm sure everything possible will be done to trace them."

"You don't understand," John protested in desperation. "My friend has been absorbed into a different time period. She's beyond reach and no amount of searching will ever find her."

On hearing this, the officer began to seriously doubt the man's state of mind, but he, recognised his extreme distress and remained sympathetic.

"Could you perhaps tell me your name, sir, and where you come from? If we could get in touch with your family perhaps they might be able to help."

For a while his suggestion drew no response, but then suddenly and unexpectedly, John burst out:

"My name? You want my name! What the hell does my name matter? Don't you realise that when I came into this cemetery I didn't care if I lived or died...? No," he muttered abjectly. "How can I expect you to understand?" His voice dropped to a point where the words were barely audible. "But, for what it's worth, my name's John... John Harper."

"Well, John," replied the officer as he sat up,

"things may look bad now and, of course, I can't begin to appreciate what you've been through, but I can tell you that life's always worth living." Then, without waiting for a reply, he added, "Now, if you're feeling a bit stronger, perhaps we could try to make it to the station?"

John responded obliquely by looking up at the sky and then south in the direction of the coast.

"No darkness."

"No darkness," affirmed the officer. "I think that, for whatever reason, it's withdrawing towards the edge of the atmosphere. Although, if you look carefully, you can still just about make it out – let's just hope it never returns."

As John struggled to his feet, it became obvious that he was still very weak, which obliged the sergeant to again take virtually his entire weight. Fortunately, the man who had originally drawn John to his attention came forward and offered to help. Even with this very welcome assistance, by the time they had reached the station, the officer was on the point of collapse. Faced with the sorry-looking trio, the duty constable behind the reception counter immediately raised the flap and rushed forward to help.

"I thought you were getting a bit late, Sergeant. Your shift ended hours ago. Where on earth have you been and what's happened? No, never mind – let me first get this young man to a reception room so that I can have him checked over. He looks in a bad way. In the meantime, get yourself sat down – you don't look in much better shape yourself."

With John comfortably settled, the Constable returned to the entrance foyer. "I must say," he observed, "that young man looked pretty rough. I mean he's half frozen and barely has the strength to stay upright. Where did you pick him up and how on earth did he get in such a state? I couldn't detect any alcohol. Has he been attacked?"

"No," came the weary answer. "It's nothing like that. Nothing so straightforward. But 'pick him up' is the operative expression. He's all of six foot and no lightweight, I can tell you. In fact, if I hadn't had the help of..." He looked round, but the Samaritan had quietly slipped away. "I was going to say, had I not had some assistance, I doubt if I'd have made it." He paused to catch his breath. "Anyway, the first time I saw him, he was in St Andrew's churchyard of all places. I think he must have spent the whole night out there. Can you imagine that? He was desperately cold and suffering from hypothermia. In fact, at first, I thought I was dealing with a corpse."

Just then, a constable appeared from the kitchen with a steaming hot mug of tea and the duty officer paused to take a long drink while requesting one for his exhausted colleague. "He's either badly deluded," continued the weary sergeant, "or has actually had a terrible and very real experience which I believe may be connected in some way with yesterday's difficulties." He gave the duty officer a straight look before continuing. "He said, and I believe it, that when he went into the cemetery he didn't care whether he lived or died – can you even begin to imagine his state of mind to do something like that?"

At this, both men fell silent for a moment before the duty constable replied:

"Did he offer any explanation for such behaviour?"

"All I could make out," the sergeant observed, "was that he had lost contact with some young woman called Jill. He went on and on about her and how she was forever beyond his reach – mind you, I'll let the young man himself fill you in on the details because, I can tell you, it beggars belief. I think perhaps his mind may have been affected in some way. Anyway, she's another one to add to the list of missing persons."

At this, the station officer suddenly looked as though something had occurred to him. Tapping a pencil irritatingly against his teeth, he sifted through the in-tray before snatching up one of the transcripts.

"What did you say this young man's name was?" he asked sharply as he glanced up.

"Well, he called himself John Harper. I managed to get that much from him – although he never gave any indication where he came from."

"This report," exclaimed his colleague excitedly, "came in last night and relates to a missing girl called Jill who comes from the Portslade area. Believe it or not, she was also last seen in the company of a Mr

Harper – now that *is* too much of a coincidence." He paused for a moment in mid flow. "Look Sergeant, you're exhausted. Get along home and leave the rest to me. I'll get in touch with our Portslade branch straight away."

Chapter 7

ABOUT THE SAME time that John had been found in St Andrew's graveyard, Jill's mother finally managed to extricate herself from the armchair where she had spent a long and restless night. The mantelpiece clock reminded her it was time to rouse the children, but she felt little inclination to start what she knew would be a very difficult day; the problem of what to tell little Anna being not the least of her worries.

Times like this made Rita regret the loss of her husband because now she had no one to turn to for support. Ostracised for her indiscretions, she had frequently considered leaving the neighbourhood altogether.

However, once she had her young daughter safely settled with a local school friend and Anna in her pushchair, Rita made a beeline for the local phone box where, filled with trepidation, she shakily dialled her daughter's college. At first she was told to wait while enquiries were made in the relevant department. After an interminable delay, she was politely informed that

Jill had failed to register both yesterday and today. So, numbed with disappointment, she replaced the receiver without a further word and stepped dejectedly back out into the street.

Finally, upon returning to number 62, she was surprised to find a white envelope protruding from her letterbox, the contents of which proved brief but pertinent.

'There has been a new development. Please contact the police station.'

The old sergeant, it seemed, had proved as good as his word and she left immediately with fresh hope. All this time, little Anna had remained confined and uncomplaining in her pushchair although, irritatingly, upon arrival Rita found the small police station reception area packed and was forced to wait her turn. It was frustrating, but finally she reached the counter to be greeted by a pleasant-faced constable, probably, she guessed, somewhere in his mid-fifties.

"I believe," she asked eagerly, "that you may have some news about my daughter."

"And what is your daughter's name?" enquired the officer politely.

"Jill. Jill Bower," she asserted quickly, but then, almost immediately, realised from his expression that the name conveyed little meaning. "Oh, you must know about my daughter," she added with a touch of exasperation. "I came here late last night and told the old sergeant she was missing."

"Ah!" he exclaimed more positively. "Anything of that nature would have been recorded in last night's log." He began to thumb through a thick ledger lying by the phone.

"There it is," he said slowly after running his finger down the most recent entries. But then, to her crushing disappointment, added, "There's nothing here other than what was written yesterday."

"Oh, but there must be," she insisted desperately as she thrust the old sergeant's note in his hands. "I found this in my letterbox this morning."

"'There's been a new development,'" he mused, glancing at the handwritten sheet. "Well, that's certainly the Sergeant's handwriting... I wonder..." And with that, he reached for the upright phone and began to dial. Silence followed as it rang at the other end but finally he spoke.

"Sergeant – it's Constable Hawkes from the station." He then described Rita's note. "I see Sergeant," he said eventually. "I understand. Thanks very much." The one-sided conversation had conveyed very little for Rita who was desperate to know what had been said. "It seems," explained the constable as he replaced the receiver, "that a message did, in fact, come through from Hove Police station earlier this morning concerning the apprehension of a Mr John Harper at about 8.30am. Apparently, he was picked up in the area of St Andrew's Church. By the way, that's along Church Road near the Hove Town Hall. Now, I would assume he's the same person mentioned in last night's memo." The officer pulled a face and shrugged. "Really, the sergeant should have told me about it but, then again, he's well into his seventies so... anyway," he stressed, "I'm sorry. I hope some of this has been of help."

"Yes, it has. Although it's very much at odds with the facts as I know them. Tell me," she pleaded, "was there any mention of my daughter?"

The officer shook his head.

"I'm sorry, I'm afraid not but I can always phone our Hove branch and request more details if you'd like me to."

However, by the end of the second call, it was clear that the only additional information available concerned John's apprehension in St Andrew's graveyard itself.

"And nothing about my daughter?" she asked desperately.

But the officer shook his head.

"I'm afraid not."

The news left Rita feeling not only disappointed but also bitterly resentful.

"That young man," she exclaimed, "collected my daughter in his car yesterday morning and I haven't seen or heard from her since. I'm sick with worry – I'll have to go straight to Hove and find out just what's happened to her."

"I'm not sure," volunteered the Constable, "whether the normal bus services have been resumed after yesterday's chaos but," he offered, "I come off duty at midday and would be happy to give you and the little girl a lift. You see I'm only on loan from Hove and I live quite close to the station anyway."

It was a kind gesture and, although bitter experience had made her wary, she nevertheless graciously accepted his offer. In fact, when the time arrived, she felt quite relieved to take her place in the front of his spacious Triumph car. And with little Anna comfortably perched on her lap she said admiringly:

"You are lucky to have such a beautiful car. It's so stylish."

"I'm afraid," admitted the officer, "it's really a bit self-indulgent and, to be honest, I can't really afford to run it. Petrol is very expensive and that's supposing you can even get any. But," he added with an appreciative smile, "I love the old girl. Now, more to the point, I understand the seafront road has been opened but I think I'll play safe and take the middle route along Church Road."

Therefore, Rita found herself inadvertently retracing the final part of John's fateful journey. Drawing close to its western end, the officer became obliged to stop at the traffic lights where he impatiently awaited the green signal – the same traffic lights, in fact, that John had so desperately searched for barely twenty-four hours previously. Finally, as the lights allowed them to move forward, it brought them within fifty yards of the actual spot where the old car had simply refused to go any further.

"Wait!" cried Rita suddenly. "I think that vehicle parked just ahead belongs to John."

"Are you sure?" queried her companion.

"Yes, yes, I'm quite sure," she confirmed excitedly. "Could we just pull over for a moment?"

As they got out to approach the Ford, it somehow seemed the ancient vehicle conveyed an aura of silent abandonment while, conversely, at the same time, it screamed out a terrible and fascinating enigma.

"Strictly speaking," observed her companion, "this vehicle constitutes police evidence and really it shouldn't be touched."

"I don't care! I really don't care," she replied almost hysterically wrenching open one of its rear doors. "Look, my daughter's lunchbox."

And there, sure enough, resting on the worn upholstery, was the old Oxo tin she always used for her daughter's sandwiches, but after frantically prising open the lid she found its contents remained completely untouched. Desperately, she scoured the remaining interior for some clue – any clue, in fact, that would indicate her daughter's fate. But the stubborn old relic refused to offer the slightest hint of the terror it had so recently witnessed.

"Mrs Bower," said her companion gently, "if you could take charge of Anna for a minute, I think I've spotted something."

Opening the passenger's front door, he reached in to pick something up off the floor.

"My daughter's face powder," Rita exclaimed,

taking the mock tortoiseshell container. "I gave it to her only last Christmas."

He looked thoughtful.

"You say they were on their way to Brighton Art College – now, I can understand why they took the middle road because, with all the problems along the seafront, I would have done the same thing, but I wonder what caused them to stop, and why here of all places? Then, of course, there is the question of where they went and why – although, of course, we know where John ended up. And look, even the keys are still in the ignition. It gives you the impression that for some unknown reason they left in a terrible hurry."

Although not involved in any official capacity, the officer was nevertheless very curious. He also felt a certain sympathy for Rita and, standing by the car, he carefully glanced around the immediate area.

"Now, it was confirmed on the phone," he mused, "that John had been found earlier this morning in St Andrew's graveyard. Well," he added pointing along the road, "that's the church just up there on the left." He shook his head. "But it beggars belief why he would want to spend the night there – especially as he had this car. Even more to the point, why didn't he just go home?"

"Well!" exclaimed Rita. "I was given to understand that he was in Brighton General Hospital all night so how on earth could he have been in two places at the same time?"

Her new friend just shook his head in bewilderment.

"I wonder if they broke down," he muttered, climbing behind the steering wheel and turning the ignition key. But the recalcitrant old engine sprang into life at his second attempt out of sheer perversity. He passed a hand questioningly through his hair. "Well, at least we know that wasn't the problem... mind you, I shudder to think of my superior's reaction when they discover I've been tinkering with the evidence. But that aside, it's always possible they had some sort of row, although even that doesn't quite explain what we've got here. The only person with the real answers, of course, is along the road in the police station."

"Well, if we're going to get there, I've got to watch the time," stressed Rita anxiously, "because I'm due to pick up my daughter from her friend's at four o'clock."

"It's almost 2.30pm now," he replied checking the Town Hall clock, "so it's going to be a bit tight, but I can always remain at the station until you've finished and then run you back because I don't think you'll make it otherwise."

"Are you sure?" she smiled. "You've been so helpful already. I feel I'm imposing."

"Well, certain it is," he assured her, "I've got nothing else planned and, to be quite honest, I'm as fascinated to find out what's going on as you are. It also seems to me you could do with a little help."

* * *

In the meantime, when Jack and his wife came to leave the hospital, they found themselves effectively stranded. Although the threatening twilight had lifted, there were still no buses available and Brighton railway station was some three miles distant. It represented a long haul for the exhausted Violet and something she could well have done without. Even by the time they eventually reached the ticket office, they had a further hour's wait for one of the few trains that still remained in service. The reverberations of yesterday's chaos had obviously affected everything and everybody.

Finally arriving home, they were surprised to find the ever-faithful Mrs Grimshaw still in charge of the shop even though it was her day off. However, by this point, Jack's wife was close to collapse from a combination of anxiety and lack of sleep. Whereas her husband was endowed with a stronger and better constitution. This was just as well because, as they walked in through the front door, their assistant handed them a telegram.

"Now what?" gasped Violet, sinking wearily down onto their little settee.

Tearing open the plain buff envelope, Jack drew a sharp breath.

"Apparently," he observed slowly, "there might be some good news. It simply says here that a young man fitting John's description has been detained by Hove Police."

"Oh Jack!" she cried, immediately getting to her feet. "We must go to him at once."

"There's no 'we' about it," objected the elderly tradesman. "You're to stay here. You're in no condition to go anywhere."

Hove Police station was a spacious and pleasant experience when compared to its Portslade counterpart and, with two officers in charge, Rita was quickly able to explain the purpose of her visit. As she was speaking, she caught sight of Jack coming in through the main entrance. He had arrived at virtually the same time courtesy of his faithful old trades bike.

After apologising to the attendant officer, Rita rushed across the reception hall.

"Oh Jack, I'm so pleased to see you!" she exclaimed breathlessly. "I just don't know what's going on – my daughter's missing and I've been unable to contact anyone. Where have you all been? Please tell me, have you got any news?"

With her long blonde hair in disarray and obviously distressed, Rita presented an enticing proposition for any man. Despite himself, Jack felt his male instincts surge. In the past, the elderly milkman had always been aware of the danger, and although one of his regular customers, he had invariably kept business with her on a strictly formal basis.

"I'm sorry, Mrs Bower," he replied apologetically.

"I wish I could help. But all I know is that my own son has been missing and, as regards your daughter, I'm afraid I have no knowledge of her whereabouts at all.

"But you must have some idea," she said desperately. "Your son picked her up for college only yesterday morning. She can't just have vanished."

"I can only say," Jack answered slowly, "that I hope the young man they're holding here turns out to be my son and that he can tell us what's really happened."

"But I heard he was in hospital," she objected. "How can he be here? I'm confused and sick with worry."

"You're not alone," the veteran solider responded shortly. "I don't understand it any more than you do. That's why I'm here – to get some answers."

"Well," came an unexpected voice. "I've spoken briefly to the man in question and I can tell you there is still a lot that needs explaining."

Jack turned to find himself once again face to face with the formidable Detective Sergeant Hobbs who hadn't endeared himself the first time round.

"Meaning?" snapped John's father.

"Meaning," stated the detective abruptly, "that the man being held here probably is your son. Whether he's the same person reported missing from Brighton General Hospital is another matter and, as far as I'm concerned, irrelevant. At the moment, my problem is his total inability to give a coherent account of what led up to his apprehension in St Andrew's graveyard."

"Well, just what sort of explanation would you like?" snapped his father.

"What I would like, Mr Harper," retorted the detective, "is a satisfactory reason for Miss Bower's disappearance and just what he means when he talks about her being trapped in some mythical limbo, because, sir, that is the ramblings of a disturbed mind."

On hearing this, Rita stepped forward anxiously.

"Look, I'm Jill's mother. What do you mean my daughter's trapped? Trapped where? Trapped how?"

"I'm sorry," apologised the detective. "I didn't realise who you were. All I can tell you is, that the man I spoke to in the interview room appears slightly deranged and, at the moment, it's difficult to take anything he says seriously. However, he seems to have been through some sort of trauma that might have affected his mind. I just hope we can find out what really happened when he's had time to recover."

This wasn't good enough for Jack and he took a step forward, only to be abruptly stopped by the unexpected and warning sound of his wife's voice.

"No! Don't even think of it!"

Breathless and unnoticed, Violet had arrived just in time to witness the confrontation. Although the detective was not easily intimidated, he perhaps unwisely was returning Jack's aggressive stare.

But Rita had been struck a mortal blow that only a mother could feel.

"You don't think," she asked ashen-faced, "you don't think he's done something to her, do you? Oh please! God, no!"

"Mrs Bower," assured the Detective, "I'm confident he wouldn't do her any harm; quite the opposite in fact. He seems completely devastated by her disappearance – but, having said that, he's the only link we've got with her and, therefore, I have recommended that he be detained pending a full investigation."

"And how long's all that supposed to take?" demanded Jack.

"Well, Mr Harper," came the sarcastic reply, "I'd hesitate to put an exact date on it, but at the very least, I've suggested that he should be held here while there is a comprehensive search of St Andrew's cemetery and the impoundment of his car for forensic tests."

The implications of all this only further infuriated Jack and he demanded to see his son immediately.

"That's not something I would recommend," retorted the detective caustically. "His immediate needs are a physical check and psychiatric help."

"I'm not interested in what you happen to think is advisable," shouted back the old sergeant. "If it's my son you've got here, believe you me I'm taking him home as of now. You do realise of course, I suppose, there's no way he can be detained without specific charges."

It was not strictly accurate and the detective knew his facts.

"Mr Harper, I have no jurisdiction in the Hove area and it's not up to me if he's detained or not. I have made my recommendations to the Chief Inspector and he will decide on an appropriate course of action."

But, as Jack made to continue, the Detective raised a hand indicating that the discussion was at an end. Rita, however, was beside herself.

"What are you arguing about, for heaven's sake?" she almost screamed. "Don't you realise I've lost my daughter!"

"Try not to upset yourself too much, Mrs Bower," Violet said gently. "I'm sure when we see John he will be able to tell us where she is."

In the meantime, Jack had become bemused by his wife's unexpected arrival.

"How on earth did you get here? I thought we'd agreed that you'd stay at home and rest.

"I'm sorry, Jack, but I had to come. I just couldn't bear the uncertainty of it all and Mrs Grimshaw has been so good. She's agreed to stay on at the shop. Then her husband kindly offered to drive me here. I don't know what we'd have done without them – but tell me, what's happening about John?"

"I wish I knew," responded her husband. "I've yet to have the luxury of finding out." Then, thoroughly irritated, he strode purposefully towards the reception desk. "Excuse me. I want to speak to whoever's in charge," he demanded bluntly – to which the attendant officer gave him a disdainful look.

"If you'll be patient for a moment sir," he replied in a restrained voice, "I will try and find out if the Chief Inspector can see you."

During all this wrangling, Constable Jim Hawkes had remained patiently in the background amusing little Anna as best he could. But Jack's latest outburst caused him to exchange a knowing look with Rita as he reminded her about the time.

Finally, the anxious parents found themselves on the inside of the door marked Chief Inspector Issacs; a man whom Jack instantly recognised as being of a very different calibre to Sergeant Hobbs. Inviting them to sit down, the senior officer took pains to make their individual acquaintance before leaning forward on his desk to address Rita.

"I do sympathise with your situation, Mrs Bower," he said kindly. "You must be extremely concerned about your daughter. Now, as I understand it, when you reported her missing she was allegedly in the company of a Mr John Harper. Well," he continued, "I have every reason to believe the man brought in earlier this morning is the same person. I also believe that, for a time, there was even some doubt about his whereabouts, which can't have helped."

At this point, he was interrupted by a knock on his door; whereupon, in answer to his summons, an officer from the motorcycle division immediately entered. Still wearing his crash helmet and with the straps hanging loose, he carried a chilling message.

"Excuse me, sir," he blurted out breathlessly, "but I thought you should know that two unidentified bodies have been discovered near the Hove–Portslade boundary."

"Exactly where on the boundary, Constable?" asked his superior, obviously irritated by the sudden intrusion.

"Well, sir, I've come straight from the location. It's at the bottom of the canal embankment along the seafront road. The ambulance unit was still there when I left but it looked to me as though they had both been killed by a fall from the pavement above. It's almost a vertical drop at that point, although I should stress, they were separate incidents because the bodies were about half a mile apart."

"Thank you, Constable, but tell me before you go, was there anything to suggest what might have happened?"

"Well, it's not for me to speculate, sir," replied the patrolman, "but the fencing along that stretch was badly damaged and much of it is lying in the canal with a lot of other debris. I think, perhaps, they got caught up in the drag of that darkness which caused us so much trouble yesterday. They probably just got sucked over the edge." Hearing this, the

Chief Inspector made no immediate reply but looked reflectively at his desktop. "Will that be all then, Sir?"

But, with the current case in mind, the Chief Inspector had one final question.

"Did you happen to notice the age of either of the victims?"

"From what I could see," came the thoughtful reply, "one of them appeared to be a man of about fifty. He might have been a bit more. The other person was much younger; a woman probably in her mid-twenties or thereabouts." The motorcyclist shook his head. "Very sad. She was such an attractive-looking girl too."

The possible implications of this latest information were too much for Rita and she burst into tears while, motivated by maternal empathy, Violet rushed forward to put a comforting arm around the stricken woman. Rita looked up, her eyes awash with anguish. "When you see this young man," she pleaded, "please ask him what's happened to my Jill – that's if she's not already dead."

Violet turned to look despairingly at the Chief Inspector.

"You all come from Portslade," observed the officer, "and, as I was about to say earlier, you probably can't appreciate the chaos and panic we experienced yesterday in the southern parts of Hove and Brighton." He indicated a window behind his high-backed chair. "I stood there around 10am and I saw people outside milling about desperate to escape the strange dark phenomenon that's been in the news so much lately." He paused before stressing, "I could see it approaching above the rooftops where it hung like a great black pall over the entire length of the road, literally turning day into night. And, within minutes, the whole area became deserted. It was a terrifying sight and, to be honest, I felt tempted to run myself. But it wasn't just its deadly appearance," he continued, "it was the terrible magnetic force that dragged many people off their feet and some of them were actually sucked up into the air. So I suspect the final toll will be quite high. The two people found today may well be only the beginning." He paused momentarily to look at the distraught mother. "I tell you this, Mrs Bower, because it makes the probability of this girl being your daughter less likely."

"All the time we sit here endlessly chewing the probabilities," protested an irate Violet, "we could well be finding out the actual facts from my son, presupposing it is my son you've got here. Now please, is it possible to see him?" she demanded.

"Well!" exclaimed the Chief Inspector patiently. "The doctor's with him at the moment because I deemed a medical examination essential."

"Excuse me, sir," queried the now marginalised motorcyclist. "But will it be in order to return to my duties?"

"Yes, yes. Of course, Constable. Please do. And thank you," he replied with a dismissive wave.

As the poor man left, he almost collided with the doctor returning from John's assessment.

"I've had a good look at this young man," explained the medic, "and, I think, physically, he's recovered sufficiently to go home, but his mental condition, I'm afraid, is a somewhat different matter. At the very least, I would recommend some serious counselling."

After thanking the doctor, the Chief Inspector rose slowly from behind his desk.

"I think, under the circumstances, Mrs Harper, it would probably be best for you to see John and confirm he is your son. Nobody knows a man better than his mother. So, if you would like to follow me."

But, as they were about to leave, Rita gripped Violet's arm to make a final desperate appeal.

"Please, please, Mrs Harper, try and find out about my daughter."

After closing the door, the senior officer spoke to Violet confidentially.

"I'm afraid what I said in there was partly to reassure that poor woman, but there are several aspects of this case which I need to draw to your attention." Reaching the rear reception room, he indicated several chairs lining the corridor. "Please, do take a seat for a moment Mrs Harper. You see," he observed, sitting down beside her, "I have no reason to detain your son – although it's been suggested 'in some quarters' that I should. However, you must understand the girl he was with has disappeared under questionable circumstances. Now, when you see him, it may well be that he can furnish us with a satisfactory explanation. But if not," he warned, "and the girl fails to materialise, then it leaves him under suspicion. The last thing I want to do is alarm you, but it could become a murder investigation." In the deafening silence that followed, he leaned forward to rest his forearms on his legs. "I have known Jim Hobbs for a number of years and, despite his brusque manner, he is a very competent officer. Like me, he played down his concerns for the sake of Mrs Bower, but I know he is far from satisfied with the facts as they stand." Finally, the Chief Inspector sat back to look directly at the horrified Violet. "I know it's been a difficult time for you, but I felt it my duty to point out the realities of the situation."

"Look, Chief Inspector. For the second time, can't you understand I'm desperate to see my son? Surely this can wait till later."

"Yes, I'm sorry," he apologised.

And with that, he got up, but his departure left a distraught Violet facing the ordeal of John's door on her own and, as she went to open it, she hesitated uncertainly. Was it really possible, she wondered, for the man on the other side to be her son, especially after how she remembered him in Brighton General Hospital only hours previously. Could this man the police doctor had pronounced fit to go home really be the same person? It seemed inconceivable.

With a hand on the doorknob and her forehead pressed hard up against the cool woodwork, she continued to hesitate and only a supreme effort of will finally enabled her to push the door open. Fearfully looking around the room, she caught sight of a figure huddled in a blanket and crouched over the fireplace, but instinctively she knew it was her son. Hearing the door, the man looked up slowly but immediately broke into a smile of relief as he caught sight of his mother. Even before he could get to his feet, she had rushed across the room to embrace him in a fierce hug.

"Oh, John!" she exclaimed. "It's so good to see you. I've been absolutely frantic."

A thousand desperate questions burned in her mind and she so badly wanted to scream, "How could you have been in the cemetery all night while at the same time be dying in the intensive care department of Brighton General Hospital?" But Violet was, nevertheless, a perceptive and intelligent woman and wisely decided not to 'muddy the waters', but rather concentrate on the immediate situation.

"How are you, John?" she asked, taking him by the shoulders and studying him intently. "They tell me you spent the night in a churchyard. I don't understand. I mean, you must have been absolutely frozen – why on earth didn't you come home? But, more than that, I must ask you what's happened to Jill because she didn't return home last night and her mother's here in the reception area worried out of her mind – you haven't done anything... well?"

"Mum!" he objected angrily. "What do you take me for? You know how much Jill means to me."

He slumped wearily back in his chair. "It's bad enough with that man Hobbs thinking I've done her some mischief," he protested. But then his words seemed to take an incomprehensible turn. "I've lost her, Mum. She's the only woman I've ever loved and I've lost her."

"Oh, don't be so ridiculous John," she replied with an irritation borne out of fear. "What do you mean you've lost her? Lost her how? How could you possibly lose her?"

"I can't begin to describe it," he replied in an almost mantra-like tone. "I could see her, Mum. I could see her. But I realised she couldn't see me because suddenly it seemed as though both the car and myself no longer existed for her." At this, Violet felt her mind recoil at her son's seemingly demented account. "She tried to speak, Mum, but she had already been drawn into an illusory world which had surrounded us. Can you even begin to imagine how she must have felt? I saw the hysterical terror on her face as she screamed and screamed, but I couldn't hear a sound. You see, she was totally beyond my reach. I couldn't touch her," he sobbed, "or offer any comfort. I even tried putting my arm around her but there was nothing there, Mum. Nothing. Her body no longer had any physical substance."

The disjointed ramblings began to make Violet appreciate the doctor's concern over his sanity, but seeing her expression he looked at her imploringly. "It's true, Mum. I don't care how it sounds. As God is my witness, that's just what happened."

Torn between loyalty and total disbelief, Violet felt unsure how to respond, although, finally, her gut reaction prevailed.

"I do suppose," she insisted, "that you realise no one in their right mind will believe a word of all that nonsense. They'll simply think you're insane or deliberately trying to cover up something sinister." Unable to suppress her fears or irritation any longer, she added bluntly, "And, in any case, what on earth possessed you to stay in the cemetery all night?"

"What on earth possessed me?" he protested almost hysterically. "I'll tell you what possessed me. You don't seem to realise the situation I was in. We'd found ourselves completely surrounded by some sort of phantom imagery of a bygone age." He shook his head agonisingly. "You can't imagine such an experience. There was no sound, no colour, in fact all normality as we knew it had ceased to exist. Worse, there were no means of knowing how far it all extended. I didn't even know if our homes still existed." He smashed a fist into the palm of his hand adding bitterly: "I had such high hopes for our future. I took to Jill's daughter straight away and, as far as I was concerned, it was to hell with what the neighbours might think. I was determined to be a good dad for her." But then, sensing his mother's thoughts, he added, "They won't find a body, Mum, if that's what's worrying you. They can't because she no longer exists as we understand it."

As he spoke, however, the Chief Inspector reappeared in the doorway.

"Everything going all right?" he asked pleasantly.

But, fraught with uncertainty, Violet momentarily refrained from comment for, with her son's life in possible danger, she was frightened to say the wrong thing. However, sensing the officer to be a decent man, she decided to take a risk and unburden the impossibility of their situation so she wearily turned to John.

"Go on. Tell the Chief Inspector what you've just told me."

Looking askance at his mother, he reluctantly complied. While the chief officer listened, Violet carefully watched his face for any reaction, but saw little change in his professional expression – a fact clearly reflected in his response.

"From a legal point of view," he observed evenly, "there would be a need of validation or proof of what you've alleged. But, in the circumstances as you describe them, I imagine this would prove somewhat difficult. On the other hand," he continued, "if the young lady in question is found among the victims of yesterday's difficulties then, obviously, you would be in the clear, but," and he looked pointedly at John, "if she is found to have died in suspicious circumstances

151

then you may well have some explaining to do." The officer paused as if to ensure that Violet's son had fully understood the implications of what he'd said, before adding, "We'll finalise things in my office but I must emphasise at this stage that, although I'm releasing you, you must remain in the Brighton and Hove area in case I need to question you further."

However, as the trio re-entered his office, Rita pounced.

"John!" she almost screamed at him. "Where is my daughter? What's happened to her?"

The critical moment Violet dreaded had arrived and she again looked imploringly at the Chief Inspector.

"Mrs Bower," he said kindly. "Let me try to explain. The fact is, this young man is not in a position to help you. He was caught up in the darkness we were discussing earlier and lost all sense of time and location until he was picked up this morning. Now, I suspect at some point he and your daughter became separated in the confusion and that she is probably still out there somewhere. It's just a matter of time before we find her and, when we do, you'll be informed immediately."

Violet had to admire the delicate path he had woven between fact and fantasy, with no trace of the formal 'We are conducting further enquiries' she might have expected. Essentially a ploy for time, however, it did little to placate Rita's fear-fuelled anger and she again tore into John.

"I had you in my home," she shouted bitterly, "and made you welcome. Is this how you repay my hospitality? You've deprived me of my daughter and what about little Anna? What can I tell *her*?" The venom in her voice was tangible. "You pretended you were fond of that little girl. How could you?"

Mortified, John did his best to protest, but Rita was beside herself. Fortunately, though, in the middle of her tirade, the Chief Inspector's phone suddenly trilled into life and, after listening carefully, he endeavoured to speak to the irate mother.

"Mrs Bower, if I could have your attention for a moment. The constable who accompanied you here is still waiting in the reception area with little Anna and it seems she is becoming increasingly fractious. But, more importantly," stressed the officer, "he says if you don't leave now you will be too late to pick your daughter up from her friend's."

Rita clapped a hand over her mouth in anguish.

"Oh, how awful. That poor man. I'd completely forgotten. And he's been so good." But, as she left, she made one final desperate appeal. "You will let me know immediately if there's any news about my daughter, won't you? They have my details at the reception."

The Chief Inspector raised his eyebrows at her exit and expelled a long breath.

"That was an opportune call to say the least, although she has all my sympathy. It is also opportune because I wish to discuss a few issues that would be better she didn't hear." Then, looking at John, he added, "I think it might also be helpful if you waited in the reception area." But even then, and with the office to themselves, he still spoke in subdued tones. "I'm afraid, as part of my enquiry, I need to touch on certain, and perhaps sensitive, areas, so I do hope you'll bear with me." He paused for a moment to allow time for Violet and Jack to absorb the implications of what he'd just said. "For example," he continued, "I need to know if your son has any unofficial record of violence or mental instability. I'm sure you both appreciate that what he has said so far throws serious doubt on his state of mind."

It was not the kind of question that parents readily want to hear and Jack was no exception.

"Well, he can certainly stand up for himself if that's what you mean," emphasised the old soldier. "Or he wouldn't be my son."

The Chief inspector had already assessed Jack's disposition and tempered his response accordingly.

"I understand that, Mr Harper, but I'm referring to gratuitous violence or sudden bouts of uncontrollable anger that could lead to an assault or worse."

Violet looked at her husband and shook her head.

"There's never been anything like that," she assured him. "A few schoolboy rucks but that's about all."

However, the senior officer had not finished.

"Could you also tell me if there's ever been any history of psychological problems?"

"I should think not!" snapped his father who was fast becoming increasingly irritated.

"It's my duty, Mr Harper," persisted the officer, "that I'm clear on all possible aspects of the case; to do less would be a failure of my responsibilities to all parties concerned."

"We do understand. We really do," interceded Violet while giving her husband a look of disapproval. "But I can assure you there's no record of any mental disturbances anywhere in our family."

As they made to leave, she turned in the doorway and looked back at the Chief Inspector to give him a lingering smile. "Thank you so much for your help and understanding," she said gently. "I want you to know I appreciate it."

She would have said more, but knew it would have been inappropriate. In turn, he responded with a slight nod and the hint of a smile as the door quietly closed.

Unwittingly and unknowingly, they had left behind a silent emptiness in which the Chief Constable suddenly, and perhaps unexpectedly, found himself prey to his thoughts. With a sigh, he sank slowly down into the high-backed swivel chair behind his desk and leaned back as he contemplated his official, yet somehow vacuous, surroundings. He tried to extract some intrinsic significance from it, yet all the while knowing there was none to be had.

Finally, he reached down and withdrew a framed

photograph from his desk drawer, which he placed on the top. A young woman smiled out at him with large wistful dark eyes. Somewhere in the early twenties, her beauty was enhanced by long shadowy tresses of hair that reached past her shoulders – her resemblance to Violet Harper was unmistakable.

Only on rare occasions did the Chief Inspector look at the portrait. The memories were too painful for, within a year of their marriage, she had suddenly fallen ill and died quite unexpectedly. Even now, some three decades later, his sense of emptiness remained virtually undimmed. After several minutes he reverently placed her picture back in the drawer and gently closed it shut.

Momentarily shelving the demands of the day, he got up and moved across to the window that overlooked Church Road and, standing there with hands clasped behind his back, he stared fixedly down at the street below. Oblivious to his feelings it seemed, the impersonal world outside was gradually returning to normal.

When Rita left the station, she felt as though her world had collapsed. John would not, or could not, explain her daughter's absence and, in her heart she feared the worst. Indiscretion, she felt, had robbed her of her husband whom she still loved; and now, Jill – her beautiful girl and great consolation – had also gone.

In stark contrast, as Violet and Jack stepped out into the October sun, they were delighted to be reunited with their son – even though they knew their problems were far from over. Then, with John seated safely in the front of a London-style taxi with its interior glass partition, they enjoyed a brief, confidential, time together during their journey home. As Violet settled in the back, Jack, in time-honoured tradition, put his arm around her shoulders and pulled her close.

"Oh, that poor woman," his wife whispered. "It must be absolute hell for her. And then there's those two little girls – she's all on her own you know – I must try to find time to call round and see her."

"It's been tough on everyone," he agreed, "and she certainly has my sympathies. But it's put John in a difficult situation – not to mention the fact that you've had virtually no sleep for the past twenty-four hours. Now, when you get home you're to do absolutely nothing until tomorrow."

A comfortable silence ensued as they were driven back along Church Road. The ride in itself was a treat, for taxis were a rare luxury in the immediate post-war period. Jack was the first to break the quiet.

"Did John happen to offer any explanation about his disappearance from the hospital?"

"None," she replied nestling against his neck as she recounted their son's extraordinary description of the previous day. "And I can tell you, he was absolutely adamant that he never came home yesterday – can you believe that?" she shrugged. "So where do you go from there? Anyway, it was useless to make an issue of it because my main concern was to find out about Jill. I don't know, but the whole thing just doesn't seem to make any sense."

Jack responded by peering sideways through the car window as if somehow hoping to find answers from outside.

"Well, at least," he observed finally, "that shadowy threat seems to have lifted."

"It makes you wonder though," replied his wife, "whether the horror of yesterday affected all our minds in some way and we imagined the whole episode. Or perhaps Detective Hobbs' assistant was right when he suggested that John might have projected a crisis image of himself which eventually just faded away. It would certainly explain those empty bed covers – I don't know," she repeated wearily, "I doubt whether we'll ever know what really happened. But," she stressed anxiously, "it's John's future that worries me. Do you realise that, if Jill's body were to be found, it's quite possible he could face a murder charge and that means he would hang if they found him guilty?"

Jack had obviously not thought of this eventuality and looked visibly shaken.

As Violet finished speaking, the taxi turned south towards the seafront where, straight ahead, lay the

Channel, shimmering and azure in the late autumn sun, with no trace of the previous day's menace. Now the bright sky reflected nothing but tranquillity, and momentarily Violet felt her spirits rise.

"Oh, Jack," she whispered. "Thank God it's over." But then, lifting her head from his shoulders, she added, "Except that it's not over, is it? Not for us. The effects remain. The only reason John has been released is lack of evidence and that could change at any time. It means," she added, "being afraid that every time someone knocks on the front door it could be the police come to arrest him. Do you realise, Jack, we'll be living in daily terror and can you imagine the neighbours' reaction if they caught even a whiff of any suspicion? I tell you, our lives would become unbearable. In fact, I think we would probably have to move."

The neighbours' opinions, provided they did not adversely affect his business, had never carried much weight with Jack.

"I think," he replied slowly, "we need to examine the realities of what we're facing. There's a clear choice between accepting John's improbable account, or even less likely the possibility of murder. And, the fact is, I just don't think he's capable of murder."

"I just hope you're right," sighed Violet.

By 6pm, their taxi reached the coast road where the driver found it difficult to avoid the previous day's debris, which still lay strewn across the highway. Meanwhile, Jack again turned his attention to the side window with its unobstructed view of the sea. By now, the sun was beginning to go down as he casually glanced up at the sky. Just as he was, about to turn back to his wife, he suddenly caught sight of a small but familiar darkness against the deepening blue. Radiance from the sinking sun had initially obscured it, but as Jack leaned forward for a more careful look, it was inescapable.

Miniscule compared to the original threat, it nevertheless hung there as a stark reminder of yesterday's chaos and, contrary to their first impressions, had obviously not completely faded out of existence. Fortunately, his wife's position in the taxi obscured her view and Jack decided not to disturb her new-found peace. Instead, he determined to get a clearer picture of the situation after Violet had gone to bed by listening to the late-night news.

Finally, after pulling up outside their home, John turned in his front seat to give both his parents the thumbs-up sign. However, it was Mrs Grimshaw and their daughter Margaret waving to them from inside the shop that really seemed to restore a sense of normality. Although, in reality, things would never be quite the same again, as Violet and her husband were bitterly destined to find out.

By the time they got indoors, it was fast approaching 6:30pm, which meant that, apart from a short nap on the hospital bench, Jack had been on the go for some thirty-six hours; and even with his iron constitution he was beginning to feel the strain. Violet, meanwhile, despite her brief rally in the taxi now felt completely exhausted, and so, after thanking Mrs Grimshaw for her support, she made straight for the bedroom. This, of course, left the thoroughly depleted Jack with the thankless task of explaining John's seemingly miraculous recovery. Although he finally just took the easy option.

"My wife will tell you about everything in the morning," he managed in response to their assistant's incredulous expression.

He was fast reaching a point of exhaustion where nothing really mattered anyway. So, with his intention to listen to the late news now out of the question, he made his way unsteadily to the foot of the stairs where, clinging on to the banisters, he wearily turned to his children.

"John, Margaret. I know you've both had a hard day but your mother and I are about finished, so I'll just say, all my love and goodnight."

Then, with a chorus of, "Goodnight Dad, we love you," ringing in his ears, Jack finally made it to the bedroom.

The drama and exhaustion of the previous two days had, of course, made no allowance for Jack's normally punishing routine. However, despite his weariness, years of self-discipline ensured he was awake by 3.30am, although, lying there with his head buried deep in the pillow, he longed to just turn over and drift off back to sleep.

With daybreak still a long way off and taking care not to disturb his wife, he swung his legs out of bed before reaching for his tired old brown dressing gown. But even as he pulled it around his shoulders, he suddenly remembered his intention to listen out for the previous night's news. So, after a quick shave and some two hours' work in the dairy, he slipped back into the house and switched on the old wireless set.

It was fast approaching 6am, and he should have been out on his rounds but, anxious to hear the early morning broadcast, he put such thoughts to one side while taking care to be quiet and not disturb the family upstairs. The last thing he wanted was to bring his wife down in the middle of any possible bad news. However, despite his best efforts, he omitted to adjust the volume and the set suddenly boomed out all over the room. Frantically reaching for the sound control he strained to catch any noise from overhead, which might indicate that someone had been disturbed, but, although he listened carefully, there was nothing and he breathed a sigh of relief.

With the wireless barely audible, Jack was obliged to put his ear hard up against the set, but the effort proved worthwhile for, immediately after Big Ben had struck the hour, the newscaster came straight to the point.

"This is the *Six O'Clock News* for Sunday the

12th of October 1947. It is now some three days since the heavy darkness prevailing over the Atlantic and along the south coast first came to worldwide attention. However, the latest reports available seem to suggest that these masses have inexplicably lifted high above the earth and are now moving towards the outer limits of the atmosphere. "Normally in these circumstances," continued the announcer, "we would seek the opinion of Professor Sinclair but, unfortunately, he was unavailable for comment and instead, we are grateful for the observations of his deputy."

The university man's tone proved measured and cautious.

"What I'm about to say concerning the apparent reprieve from the Atlantic problem and its associated difficulties, are the joint opinions of myself and Professor Sinclair. However, I must stress they are not proven fact. The question we now face, of course, is just what has caused these masses to suddenly move away from the earth's surface and the answer, we think, might lay in the fact that yesterday marked the moon's closest point to the earth during its monthly cycle. Technically, this is referred to as a perigee, which, in practical terms, means the moon was exercising its maximum gravitational pull. Now, both the professor and I believe this has been responsible for drawing the threat out towards deep space where, of course, it will be virtually harmless..." A smile entered his voice. "It's ironic, perhaps, that

163

these gravitational entities have probably become victims of gravity itself."

Jack had heard enough and reached to switch it off before sinking back in his chair with a deep sigh. His relief, however, was cut short by the unexpected sound of his wife's voice.

"Jack – what on earth are you doing listening to the wireless at this hour of the day?" Unnoticed, Violet had entered their small living room and appeared far from finished. "I do suppose you realise it's approaching 6.30am and that a lot of your customers rely on their early morning delivery."

Her husband knew all that only too well and pulled a face that reflected a combination of schoolboy-like guilt and a smile.

"I know, love," he murmured gently, "I know. And I'm just off – but you see," he added tenderly, "yesterday in the taxi, something came to my attention and I thought I'd just check it out before you were caused any more anguish..."

He had no chance to finish for she reached up with her arms to hold him so tightly that he could hardly breathe. And so, early that Sunday morning, with the dawn streaking the night sky, they yet again enjoyed a brief moment of the special magic they had first forged so long ago.

Chapter 8

EVENTS OF THE weekend had thoroughly depleted Violet. However, she nevertheless determined to face Monday with fresh hope, even though it was the 13th of the month.

As usual, business began promptly at 7.30am but, upon entering the shop, she instantly became dazzled by the rising sun. Her little store faced due east which had always made it vulnerable to early morning glare and, normally, Jack would have pulled down the shop blinds before setting out on his rounds but, today, with so much on his mind, he'd obviously forgotten. She'd barely completed the task herself, before the arrival of Gwen come to collect her daily 'pinta'.

"Good morning, Violet. Another lovely day, but I can tell you it's quite a relief to get away from that sunlight because it's enough to blind you out there."

It was a reassuringly routine start to the day, which helped. But the comforting beginning was short-lived. After a steady stream of customers, old Mr Baker burst in just after 10am.

"Ah, Violet!" he exclaimed, busily waving a newspaper about. "Have you seen this morning's *Daily Mail*?"

But Jack's wife, who obviously hadn't, shook her head while, at the same time, suspecting she was about to become acquainted with the copy in the old boy's hand. Upon glancing at the stark headlines, she felt herself go cold, for there dominating the front page were just three terrifying words:

'WAS IT MURDER?'

Taking the paper, she spread it out on the counter and turned to page two which gave a brief account of the ten people who had fallen victim to the recent sea threat. It appeared that, although they had been drawn into the vortex, their bodies had now all been accounted for. The article then moved to its main theme concerning a Brighton girl student who had mysteriously disappeared. Much of what followed amounted to little more than lurid speculation, with her companion being described as a dangerously disturbed individual who was unable to give a reasoned account of her whereabouts. Fortunately, the report failed to identify either the girl or who she had been with, but went on to suggest that murder might have been committed under the cover of the weekend's mayhem. It was Violet's worst fears staring out at her in cold print. Slowly, she handed the paper back to her customer.

"Bit close to home, don't you think?" observed the old muckraker, who obviously had no idea as to just how close it really was.

Poor Violet, however, was too distressed to answer, for the more she thought about it, the worse the situation seemed to appear. Although Mrs Grimshaw's discretion over the article could be relied upon, she knew only too well the same could not be said of Jill's mother. Feeling quite faint, Violet just about managed to serve the old boy before withdrawing to the small living room behind the shop where, sitting alone on the old settee, she fervently hoped for a pause between customers. Desperately shocked and worried, she reached into her handbag for a cigarette. While virtually a non-smoker, she nevertheless drew gratefully on the smouldering tobacco. Jack was still out on his rounds and with John too depressed to attend college, she had no alternative but to hang on until the arrival of Mrs Grimshaw at midday.

But as the hands of the living room clock approached 11am, the sound of the shop bell brought her once more reluctantly to her feet. Crossing the hallway into the store, she became horrified to find herself face to face with none other than Jill's mother. Despite the shock, however, Violet had to admit that here was a woman of stunning physical appeal, yet who, at the same time, radiated a certain vulnerability in the way she clutched the hand of the little girl by her side.

"This is Anna," began her visitor gently. "She's my granddaughter and, as I'm sure you must be aware, I'm desperately worried about her mother." Rita paused for a moment as if to let Violet absorb her emotional distress. "I wondered," she pleaded, "as one mother to another, whether you've managed to find out anything about my Jill?"

The sheer sadness and desperation in the woman's voice temporarily obscured Violet's own anxieties and, in a moment of empathy and to avoid being interrupted, she lifted the counter flap and invited her visitor through to the rear room. Once, Rita was comfortably seated, she attempted to converse with the woman who seemed to hold so much power over her son's future.

"Although I'm afraid we hardly know each other," began Jack's wife, "I'm aware that your daughter and my son are very close and I want to assure you that both my husband and I are certain he would never have caused her any harm."

Anna sat quietly by her grandmother as Rita began to pour out her anguish.

"That may well be the case, but you must realise the last time I saw my daughter was on Friday morning when she left for college with your son and I've heard nothing from her since. Surely," she added desperately, "John must know something of what happened to her."

Violet drew a deep breath and took a seat opposite.

"I believe he may do," she confided slowly, "but before I say any more, I must stress that these past three days have been just about the worst I've ever experienced. I won't go into detail, but at one point I thought my son was dead so, believe me, I do know what you must be going through. But with regard to your daughter, all I can tell you is what John told me." However, the very incredibility of what she was about to disclose made it impossibly difficult and the sudden sound of the shop bell came as a relief. "Excuse me," she apologised. "I won't be a moment."

It was, of course, but a brief respite before she was again faced with her visitor.

"As far as I know," Violet began hesitantly, "I believe my son and your daughter were still together after John left the coast road – although I'm afraid, what happened after that..." But, as she endeavoured to relate the 'subsequent events', it became increasingly obvious she was wasting her breath because Rita just angrily rose to her feet with a look of total disbelief.

"I had hoped," she said bitterly, "that you might have had some reassurance to offer, but unlike you, I happen to live in the real world and not in some fantasy existence."

By this time, she was shaking with emotion, and although Violet did her best to placate the distressed woman, it was all to no avail because Rita just grabbed her granddaughter's hand and stormed out without a further word.

Meanwhile, John had his own emotional problems to contend with and, sick with worry over Jill, he decided on a sentimental journey that would once again take him under the railway embankment and to the local recreation ground. Well before 10am and with the sun still low in the sky, he reached the wrought-iron gates of the park and entered with a heart that grew heavier with every step. Finally, he stood gazing down at the bench he had once shared with the girl he loved. He paused to look sadly over the green and neatly mown grass towards the tea rooms before slowly and dejectedly sitting down as the memories flooded back; memories of the girl who had so exceeded anything he could have dreamed of. Remembering the birds, he looked about but there were none to be seen. Even they, it seemed had foresaken him. He again focussed on the tea rooms and remembered their time there together while, in his mind, he could still hear her voice.

'Now you know, John, why I love you a hundred times.'

A certain tranquillity pervaded the park but it was suddenly disturbed by the gentle chiming of church bells. While a welcome intrusion, he somehow instinctively knew they heralded the time for him to return home. Rising to his feet, he made his way slowly back towards the entrance while vowing to return the following Sunday. Retracing his footsteps, he found himself again at the head of the steep slope which led down towards the Cattle

Arch; at which point, he paused to idly study the semi-circular-topped structure and its ancient grimy brickwork. The whole area had formed part of his happy childhood, yet today he perceived it through a melancholic mindset which coloured everything. Even raising his eyes to the seemingly forever-blue sky did little to raise his spirits. In fact, its very brilliance only served to deepen the shadow that enveloped the underpass entrance. Bitterly, he wondered why fate had decreed that he should be the one left behind and how a freak of physics had caused his present misery. However, aware that such speculation achieved nothing, he reluctantly continued towards home.

Two uneasy days were to follow before the 'consequences' of Rita's recent visit began to make themselves felt. By Wednesday, the drop in trade had become noticeable – evidence that her venom had already begun to spread.

A week later Violet rose around 6am, albeit after a very poor night of troubled thoughts. The uncertainties over John had fuelled her fears to almost breaking point and left her feeling utterly drained. In addition, she had woken up to a splitting headache. The prospect of another uncertain day in the shop seemed almost too much and she slowly sank down on to one of the kitchen chairs. However, after several minutes, she remembered that Mrs

Grimshaw was due at 9am and, slightly cheered, she got to her feet in the pursuit of a coffee. But, as she crossed the floor, the very effort seemed to intensify the throbbing in her head, while after collecting her drink from the stove she made an unsteady return to her seat where she became overwhelmed by waves of nausea and faintness. Fortunately, at this point Margaret put in an appearance and, although expecting her breakfast, she was quick to realise her mother was far from well.

"Mum, are you all right?" she enquired anxiously.

Violet, who had been resting her forehead in her hands, looked up and did her best not to alarm her daughter.

"Oh, I've just got a bit of a headache, love – that's all. Nothing to worry about."

But Margaret, who was by now approaching thirteen, refused to be so easily deterred.

"Mum, you look absolutely awful. Why don't you go back to bed? I'll look after the shop until Mrs Grimshaw gets here."

Violet, however, would have none of it.

"That's very sweet of you love, but your place is in school – and that," she added with a certain emphasis, "is where you're going."

"Well, will you at least see the doctor then?"

"I promise. I'll get Dad to contact him directly he gets back. But, in the meantime, I wondered if you could try and get that brother of yours out of bed."

Margaret rolled her eyes.

"I'll have a go, Mum, but you know what he's like." And with a nod, her daughter made for the stairs.

The conversation had taken the time to well past 7am, but even so the weary Violet decided to leave it as late as possible before opening the shop. Earlier she had taken two aspirins, but the pain in her head remained unabated. However, to her surprise, Margaret actually managed to prise her brother out of bed, but he was in a foul mood by the time he reached the kitchen.

"Mum – where's my breakfast?" he demanded irritably.

"John!" his sister shouted back. "Can't you see your mother's poorly?"

"Sorry, Mum," he mumbled. "You know what I'm like in the morning – anyway, what's the matter?"

He made it sound like an afterthought, and Violet found his apparent lack of concern quite hurtful.

"John, I've found the last few days almost unbearable," she exclaimed angrily. "You know I'm worried sick over Jill's disappearance and now I'm afraid the neighbours might be connecting you with her possible death. I've also got the most terrible headache. To be honest with you, the strain of it all is getting me down."

He took a seat with a contrite expression.

"I'm sorry, Mum," he apologised again. "I suppose I'm so taken up with my own misery that nothing else

173

seems to matter. Don't worry though – I'll get my own breakfast."

It fell quiet for several moments before Violet spoke again.

"Margaret, it's time you were getting ready for school or you'll be late." Then, turning to her son, she added, "Perhaps you could nip into the shop, John, and get me a packet of cigarettes?"

Now very concerned about his mother, he rose to leave the kitchen table.

"Are you sure you'll be all right Mum? None of all this is worth making yourself ill over, you know." John had caught sight of last week's *Mail* and he hastened to try and reassure her. "Look – the neighbours and the newspapers can speculate until the cows come home, but they'll never be able to prove a thing."

His mother looked and sounded weary.

"It's not a matter of proof, John. It's how people think and that's what governs their actions. Now, if you'll just be kind enough to get me those cigarettes, I'd be grateful."

John thought he detected a certain fatalism in his mother's voice and, as he crossed their small hallway in the direction of the shop, he experienced an apprehensive tightening in the pit of his stomach. However, that was nothing compared to what awaited him in the little store. Upon opening the door, he immediately realised the whole place was enveloped in an unnatural gloom. However, the cause quickly became apparent as he glanced towards the large plate-glass windows, which, to his horror, were covered with great swathes of white paint. Racing for the customers' entrance, he stepped outside to be confronted by the vicious-mindedness of the local populous; for there, in great two-feet-high lettering, was the raggedly scrawled word 'MURDERER' – and, not content with that, the perpetrator had also randomly splashed paint over the entire window Momentarily transfixed, John could only stare incredulously at this desecration of his parents' property. No stranger to local petty-mindedness, he was, nevertheless, appalled at such disrespect towards his mother and father who had loyally served the community for so many years.

But the clock had been ticking and, by now, it was fast approaching 8am: time when people were beginning to get out and about on their way to work.

"Very nice, I'm sure!" came a sudden sneering voice.

Spinning round, John found himself barely feet away from one of the local undesirables who, at the best of times, were never in short supply. About his own age, John had a vague idea that this particular specimen owed his origins to somewhere in Norway Street. Frustrated over the loss of his beloved Jill and worried about his mother, the shop window episode had proved the last straw. Striding across the pavement, he grabbed the mouthy offender by the shirt front.

"What did you say?" he snarled, as in a burst of uncontrollable fury he felt his knuckles smash painfully into his adversary's teeth. The youth staggered back, and although managing to stay upright for a brief moment, finally collapsed at John's feet. Amazingly, although the incident had taken place in broad daylight and in front of a number of passers-by, nobody, it seemed, was prepared to take a blind bit of notice. It would not have bothered John if they had because, without a second glance, he turned and re-entered the shop.

Gradually, however, the pain in his right hand began to penetrate the mists of anger and, looking down, he could see blood dripping from his knuckles onto the shop floor. Unfortunately, at this point, his mother, who had been patiently waiting for her cigarettes, finally decided to find out what was taking him so long. Entering the shop with its reduced light, Violet was horrified to see John gazing down at his bloodied hand.

"What on earth's going on and what's happened to the windows?" she cried almost hysterically. John responded by doing his best to propel her back towards the kitchen. "John!" she pleaded desperately. "Will you please tell me why the shop windows are covered in paint and, more to the point, why is your hand all covered in blood?"

"Oh, it's nothing, Mum," he assured her casually. "I just happened to catch some idiot splashing paint over the shop front and I whacked him, that's all."

"Look," she protested anxiously, "that sort of behaviour does nothing to help your case with the police. You know only too well the Chief Inspector at Hove is likely to send for you at any minute. He already suspects the worst and now you go and... and..."

Violet faltered and, much to John's alarm, her speech suddenly became broken and incoherent, while, to his absolute horror, he noticed the right side of her mouth slowly beginning to sag. Fortunately, Margaret was well on her way to school while Mrs Grimshaw had just let herself in to take over the shop. Closing the front door, she caught sight of the stricken John.

"Are you all right?" their assistant enquired. "And what on earth's happened to the shop front?"

But scarcely were the words out of her mouth, when she caught sight of Violet sitting upright at the kitchen table. Terrifyingly, the shop assistant realised from her expressionless eyes that she was unconscious. Even more distressing was the intermittent vomit that slowly trickled from the corner of her mouth.

Violet was in the process of having a stroke.

That evening, two troubled people gathered in the lounge behind the shop where, understandably perhaps, the sole topic of conversation revolved around Violet's health and the early morning paint episode. Jack had always been a tower of strength for his family, but tonight as John studied his father, he realised just how vulnerable he could be. He was also no fool and had long realised the great love that existed between his parents. Violet had been taken to hospital late that morning, but was still unconscious when they left around 4pm.

"Do you think Mum'll be all right, Dad?" he ventured quietly.

His father shook his head before responding with misery-filled eyes.

"Well, you were there. You heard what the specialist said. Your mother can't stand any worry because it sends her blood pressure far too high and that," he added grimly, "will probably lead to her early death." He turned away with a voice choked by emotion and shook his head. "Your mother has always been the nervous type," he almost whispered. "I realised that right from the start and I've always tried to shield her from the darker side of life."

Again, he shook his head in a hopeless gesture. "But this episode over you and that girl has been the last straw – she's worried sick that you might be arrested. She's worried over the effect of everything on trade. She's even afraid that things could become so bad that we'll have to leave the area. And now this business with the shop window... Oh! And, by the way – while I'm at it, what the hell were you thinking, laying into somebody right outside the premises? Have you got no brains at all?"

"He asked for it, Dad. He really did."

But his father was obviously disgusted, and instead of replying got slowly to his feet and made for the foot of the stairs.

"Goodnight," he just about managed. "I'll see you in the morning."

Two weeks were to pass before Violet's release from hospital, and then it was only with the strict instructions that she should be kept absolutely quiet. In the meantime, their loyal assistant, Mrs Grimshaw, had taken full responsibility for the shop while John had absented himself from his studies in order to care for his mother and the needs of his younger sister.

The busy world that normally revolved around the shop at 2 Gordon Road now virtually ceased to exist, although there were a few notable diehards such as Gwen and old Mr Baker, who obviously still enjoyed the opportunity to drop in and rake over the gossip.

Wednesday 5th November – the day after Violet's return – saw Mrs Grimshaw behind the counter by 7.30am sharp. The dour Welshwoman had never been one to stand for any nonsense, a fact borne out at the arrival of her first customer.

"Good morning, Gwen."

Her greeting was short and formal.

"Oh!" exclaimed the newcomer. "No Violet?"

"No Violet," repeated the assistant. "Now, what can I do for you?"

"Is she...?" But then, as if in answer to her own unspoken question, Gwen added, "Mind you, I don't think I'd want to face the public with all the scandal that's been going on about her son." She frowned slightly and shook her head, before adding with a touch of self-righteousness, "I told Violet some time ago that if her son insisted on going out with that girl from Norway Street, then sooner or later it would lead to trouble. I tell you, that family at number 62 are nothing more than..."

But her tirade was cut short.

"Gwen, I'm not the least bit interested. Now, if you'll please tell me just what you came in for, I'd be obliged."

Subdued by Mrs Grimshaw's sheer bluntness, the customer reached for her pint of milk from a nearby crate, placed the requisite sixpence on the counter and left without another word.

For the first half of November, trade in Jack's shop continued to be virtually non-existent, which allowed Mrs Grimshaw to spend much of her time caring for Violet who had improved but was still far from well. Being a perceptive woman, she kept shop matters to herself, but couldn't fail to notice how some of the neighbours looked at the property as they passed by.

Towards the end of the month John was recalled to Hove Police Station on a number of occasions, with one interview proving to be extremely harrowing as the officer in charge made a concerted effort to undermine his account about Jill. In the absence of a body, however, there seemed little the police could do. The sergeant also broached John's recent attack on the youth outside his father's shop – although how this had come to their attention was a complete mystery. Nevertheless, John was quick with an acid reply.

"And witnesses?"

The officer's face told him he had scored – although the look of suspicion and scepticism it engendered proved how right his mother had been.

Despite the days remaining bright, their length grew ever shorter as the month of December finally got underway. 1947 was approaching its death throes, and in the same way the summer heralded such beautiful weather, the winter proved to be one of unremitting cold and heavy snow.

In this respect, Jack's little corner shop offered something of a convenient refuge compared to the snowbound alternative confronting anyone attempting to visit the main shopping street. However, the upturn in trade this engendered only thinly disguised prevailing attitudes, which could, on occasions, amount to outright rudeness; a prime example being old Mr Dean – the insensitive, grubby-looking individual that Violet had always found so distasteful. Entering the shop, he leaned his elbows indolently on the counter.

"Oh, you're still here then, Mrs Grimshaw," he observed offhandedly. "I must say I'm surprised, bearing in mind the circumstances and all."

"If you don't mind," retorted the irritated assistant, "the counter is reserved for serving customers thank you. So, if you would be so kind..." She emphasised the rebuke with a dismissive wave. At this, the disreputable visitor slowly drew himself upright, but she had not finished. "Now, if you'll just tell me what you came in for. If not, please move out of the way because I have other customers to attend to." For a brief moment, he stood his ground before gradually retreating with a final snipe.

"It won't go away, you know. Feelings around these parts are very high and a lot of people think that son of hers should be behind bars. What with killing that young woman and all. Mark my words – he won't get away with it."

"If you take my advice, Mr Dean," she retorted pointedly, "I wouldn't let Violet's son hear you say that sort of thing. In any case, if all you've got to offer is rudeness, I would ask you to get out and never enter the shop again."

It was enough, and the belligerent lost no time in leaving – although the following customer had been quick to raise her eyebrows at the unpleasant exchange.

"I hate to say it, you know, but I'm afraid there's an element of truth in what that man said."

The shop assistant ignored the remark and simply

enquired if she could be of assistance. The whole incident, however, served to underline something she already knew only too well. Local people were angry about the apparent ineptitude of the police in bringing John to justice.

Later on, as she was about to close, Jack stepped in through the shop doorway looking absolutely exhausted. Accompanied by a flurry of snow, he sank gratefully onto the customers' shop chair normally reserved for the likes of old Mr Baker.

"Do you know," he said, wearily brushing the icy snow from his overcoat, "I've been on the go for nearly ten hours and all I've managed to cover are a few local streets. As for the rest," he shrugged, "I'm afraid they'll just have to go without. It's damn nigh impossible to get through the snowdrifts and," he stressed, "the stuff's still coming down. It's just as well you only live a few doors away because otherwise I don't think you'd make it – anyway, that's enough of me. How's my wife been today?"

"Well, Jack, to be honest, I just don't know," she replied. "Because I've been tied up with customers all day. But I'm sure if there was any change, John would have been the first to let me know."

For a moment the old Sergeant looked a bit disgusted.

"Lovely isn't it," he muttered, "how people's principles fly out the window the moment their bellies come under threat."

His assistant smiled.

"I know only too well what you mean, but I should mention what I told Mr Dean in the shop earlier – honestly, that man absolutely stinks. No wonder your wife can't stand him – and rude! Anyway, I'm afraid I told him to get out and stay out. I'm sorry," she added, "but I honestly think that we're better off without him."

Jack nodded and got to his feet.

"That's okay by me. You're in charge, so I leave that sort of thing to you. But now, if you'll excuse me, I must see how my wife's getting on."

"But, Jack," she insisted, "just before you go, I feel I need to tell you that there's a lot of antagonism out there over your son and that girl from Norway Street – I mean, the way some people glare into the shop as if they really hate the place."

He pursed his lips and looked out towards the street.

"They probably do," he nodded. "But the fact is, that's just something we've got to live with – and, in any case, there's nothing any of them can do about it. I believe my son," he added emphatically, "and they can think what they damn well please."

The stoic old sergeant meant every word, but in saying there was nothing any of them could do, he was sadly mistaken.

On the night of December 23rd, the constant downfall of snow suddenly erupted into a raging blizzard, which, together with the vicious wind howling in from the north-east, finally reduced movement to a standstill. Jack, therefore, had no alternative but to admit defeat and abandon his deliveries altogether. In any case, many of the glass milk bottles were splitting open as their contents expanded in response to the bitter cold.

The foul weather, however, combined with Violet's illness and the ever-present threat of John's arrest, gave the Harper family scant cause to celebrate the festive season. Moreover, business on Christmas Eve again dropped to virtually zero, with few locals venturing out into the impossibly snowbound conditions. Even so, Jack was adamant that his shop should remain open, albeit without the faithful Mrs Grimshaw, who had taken the day off for the pending festivities.

This meant, of course, that the old soldier had been left in charge but, by the end of a soul-destroying day, he was only too glad to lock up and switch off the lights. But then, after finally being satisfied that everything was secure, he took time off in the semi-darkness to gaze through the shop windows at the snow scene outside and to think. To think not only of life in general, but to wonder why his family and business were in such a chaotic state. And this after his having worked so brutally hard to achieve success. In addition, perhaps the hardest thing to bear was the knowledge that his lifelong sweetheart lay seriously ill upstairs.

The lamp post across the street which normally illuminated the area quite adequately, now appeared little more than a faint glow as it struggled to penetrate the dense wall of falling snow. Jack, who's mind was consumed with sadness, allowed his thoughts to slip back; back to earlier and happier times when John had been much younger and they had all celebrated the season in time-honoured tradition. This year, however, there was no Christmas tree to decorate; nothing at all in fact to mark the season of goodwill and, with a feeling of utter emptiness, he turned to leave the shop while thinking that things just couldn't get any worse. Crossing their tiny hallway, he nearly bumped into his son.

"How's your mother been today?" he enquired flatly.

"She's okay, Dad." he replied. "Yeah, she's okay."

"Well, I'm going up to see her and I probably won't be down again until later, so I'll let you sort yourself out over food and things, okay?"

His son nodded dumbly as his father made his way upstairs to the bedroom and his ailing partner. Never quite sure what to expect, Jack gently opened the door, but there, to his relief, he saw his beloved wife sitting comfortably propped up on a bank of pillows with her abundant silver-streaked hair sweeping down to her waist. She had been busy reading her favourite women's magazine, but immediately upon seeing her husband she put it down and reached out with open arms. After a prolonged embrace, Jack sat on the edge of the bed.

"Make no mistake, my love, you're in the best place, believe me. The whole area's virtually buried in snow – and cold – you wouldn't believe it."

"I would," she retorted. "I had a sneaky look out of the window and I can see what it's like only too well." Then, pointing to their small grate, she added, "If it wasn't for that little fire and the endless supply of hot water bottles courtesy of our John, I think I'd have frozen to death."

"Well, that's the price you pay for living in a corner property," he smiled.

Normally used to a long heavy day, Jack was not particularly tired and midnight struck before he felt the need to retire. Finally, with 1am approaching, he began to drift off into the outer fringes of sleep, although Violet had been in a deep slumber for several hours. As he coasted through a shallow dream, he was suddenly brought bolt upright in bed by the noise of breaking glass. Its sharp, high-pitched shattering sound was unmistakable, and leaping up to grab his dressing gown, he rushed onto the little landing where John joined him as he reached the head of the stairs.

"It's the shop window, Dad!" he shouted. "I'm sure of it. It's just below my bedroom." Even as he spoke, there came a second, louder splintering crash. Racing down to the ground floor, John again shouted back to his father. "They're smashing the main windows, Dad."

Flinging open the shop door, John switched on the lights to reveal a state of complete devastation. Two great jagged black holes had appeared where there had once been windows, while shards and fragments of glass lay everywhere. In addition, much of the soft goods, such as bags of flour, had been totally ruined by the flying splinters. In the meantime, the perpetrators had lost no time in making themselves scarce – although, in the distance, they both distinctly heard the sound of a male voice.

"You murderer. You bloody murderer!"

John's gut reaction was to go out into the street, but Jack restrained him.

"Leave it. You don't know how many there are and, in any case, you'd never catch them in all that snow."

"Dad," he protested. "You can't just let them get away with it."

"We've got no option, John," his father replied bitterly. "We just can't fight every thug and malcontent in the area." With the plate-glass windows gone, there was now nothing to stop the bitter north-east wind driving great flurries of snow directly into the little store. "I'll have to try and fix some of the old war-time shutters over those holes before the whole stock is completely ruined," he added urgently.

But scarcely had he finished when a deep sigh-like cry caused him to spin round in time to see his beloved wife crumple slowly to the ground where she lay inert across the threshold dividing the shop from their hallway.

Violet was dead.

Chapter 9

WHEN JILL FOUND herself separated from John and drawn into the intangible, shadowy world of a bygone era, all sense of reason deserted her as an unimaginable thrill of terror closed in. Virtually frozen into immobility, she could only stand on the kerb and scream.

"John! John! Don't leave me here. Please don't leave me here."

But her desperate pleas were to no avail, for he could no longer hear nor contact her. Only moments earlier, she had been settled in the relative comfort and security of his car. Now she could only stare uncomprehendingly at the vacant space it had so recently occupied. Repeatedly, she screamed her anguish at the empty air until at last, emotionally exhausted, she sank slowly to the pavement in unutterable despair. Finally, the tears came, accompanied by deep rending sobs as she buried her face in her hands. This alone could not shut out the alien sounds that pressed in on every side, nor could it help her escape the suffocating intensity of the whole nightmare. How long she hung suspended in that mental hell she would never know. Somewhere in the distance the town hall clock chimed the hour, but in her anguish, it didn't even register.

Meanwhile, on the far side of the road, her terrified screaming had drawn the attention of a passer-by who turned to his lady companion.

"I think it's that poor girl over there by the kerb," he observed, indicating Jill's crumpled form. "What on earth's the matter with her?"

Street vagrants, drunks and various social dropouts were not an uncommon feature of the Victorian scene and in a hard, unfeeling society, many people found it difficult to keep abreast of even basic necessities. Therefore, human distress like this tended to draw little attention. Even so, the lady's reaction was immediate.

"Well, let's go over and find out," she replied briskly as she made to cross the road.

Arriving on the far side, they were alarmed to see the extent of Jill's distress and the man reached to undo the cords of his long cloak before placing it around her shivering frame. The standard remedy for most ills in the 1880s was brandy, and the Samaritan lost no time in unscrewing the top of his hip flask. He meant well, although he had no inkling of what he was dealing with, and as he brought the container to her lips, she instinctively lashed out blindly and sent the flask flying from his hand. Caught off guard, her helper staggered back, clutching at the burning fluid in his eyes.

"Don't touch me, don't touch me," she repeatedly screamed hysterically. "You're all dead. Don't you realise? You're all dead. You've been dead for years."

Stunned by her ferocious outburst, the Samaritan turned to his companion and raised his hands in a token of despair.

"I don't think there's much we can do. She's either hysterical or had some kind of mental breakdown." Standing there in his soaked waistcoat and with the brandy dripping from the brim of his top hat, his companion found it difficult not to laugh.

"I'm sorry," he said irritably, still dabbing at his eyes, "but I fail to see anything funny." It was a vain attempt to restore some sense of dignity. But finally giving up, he reluctantly broke into a smile himself. Meanwhile, Jill had again reverted to the self-protective ploy of burying her head in her hands. "There's more to this than just her strange behaviour," the man observed. "I mean, have you ever seen a woman dressed like that – in tight black trousers?"

"I'm not interested in her outfit," protested his friend. "I'm here to help her and, by the look of it, she needs all the help she can get."

And, with that, she stooped down to try a more feminine approach.

Meanwhile, the tiny kerbside drama had acted as a magnet for the curious, but while some expressed a genuine concern, others were far less charitable with one unsavoury, bloated individual enquiring sarcastically if the girl was drunk. This was not an unreasonable assumption, for late Victorian beer halls far outnumbered the churches and alcoholism was rife right across the social divides. However, it was the speaker's derisive tone that so irritated the Samaritan, especially as the blotchy-faced individual was such an obvious imbiber himself, and he stressed, pointedly, that alcohol was not the problem.

"In some ways, I wish it was intoxication because I'm not quite sure what we're dealing with."

"Well, if she ain't drunk," he sneered, "she's probably deranged. Did you hear her?" he called out to the small crowd. "She was yelling at some bloke that wasn't even there. I tell you, she's mad; probably escaped from the county asylum at Haywards Heath."

Feeling unable to cope with such uncharitableness, the man turned back to his companion and her attempts to comfort 'the girl by the roadside. He knew from experience that, if anyone could help, she was the best qualified. In his role as a church minister, he had always found her empathy and natural love of people a huge support.

Hearing the gentle female voice, Jill momentarily looked up in the vain hope that, perhaps, normality had somehow reasserted itself. But, in doing so, she was only to find that nothing had changed and that she was still marooned in the dim, gas-lit high street with its rhythmic clatter of horse hooves and the all-pervading smell of animal dung. In fact, if anything, the woman's close proximity only served to intensify the sense of unreality. In the poor light, she could just make out her dark, ankle-length period dress with its white lace trim and a wide-brimmed floral hat that completely overshadowed her features. But even in the midst of her distress, Jill found herself beginning to respond to the stranger's obvious sincerity and, sensing her slight breakthrough, the woman ventured to introduce herself.

"My name's Rose and this," she added in a lyrical Welsh accent, "is my husband – the Reverend Michael Hewish." Jill had no means of knowing it at the time, but this would prove the beginning of a very close friendship. "We're here," she continued gently, "solely to try and help –nothing more."

At this, Jill ventured to look up with a tear-stained face. "Could you perhaps tell me your name?" Rose continued gently.

"Jill," came the hesitant reply. "My name's Jill." Then added after a long pause, "But you see, I don't belong here – I just don't belong here."

Her voice sounded strange even to her own ears, but it signified an attempt to communicate with this ethereal existence and, by implication, an attempt to identify with it.

"Well, Jill," replied the minister's wife, "you're obviously very upset. Could you perhaps tell me what's the matter? You say you don't belong here – is that the problem?"

The almost impossible question, left Jill at a loss and Rose was quick to see the hesitation. "Never mind. The important thing is to get you back to your family and if you like, my husband would be more than happy to take you home in our little buggy."

Unknown to Rose, her words held a desperate poignancy.

"That's my problem you see... I'm not sure if my home, or even my family, still exists."

The unbelievably strange remark made Rose exchange glances with her husband and left her unsure quite how to respond. So, getting down onto the pavement, she just sat there for a few minutes in a companionable silence. A socially erudite woman, Rose was quick to realise that any progress might depend on something they had in common and she glanced up at the clear night sky.

"You know, Jill, it's been such a lovely October this year."

The words held a familiar ring and, for a split second, everything felt almost normal. But it was enough.

"We had a lovely autumn where I come from," Jill agreed. "The sunny days just seemed to go on forever."

Rose smiled, but deemed it better to say no more for the moment, which left the two oddly assorted women just sitting by the roadside in an atmosphere of togetherness. Eventually, judging the moment to be right, Rose risked a more probing question.

"Can you tell me, perhaps, where you come from or how you came to be here?"

With her mind still reeling, Jill turned to her companion.

"I really don't know what to tell you... because, whatever I say, you'll think I'm insane. In fact," she added, "if I'm honest, I'm beginning to doubt my own reason. I heard what that man had to say about me just now and I suspect he might be right."

Mindful of the brandy episode, Rose, nevertheless, cautiously took her hand in a gesture of solidarity. However, this time there was no violent reaction for, as Jill experienced the warmth of genuine flesh and blood, any doubts about her companion's reality finally vanished.

"That was a very hurtful thing to have to hear," sympathised her new companion, "because that man knows absolutely nothing about your circumstances. I'd just ignore him – he's obviously a nasty piece of work with nothing better to occupy his mind." Then, after a pause, she added, "If you feel able to tell me what's the matter, I'm sure we can help and, I promise, we won't think you're mad."

As she spoke, Rose loosened the ribbons of her hat before removing it all together. It was an act of self-revelation and Jill found herself gazing at a middle-aged woman with an abundance of grey hair piled high on her head and a slightly plump but kindly face. Gradually, and a little incoherently, Jill attempted to describe the horrors she had been through, before adding finally:

"So you see, I'm forever separated from the things

I know and everyone I love." Fortunately, Rose possessed sufficient presence of mind to contain her natural reaction. For despite her promise, she experienced severe doubts about Jill's state of mind – a fact the stricken girl was quick to sense. "You don't believe me, do you? But then again," she sighed resignedly, "how could you?"

The gentlewoman was not a liar. Therefore, she chose her words carefully in order to preserve their fragile rapport.

"I'm sure what you've told me is in good faith and I accept that. However," she smiled, "you must admit, it's a bit different, to say the least."

Her last words, however, were virtually drowned out by the raucous voice of the fat man who still refused to mind his own business.

"What did I tell you?" he sneered. "The woman's nuts. In fact, Mrs, if you ask me, you're just as barmy to listen to her. Just pack her off back to the asylum where she belongs."

Unsteady and now with a whisky flask in his hand, the reprobate's remark drew a swift rebuke from Rose's husband.

"I think, Sir," he observed imperiously, "that your behaviour is totally inappropriate. Take your liquor and go. Your conduct as an Englishman is a disgrace to Her Majesty."

Cowed by the admonition, the degenerate fell momentarily silent. Then, after taking a further swig from his flask, he lurched away, muttering derogatory remarks about certain ministers of the church. Meanwhile, the still-fragile Jill turned to her new friend.

"Just take no notice," stressed Rose. "The man's obviously drunk. But now," she encouraged, "let's try and get you up. It's turning a bit chilly sitting here, so I think it would be a good idea to take you back to the Vicarage for a warm meal and a good night's rest. Then, in the morning..."

Before she could finish, however she was again interrupted, although this time, it was by the local police.

"What be going on 'ere then?" chimed a mellow West-Country-sounding voice. "Have you people got no beds to go to? Move along now, I say – you're blocking the public way." As the few remaining onlookers drifted off, the officer found himself surprised to see the minister and his wife. "I didn't realise it were you, Reverend. Is sommat up?"

Glancing towards the inordinately tall speaker, the minister immediately recognised one of his congregation.

"Hello there, Arthur. It's good to see you because you're just the man we need." Then, indicating Jill and his wife, he added, "This poor young woman seems to be lost and very distressed. We would be only too glad to take care of her, but I think in the meantime, it's important that we establish her circumstances and identity."

Unnoticed by the little group, the sky had slowly

clouded over and was now beginning to ooze a steady drizzle. In response, the officer pulled his cape tighter as the dim street lights began to reflect in the wet pavement. Then, glancing up at the falling rain, he observed:

"Desperately needed. But let's get yon girl down to the station before she becomes drenched. She don't seem none too well equipped for this sort of weather." He gave the minister an odd look. "Come to that, Reverend, she don't seem none too well dressed for any sort of weather."

Finally, as Jill regained her feet, Rose stooped to retrieve her shoulder bag from the gutter. It was the one remaining link with normality which she clutched gratefully and so, with Rose's comforting arm around her shoulders the little group moved off through the rain towards the police station. As Jill turned to go, she paused for a final look back in the hope that maybe... just maybe... But there was nothing.

As they approached their destination, Arthur was at pains to describe the frequency of accidents along the busy Church Road, and he explained how, at first, he feared the crowd around Jill might have signified yet another victim.

"If you arst me," he stressed, "there be far too many 'orses about these days and I reckon someone's gonna get killed if sommat ain't soon done aboot it. Anyway," he added as they entered the station, "yon sergeant will see you reet. Meanwhile, I best be gettin' back on me beat. Nice to see you, Reverend – I'll be there for mornin' service on Sunday. Never fear."

Then, with a brief wave, he melted away back into the darkness of the night. Watching him go, the minster murmured to his wife, "There goes a good man. One of the best."

The spacious station interior proved almost as inadequately lit as the street outside. Even so, it was difficult not to miss the sergeant's enormous girth as he dozed fitfully at the reception counter. Equally impressive was his vast drooping moustache. He'd been an intermittent churchgoer for years and his massive facial hair with its regular manhandling had always fascinated Rose, although she suspected its maltreatment was probably an outlet for the frustrations of his job. His leaner colleague, however presented a sharp contrast and was quick to impart a nudge to his superior's ribs upon their entry. It soon became apparent though that the sergeant's blatantly dilapidated exterior did nothing to impair his proficiency as a police officer.

"Hello there, Reverend!" he exclaimed as he suddenly recognised Michael. "What brings you and your lovely lady wife here at such a late hour? Is there something I can do for you?" But then, catching sight of the dishevelled Jill, he asked, "Is that young lady quite all right?"

"The fact is, Sergeant," Rose confided, "I'm glad

it's you on duty because you're one of the few people I know capable and flexible enough to handle this poor girl's difficulties." She turned to her husband. "Michael – would you be kind enough to sit with Jill in the waiting area for a few minutes while I have a quick word with the sergeant?" But even then, with the two of them out of earshot, she still spoke in lowered tones.

"Tell me, Sergeant, have you by chance had any recent reports of someone missing from the Haywards Heath mental institution?"

Although obviously surprised by the question, the officer shook his head while confirming there had been none to his knowledge.

"Why do you ask, Rose?" he queried.

"It's most extraordinary," she replied. "You see we found this young lady further back along Church Road – just by St Andrew's Church – and she was in the most terrible state."

The sergeant glanced curiously over towards Jill, where she was waiting patiently with the Reverend Michael, and he raised his eyebrows in approval.

"Very attractive young lady if I might say so," he observed. "Strange clothing, though. I don't think I can ever recall seeing a woman dressed quite like that before."

"That, Sergeant is part of the problem. But tell me first, have you ever heard of anywhere in the Portslade area called Norway Street?"

But again the officer shook his head.

"No, I can't say I have. But if you're talking about the land between the railway line and the sea, there's nothing much there except 'Old Goacher's' rundown farm. There's the old village of Portslade further north of course, but I've never heard of any road by that name. Why, is it important?"

"It's important," emphasised Rose, "because that's where the young lady claims she comes from."

"Well, that's not possible," shrugged the sergeant, "because there's no such place."

Rose was quiet for a moment.

"But that doesn't mean to say there never will be," she insisted.

"Sorry, Rose. You've got me there. I don't understand."

"Look Sergeant – I'll be perfectly straight with you. Ridiculous as it sounds, this girl genuinely believes she belongs to a different time. Some period in the future, as far as I can make out – I know, I know!" she stressed, raising her hands. "But the fact remains, that's what she believes and that's the address she gave. Now," added Rose, "she's either suffering from some form of mental delusion, brought on perhaps by a personal tragedy – or – unbelievably, she's telling the truth. Whichever way it is, I feel it my duty to look after her and try and reunite her with her family – wherever and whoever they may be."

"You're a good woman, Rose, and that's a fact, although it's not something I'd like to take on," muttered the officer, tugging at his moustache. "But if, as you say, she may have had a mental breakdown, then sooner or later someone will report her missing. In which case, of course, I will get in touch with you immediately." At this, the officer paused and looked thoughtful. "Rose," he said suddenly, "bring the young lady through to the rear reception area – I've got an idea."

Although nowhere near as spacious as the main service area, the room proved to be a good size and somewhat better lit, while at one end a map of Sussex virtually dominated the entire wall.

Conscious of Jill's distressed state, the portly sergeant spoke gently.

"Now, young lady. Mrs Hewish has explained some of your difficulties and, if I can, I will try to help." Then, pointing to the wall chart, he added, "This map shows all the local towns and villages for miles around and I wondered if, perhaps, you could identify your home area?"

However, even with Rose's encouragement, Jill remained desperately disorientated as her mind strove to cope with the insaneness of it all while the sheer vastness of the map overwhelmed her.

"Which is Portslade?" she faltered. But when it was pointed out, she could find no trace of the familiar streets she knew so well, and seeing her difficulty, the Sergeant quickly came to her rescue.

"Not there?" he said sympathetically. "Never mind. But you know where it should be, don't you?"

Unseen, he exchanged a glance with Rose. Then, being conscious of Jill's confusion, he said quietly, "I see you have a handbag with you. Do you think, perhaps, it might contain some sort of clue as to where you come from?"

Jill shook her head.

"I've only got a small bottle of aspirins and my college enrolment form. There's also a few bits of loose change."

Again the sergeant spoke with care.

"Would you mind very much if I had a look?"

In response, Jill opened her shoulder bag and emptied its contents on to a nearby table whereupon the officer immediately reached for one of the coins before crossing the room to scrutinise it under the wall-mounted gas lamp above the fireplace. Then, momentarily excusing himself, he made his way back to the reception area for a word with his fellow duty officer.

"George, can I drag you away from that paperwork for a minute? I'd like your opinion of this coin."

Reluctantly, his colleague adjusted his pince-nez, and after a cursory glance he just handed it back.

"Well, what can I say? I mean, it's a penny piece – so what?"

"Never mind the 'so what'!" exclaimed the irritated sergeant. "I want you to take a proper look."

Chastened, his subordinate again reached for the coin.

"Well," he observed sceptically, "it says here 'George the fifth', which is insane of course because

204

it sounds as though it could be our Queen's second-eldest grandson." At this point, his patience seemed to run out. "Look, Sergeant, I'm not going to speculate on this sort of lunacy because it's probably just a mistake at the mint."

"But what if it's not a mistake, George? What if it's genuine? Where does that leave us?"

"Sergeant," he continued in the same exasperated tone, "does this by any chance have something to do with that girl who was in reception just now? I couldn't help but overhear some of what was being said. But it's a lot of rubbish. People don't move about in time – it's absolutely absurd. Surely you aren't taking any of it seriously?"

"The fact remains," stressed his superior, "that this coin comes from her handbag and I don't think a mistake by the mint is an adequate explanation."

"I agree, it seems strangely circumstantial," argued his colleague, "but that's all it is. In my opinion, the girl's disturbed and in need of medical attention. It's not really a police matter at all. If she's a deluded vagrant, then her only recourse is parish relief or the workhouse."

"That sounds a bit callous, George, if you don't mind my saying so. Suppose she were your daughter? Is that how you'd like her treated? I doubt it. Anyway, I want you to take a look at the rest of her belongings."

The remainder of Jill's coins only served to emphasise the sergeant's dilemma when he indicated the date on a shilling piece. Both officers agreed it was English, but the 1945 date and reverse-side profile of George VI left them utterly bewildered. The Sergeant then turned his attention to the enrolment form.

"Listen to this, George!" he exclaimed. "It certifies Miss Bower as being a registered full-time student of fashion design at Brighton College of Art for the academic year 1947 / 1948. Now what the hell do you make of that? I didn't even know such a place existed."

"It doesn't," agreed George. "Although, I've heard of plans to build something along those lines in the Grand Parade area of Brighton. I think it's being proposed as an educational move to promote the commercial aspects of the arts and crafts movement. I don't know about you but I'm beginning to feel distinctly uneasy about this, because reason tells me it's all impossible."

The sergeant drew a deep breath.

"How on earth do you think this poor girl must feel?" he murmured quietly as he turned to the minister's wife.

"I don't begin to know what's going on here or what to advise. I feel faced with something completely beyond my understanding. Factually, of course, if this young lady is displaced in the sense of being homeless and without any means of support, then her only recourse, I'm afraid, is the workhouse." He shrugged. "It's hard, I know, but there's no other option."

"Well," countered Rose determinedly, "fortunately she does have another option because I could never live with my Christian conscience if she ended up in such a dreadfully bleak place. No," she stressed, "the young lady will have a home with my husband and I for as long as it's necessary."

The sergeant nodded and caressed his prestigious moustache.

"Well. For what it's worth, Rose, I think this young woman is probably a genuine case, but as a police officer, there is only so much I can do and I also have to be careful in case my own sanity becomes called into question. However, I do wish you both good luck because, how her mind will deal with it..." he shook his head, "... I just can't begin to imagine. But I do know, Rose, she couldn't be in better hands than with you and the reverend."

"Well, thank you Sergeant, and thank you for all your help." She lowered her voice. "I think it better perhaps if we keep this matter between ourselves. Oh, and while I'm at it – don't forget the church service starts sharp at 11am on Sunday, so hopefully we might see you."

The moustache twitched.

"I'll do my best, Rose, I promise."

"Now, Jill!" she exclaimed. "You must be one very tired young lady so let's get you straight home. It's not far."

Sure enough, the Vicarage, which also fronted Church Road, proved to be barely a ten-minute walk from the police station. This was just as well, because Jill was utterly exhausted. In the darkness, she could just make out a large stone-built church with a spire that tapered high into the night sky. But it was the house with its bright welcoming lights that really caught her attention.

"Ah – good!" exclaimed Rose. "Josie's obviously still up. She'll be wondering where we've got to, it being so late and all. Oh, by the way, I should explain Josie's our housekeeper and been with us for more years than I can remember. In fact, I don't know what we'd do without her and she's such a wonderful cook."

Despite all the distraction and her own weariness, John was still very much on Jill's mind and she, again, felt drawn to look back towards the spot where they had become separated. She desperately wondered what had happened to him and whether he was still trapped in the halfway limbo which, for her, had now become a reality.

Entering the great oak front door, she immediately found herself confronted with the largest hallway she'd ever seen. Lighted gas mantles revealed a host of ornate doors leading off to various parts of the house. In the far corner, stood an imposing grandfather clock with hands that pointed at 12.15am and, even as they moved down the hallway, the quarter began to strike.

"It's all so big!" exclaimed Jill who, despite her exhaustion, felt quite overwhelmed.

"If I'm honest," replied Rose, "I sometimes think it's far too big because there's only Josie and myself to keep it all clean – ah!" she exclaimed warmly. "And here she is now. Josie, can I introduce you to Jill? She's going to stay with us for the foreseeable future and I'm sure you will help to make her feel at home. I won't go into details, but she's just come through the most desperately difficult ordeal. But anyway, never mind that. Would you be an angel and make up a bed for her in the spare room while I fix the supper? Oh – and perhaps you could also put out a jug of hot water in case she would like to freshen up before going to bed."

A little like Rose, Josie turned out to be a rather plump, but pleasant-faced woman in her mid-forties. Dressed in the traditional long, dark frock and frilly-edged white apron, she extended her hand in a gesture of welcome.

"Hello, Jill. Welcome to the Vicarage. I do hope you have a nice stay with us and if there's anything I can do, please don't hesitate to let me know."

Again, it all seemed so terribly real and natural that, fleetingly, Jill found herself accepting the situation as almost normal. But then, as Rose invited her through to the kitchen, her husband excused himself before bidding them goodnight and retiring to bed.

"Pay him no mind, Jill," smiled her host. "He's got an early start with the church deacons. But, far more importantly, let's see about a cup of tea – you know, I sometimes think there's something about a nice cup of tea that helps to make our troubles seem just that little bit easier to bear."

If the hallway had been a surprise, it paled when compared to the kitchen, which, to Jill's parochial mind, appeared almost ridiculously huge. Brilliantly lit with numerous glass-funnelled oil lamps, it was dominated by a magnificent table whose top had been scrubbed to a gleaming white. It was the largest table she'd ever seen. Its only real competition came from the massive oak dresser that groaned under the weight of numerous pieces of Wedgewood china.

At the far end, two large sinks were flanked by what she took to be a water pump, for there was no sign of any taps. Immediately adjacent stood an enclosed iron fireplace. Although, at this stage, she had no means of knowing it was the kitchen range where Josie practised her many and varied culinary skills. Finally, above the stove area hung neat rows of copper pans, polished to a mirror finish.

"It's unbelievable," she gasped. "Our little kitchen at home is so small you could reach out and touch both sides at the same time."

"Well, strictly speaking Jill, it's not entirely our kitchen as such," admitted Rose. "We do lots of church catering here and it's also a venue for the deacons' meetings so the place often gets quite crowded, but we don't mind because Michael and I love all the activity. But now, on a more personal note, I've asked Josie to hunt out one of my nightgowns for you. I just hope she can find one to fit because, by most standards, I'm quite tiny if a little on the plump side," she smiled.

"You've been so good, Rose. I don't know what I'd have done if you hadn't been there for me."

"Well, if we can't be kind to each other," replied her new friend briskly, "we shouldn't be here in the first place. That's all I can say."

Tentatively taking a seat at the vast table made Jill suddenly aware of just how long it had been since breakfast. While finishing her welcome meal, she was surprised to see Rose emptying red-hot coals from the fire into what appeared to be one of the frying pans.

"Rose. If it's not a silly question – what are you doing?"

"Oh, you've probably never seen one of these," replied her host. "It's to help you get off to sleep. See, it's got a copper lid which you close down so, and then you can warm yourself without getting burned. We call it a bed-warming pan... Anyway," she added brightly, "if I carry it, can you take one of the lamps. Then we'll make our way up to your room. You must be absolutely exhausted by now."

Threading their way back along the panelled hallway and up a wide staircase, they finally entered quite the most exquisite bedroom Jill had ever seen. Even in the subdued lamplight she could make out brilliant white embroidered curtains held back by matching ties and, flanked by oak panelling. The large windows looked directly out over Church Road.

White wickerwork chairs stood either side of the bed, which had its covers partly drawn back to reveal spotlessly clean sheets. At the far end of the room, there was a low table graced by a large, beautiful jug and bowl, which were decorated with floral motifs in green, white and gold.

"Now I'm sure you'll be quiet and comfy enough in here," promised her host as she drew the curtains and slipped the bed-warmer between the covers.

Again, everything seemed so deceptively normal, which made it hard to believe how, in her own reality, this scene and even the vibrant Rose herself, would have long since vanished without trace.

"When you are ready to settle down for the night, remember to put the pan on the washstand for safety," advised Rose. Then, turning to the oil lamp, she explained, "If you want a brighter light, turn this little wheel at the base. To extinguish it, just cup your hand round the top of the glass like so and blow down the funnel."

She paused to place her hand on Jill's upper arm and gave it a reassuring squeeze. "It's going to be lovely to have you with us, so please don't worry about a thing." She shook her head. "I can't begin to imagine what you must be going through or how impossibly difficult and strange it all must seem. I just wish I could do more, but remember, Michael and I are down the hallway. So, if it all gets too much, please don't hesitate to knock on our door. Now, tomorrow, there's no reason why you shouldn't have a good lie-in. So, I'll just say goodnight and look forward to seeing you in the morning."

Then, with a parting smile, she gently closed the door and left Jill alone in the strange room with her thoughts and where the enormity of her situation closed in with a vengeance. Rose's stabilising influence was gone, and she was left to fight the turmoil of her mind alone. Eventually, sheer exhaustion prevailed; and mentally and physically spent, she collapsed on to the bed, bereft of sufficient energy to even undress.

Meanwhile, as Rose approached her own room, she could see a chink of light under the door. She curiously entered and was surprised to discover her husband still sitting up in bed busily reading.

"Michael!" she exclaimed. "I thought you were supposed to be tired. You know you've got an early start in the morning – what's the matter with you?"

"I don't know," he sighed, removing his glasses. "I just can't get that girl off my mind. None of it seems to make any sense. I mean, take that money for example; reason dictates she's a fraud, but if that were the case, how on earth could she have got the coins in the first place? And, even if someone else had forged them, what would be the point? What's there to be gained?" he shrugged. "I don't know, I mean, she certainly doesn't strike me as the type who would seek sensationalism."

"She's not," retorted his wife emphatically. "Neither, might I add, is she a fraud – but look, as you're still awake, why don't you make yourself useful and help me with this wretched corset. It seems to get tighter and tighter as the day goes on and for the life of me I can't get it undone."

"You do realise," her husband smiled, "that this performance is fast becoming a nightly ritual. I hate to say it, darling," he added with a gentle poke at her ribs, "but we have to face the reality of your gradual expansion."

"Don't you dare be so rude, Michael!" she shouted angrily. "And, in any case, you can talk. Where would you be without those tight waistcoats under your surplus? Imagine the sins *they* conceal. It might fool the women in the congregation but it certainly doesn't fool me. Their lofty illusions of you would go straight out of the stained-glass windows if they knew the half – urrgh, that's better," she then sighed gratefully as the stays finally relinquished their vice-like grip.

Michael looked amused as his wife sank thankfully onto their bed and enquired if all the suffering was really worth it. But his question was only graced by a dignified silence.

"You do realise, I suppose," he observed more seriously, "that if that girl turns out to be genuine, then she is unique and defies all the known laws of logic and physics, which would be a real opportunity for the scientific community."

"Look, your Reverendship," retorted his wife, "Jill is not a scientific curiosity. Neither am I going to allow her to be exposed to any sort of degrading enquiry. So, let's not be having any more of that.

To all appearances, she must remain a distant relative who happens to be staying with us. She's a vulnerable human being in the midst of the most terrifying ordeal, and it is our Christian duty to reassure and support her in every way. I mean, can you imagine the state of her mind and what she must be going through? To be honest, Michael, if I was in her position, I don't think I could cope. In fact, I wouldn't be surprised if she doesn't have a complete mental collapse. The human mind just isn't designed for that sort of stress." Her voice briefly trailed off for a moment before she observed wistfully:

"She's an anachronism in the universal order, isn't she, Michael? And I suppose that, sooner or later, the error will correct itself and then she will be gone."

"Does that really matter?" observed her husband a little surprised by her tone. "If she became able to return to her family, shouldn't we be glad for her?"

"Well, of course we would be," admitted his wife. "I suppose I'm just being a bit selfish that's all." At this point, she paused to stare vacantly at the dark pall of the window opposite. "Oh, I know I've got Josie," she added finally, "and I'm very grateful. But, you know, in some strange way I identify with Jill as though she were my own daughter. She's about the right age and such a lovely girl. I suspect I'll always remember her – silly I suppose after having only known her for such a short time."

"You're not being silly," Michael sympathised,

taking her hand. "I know only too well how you've missed out on motherhood and yet you've never once complained. But," he added suddenly, "it did feel horribly eerie this evening when she suddenly screamed, 'You're all dead'." He shivered slightly. "It's the stuff of nightmares, although under the circumstances, I suppose it's the sort of thing you might expect." He smiled. "However, having said that, if my backache's anything to go by, I can tell you I feel very much alive and hurting nicely thanks. Come to think of it though – what year did she say she came from? 1947? Let's see," he speculated. "If I live that long it would make me around a hundred and seven – not a very likely scenario. But I wonder what made her choose 1887 of all years. I mean, why not earlier, like 1787, or even further back?"

"Really, Michael," Rose retorted. "You do talk utter rubbish sometimes. Surely you don't suppose for a moment that she had any say in the matter. She's a victim of circumstance. But then," she added, almost as an afterthought, "it does make you wonder ,because if she's with us now, does it mean her generation has yet to be born or do we all somehow coexist in our own particular time frames? I don't know. The more I think about it, the more muddled I become." She suddenly frowned in response to a worrying thought. "And how does all this sort of thing relate to our faith? I bet they never discussed problems like that at your seminary."

In response, Michael roused himself up on his elbows, his tiredness momentarily forgotten.

"No, they didn't," he agreed. "Well – not in so many words. But I think when you speak of time or sequence it represents part of the order in which we exist – although it was no accident and, without it, there would be unimaginable chaos. Yet atheists take it all for granted. But, of course, a time structure has severe limitations, like the apparent division between generations and the loss of people we love. For the time being at least, that's just something we have to accept. But with regards to your question, I think the answer is probably no and that Jill's generation has yet to be born. Paradoxically, though, I believe from the perspective of eternity, we all very much coexist, although it seems this young lady has fallen victim to some minor rupture in the normal passage of time and has caused a limited and, I hope, temporary, overlap of the two periods. Does that help Rose? Rose!"

But Rose had drifted off into a timeless zone of her own.

"Well, thanks for listening," he muttered under his breath as he collapsed back onto the pillow. "It makes me wonder sometimes why I even bother."

Chapter 10

THE FOLLOWING MORNING, Jill awakened to the discomfort of blinding sunlight piercing her closed eyelids. Looking up, she could see it streaming through a chink in the curtains. Blinking against the glare and momentarily disorientated, she briefly gazed around the beautiful rose-tinted room. But then, prompted in part by the rhythmic clip of horse hooves from the street below, her memory suddenly and agonisingly surged back and a brutal panic caused her heart to race. Immediately she sat up and clutched at her chest, her mind seething with the problem of how to get back home.

Desperate to quieten the mental turmoil, she frantically tried to recall Rose's reassuring voice from the previous evening. Only gradually did the raw terror subside, helped by the timeless, mellow chimes of the grandfather clock as they echoed through the cavernous but tranquil house. She could not know, however, that her own mental hell had been more than matched by that of her beloved John, who had spent a broken-hearted night out in the open. Lying back briefly, it suddenly occurred to her that she had given virtually no thought to her little daughter or the distress her absence would be causing back home. But it was a self-recrimination cut short by a gentle knock at the door and the sound of a feminine voice enquiring if she was awake.

"Just a minute," Jill called out before rushing across the room to check her appearance in the mirror above the washstand.

A restless night spent fully clothed had taken its toll and she frantically endeavoured to offset the worst of the damage. Finally, opening the door, she found Josie patiently waiting with her breakfast and a scrubbed appearance that was tangible.

"Good morning, Miss Jill," she said brightly. "Did you sleep well?" Then, without waiting for a reply, she added, "My – it looks like another lovely day. I can't remember such a beautiful October."

To which Jill unwittingly replied:

"It's strange, but the October I left behind was just as lovely."

Slightly puzzled by the remark, Josie nevertheless proceeded to place the breakfast tray by her bed before crossing the room and drawing back the curtains to reveal the full graciousness of her spacious surroundings.

"Now," said Josie in her upbeat mode, "Mistress Hewish has told me there's no hurry, but I do know she's planning a shopping trip to Brighton later on. Although I'm not supposed to tell you, I believe she's hoping to take you along and buy you some new clothes. Between you and me," she added with a knowing smile, "I think she's quite looking forward to it. She's such a generous and lovely person; everybody's very fond of her."

Moving to the washstand, Josie collected the large jug and bed-warming pan before taking her leave with a promise to return shortly with hot water.

Some time later and with a certain trepidation, Jill finally made her way downstairs in search of Rose. Her lack of familiarity with the Vicarage was not helped by its sheer scale. However, as she ventured down the hallway, her attention became drawn to the melodic sound of piano music emanating from a partly open doorway. Screwing up her courage, she risked peeping inside to see her host seated at a baby grand and silhouetted against the morning light of a huge bay window. Expertly running her delicate fingers over the ivory keys, Rose seemed lost in the music and Jill decided to wait for a suitable pause before announcing her presence.

"Good morning," she ventured finally. "I do hope I'm not interrupting your playing."

She need not have worried for, swivelling on her stool, Rose immediately got to her feet with a warm smile. It was a welcoming gesture that gave Jill her first real opportunity to see her mentor properly.

By no means a tall woman, Rose was immaculately groomed with silver-streaked auburn hair parted in the middle and combed to form twin oval braids at the back of her head. Although what really caught Jill's attention was the full-length cream taffeta dress with its figure-hugging bodice that served to emphasise her friend's small waist. The whole outfit was complemented by delicate ruche-work set at the cuffs and the neck. This sudden exposure to Victorian elegance made Jill feel quite shabby as she gazed down at her black trousers and crumpled white blouse. Instinctively, she put a hand to her tousled blonde hair, conscious of how unkempt she must appear, but Rose's warmth was quick to dispel any sense of embarrassment.

"Oh, Jill. How lovely to see you," she exclaimed. "Please do forgive me for being such a poor host. Only I find piano-playing in the early morning so relaxing. It somehow seems to set the tempo for the rest of the day." Then, holding out both hands in welcome, she crossed the room to give Jill a gentle kiss on her cheek. "Now," she said brightly, "I do hope Josie hasn't mentioned it, but if you feel able, I'd like to take you on a little shopping trip." However, upon catching her guest's expression she added, "Oh, she has told you, hasn't she? She really is naughty, but I should have known better, because she's always found it difficult to keep a confidence. Ah well, never mind – but if you've had your breakfast and feel up to it, we could make a start."

For a moment, Jill hesitated. The shock of the past twenty-four hours had left her bewildered and very fragile, while the inner struggle remained indescribable with intermittent urges to scream uncontrollably. Sensing the problem, Rose put a comforting arm around her shoulders.

"I'm sorry," she sympathised. "Perhaps I'm trying to rush things. I can well understand if you feel unable to face the outside world because it's bound to seem very different from how you remember it. So, maybe we should wait a few days."

But, behind Jill's desperate sense of disorientation lurked a burning curiosity, a curiosity to see how life functioned in the area long before she was born.

"No," she stressed emphatically. "This is something I shall have to do sooner or later – so let's make it sooner."

As they approached the front door, they came upon the Reverend Michael busily adjusting his top hat and admiring his reflection in the hallstand mirror.

"Vain," murmured Rose. "Pure male vanity." It amused Jill to see how he checked and rechecked the angle of his hat to ensure it was just right, before reaching for his walking cane. "Although," exclaimed Rose adamantly, "he's not going out like that," and she proceeded to dust the back of his frock coat with a stiff hand-brush. After he had gone, Jill enquired if he really needed a walking stick. "Style," smiled Rose succinctly. "It's all about style and making the right impression. But," she added, "who he's trying to impress...?" and she shrugged.

Once outside, Church Road in broad daylight did

indeed present a very different proposition from the one she knew about, with the people and their way of life seeming almost alien. Noise ranged from the grind of iron-rimmed wooden wheels and the rhythmic clip of horse hooves to cries of drovers as they constantly urged their animals to greater effort. The diversity of transport alone left her breathless. Stately-looking four-wheeled carriages drawn by matching horses mingled freely with handcarts, many of which were piled high with various merchandise; evidence, if it were needed, of the eternal class divides.

Then there were the cyclists weaving their way through it all; perched high on their peculiar-looking machines, which she instantly recognised as Penny Farthings, they required skill and concentration – a fact admirably demonstrated by one rider who nearly lost control when he raised his hat to Rose.

In addition there was the elegant and unhurried way the obviously more wealthy women moved about in their long dresses, accompanied by their stylish gentleman escorts. They spoke eloquently of a graceful but lost way of life. Her poignant observations, however, were suddenly interrupted by an excited Rose.

"Look, Jill. It's our bus. This one will take us right to the centre of Brighton. I know you'll just love it," she enthused. "There are lots of stores where we can have a good browse and several of them have their own restaurants and even a small orchestra. I can't wait to show you around."

As the driver of the approaching vehicle reined in his team, it gave Jill her first real opportunity to study a horse-drawn bus, but it was a sight that left her with a mixture of curiosity and pity: pity for the two tired-looking horses forced to drag such an obviously excessive load. Standing there while the passengers embarked, they seemed only too grateful for the brief respite and hung their heads in a gesture of weariness. Steam rose from their heaving flanks and the smell of their sweat was pungent. It made Jill wonder why only two horses were forced to pull so many people, mindful perhaps of the six-in-hand western-style stagecoaches she'd seen at the local cinema. Obviously not well fed, she could well imagine their soulful eyes behind the dark blinkers of their harnesses. Instinctively, she stepped from the pavement to pat the nearest animal as it inclined its head in her direction but then only to be quickly rebuked by the surly driver.

"Are you gettin' on this bus or ain't ya?" he demanded. "I dunno if you realise it, but I've gotta run this thing on time and I can't hang about while the likes of you pander to these lazy creatures."

Temporarily taken aback by this unexpected rudeness, Jill turned to see the grubby, unshaven speaker perched high up in front of the vehicle. She felt her eyes begin to sparkle with anger. Caught up in the immediacy of the moment, the unreality of the situation vanished from her mind.

"Sir. Your horses look half-starved and exhausted,"

she exclaimed. "Can't you see how tired and overburdened they are? You should be absolutely ashamed." But then, impetuosity caused her to make a potentially critical error. "Where I come from," she then almost shouted, "the authorities would not tolerate such cruelty and people like you would end up in prison."

Fortunately, the subtle implication was wasted on the irascible driver and he impatiently flicked his long whip over the tired team to urge them forward. But then, as the whole shaky-looking edifice moved off, he turned to deliver a final insult.

"I dunno if you know it Miss, but it's about time you learnt to mind your own business and, what's more, try dressing like a woman for a change instead of flaunting yourself around like a man."

"How rude!" exploded Rose. "There was absolutely no cause for that sort of unpleasantness. I agree with you. Those poor animals looked completely worn out. It's just sad there's nothing we can do about it."

However, as their transport disappeared down the road, she observed resignedly, "I'm afraid that means we'll have to walk – but it's a lovely day, so they can keep their wretched bus."

"I'd love to walk," agreed Jill. "In any case, I couldn't bear the thought of adding my weight to the misery of those sad horses."

So, defiantly linking arms, the two 'girls' strode off towards the main shopping street. However, the adverse reaction to Jill's appearance was not only confined to the bus driver, and the blatant disapproving stares she constantly received only served to remind her of how peculiar she must appear in the eyes of the prevailing mindset. Worse, as they approached their destination, two elderly women in particular infuriated her when they actually stopped to watch as she walked by, and it prompted her to ask sarcastically if they'd seen enough.

"Well, I never," gasped one of the women. "I've never been so insulted."

"Oh, come on Jill," exclaimed Rose. "Just leave them. They're probably a pair of sour old spinsters with nothing better to do. It's sad."

By this stage, Church Road had given way to the Western Road of Brighton, and it quickly became apparent that even in 1887 it was the commercial heart of the area. In her own day, it had consisted largely of huge department stores, whereas now, she became fascinated to see endless rows of little shops inundated by swarms of customers.

Tiny sweet stores rubbed shoulders with harness-makers while greengrocers vied for attention with the hardware outlets. Moreover, everywhere she looked it seemed that various proprietors were hell-bent on festooning the outside of their premises with grotesquely large displays of merchandise. Butchers, in particular, appeared determined to obliterate their shopfronts with almost obscene displays of bloodied meat carcasses. The whole scene, in fact, seemed such a far cry from the austerity of 1947.

Against all this feverish activity, the incessant clatter of horse hooves and cries of traders combined to generate an almost carnival-like atmosphere.

"You can't believe it all, can you?" said Rose with a sudden flash of insight. Stopping impetuously on the busy pavement, she took both Jill's hands and murmured quietly, "You really have come to visit us from somewhere else, haven't you? I know that now. Forgive me if, at first, I doubted you, but now I'm sure. Sure that somehow, some way, fate has brought us together; and you know, from my own selfish point of view, I'm glad to have your company." But then she added with a hint of sadness, "However, I feel it can't last, for instinctively, I know that sooner or later you'll have to return to your own time and your own family." She paused reflectively:

"You see, I've never had any children of my own – so if I may, while you *are* with us, I'd like to be your surrogate mum." The hug she then received, however, rendered any words irrelevant. "Anyway," she emphasised, "we must remember the purpose of our trip... which is a little farther on."

'A little farther on' proved to be the multi-departmental store of Hanningtons – a vast emporium which operated on several floors. Accessed by numerous entrances, its endless and impressive window frontage displayed every conceivable kind of saleable goods.

"Oh, this is very much how I remember it," enthused Jill. "We always thought this store was the biggest and best in Brighton."

Its revolving doors whirled continuously courtesy of an endless stream of customers laden with beribboned boxes and various luxury goods. The whole store, in fact, conveyed a prosperity peculiar to the more privileged section of Victorian society. This nouveau riche owed their wealth to the new industrial age and a rather dubious exploitation of Britain's overseas colonies.

Grabbing her elbow, Rose gently drew her attention to the lavish window display of dresses and gowns.

"Oh, you'll be absolutely striking in any of these," she exclaimed excitedly. "Just look at the one on the far right. It might have been made for you – that dark material would contrast perfectly with your colouring and you are so naturally slim." It was an observation that conveyed a touch of envy. "You won't need any painful corsets – oh, but there's me babbling on about what you should like. Take no notice – I tend to forget how strange all this must seem to you."

"I must admit," smiled Jill, "it does feel a bit like a museum display." But, quickly realising how gauche that must have sounded, she hastily apologised. "I'm sorry Rose – I didn't mean to be rude. But, you see, the only time I've ever seen dresses like these have either been in historical films or books. Of course, these dresses are absolutely beautiful and I admire them enormously. In fact," she added wistfully, "they have a stylishness quite unknown to my generation. Where I come from, there was very little grace or elegance. Everything had to be purely functional with a strict economy of materials. The last war drained us all. There was nothing to spare – in fact, everyone had to struggle to even survive."

"The war?" queried Rose.

"Oh – I'll tell you about that another time," Jill replied evasively. Then, conscious of her host's enthusiasm, she quickly changed the subject and indicated one of the mannequins. "I quite like that blouse with the long dark blue skirt – but just look at the waist. Surely that can't be natural."

"It isn't!" cried Rose indignantly. "Believe you me, we ladies really suffer trying to emulate such impossible ideals. I tell you, pride does feel pain. It can be absolutely hell sometimes – but come on, let's go in, then you can try it."

Once inside, it seemed the staff couldn't do enough to please and it became obvious to Jill that Rose was a familiar and valued customer. However, after drawing the changing room curtain, she hesitated to gaze at the strange costume. The sight of it engulfed her with a terrifying sense of unreality. Although, as she reluctantly pulled the long skirt up around her waist, she had to admire the elegant way it swung from her hips, and despite herself, by the time she'd buttoned the stylish floral white blouse, she unexpectedly felt quite elated.

But, if *Jill* had been pleased with the result, Rose became almost ecstatic when she finally stepped from the cubicle.

"I knew it, Jill," she enthused, "I just knew it! You look absolutely stunning – don't you agree, ladies?" she asked, turning to the fawning staff.

"I must admit, Rose," confessed Jill, "that I was a bit unsure about it all at first. But now I just love the elegance of the long skirt and it goes so well with the blouse. Although you don't think perhaps the skirt's a bit on the long side, do you?"

"No. Absolutely not," her new friend assured her. "It's perfect. You see, all skirts and dresses should just, and I mean *just*, brush the floor without any sense of drag and that's what it does. Now," she added, "you have the most lovely thick hair, but it needs fashioning to harmonise with your new outfit and Josie is just the person to do it. But first we need a selection of stylish hats for you – preferably ones with a wide brim and bold ribbon ties."

Despite the momentary exhilaration, Jill had been quick to recognise the clothes for their symbolic significance and how, by wearing them, she was effectively becoming a 19th century middle class lady. However, she failed to recognise the danger of undermining her true persona; a factor which could eventually lead to an identity crisis. But that was something she would have to face later on.

Now, it's probably true when any of the fair sex find themselves let loose in a huge clothing store, there's a serious chance of expense becoming a secondary consideration. The two new friends were no exception as they rapidly became engulfed in a tide of purchases. However, the expense began to worry Jill as Rose finally arranged for everything to be forwarded to the Vicarage.

"Rose," she ventured tentatively, "you do realise, that I have absolutely no way of repaying you. The little money I have would be quite useless here."

"Jill," she replied gently, "the cost is not a problem compared to the difficulties you would face if we don't help you blend in with our time. You've experienced a little of it already." Then taking Jill to one side she added earnestly and quietly, "You know, I believe that you're not here entirely by accident and that there's some underlying reason for it, which makes it imperative for me to support you in every way possible. Perhaps you have a contribution to make to our lives or there are lessons you have to learn. I don't know. But, either way, you can't do it if people view you as peculiar in some way."

At this point, Rose had an idea.

"You've no means of knowing it, Jill, but Michael and I have long realised I need assistance with the parish work. Visits to the elderly and that sort of thing. I just wondered if you might like to help me out from time to time, because if you do, I'd love to have you along. And," she smiled, "that would be more than payment. What's more, it could also help you to adapt to your extraordinary situation. Anyway, it's just a suggestion and something you might like to think about. But now, changing the subject," she exclaimed with sudden relish, "how about some lunch? I don't know about you, but I'm feeling quite famished after that long walk. It's just unfortunate, though, that the restaurant in this store is on the top floor and may cause you some difficulty with your long dress. Anyway, if you follow me I'll show you what I mean." And sure enough, upon reaching the foot of the stairs, Rose dutifully proceeded to demonstrate how a lady should make a graceful ascent, Victorian-style. "You need to raise the hem of your dress so – just clear of your feet – to allow for easy movement. But never," she stressed vigorously, "never at the expense of exposing an ankle, because that is just not the done thing."

The restaurant itself proved an almost surreal experience which began with the rousing strains of a Strauss waltz as they mounted the wide, curving, stairway. Gently lifting her long skirt with both hands in the classic tradition made Jill feel almost like walking in a dream. Upon entering the dining area itself, her attention immediately became drawn to a great glass dome that spanned the entire area and the almost equally impressive columns that lined its perimeter. At the far end of the restaurant, she noticed formally dressed members of the orchestra setting the mood with their melodic music. The whole experience, combined to create an atmosphere of unhurried opulence, which was further enhanced by the graceful palms interspersed among the tables and set at either side of the orchestral stage.

Spotless white linen covered the numerous tables each of which was graced by individual candelabras and other matching silver accessories. Although the restaurant was by no means full, the patrons who were present conveyed an air of relaxed prosperity, some of whom were engaged with their lunch while others just sat nonchalantly about listening to the music or enjoying a cigar. Spellbound, Jill had to be nudged by her companion who was anxious to secure a good seat.

"I thought it might be crowded by this time of day!" she exclaimed. "But it seems we're in luck."

She indicated a vacant table by one of the windows.

"Look – the one over there. It couldn't be better. It's far enough away from the orchestra to hear ourselves speak."

The strange, yet seemingly natural, familiarity of it all was almost overwhelming, for it might have been her mother speaking. As her mind instantly refocussed, she began to wonder how long it would be before she accepted her peculiar situation without question.

However, arriving at the chosen table, she quickly discovered how she had yet to master the art of sitting down gracefully in a long dress.

"There we are," breathed Rose, obviously glad to finally take the weight off her feet. "Now, what shall we order?"

They had barely made themselves comfortable, however before a smartly dressed waiter appeared who, complete with the traditional napkin draped over his forearm, proved to be the personification of good manners. As Rose placed their order, Jill's attention became distracted by the arrival of two very fashionable couples at a nearby table and she left her companion to make the final choices. The taller of the two men, in particular, caught her attention. Although of similar height to her John, he was strikingly handsome with thick wavy dark hair and long sideburns that complemented his well-sculptured face, while his equally impressive outfit reflected the best taste of the age. But what really fascinated Jill was the group's ritualised display of etiquette and how the immaculately dressed women just stood behind their chairs awaiting the removal of their expensive fur wraps before deigning to sit down – and that only after their escorts had drawn back their chairs.

"Jill," hissed Rose. "You're staring."

"Sorry – I didn't mean to, but I just can't get over how courteously the women here are treated. It's all so different where I come from. My generation seems to have lost the art somewhere between the two Great Wars."

"*Two* Great Wars?"

"Oh. Take no notice, Rose – I was just thinking out loud again. Don't give it a second thought." At that moment, however, their coffee arrived and

Jill began to unburden herself about Anna. "Rose, I haven't told you about my little daughter, have I?" she said with a touch of wistfulness. "She's only three and I'm desperately worried how my continued absence will affect her – everyone at home must be sick with worry and there's absolutely nothing I can do. I feel so helpless. There's no way I can contact them and they will probably think I'm dead by now."

Rose didn't immediately reply, but reached across the table to take her hand.

"I didn't realise you were married, Jill. Oh, you poor thing. It must be an absolute torment for you – but tell me," she asked gently, "what's your little girl's name?"

The poignant question resonated back to an earlier coffee occasion in the local park when John had asked the same question. But all that felt so long ago now and, for a brief moment, the sadness of the situation threatened to engulf her.

"She's called Anna," Jill managed finally. "She's lovely, but the fact is I just don't know who will look after her, because my mother has a job and can't be with her all the time."

"But what about your husband, Jill? Surely he will be able to help, or…" For a moment, Rose hesitated. "Or was he killed in one of the wars you mentioned?"

"No, he wasn't killed," she admitted reluctantly. "And neither was he my husband, which I know must sound dreadful. But, in any case, I haven't seen him for years and I've had to bring my daughter up on my own. You see Rose, Anna is what you would call illegitimate."

Jill was only too aware of the stigma attached to unmarried mothers in the post-war England of 1947, let alone during the puritanical Victorian era. So she could well imagine how Rose might react and, indeed, for a moment, she felt the grasp on her hand begin to slacken. But there was more to her friend than a mere reflection of the age because, almost immediately, the grip returned, stronger than ever.

"You know," said Rose, deliberately appearing oblivious to what she had just heard, "things have a habit of working themselves out even in the worst circumstances. People can prove surprisingly capable. Especially when they have to – oh," she exclaimed, "I have no doubt your mother will find it difficult at first, but somehow I feel she will find a way to cope. We women can be very resourceful, you know." She paused to study her companion before adding, "However, I suspect your mother's real problem will be coming to terms with your loss and, I must admit, I don't know the answer to that."

Jill idly stirred her coffee in response.

"I don't think there is one," she observed quietly.

Then, reaching to pick up her cup, she suddenly froze as, to her horror, she found it had become impossible to grasp the handle. In disbelief, she tried again but the cup had lost its solidity. It had assumed the all-too-familiar terrifying intangibility she first encountered at the newsagent when the whole-wretched nightmare began.

Alerted by her ashen expression, Rose enquired what was wrong, but all Jill could now hear was the same intermittent static she had first encountered the night of her separation from John. Petrified by this sudden turn of events, she looked frantically around the restaurant but its very definition was beginning to become indistinct as she felt herself slipping ever further back into the insubstantial world of a phantom existence. Almost hysterical with fear and uncertainty, she hovered, mentally suspended in an indeterminate netherworld – a victim of the caprice of time.

"Jill, what on earth's the matter?" cried Rose in alarm as she watched the ethereal change in her companion. Her horror was only compounded when she found her friend's hand no longer had any substance. It was too much. Although a woman of strong faith, she found herself unable to withstand such an assault on her reason and began to scream uncontrollably.

Whether or not this terrifying ordeal had been the precursor of a return to her own era, Jill would never know, because Rose's piercing screams somehow had the effect of jolting her back on to an 'even keel', and the threat receded almost as quickly as it had begun. However, short as it had been, the devastating effect had left her feeling weak and emotionally exhausted. But bad as she felt, she instantly realised how traumatic the episode had been for Rose because her friend now lay prostrate across the table in a dead faint with her hand, hauntingly, still reaching out in a symbolic gesture of support.

Prior to her sudden screaming, the restaurant had been oblivious to the unfolding drama at the table by the window. Now, the sheer unexpectedness of it generated an instant impenetrable silence – a silence quickly shattered by the outbreak of curious chatter. To Jill's discomfort, she found herself at the centre of a lot of unwelcome attention. However, not a soul moved to offer any assistance for, while many looked, they seemed loath to become involved.

Seeing Jill's predicament, the tall, dark stranger at the adjacent table immediately rose to his feet and came over.

"May I be of help?" he volunteered with a slight bow and in a deep cultured voice. "Because, if I'm not mistaken, this poor lady is the wife of the Reverend Michael and they are both dear friends of my family."

Catching her breath, Jill found it difficult to repress a fleeting reaction to his charisma. However, not content to wait for a reply, the gentleman moved quickly round the table and lifted Rose back into a sitting position. At the same time, he beckoned to his female companion.

"Charlotte, may I ask you for some assistance?"

Appreciative as she was, Jill couldn't help feeling marginalised, although she duly moved to one side as the expensively dressed woman reluctantly got to her feet and approached their table. As she did so, Jill could sense her resentment which, she suspected, in some way related to herself. Although, why she couldn't imagine, because here was a beautiful young woman whose ornate silk dress rustled at her every move and whose expensive perfume was obvious to everyone.

Arriving at Jill's table, Charlotte took one disdainful look at the unconscious Rose and, ignoring Jill, spoke directly to her escort.

"Really Alistair, I'm not a nurse you know," she observed imperiously.

"I realise that," he replied, choosing to ignore her attitude. "But this dear lady needs help with her breathing and I wondered perhaps if you would be kind enough to loosen her bodice – it's no wonder women faint in these wretched things. They can't get enough oxygen to their lungs."

Charlotte's distaste for the task was blatant and Jill immediately stepped forward to help. In response to which the handsome stranger smiled briefly before reaching for his brandy flask to moisten Rose's lips. At first, this seemed to have little effect, but as the burning liquid caught the back of her throat, Rose started to cough and then, to Jill's immense relief, slowly opened her eyes. Still supporting the semi-conscious woman, the stranger turned to Jill.

"My apologies. I'm afraid we've not been formally introduced. But, perhaps, that is my loss and something that could be rectified on another occasion. In the meantime," he continued, "I suggest we get this dear lady down to my carriage. It's just outside the main entrance. And then we'll take you both back to the Vicarage."

In all her experience, Jill had never met such eloquence but, before she could dwell on it, he had effortlessly gathered Rose in his arms and made his way out of the restaurant down towards the exit. But by this time, Rose was fast recovering and began to protest. However, this was a gentleman among gentlemen and he would have none of it.

Parked opposite the department store stood a four-wheeled, open-topped landau carriage, drawn by a pair of magnificent grey horses. And from their scarlet head plumes and gleaming harnesses to the matching interior upholstery, it presented a breathtaking spectacle of wealth.

Upon recognising Alistair, the driver immediately descended from his seat and touched his top hat before opening the carriage door. This was the privileged side of life which, to the working-class Jill, provided a window into a world beyond her imagination. Alistair gently lowered Rose with extreme care onto the rear seat before proceeding to cover her from the waist down with a thick tartan rug. Only when completely satisfied with her comfort did he turn to the driver and, although obviously the man's employer, he nevertheless spoke in the most courteous terms.

"Albert – would you be kind enough to take Mrs

Hewish and her companion to St John's Vicarage? She's had a nasty turn and I'm a little concerned. So when you arrive, do see her safely indoors and explain the situation to Josie the housekeeper. She'll know what to do. Oh – and please tell her I'll call in later to check that Rose has quite recovered."

"Very good, Mr Gregson, Sir," he replied, again touching his top hat. "Would you also perhaps like me to call out a doctor for her?"

"I don't think that will be necessary at the moment, but thank you for the thought, Albert. I appreciate your concern. No – just see her home and come straight back."

Finally, sitting in the deep upholstery opposite Rose, Jill found it difficult not to appreciate the luxury of the carriage, for it was truly an exhilarating experience as it glided effortlessly over the uneven road surface. It all seemed a far cry from John's old Ford, but her chief concern was for her traumatised friend and she leaned over to take her hand.

"How are you feeling, Rose?" she asked anxiously. "I'm so sorry to have given you such a terrible fright. I'm afraid it was all my fault and the last thing I would have wished – especially after how good you've been to me. But it seems, for whatever reason, I'm caught up in something I don't understand and can't control."

But, with the colour returning to her cheeks, Rose responded with her usual warmth:

"Please. Don't you dare blame yourself," she

insisted. "At least I've seen what you're up against first-hand — but," she sighed, "you know, for a dreadful moment back there I really thought we were going to lose you." Still obviously shaken by her ordeal, she leaned back in her seat and smiled before adding, "But I'm oh so thankful that we didn't."

Chapter 11

WHEREAS JILL'S FIRST day involving the Hanningtons episode had felt interminable, subsequently the time seemed to pass at an ever-increasing rate. However, her mental state remained extremely precarious. Devoid of any reference to her previous life, maintaining any sense of normality was a moment-by-moment struggle and she continued to rely heavily on the stabilising influence of Rose. Yet, despite the enormity of her ongoing ordeal, she couldn't help but become increasingly aware of the sharp social and economic divides which so beggared late 19th century Victorian England – a place where the women's rights movement was still some way off.

However, in their ecclesiastical position, Michael and Rose enjoyed a relatively insular existence and, initially, this shielded Jill from the seamier side of the era. But, as she became increasingly involved with the charitable work of the parish, she quickly discovered the meaning of real deprivation. It was also a shock to find that universal education for children was yet to become available. In addition, it appeared that, apart from marriage, the average working-class woman had little choice between in-service drudgery and life in a nunnery. She was also becoming acquainted with the devastating effects of the then-unconquered killer diseases such as smallpox. Typhoid had also robbed Queen Victoria of her husband, Albert, earlier in the century – proof if it were needed that these sicknesses held no respect for social class.

Although deeply affected by these conditions, Rose was obviously determined to do all in her power to alleviate the suffering caused to members of her husband's parish. A fact emotionally demonstrated one evening during supper-time in the Vicarage kitchen. Following a lull in conversation, she took the opportunity to voice her concern over one of her 'old ladies', as she called them.

"Michael? Do you remember I recently spoke to you about poor Martha?" Then, seeing her husband's blank expression, she insisted with a touch of irritation, "Oh, Michael – you must remember her. She's never missed a Sunday service during the entire time we've been here. Well, anyway," she continued as the penny finally appeared to drop, "the poor woman is in her mid-seventies now and crippled with arthritis, which means she can't get about as she used to. But the point is, the Johnson family now want her out to make way for someone younger. I can't believe it," she added passionately. "After all those years of faithful service in that huge house – working God knows what hours – that's how they thank her. Mind you," she added disgustedly, "her home has only ever been a cramped and damp basement room. It's no wonder her joints have given out. But the question is, Michael, what's to become of her? She has no husband or any family that I know of. Or, for that matter," Rose added after a reflective pause, "what becomes of any of us when we are of no further use?"

The haunting question hung heavily in the ensuing silence, but it was a question that stridently demanded an answer. It also conveyed a starkness that shocked Jill into a sudden appreciation of the real suffering of other people. An appreciation that momentarily eclipsed her own problems and, like Rose, she looked at the minister for his reaction.

However, to her surprise, his response was muted and cautious. This was because, in reality, there were no solutions at this stage of England's social development and he pulled uncomfortably at his clerical collar.

"Rose," he began defensively, "we have been over this ground many times. Martha, God bless her, is barely the tip of a monumental human problem that surrounds us on every side, and it's something the Christian world has failed to fully address." His voice trailed off for a moment.

"It's no good looking at me like that Rose," he protested, as he caught sight of his wife's expression. "What do you expect me to do? Turn the Vicarage into some kind of hostel for the homeless?"

"Michael!" she retorted. "For goodness sake. Don't go overreacting. What's to stop poor Martha staying with us? Heaven only knows, the place is big enough. Just ask Josie."

Her husband adamantly shook his head.

"The Bishop wouldn't hear of it. In any case, who would take care of her should she become totally incapacitated?"

"The Bishop!" his wife almost exploded in disgust. "Don't talk to me about that man. Tucked up in his palace – what does he know or care about the Marthas of this world? When his time comes, it'll be off to some comfortable country retreat no doubt; waited on hand and foot, while the likes of Martha can be left to die a lonely death of cold and neglect in the local workhouse or, worse, on the streets or under the West Pier."

The following potent silence was tangible and even brought the ever-busy, upbeat Josie to a momentary standstill – mindful, perhaps, of her own vulnerability in this respect. But the quiet was suddenly and unexpectedly broken by Jill.

"I would be happy to help look after her." Then, surprised by her own impetuosity, she added quickly, "I could share my room, which would enable me to keep an eye on her."

At first, the offer drew no immediate response and she hesitated.

"Well, at least it's an idea," she finally ventured uncertainly. "Surely we can't let the poor woman just end up homeless?" She looked intently at the minister. "I was on the street, remember, and you rescued me. So, yes, I would be prepared to help. Although, of course, we have to bear in mind what happened at Hanningtons and the possibility that I might suddenly be drawn back to my own time."

Deep down, Jill realised her suggestion signified yet a further shift from the involvement with her previous life to one with her new friends. She also suspected that it arose, in part, from her relationship with Rose, whose warm Welsh personality she found so reassuring.

"Jill," Rose exclaimed finally, "that's a very kind gesture, but it could involve a lot of responsibility you know – and then there's – well – there's your own life to consider. What about your little daughter, for example?"

In response, Jill looked earnestly at her friend.

"I often think about her, Rose, and the very real possibility of never seeing her again. But," she then stressed, "my little Anna is not here and Martha is. My reality is the here and now. Although one day I might go home, in a strange way I'm beginning to hope it's not too soon. I suppose it's a bit like living in different worlds and eventually I might have to make a choice between the two."

Rose nodded and smiled before turning to her husband.

"Well, Michael," she asked passionately, "does it really take a stranger to show us our duty?"

Her words put the minster in a difficult position and he looked defensive.

"Rose," he protested with a touch of finality, "I can only advise you that we run the risk of a severe reprimand by the bishop if we take in unauthorised guests."

His wife dismissed the warning with a wave of her hand.

"Michael, I'd rather take that chance than abandon poor Martha to her fate. So it's decided!" she exclaimed brusquely. "When the time comes, Martha will become part of our extended family."

Realising the futility of further argument, the deflated minister sank further back into his chair and remained quiet for a while before getting up the courage to raise another controversial topic.

"Rose," he finally ventured tentatively, "please understand it is not my purpose to criticise, but I'm becoming increasingly worried about your frequent visits to Foredown Isolation Hospital. Oh," he added earnestly, "I know you go there for all the right reasons, but you do realise, I suppose, that the consequences could be horrendous because, sooner or later, there's a risk that you're going to succumb to one of those diseases and spread it among a lot of innocent people."

Rose looked momentarily contrite, knowing it to be a valid observation.

"I realise that, Michael," she answered quietly. "I am aware of the dangers, but you must remember we have people from our congregation in that hospital and some of their families are often too frightened to visit the place. If we abandon them, they have no one and I have to ask myself, what are we really about? A church that only exists for healthy people? I don't think so. 'Sick and ye visited me not'. Remember?"

Again, Michael was quiet before replying:

"I'll leave it to your absolute discretion, of course, Rose, but I think you should be aware of my concern."

By this stage, Jill was becoming quite tired and decided to leave them to their differences.

"Well, I'll say goodnight, Michael and Rose. I'm afraid I just can't stay up any longer. But thank you both for having me."

"Goodnight Jill," smiled her friend, "but there's no need to thank us. It's an absolute pleasure to have you."

Finally in bed and despite her tiredness, Jill found sleep to be an elusive prey as, once again, the unreality of her situation closed in. Somehow things seemed easier during the day when she was busy with various people and other activities. Tonight proved to be particularly bad. Gazing around at the rose-tinted bedroom now gently bathed in gaslight from the street below, she desperately attempted to push the turmoil from her mind and concentrate instead on the day's events. She pondered her wisdom for offering to help Martha and wondered if she'd been a little too impulsive. Certainly, it seemed unthinkable for someone old and frail to face life on the streets, particularly in the depths of winter. She, personally, had a dread of the cold and bitterly remembered the icy conditions of Christmas 1944, which had proved to be the coldest on record.

Jill felt her dilema growing over her attachment to life at the Vicarage. She admired the Reverend Michael and found increasing satisfaction with helping Rose, but she very much questioned whether this really justified a desire to spend the rest of her life in what was, after all, a shadowy existence in a bygone era. She leaned back on the pillows and sighed, realising that the longer she stayed, the more natural it would all become and the more engrossed she would find herself in the various everyday activities. Restlessly she thought of little Anna's unhappiness and castigated herself for even contemplating deserting her. Her mind drifted back to the man she'd left behind. Where was John now, she wondered? Did he make it back safely the night they'd become separated or was he still trapped in that indeterminate netherworld? Her only certainty was she loved him and that was all she had, for she knew, in all probability, she might never see him again.

Nostalgically she cast her mind back to that beautiful autumn Sunday in the recreation ground, and with her eyes misting over, she recalled John's words which all seemed so prophetic now:

"You know," he had said, "this will always be

our special place and when we're apart and thinking of each other, we will remember this day together. It will forever be a private meeting place in our hearts..."

Sleep was now impossible, and Jill glanced at her watch – its familiar face being one of the few precious links she still had with normality. It was just possible to make out the big hand pointing at five minutes to midnight. Swinging her legs over the side of the bed, she crossed to the window overlooking Church Road. Even at this late hour, the street lamps still burned in the now deserted thoroughfare while the ceaseless clatter of horse hooves had long since died away to leave an almost eerie calm; a silence that seemed to somehow amplify the sound of a lone horseman as he rode past under one of the street lights. An anonymous rider in the dead of night, travelling she knew not where. Closing the window and gently resting her hand on the heavy curtain, she continued to gaze down at the lamplit scene while murmuring:

"I'm sorry, John. I can't change the way things are. But one thing I promise you, should I not make it back, I will always remember in my heart. I also trust that even if you find someone else, you will never forget me."

Overcome, she felt the tears prick her eyes but made no attempt to brush them away.

* * *

As the weeks passed, Jill's experience of working with Rose drew her ever deeper into the rhythm of parish life. Over time, her network of contacts increased, as did her confidence and, anxious to share Rose's burden, she slowly attempted solo visits to the elderly and various other people in need. She found loneliness to be a common problem and invariably received a warm welcome wherever she went. The parish covered a large area and included a number of working-class and severely deprived districts, which made Jill wonder how Rose had ever managed on her own. Even with their combined efforts it frequently became a matter of priority and this eventually led to her unsuitable involvement with a family devastated by smallpox.

It transpired that the husband worked as a low-paid clerical assistant and his wife had been obliged to take in laundry to augment their meagre budget. During her visit, Jill discovered that their youngest child, a little girl, had just died from the deadly virus, while sadly, the man's wife was in the final stages of its unrelenting grip. Overwhelmed with the magnitude of the tragedy, Jill struggled to do her best, but quickly realised how ill-equipped she was to offer any real help. If anything, she felt like an intruder on the family grief. The father's agony had been compounded by his inability to even afford decent funerals, and as Jill later discovered, this meant a pauper's grave.

It had not taken her long to realise that evening

supper at the Vicarage enjoyed an almost ritual-like tradition and often acted as a forum for the day's events. Sometimes Rose would invite several of the church deacons who, together with their wives, would carry on various discussions into the late hours. It was one such night, that Jill, perhaps foolishly, chose to describe her experience with the stricken family.

"As you probably know," she began tentatively, "I'm relatively new to the charitable work of the church and up till now I think I've been able to make a reasonable contribution. Today, however, I felt at a loss." And, with that, she proceeded to explain her difficulties with the bereaved husband. "I mean," she concluded, "what could I possibly have said or done in such a situation? Words just seemed so inadequate – but a pauper's grave for his wife and little girl? I don't really know what that involves. Although it sounds pretty awful... I have a daughter of my own about that age... how can such things be allowed to happen?"

She turned to Rose.

"You or Michael would have known what to say, because you have so much more to offer, but I'm not so familiar with the Christian faith. Partly, I suppose, because church attendance was not very popular after the war, which undermined people's faith, but my real point is," she added earnestly, "can you really allow that poor little girl to have such a miserable end?"

A sentiment to which Rose was quick to respond.

"Jill," she stressed, "I must apologise for allowing you to walk into such a deplorable situation, but I'm afraid I didn't know how bad it was. That's no excuse, I know, but someone had just happened to mention in passing that the family was experiencing difficulties. I'm sorry. I should have checked it out first. But with regards to the little girl, I'm sure we can arrange a more respectable send-off for her, because the funeral can be paid out of church funds."

It was a suggestion that proved readily acceptable by all those present. However, one of the deacons was quick to express serious reservations about some of Jill's remarks. Less gracious and more critical than his colleagues, he looked at her questioningly.

"I think," he began slowly, "that I speak for everyone present when I express gratitude for what you have been doing, because we all know that it has long been more than Rose can comfortably manage on her own. Even so, the deacons and I know very little about you or where you come from – although, arguably perhaps, that shouldn't really matter. What does concern me, though, is that by your own admission, you seem to know very little about the church, which to me at least, begs the question of your suitability for this sort of work in the first place. After all, you say how difficult you found this recent case. What also seems strange is that you've never heard of a pauper's grave. Surely," he added searchingly, "that's common knowledge, isn't it? But not only that, you mentioned widespread atheism and something about a war, but, I mean, what war? There's been nothing major to speak of since the American civil conflict and that's some twenty years ago."

It was an awkward moment and Rose moved quickly to counter the threat.

"That was a bit uncharitable, Edward, if I may say so. Especially after all this young lady has done to help us. To start with, you obviously don't know that she comes from a wealthy and sheltered background, where paupers' graves would hardly constitute everyday conversation."

It was, of course, a lie, and she fervently hoped her Maker would understand. "What's more," she continued, "it might interest you to know that three of her relatives lost their lives fighting for the southern cause as did tens of thousands of other young men. So, yes, people do sometimes question God's goodness."

Although the fabrication continued to prick her conscience, Rose, nevertheless, desperately hoped it would be enough to silence the inquisitor but, although Edward nodded, he looked far from convinced, and at this point, Jill glanced at her friend and grimaced.

"Perhaps the gentleman is right. How can I do the job properly without a church background or talk to people about something I'm not sure even exists?"

It was a courageous, if perhaps an inappropriate, thing to say in a Vicarage yet somehow it carried a ring of honesty that echoed an eternal human uncertainty. However, Rose was again quick to respond.

"We all have our doubts, Jill," she confided. "Believe me. But it might be an idea for you to at least find out what we're about. Then you'd be in a better position to make a reasoned judgement."

"Since your arrival here," added her husband, "Rose and I thought it better to let you take your time and settle in. The last thing we wanted was to rush you into church, but under the circumstances. It might be worth your while to explore the motivation behind our work. Who knows," he smiled, "you might find our faith more acceptable than you think."

Alone in her room later that evening, she again experienced the now familiar sense of disorientation and sadness. In order to counteract this, she tried to imagine being on holiday in a strange land and that, by the end of her stay, she would return home. But, tonight, even that ploy failed and sinking onto the bed, she suddenly felt overwhelmed, for everything she could see and touch directly contradicted what she knew to be the facts. Even her dear friend, the vibrant and dynamic Rose, was in reality no more than an apparently substantial illusion.

Rising from the bed, she approached the dressing table with its large oval-shaped swivel mirror. Even her reflection seemed to be a lie as she gazed at the image of an essentially middle-class Victorian lady. Slowly she unpinned her piled-up blonde hair, which, once free of its constraints, cascaded down about her shoulders. That was her; that was the girl John had fallen in love with. Reaching for a brush, she proceeded to coax it back into the style he had so admired. Moving to the washstand, she took the ornate china jug and poured out a bowl of warm water; faithful Josie, she thought. Although, as she touched the handle, it reminded her that at any minute it could suddenly assume the same intangibility she'd experienced with the coffee cup.

Another means she had adopted to offset these bouts of melancholy would be to stand by the window that overlooked Church Road. Indeed, as the weeks passed, it had gradually assumed an almost portal-like significance, which allowed her to gaze east towards the spot where she had finally lost contact with John.She felt, in some way, that it offered a tenuous link with him.

Things had seemed so simple when they had been together. It had been a relatively carefree, fun-loving relationship; both agnostics, religion just hadn't seemed relevant somehow. Her present circumstances, however, were very different. Here she had been brought face to face with the stark realities of existence and the experience had profoundly affected her outlook on life. Of one thing she was certain: should there ever be the chance to return home, she would be returning as an entirely changed person.

She turned from the window with a sigh, remembering when they had first met and how life had suddenly assumed a whole new meaning of excitement and expectation. She'd known instinctively that John would be loyal and considerate, and so it had proved. Above all, he had shown himself non-judgemental, loving not only herself but also possessing a pleasing way with little Anna. But then fate had cruelly intervened and snatched him away, so now all she had left were the might-have-beens.

Chapter 12

EVEN WITH THE approach of late November, the weather continued to be summer-like and the following Sunday proved no exception. Warm, crystal air vibrated to the clamour of church bells calling the faithful to worship – although the previous night had witnessed a distinct chill, as was testified by lingering patches of frost that still cringed behind the various tombstones.

Jill could almost feel the freshness and, she had to admit, a certain sense of sanctity, as she and Rose, accompanied by the ever-faithful Josie, made their way towards St John's. While feeling still somewhat conspicuous in the bonnet Rose had all but insisted she wear, Jill nevertheless knew her decision to attend had been the right one. Church attendance, it seemed, had been a popular pastime in the late-Victorian era for, as they approached the main entrance, she noticed groups of people queuing to go in. However, she couldn't help but wonder if some of them just saw the occasion as an opportunity to display their fashionable outfits. Parasols and top hats abounded, while some of the women's dresses were quite breathtaking.

Voices mingled with the sound of the bells and once again, Jill couldn't help but notice how warmly Rose was greeted by virtually everyone present – so many people wanted to talk to her that it made her feel almost superfluous.

Once inside the church, however, it was a quite different atmosphere, with the subdued silence being enhanced by gentle background organ music, while the dimness of the vaulted interior further helped to generate a sense of awe. If people spoke at all, it was only in the very hushed of tones.

Finally, as Jill's little group took their seats, the organ suddenly picked up tempo, to announce the entry of the Reverend Michael who was now attired in his full clerical vestments. Slowly and with measured tread, he led the choir down the aisle towards the altar situated at the eastern end. It was all such a new experience for Jill and she watched the colourful ritual with fascination.

After the service, they were among the first to emerge and, blinking against the low strong sunlight, were soon joined by Rose's husband. The reverend was obviously anxious to communicate with and encourage the members of his congregation. Feeling left out, Jill found herself relegated to conversing with Josie, for Rose and the minister were again besieged by parishioners all vying for their attention. But it was a situation about to dramatically change as Jill caught sight of a vaguely familiar figure edging his way towards Rose. Tall and distinguished, the man spoke in a low, cultured voice:

"Good morning, Rose. What a glorious day."

"Indeed it is," her friend replied. "And may I say how good it is to see you. Did you happen to attend the service?"

The stranger raised his hand in a defensive gesture.

"What can I say?"

"Well then," she replied, "to what do we owe this honour?"

"That, Rose, brings me to a point of confession."

"Confession?"

"Yes, confession. Because, you see, my brother tells me that, of late, you have been covertly entertaining a newcomer at the Vicarage."

"That's very true," she smiled. "And, I might hasten to add, that it's been a great pleasure, but by no means a secret one."

"The point being, Rose," he continued, with a touch of mock solemnity, "is that I'm given to understand your visitor is not only a young lady, but also a very beautiful one – which begs the question, why have I not been introduced? And that, you see, is something I'm here to rectify." But, before Rose could reply, he glanced over towards Jill. "Now, from my brother's description," he added admiringly, "I would say *that* is the young lady in question. But, never mind – I will do the introductions myself."

Jill, however, was finding the whole situation rather embarrassing and, worse, became alarmed to feel an unbidden excitement, which only intensified as the stranger got closer. Possessing the appearance and movement of an athlete, he was also probably the most handsome man she had ever seen. Immaculately dressed for the period, his only hint of ostentation seemed to be an elaborate waistcoat and a matching cravat that sat between the high wings of his spotless white collar.

The experience was such that, for the first time since her separation from John, she became completely oblivious to her unnatural situation. Even her immediate surroundings seemed to fade as she caught herself gazing into his brown eyes: eyes that matched his thick, wavy dark hair and long sideburns. However, when he bowed and removed his top hat in a sweeping gesture, it all suddenly seemed a bit theatrical and she felt a hint of caution as she smilingly returned the overture with an exaggerated curtsey.

"I'm afraid, young lady," he began in the same smooth voice, "that I have you at a slight disadvantage because, you see, I already happen to know your name." He paused for a moment to lean heavily on his ornate silver-handled cane. "You see," he continued, "my brother has spoken of you at great length and, I might add, on a number of occasions – which is most unusual for him, for beautiful women are far from rare in his world."

"I see, sir," she replied with a certain flippancy.

"And what about your world? Is that also overpopulated with beautiful women?"

The remark broke his veneer of play-acting.

"In my world," he replied soberly while gazing up at the impossibly high steeple of St John's, "in my world, there are no ladies – beautiful or otherwise – because I never have the time." But, having said that, he continued finally, "I still became intrigued by my brother's description of a certain lady at the Vicarage and," he smiled with a twitch at the corner of his mouth, "I believe I'm talking to her right now."

"I believe you're right," she confirmed mischievously but then, with a sudden flash of insight, she asked, "Tell me. What's your brother's name?"

"Ah!" he smiled. "He goes under the name of Alistair – all whitewash and fine manners, if you'll pardon my saying so; very good at everything and does far too much of it for his own good. I believe you had occasion to meet him several weeks ago in Hanningtons."

Suddenly, it all fell into place as she recognised him as a slightly older and even better-looking version of the man who had so briefly captivated her attention in the department store. Moreover, if anything, he appeared even taller than his brother.

"Whereas for me," continued the stranger, "well, I'm just plain Greg – although, officially, I'm known as one Frederick Oliver Gregson: far too pretentious though for my liking, so I prefer to be known as just plain Greg – but enough of me. It is you I've come to see and find out about. Now, for a start, you seem to have sprung from nowhere." He again smiled his wry smile. "So, tell me. Where have you been hiding? Very naughty of Rose to keep you all to herself."

His good-natured remarks, however, had come a little too close for comfort.

"I've not been 'hiding away', sir, as you put it," she objected, "but busy trying to help poor over-burdened Rose." But then, and not for the first time, she became a little impetuous, "It's the kind of work, sir, that someone of your obvious status would probably know very little about." However, she immediately regretted her hasty remark when seeing the hurt on his face; too late, she realised his apparent flippancy concealed a deep inner sensitivity. "I'm sorry," she pleaded. "I had no right to say that – it was unforgivable. Please – I'm sorry."

But it really was too late; the damage had been done, as was evidenced by his reply.

"I'm sorry you think of me like that, Jill." It was the first time he'd actually spoken her name and, somehow, he made it sound very special. "You see," he concluded, "I'm not actually from this parish, but further west towards the Portslade area. Our tenant farmers have experienced a succession of devastating harvests and severe bouts of illness among their livestock. This endless summer weather has brought a lot of misery to the agricultural world. In fact, things have been so desperate on our farms that even some of the children have been in danger of going hungry."

Cradling the ornate silver cane in his left hand, he seemed to study its intricate design as if seeing it for the first time.

"Contrary to your opinion," he said eventually, "my time has been completely taken up with giving all the support I can – it's left me with very little opportunity for anything else, until now, when I thought that, perhaps..."

Then, with a slight bow he turned suddenly and unexpectedly on his heel before slipping away among the few remaining parishioners. Caught by surprise, Jill could only watch him go until he was completely out of sight. Even then, she continued to look with her feelings in absolute turmoil.

"That," exclaimed Rose with a nod of approval in his direction, "was someone very special. It's funny though," she observed, still gazing towards the church gate, "he never normally attends the morning service. In fact, it seems he wasn't among the congregation today. So, do you realise, young lady, he must have come here especially in the hope of seeing you?" At that point, she became very emphatic. "You should be honoured. There's hardly a single woman in the county who wouldn't give their right arm to catch his attention and," she added knowingly, "from your expression it looks as though he's made quite an impression on you."

"Oh, Rose. You're exaggerating," Jill replied a little over-hastily.

"Possibly!" exclaimed her friend. "But it might

interest you to know, that was the eldest son of Brigadier Gregson – they're one of the wealthiest families on the south coast, but unlike most landowners, they care for the people who farm their properties. Oh," she continued, "I know he sometimes seems a bit of an exhibitionist, but I think it's just a cover for a sense of insecurity."

"I realise that now, Rose," she replied miserably. "But, unfortunately, not before saying some pretty awful things. So, it's all a bit late now, I'm afraid."

"Well, all is not lost," observed her friend brightly. "You'll just have to be honest next time and tell him you're sorry."

"I very much doubt whether there'll be a next time," replied Jill.

The same night again saw Jill at the sentinel position by her bedroom window, only now circumstances were far more complicated because, try as she might, she found it virtually impossible to dismiss the handsome stranger from her mind. Although she hated to admit it, Greg had got through to her emotionally and this despite her deep ties with John. In her experience she had never met such a cultured man who carried himself in the matchless style she had witnessed that morning. His tailored period costume and the lithe way he moved made it difficult not to compare him with John who, if she was honest, often didn't care what he looked like.

Although completely faithful, she knew he could also operate on a short fuse and, as such, was not a man to be crossed. While, with Greg, she had found a sensitive and refined gentleman who belonged to a way of life she could only dream about.

Emotionally confused, she felt angry for letting such a brief encounter come between her and the man she loved. Feeling thoroughly unsettled, she finally lay back in a vain attempt to find escape in sleep.

Attending church the following Sunday morning, Jill felt even more annoyed to find herself glancing about for any sign of the stranger. Although she looked carefully both before and during the service, she could see no sign of him.

Sensing what she was doing, Rose leaned over in the pew.

"Looking for someone, Jill?"

As the weeks slowly slipped away, Jill found herself ever more involved with various daily activities, as well as making new female friends in the congregation. The Christmas of 1887 and all its demands was fast approaching, so there seemed ever less time to dwell on the reality of her predicament. Even the morning ritual of getting dressed in her long Victorian costume was now fast becoming routine.

However, this growing sense of involvement carried with it an unexpected twist as she began to have serious doubts concerning her memory, at times even wondering whether she really belonged to the mid 20th century at all. She sometimes felt that perhaps some terrible trauma had blotted out her true identity in favour of an imaginary future existence. After all, she reasoned, Michael and Rose had found her in a desperately distraught state. Finally, she decided to voice these concerns to Rose. However, her reaction was both immediate and firm.

"Jill. If I'm sure about anything, I'm certain that what you told us originally is correct. If nothing else, your clothes and money in your bag showed you were genuine. Remember what happened in Hanningtons? When I held your hand, it suddenly felt like trying to grasp thin air. No," she emphasised. "There was nothing imaginary about that. It was all very real and very terrifying."

With the arrival of Christmas Eve, church life at St John's reached a crescendo. Decorations and greetings cards festooned the Vicarage, while Jill found herself caught up in the seasonal excitement, rushing from one demand to the next. The church itself stood on a promontory at the junction of Palmeira Square, a large open public area close to the Brighton and Hove boundary. Built of Sussex flint, the church's elegant gothic outline and towering spire were landmarks for miles around. At night, the sparkling light from its coloured stained-glass windows served to broadly proclaim the festive season. In addition, standing at the centre of the square was the biggest Christmas tree Jill had ever seen; festooned with numerous coloured lanterns, it more than competed with the brilliance of the church.

It was the small hours of Christmas Day before Jill finally retired to bed feeling both exhilarated and exhausted – her tiredness being partly due to the deacons and a small group of friends who, intoxicated with the seasonal spirit, had stayed on after supper late into the night.

Now, as she closed her bedroom door, she suddenly felt the mood evaporate: Christmas Eve and no little Anna. Ashamed and guilty that she had been enjoying herself without a thought for her daughter, she sank down dejectedly onto the bed. How could she, she asked herself, forget her own little girl even for a moment, but especially at a time like this? What sort of Christmas would there be for Anna without her mother? She tried to picture the scene back home – the little living room with its paper-chains and the big old sock they used to hang by the fireplace. How, she wondered, would they cope without her? Worse, they didn't even know if she was still alive. How, she asked herself, would they celebrate Christmas?

Spring arrived early in the new year of 1888 and it seemed nature had been quick to take advantage of the opportunity it presented. As Jill and Rose approached the church that Easter Sunday, they found themselves greeted by a plethora of daffodils and snowdrops. Nodding in the slight breeze, the flowers seemed determined to flaunt their brilliance in the early morning sunshine while, wearing a dazzling new spring outfit, Jill felt they somehow reflected her own upbeat mood. Now thoroughly familiar with the fashions of the age, she had decided to explore some of the more exciting possibilities they offered. To this end, she had spent hours with Rose at Hanningtons before finally selecting an ivory white gown with a delicate gold trim. The voluminous skirt had been adventurous but it emphasised her slim waist while the deep-brimmed matching bonnet complemented the outfit to perfection. This and a beautiful parasol, made her feel both attractive and very feminine.

As they prepared to enter the church, however, Jill was suddenly taken unawares by a familiar voice.

"Well, hello, Jill and good morning to you, Rose."

And, spinning round, she found herself once again face to face with Greg. Suddenly caught off guard, she just about managed to falter a hesitant, "Oh... hello."

Even as she spoke, she realised just how devastatingly handsome he was. At well over six feet, he cut a striking figure and, once again, her emotions began to churn. Rose just raised her eyebrows and gave a knowing look.

"Shall we see you in church then, Jill? Or possibly a bit later on maybe...?" The innuendos were lost on her as she gazed at the newcomer, who just stood there idly leaning on his silver-mounted cane. "You had me worried."

"Worried?" she repeated blankly.

"Well," he replied with the merest shake of his head, "you're late and I thought perhaps you weren't coming."

At first the remarks seemed so banal that she didn't know what to say, but then recognising them for the play-acting they were, she smiled.

"Oh, Greg. I'm so sorry for what I said to you last time. It really was unforgiveable. Please do accept my apologies."

He smiled the smile she'd been unable to forget.

"There's nothing to forgive," he assured her while, at the same time, indicating a wrought-iron seat by the church path. "I wondered, perhaps, if you could spare a few minutes. I promise not to keep you long, so you won't miss the service."

Despite a sense of guilt, the moment she hoped for had finally arrived and it made her breathless with excitement. Taking her hand as she sat down, he then joined her – albeit at a respectful distance. The spot was unquestionably beautiful and situated beneath a number of large oak trees that also marked the churchyard boundary, while brilliant sunlight pierced the branches high above to form numerous patches right across the path and on to the swathes of daffodils lining its edges.

271

At first Greg didn't speak, but seemed content using his cane to poke at the fcw acorns still lying about from the previous autumn.

"It's funny," he said almost idly, "but nature's so prolific, which makes me wonder sometimes just how many acorns have to fall before one actually becomes a tree." He then lifted his eyes from the ground to look at her in undisguised admiration. "If I may say so, I think you look absolutely radiant." And with a sweeping action of his hand he added, "You more than complement this beautiful setting."

As she bathed in the afterglow of the compliment, he suddenly got up to cross the path and select a single daffodil, which he then handed to her without a word.

"I'm afraid, Jill," he admitted, "I'm not very good at this sort of thing – I don't know why; possibly it's a lack of practice – strange, because my brother's such an accomplished performer with the ladies. Whereas, in my case, I seem to have spent my entire life directing the estates and looking after my invalid sister." Again he glanced down at his beloved cane as if finding it difficult to maintain eye contact.

"That first time I saw you with Rose," he said quietly, "I knew." And, after a slight pause and a nod, he repeated, "I knew."

"Sorry, Greg?" she apologised. "But knew what? What was it you knew?"

This time, however, the pause was much longer.

"I knew," he said with a certain finality, "that you

were the one; the one that, almost without realising it, I had always been searching for – I can't say it any clearer than that, can I?"

"No," she replied breathlessly. "You certainly can't."

He glanced away for a moment towards the church.

"That's a beautiful building," he observed. "Although, I can never quite understand why we feel the need to keep harping back to the Gothic era for inspiration as though we have no ideas of our own." It was, of course, quite irrelevant and she quickly recognised it as a cover for his embarrassment.

"Jill," he continued, "I suppose all I can say, in the most simple terms, is that I'd like the opportunity to know you and for, well... for us to spend some time together."

It was, indeed, a simple statement, but it was enough. And her heart leapt. However, it was an elation that was quickly quelled by intense pangs of guilt, which were only made worse when she heard herself say:

"That's something I'd like very much, Greg."

In her mind's eye, she could see her John and wondered what on earth she was getting into. As she wrestled with her conscience, the faint sound of hymn-singing drifted from the church.

"I'm afraid," observed a contrite Greg, "that I've made you late for the service after all."

As if in answer, Jill removed her new bonnet and pulled at one of her blonde ringlets that Josie had so carefully teased into place earlier that morning.

"Oh, don't worry," she replied reassuringly. "I do enjoy the morning service, but I always find the interior of the church a bit gloomy, especially on a lovely day like this. So I don't feel I've missed out too much."

"It's just that I hate to upset Rose," he replied, before going quiet for several moments as if summoning up the courage to continue. Finally he spoke, "Tell me – are you able to ride horseback?"

Although totally unprepared for such a question, Jill was nevertheless quick to realise that it was a proficiency that would be expected of a woman from her supposed background, whereas, in reality, her only equestrian experience had been limited to a few girlhood excursions at the local riding stable. So she quickly decided honesty was her only option.

"I had a few lessons when I was a little girl," she admitted. "But I'm far from a confident rider and I was always very nervous. But what makes you ask?"

"Well," he answered tentatively, "I have the most beautiful dapple-grey mare and I think she would be just perfect for you."

"I see," she smiled. "It looks as though you have it all planned out."

"Well, I wouldn't say that," he observed cautiously. "But the horse I have in mind is barely fifteen hands and has the sweetest temperament. I thought perhaps we might take a ride out together some time. I don't know if you are familiar with the down-land north of here. But the Dyke, as it's known, is the highest point on the south coast and gives fantastic views right across the Sussex Weald. To the south, you can see straight to the horizon."

Exciting as it sounded, she nevertheless wondered if she would be getting out of her social depth.

"Greg," she ventured hesitantly. "I'd love to come. But you'd have to be very patient with me because I'd need to go quite slowly."

"As long as you promise to come," he insisted with a smile, "then I promise to take the very best care of you." And so it was arranged for early the following Wednesday morning. However, by now, any sounds of the service had died away and Greg reached for his fob watch.

"I fear," he admitted, "that you have, in fact, missed the entire service and it's all been my fault." He smiled. "And, being the coward that I am, I have no wish to face Rose, so I will take my leave while it's still safe."

After a slight bow, Greg strode away down the church path towards the main lychgate where Jill suddenly noticed two horses were standing waiting. One of them carried a rider and he immediately handed the reins of the spare mount to Greg who, taking control of the animal, vaulted into the saddle with one lithe movement. Then, turning in her direction, he raised his cane in acknowledgement before wheeling about and disappearing with a clatter of hooves.

In the resulting haze, Jill luxuriated back on the bench unable to believe what had just happened. The haze however, was almost immediately dissipated by the sound of a familiar voice.

"Can I be a busybody?"

Obviously anxious to find out the latest developments, Rose had made it her business to be among the first out of church.

"No, Rose," Jill retorted good-humouredly. "You definitely may not be a busybody." But then, in a quandary, she quickly relented. "Oh, Rose, what am I going to do?" she pleaded. "He's so handsome and..."

"Well, frankly," exclaimed her friend, "if I were you and had been fortunate enough to spend the last hour in the company of Frederick Gregson, then I don't think I'd be in any kind of quandary. In fact," she stressed with a hint of envy, "I'd consider myself an extremely fortunate girl. Now, look, why don't we just get back home where we can discuss the details privately over a cup of tea?"

Kind as all this sounded, Jill couldn't help but suspect that the offer concealed a certain appetite for a little vicarious romance. However, once safely behind the Vicarage front door, she was quick to convey her misgivings.

"I feel such a traitor, Rose. Greg has invited me out but I'm already committed to a man I love dearly. He's the most wonderful and understanding person you could ever wish to meet."She sank dejectedly down onto one of the kitchen chairs. "How can I do such a thing to him?"

"Well, strictly speaking," retorted her friend, "you're not actually doing anything to him, are you? Because, the reality is, he's not here and presumably belongs to your own time. I also take it from our previous discussions that he's not little Anna's father." She paused before enquiring, "Is this man by any chance called John? Because that was the name you were calling out on the night we found you."

Jill nodded dumbly.

"I'd been with him only minutes earlier when he and his car just faded out of existence and left me stranded."

"Well, if it's of any help, Jill," stressed her friend, "I feel, from what you've told me, this young man would not be the type to stand in the way of your happiness. Try to imagine for a moment, God forbid, that had he died unexpectedly, would he really have wanted you to be lonely? Possibly for the rest of your life?"

She shook her head vigorously. "I don't think so. And remember, effectively that's what we're dealing with. It's virtually the same thing. You should also bear in mind it's not a question of choosing Greg in favour of John. That really would be an agony, whereas this situation is totally different." At which point she crossed the kitchen to make their tea. "But tell me, how did you leave it with Greg?"

The answer was tailor-made to send Rose into a

spiral of ecstasy over a suitable outfit but the whole prospect had left Jill feeling very apprehensive. Even thinking of venturing onto an unknown horse was especially worrying; worse, she suddenly realised there might be the question of riding side-saddle.

"Oh!" exclaimed Rose in answer to her uncertainties. "Yes, it's the only acceptable style. You can't accompany a gentleman of Mr Gregson's calibre and expect to ride astride like a cowgirl!"

"Greg!" protested Jill. "He prefers to be called Greg."

"Well, whatever he prefers to be called," insisted her friend, "you can't ride like a man. You'll just have to get used to a long riding skirt and boots because that will be the order of the day."

The order of the day resulted in Jill looking fit to attend the most prestigious hunt in the land. Josie had again coaxed her hair into ringlets while Jill herself had chosen a low-crowned equestrian hat offset by a narrow white scarf. This, together with a dark velvet tailored riding habit, complemented her long beige equestrian skirt while Rose had all but insisted she also carry the requisite ivory-handled riding crop.

Early Wednesday morning found Jill gazing expectantly from the drawing room window for the first sign of her date. Despite the excitement, she felt slightly self-conscious in her new outfit and more than a little apprehensive. Apart from anything else, she knew she would be operating at a social level far above her own class and it made her wonder how she would cope. That was without taking into account the thorny problem of her past life, if the subject arose.

Even as these uncertainties flashed through her mind, he was suddenly there waiting outside the Vicarage gate astride a magnificent black horse. Accompanying him was a second rider whom she recognised from the previous Sunday morning. He was mounted on a smaller grey animal, which she assumed was for her, while a third, spare horse, completed the trio.

"Oh, Jill, it's so romantic!" exclaimed an all-too-familiar voice. "I'm almost jealous."

Unnoticed, Rose had quietly slipped into the room apparently determined to savour some of the romantic fallout.

"Rose," Jill hissed, "get back. We don't want them to catch us watching." Then, feeling slightly flustered, she pleaded, "Oh, Rose, what's best? Shall I wait for him to knock or shall I go out and meet him...? Oh, I don't know."

"Look," advised her friend. "Just compose yourself and wait for him to come to the house. Then, after a respectable delay – that's to give him a healthy sense of uncertainty – just open the door as if it were the most natural thing in the world. You look stunning – you just can't go wrong. Now is the time to enjoy yourself."

Unable to restrain herself, Jill rushed for the door

and slipped out into the early morning sunshine and a moment of magic she would never forget.

Seeing her approach, Greg immediately stepped down from his horse and handed the reins to his companion. Then, pausing just inside the gate and with obvious admiration, he took her right hand.

"Jill," he exclaimed excitedly, "I can only say I'm charmed and honoured, for nobody, but nobody, ever looked more stylish and beautiful than you do today."

"Why, thank you, Greg," she replied. "That was a lovely thing to say, but, if I'm honest, it's all really due to my dear friend Rose. She's helped me choose everything." And, with a similar hesitancy, she added, "I do hope you won't mind, Greg, but as much as I'm looking forward to this outing, I'm feeling very nervous. I know I mentioned it last time, but my experience with horses really is very limited."

The way she spoke reflected a vulnerability that Greg, like John before him, found so sensually appealing.

"Jill," he hastened to assure her, "you will be absolutely safe." Then, stroking the grey's neck, he added, "Her name's Cloud and she's totally reliable, if perhaps a trifle on the lazy side which, in your case, will probably be a good thing. Anyway, I'll attach a lead-rein to her bit as an added precaution."

Quite unbeknown to them and concealed behind the heavy curtains of the drawing room window, a very curious and interested Rose was busily soaking up every last detail.

By now, Greg's anonymous companion had also dismounted and, turning to Jill, he raised his top hat.

"Jill," exclaimed Greg, "let me introduce Albert. He's not only a family friend and employee but he also helps to make my life a lot easier."

"How do you do, Mistress Jill?" he smiled. "I've heard so much about you that it's a pleasure to actually make your acquaintance. May I wish you a safe and pleasant ride?" He stopped briefly before adding, "I couldn't help overhearing your misgivings, but please be assured there's nothing to worry about with Cloud. We've had her since she was a foal and a more compliant horse would be hard to find."

It was all so chivalrous and, again, she couldn't help but compare it with the behaviour of her own era.

"Well, thank you, Albert. That's very reassuring of you," she smiled.

However, at this point Greg interrupted.

"Now, may I introduce you to your horse?"

Jill knew just enough of things equine, to recognise Cloud as being an extremely beautiful animal. Dapple-grey, the mare possessed a luxurious white mane and a matching tail that virtually brushed the ground – although, what really captivated Jill were the horse's big placid eyes and soft pink muzzle that nudged her in response to the slightest attention. While she familiarised herself with her mount, Albert was preparing to leave.

"I presume that will be all for the moment, sir," he said courteously. "I will return to Merton Hall and arrange for lunch to be served around 1.30pm, as you instructed."

Albert's departure, however, signalled for Jill to mount her horse. As Rose had predicted, she found herself confronted with a side-saddle which, with her limited experience, presented something of a problem. Embarrassed, she turned to Greg.

"How do I...?"

"Oh, allow me!" he exclaimed apologetically. "It's very simple. Just stand by the horse and bend your left leg back towards me – then I can help you up."

To her surprise and relief, it was accomplished in a single easy movement and, once seated, she found the unfamiliar position quite comfortable.

"Now," he smiled, "I think we're ready to go." Taking Cloud's lead-rein in his left hand, he stepped up onto his horse. "I suggest," he continued, "we move directly north to link up with the main westbound highway. That will take us directly to the Dyke escarpment."

It amazed Jill, to discover that this main westbound highway was little more than a rutted farm track, whereas, in her own day, it had enjoyed an almost Grand Avenue-like status. Now all she could see was a distant farmhouse to the north and a large, derelict-looking windmill to the south that squeaked in protest at every turn of its slowly rotating sails. Indeed, apart from these structures, there was an uninterrupted view of rolling farmland in every direction while the slight south-westerly breeze blowing up from the sea gave a freshness she could almost taste. As it rustled gently through the grass, Jill glanced up to see a flock of birds circling high overhead in the clear blue sky. Greg, she admitted to herself, had certainly chosen a lovely day and a beautiful setting. In the meantime, Cloud's gentle rhythm together with the mare's obvious reliability, had gradually enabled her to relax and concentrate on the incredible yet still, somehow, unreal experience of seeing the landscape as it had appeared some sixty years previously.

But her thoughts were interrupted when Greg turned in his saddle.

"Are you familiar with this area, Jill?" he enquired.

"Well, I wouldn't exactly say 'familiar'," she replied guardedly. "I have been here on a few occasions and the one I most remember was as a small girl with my parents. They took me to the Dyke for a picnic one sunny summer afternoon but," she grimaced, "the only thing I remember about that was being terrified of going up and down the steep slopes. It really is very deep in the Dyke area."

"Well, don't worry," he smiled. "We won't be doing anything like that today."

The track leading to their destination was situated along a high ridge and offered breathtaking views of the coastal plain lying between the sea and the foothills. More importantly, as they moved west Jill found herself directly north of her home area and could just make out the coastal road where the terrifying darkness had first swept in from the Channel. Now, however, as she gazed at the azure sky, it seemed almost impossible to imagine. However, her obvious fascination with the view quickly caught her companion's attention, and although he had no means of knowing it, Jill was, in fact, desperately searching for any sign of her old home streets. However, it was a vain hope for all she could see were a few unidentifiable buildings and an endless vista of open fields.

Greg reined in his horse.

"It's quite a view, isn't it?" he observed. "We're about 1,500 feet above sea level at this point and if you look carefully you can just make out the canal which runs parallel to the coast. But worse," he suddenly stressed, "you see that monstrosity between the canal and the sea? Well, that's the gasworks. It was built in 1819 and it's gradually been getting bigger ever since." As he spoke, she observed a flicker of bitterness pass across his features. "My great-grandfather sold off all our rights over the foreshore to allow for that development. Although my grandfather was dead against it, apparently his father just wouldn't listen – and there you have the result. It was a terrible mistake because commercial enterprise on that scale tends to draw in other light industries and devour the surrounding district with housing to cater for their workers." At this point, his horse suddenly became restive and made to move forward.

"I can see a time," he added in the same bitter tone, "when much of this view will be nothing more than an urban sprawl and when the days of our tenant farmers will be a thing of the past."

Sad as it sounded, it was, fascinating for Jill because he was describing the birth pangs of a world she had known all her life. Twisting in his saddle, Greg quickly apologised.

"I'm sorry, I didn't mean to bore you – only it's something I feel very strongly about."

"No, Greg," she assured him, "that's fine. It's really interesting to find out about local history."

While unable to divulge the true nature of her interest, she found it ironic that her whole neighbourhood had once belonged to the man she was now with.

It took them a further twenty minutes to reach their destination, a landmark which owed its fame to a yawning chasm in the hills – although, to Jill's surprise, Greg didn't stop but rode straight on before eventually reining in on the rise of a gentle incline. However, she was quick to appreciate his decision, for the location afforded stunning views in every direction. Where they had stopped, the grassy hillside to the north sloped gently away before falling steeply to the flatness of the Weald far below. It almost seemed as if she could see to the edge of the world, for the pattern of fields appeared to stretch away to infinity. Immediately to the right stood a clump of trees whose distorted branches bore mute witness to their seasonal battering at the hands of the strong south-westerly winds. However, at this time of the year, they were besieged by masses of brightly coloured daffodils struggling to secure living space around their roots.

"Well?" enquired Greg. "Do you approve?"

"Oh, it's lovely," she smiled, gazing about. "It's absolutely beautiful."

Her companion eased himself in the saddle.

"You know," he confided, "when I find things get a bit too much, I head for this spot and just sit here to enjoy the peace." He paused as he looked around. "It's a sort of special place for me."

"And yet you brought me?" she observed.

"Yes, indeed I did," he smiled while dismounting. "Here, let me help you down. Just take your left foot from the stirrup and lift your right leg from the saddle rest. That's it. Now slide down towards me."

Again it turned out to be far easier than she had anticipated, mainly because he caught her under the arms before her feet touched the ground; an action which brought him disconcertingly close.

"Thank you, Greg." she gasped as, with lingering eye contact, he slowly released his hold.

After easing the girth-straps, her handsome companion led their horses towards the trees, where he tethered them to a nearby gatepost. Once they were secured, he reached into one of the saddlebags to withdraw what Jill had now come to recognise as a brandy flask. But, upon seeing her quizzical expression, he hastened to explain.

"This is what is known as a stirrup cup. It's used at hunt meets just before the dogs move off. But don't look so worried," he smiled. "It's nothing more than a refreshing concoction of lime and beer."

Removing his coat, he spread it out on the grass and invited her to take a seat. Unfortunately, in her long riding outfit, she found it easier said than done. However, by raising the hem of her skirt, she endeavoured to comply with as much dignity as she could muster. Finally, after joining her at an ever-discreet distance, Greg observed quietly:

"You know, I always enjoy this time of year. It holds such a freshness and a promise of the coming summer. I mean, look at the variety of colours on the slope below. I think we insult nature when we call them weeds, because they're absolutely beautiful." For a moment he looked away. "I remember my mother used to recite a poem about this time of year. It went something like:

'I long to see the buttercups appear
For then I know that spring is near
I love to see their reflective gold
As it speaks of summer days untold'

"Oh, that's so lovely, Greg," smiled Jill warmly as she leaned forward to clasp her drawn-up knees.

"You're actually quite a sensitive person, aren't you? It's a nice quality and not something I've found among a lot of men I've known in the past." Then, after a pause, she ventured, "Tell me. Do you always ride the same horse, Greg?"

He looked over at the two animals busily grazing on the new spring grass.

"I'm afraid I do," he confessed. "I suppose really it's just a mixture of habit and affection. You can keep your carriages and trains. Give me my horse any time – although, I must admit, he's not always been an easy ride and has nearly thrown me off on a number of occasions."

"And what do you call him?" she asked. "I've not heard you mention any name."

"That's mostly because he hasn't got one. Well, not a proper one anyway. I usually just refer to him as Pitch, mainly because of his colour, but also in recognition of the times he's almost had me out of the saddle." At this, it went quiet for a period and he looked thoughtful before continuing. "You mentioned the men you have known?"

"Yes," she replied slowly, sensing the remark to be a query rather than an observation. "No one special, though, if that's what you're wondering. Although, to be honest, there was someone once but he's not here now and there's no way he ever can be."

The strange remark cried out for clarification but, fortunately, her companion failed to pursue the subject, instead he asked:

"Have you been at the Vicarage for long, Jill?"

It was the sort of question she had hoped to avoid, mindful of where it might lead. So she decided to play it casually.

"Well, it must be all of six months by now but, tell me, why do you ask?"

"Oh, I just wondered," he replied absently. "Because it seems, somehow, you've suddenly become part of the Vicarage entourage from nowhere and I suppose I'm frightened you might disappear just as quickly." Taken out of context it was an innocent enough observation, but Jill found it unnerving. "Anyway," he smiled, "promise me I won't wake up one day to find you gone – because, you see..."

But he didn't finish and he didn't need to.

For a while they just sat in a comfortable silence enjoying the gentle warm breeze with Jill relaxing to its sensual feel on her face. However, amidst the tranquillity, she suddenly experienced a devastating sense of her true reality as it swept in unexpectedly and unbidden.

She glanced across at Greg busily pouring them both a drink, and became numbed by the chilling realisation that all this could be a cruel illusion. Her handsome companion, apparently so vigorous and full of life, would, in her own time frame, probably have been long since dead. The horrifying thought caused her to shiver, which Greg quickly noticed.

"You're not cold, are you?" he asked with a sudden concern.

"No, Greg, I'm fine. Really I am."

"In which case," he replied passing her a slim metal cup, "I'd like to propose a toast – to a special day on the hillside in the company of a particularly lovely young companion."

"To a special day on the hillside," she echoed with a smile, while still struggling to contend with her disturbing thoughts.

However, as Greg rose to replace the utensils, something far out over the sea caught his attention.

"Jill. Come and look at this. There," he pointed out as she hurried to join him. "Out there – on the horizon."

After following his gaze, she suddenly felt herself go cold for there, gathering over the Channel and moving steadily towards the coast, was a thunderous-looking cloud formation. The sight provoked an immediate panic attack. However, unaware of her reaction or the reason behind it, Greg continued to study the phenomenon with interest.

"That," he exclaimed with enthusiasm, "is some thunderstorm." Then, in the absence of any response, he turned in time to see his companion's eyes dilated in terror. "Jill – what on earth's the matter?" he asked anxiously. "Look, it's only a storm. It's just a particularly bad one, that's all. Honestly, there's nothing to be afraid of. It's still miles away."

However, the shock and the constant mental precariousness of her unnatural existence finally proved too much, and to Greg's dismay, she burst into tears. Reticent by nature and unsure what to do, he hesitated before instinctively gathering her in his arms and stroking the back of her head. Instinct also warned him that now was not the time for words, so he just continued to hold her gently until she finally stopped trembling and looked up.

"Oh," she gasped in a constricted voice. "I bet I look an absolute mess."

"That," he assured her, "is something you're just not capable of."

"I'm sorry," she added hastily, anxious to find an excuse – any excuse, in fact – that would explain her peculiar behaviour. "I don't know what came over me. It's just that I once had a nasty experience with a thunderstorm and it's left me terrified of them."

"I understand," he sympathised. "But I don't like to see you in such distress so let me get you back to the Vicarage before that storm breaks in earnest."

"But," she objected, "I thought Albert had arranged for us to have lunch at your home."

"Well, that's true," he admitted glancing up at the sky. "But, wherever we go we're going to get very wet – and I mean, saturated."

"Well," she countered, suddenly feeling quite determined, "if we're going to get wet, we're going to get wet. But I vote that it's on the way to your place."

"I just hope it lives up to your expectations," he grinned as they turned towards their horses.

So the memorable day sped away with an eventual

return to the Vicarage around dusk. Always the consummate gentleman, he insisted on driving her back in one of the family carriages and, upon arrival, graciously helped her to step down. It was a final act and made her feel very special. Her suspicion that his natural reserve would prohibit a parting kiss proved right with the gesture being confined to the back of her hand. Rose would explain later that it was more than just reticence on Greg's part, but an essential element of Victorian etiquette. Releasing his hold, he gazed at her in the fading light.

"I hope, Jill," he said quietly, "that you have enjoyed today as much as I have." Then, without waiting for a reply and with one fluid action, he bowed slightly before replacing his top hat and striding away towards the Vicarage gate. However, just as she began to wonder when they would meet again, he paused and half turned. "I've been wondering," he ventured slowly, "whether you have any interest in ballroom dancing?"

The sudden unexpected remark took her off guard. Although she seriously doubted if the American Swing-style she had so enjoyed with John was really the sort of thing he had in mind.

"Well, Greg..." she began.

But he was already speaking again.

"The annual Hunt Ball at the Grand Hotel – it's on Saturday the 23rd of April and starts at 9pm. I'll be here for you around 8pm. So don't forget!"

"Greg, I'd love to..." she just about managed.

"But, you see..."

At this point, her handsome escort just raised his riding cane in presumed acknowledgement of her acceptance. And that was it. He was gone with a gentle grinding of carriage wheels accompanied by the rhythmic clip of his high-stepping drove horses.

"Well!" exclaimed a voice, with a suddenness that made her jump. "Now, wasn't that something?"

"Rose!" she cried in exasperation. "Have you been standing behind the door listening? Oh – you have, haven't you?"

But hers was a mock irritation, for Jill had grown very fond of her new friend and happy to accept her vicarious appetite for other people's affairs. In any case, there was nothing to be gained from any further protest, because Rose was now in full flow.

"The annual Hunt Ball at the Grand?" she exclaimed excitedly. "Very nice. Now come on in and we can discuss all the details." So, poor Jill, who really just wanted to relax in the afterglow of the day, had no option but to comply. "You do realise," stressed her friend once they were indoors, "that this dance is *the* social event of the Sussex calendar and I can tell you, the ballgowns will be absolutely exquisite. You can't begin to imagine." A wistful note crept into her voice "I'd have loved to have gone to something like that when I was young, but my parents were just too poor to afford it." But she again became quickly reanimated at the prospect of such a prestigious event."Now," she stressed, "the first thing we must do is to find you a glamorous ballgown suitable for the occasion... and, of course, a matching fan, because there won't be a lady present without one."

So it went on and on into the small hours before, totally exhausted, Jill finally managed to excuse herself and crawl off to bed.

Chapter 13

THE FOLLOWING MORNING, while Jill was out visiting Martha, Rose happened to glance out of the drawing room window in time to catch sight of a lone horseman reining up outside the Vicarage gate. Curious, she opened the front door to find it was Albert who, having dismounted, was already halfway up the garden path.

"Ah, Mistress Rose," he greeted her in his soft Irish accent. "Good morning to you. It's another lovely day, so it is."

"And a very good morning to you, Albert," she replied brightly. "I must say, this is an unexpected pleasure. What can I do for you? Oh, but never mind. Come on in and tell me."

So, in strict accordance with Vicarage tradition, Albert found himself being conducted along the hallway and through to the kitchen where Rose promptly offered him a cup of tea. And this despite the irritation caused by his clanking spurs – instruments which she'd always referred to as works of the devil.

After inviting him to take a seat, she busied herself over the stove.

"I must say," she chided, "we haven't seen much of you in church lately."

"No," admitted her guest with a hint of guilt. "But I expect you know how things have been on the estates. It's the worst year I can remember. In fact, the past two years have been nothing short of a disaster – what with this endless drought and widespread sickness among the livestock."

"I hope that's not an excuse," she smiled.

He looked slightly embarrassed but offered no further defence.

"Rose, would you object if I smoked my pipe? I find it easier to talk with that on the go."

"Not at all," she assured him. "You go ahead and make yourself at home. Actually, I quite enjoy the smell of pipe smoke. In fact, Michael occasionally indulges himself." With that, her visitor leaned back and produced a curved clay pipe from the pocket of his long coachman's coat, which left Rose to watch the ensuing ritual with a certain fascination.

"Not many of these about now," he observed, looking at it affectionately. "This one belonged to my grandfather and I finally inherited it from my dad. So really, you see, it's quite an heirloom." After inhaling several drafts of the fragrant smoke, he looked directly at his host. "You know, I've been with the Gregsons for some thirty years. In fact, I started with them as a young groom fresh over from Ireland

and, believe you me, I was as green as they come. The Gregsons have always been very good to me and they're now like family." He paused to draw on his pipe before adding, "I say this, Rose, so you will appreciate how important they are to me."

"I can well understand, Albert," she replied. "They are very nice people."

At this point, he again reached into his pocket, but this time it was to withdraw a small leather purse, which he placed on the table.

"There be twenty gold sovereigns in that there purse," he explained. "Mr Frederick asked me to pass them on to you so as to cover the expense of costumes and such for this 'ere Hunt Ball."

"Albert," she protested. "I couldn't possibly accept such an amount of money. Quite apart from anything else, it's far in excess of what's actually needed."

At this apparent setback, her visitor took a deep breath.

"I was afraid you might say sommat along those lines, Rose. But I hope I can persuade you otherwise because, I suspect, if I were to take the money back, Mr Frederick might see it as some sort of rejection and become discouraged, which I think would be a pity. Oh, I know he's had lots of opportunities but he's never shown much time for the fair sex until meeting the young lady you've got staying here... Well, let's just say I'd like to see it work out for him."

"What amazes me," observed Rose, "is how such

an attractive and eligible man has managed to stay single for so long."

"Ah, now, to understand that, Rose," he explained, "you have to know him as a person and, more importantly, all he's been through. You see, to start with, although he doesn't like it generally known, he's naturally very shy. That's probably why I'm 'ere now. But there's also the fact that when his mother died he took it very badly and I suspect he might have felt that any affiliation with another woman might seem like – well, a sort of betrayal. It's strange, isn't it, how some people's minds work? But I'm sure that's the way it's affected him." He shook his head and examined his pipe before deciding it had gone out. Then, after striking a fresh match, drew contentedly on the smouldering tobacco. "I don't suppose," he continued finally, "you would remember the late Mrs Gregson? No." He hesitated. "You probably wouldn't because I seem to think she was a bit before your time. But beautiful! You wouldn't believe it; not only that, she was also beautiful to know. Incidentally, I understand that the young lady you've got staying here bears a striking resemblance to her. Anyway, it was a terrible loss for us all when she died so unexpectedly – it was childbirth you know. And she wasn't really that old – certainly no more than in her mid-thirties or so."

It went quiet for a moment.

"And did the child survive?" Rose enquired.

"Oh yes," he nodded. "It was a girl. They called

her Isobel. She's Mr Frederick's younger sister, although she's never been very strong." He frowned briefly. "But I think, it was an experience that left him afraid. Afraid that, somehow, women die easily and if he ever got involved with anyone he might become faced with a similar tragedy." At this point, he again indicated the purse. "Anyway, Rose. I hope perhaps now you might feel able to accept Mr Frederick's offer."

She studied his weather-beaten and lined features which spoke of hard work and long hours spent in the saddle traversing the sprawling Gregson estates. She guessed him to be a man in his mid-fifties who, even after a lifetime of service to the one family, was still very much concerned about their welfare.

"I think I understand, Albert," she replied slowly as she moved round the table to top up his cup. "And under the circumstances you've described, I would be pleased to accept the money. But tell me, just as a matter of interest, what about you and your future? As far as I know, you've no family of your own."

"Oh, I'm not concerned about myself, Rose," he replied dismissively. "Because even if I had a wife, I'd only worry about her welfare, and that's without the problem of any children. Then there's the fact that, if I haven't got a wife, I don't have to worry about losing her." He sighed briefly.

"At least that's one lesson I've learned from the Gregson household."

Gazing ahead at the neat rows of copper pans

suspended above the kitchen range, he paused to sip his tea and refill his pipe. It all took so long that Rose felt forced to prompt him.

"Er, was there anything else, Albert?"

"Well, Rose," he replied while leaning back heavily in his chair, "as it happens, there is, but I've a bit of a problem. I don't really know quite how to put it – you see, the fact is, I feel the need to ask you sommat – sommat, well, a bit confidential. Arguably you might think it none of my business, but be that as it may, I just wondered how long you've actually known the young lady in question and whether you think she would be suitable for Mr Frederick." He stopped, as if momentarily embarrassed by what he'd just said. "I suppose it sounds terrible put like that," he admitted. "But you must understand, I'm just anxious everything doesn't end up in disaster. The point is, as far as I can see, nobody actually seems to know much about her." Then, after a certain hesitation, he added, "I mean, for a start, do you even know if she's married?"

Rose was quick to reassure him.

"You're a good man, Albert, and I know you mean well, but you ask me questions which are not really mine to answer. Although I can assure you Jill has no marital ties. Having said that, let me see what else can I say. She's actually been with us now for about six months and, if it's any help, I can tell you I shall miss her dreadfully should she decide to move on. After a certain amount of thought, she added, "although I'm not at liberty to discuss the details, Jill has shown the most exceptional bravery over a recent and dreadful ordeal; an experience far more terrible than anything you or I could begin to imagine – and, incidentally, you're also probably aware that she's been an indispensable help with the parish work." At this point, Rose paused as if uncertain whether to say any more, but finally added, "In all honesty, Albert, I think that's about it. Anything else will have to come from Jill herself."

Getting to his feet, Albert took Rose's hand in gratitude before he pocketed his pipe and turned to leave.

"I hope that thing's quite out," warned Rose.

"So do I," he grinned. "Because it wouldn't be the first time I've burned a hole in my coat. Anyway, I do thank you for your forbearance. You've been very patient and helpful, and I want you to know I appreciate it – now, don't worry, I will see myself out."

Accompanied by the chink of his spurs, he disappeared down the hallway towards the front entrance at which point he turned to wave before donning his top hat and quietly closing the door behind him.

Chapter 14

THE DAY OF the Ball proved long and exhausting, even before the actual event had got under way. This was due, in part, not only to Rose's constant excitement and attention to detail over Jill's outfits but also to Josie, who worked tirelessly through the morning to get her hair 'just right', as she called it. Endless hairgrips and immeasurable patience had finally combined to produce a double pleat, set vertically at the back of her head. It was an elegant and classic style, which emphasised the clean line of her neck and shoulders. However, when the combined result was finally reviewed in the drawing room mirror, Jill had to admit it had been more than worth all the effort.

"Well, are you pleased?" asked Rose. "Because I think you look absolutely lovely." Jill's friend had just entered the room carrying a narrow jewellery box. Setting it down on a nearby table, she exclaimed, "I have a little something for you that I think will just add the finishing touch."

She slowly and carefully opened the lid to reveal

a triple row of gleaming white pearls fastened by a diamond coupling. The necklace was designed for a close fit to the wearer's neck where its intrinsic beauty would express elegance and sophistication.

As Jill delicately lifted it from its resting place, Rose explained:

"It was a gift from my grandparents to my mother on the occasion of her twenty-first birthday and I want you to have it for tonight. You see, I've never had an opportunity to wear it myself."

"Oh, Rose, it's so beautiful. I don't know what to say," exclaimed Jill as she gave her friend a hug. "I promise I will take great care of it."

"I'm sure you will," replied her friend. "And you know, really, there's no need to thank me because I'm sure you'll do it more than justice – now just hold still for a moment while I fasten it in place so we can get a better idea of the final effect. Oh," she enthused as she stood back, "it's so perfect for your colouring and slender neck."

However, even before she'd finished speaking, the Westminster chimes rang out from the direction of the front door to herald the arrival of their eagerly awaited visitor.

"Oh, he's here. He's here already!" burst out Rose, rushing headlong down the hallway.

It was almost as if Greg had come to take *her* to the Ball, and as she opened the door, there he stood – just how they had imagined: tall and immaculately dressed in tailored black frock coat and trousers which contrasted vividly with his white shirt and waistcoat. He did, indeed, cut a stunning figure of sartorial elegance.

"Why, good evening, Rose," he greeted her with a slight bow. "You make me wish I could take both you ladies to the dance – then I'd be the envy of everyone. However," he smiled, "I fear the Reverend wouldn't hear of it."

"Oh, get away with you, Frederick," she chided and blushed despite herself. "It's this beautiful young lady you've come for – and rightly so."

As she spoke, he caught sight of Jill and just stared in total admiration. It was a look that needed no words and, turning about, he proffered his arm in an open invitation.

"Madam!" he exclaimed. "Your carriage awaits."

However, her initial excitement became dwarfed by what awaited beyond the Vicarage gate. For there, standing in the dim light, stood the luxurious family carriage she had first encountered during the Hanningtons episode. This time, however, instead of there being two matching grey horses, there were four, with Albert in full livery and riding postilion.

"Oh, Greg!" she exclaimed, "I don't know what to say." Turning to look up at him she insisted, "You know, I suppose that I would have been perfectly happy to come with you in a cab or even...!"

"I know. And that," he insisted, "is precisely why I'm taking you in style."

Elated, she glanced back at the house in time to

see Rose silhouetted against the lighted doorway as she waved them off. Then, while Albert remained seated on the lead horse, Greg opened the nearside carriage door and assisted her to her seat. Finally, and only when satisfied with her comfort, did he take his place opposite. Sinking back once again into the deep upholstery, Jill coyly glanced across at her escort and thought what a consummate gentleman Greg really was; never taking anything for granted, but always treating her as fragile and precious.

"Well, young lady. Are you quite ready?" He smiled before leaning out of the window to tell Albert it was time to move off.

And so, with its lamps piercing the gathering darkness, the carriage rolled forward in the direction of the Grand Hotel. It was a comparatively short drive but Jill revelled in every movement of the well-sprung comfort; a delight somehow enhanced by the rhythmic clip of the drove horses, which seemed all the more exciting when Albert raised their tempo to a high-stepping trot.

After a journey through the relatively quiet and dimly lit approach roads, the Grand itself appeared as a blaze of light and activity. The brilliance of the main entrance revealed a long line of jostling horses and carriages waiting to disgorge their fashionable passengers. However, some of the finer-bred animals were becoming frisky at the noisy delay, with one even trying to kick over the traces and bolt. It was a nasty moment and for a while looked quite frightening, before several men managed to restore calm. Albert, on the other hand, master of the horse that he was, kept his team quiet and obedient as they waited their turn.

Finally, the time arrived to alight and Jill found the carriage door being opened by a fully liveried hotel concierge who graciously took her hand as she stepped down.

"Good evening, Madam," he greeted her courteously. "May I welcome both you and your escort to the Grand Hotel? May I also wish you both an enjoyable evening?"

However, Jill found the ballgown made it a difficult manoeuvre and, sensing her difficulties, Greg dutifully rushed to her aid and steadied her elbow as she endeavoured to compose herself for whatever lay ahead; mindful that, in her own time, the hotel had always been the preserve of the wealthy. It was an environment far removed from her own world, and painfully conscious of this class barrier, Jill knew she would have to rely heavily on Greg for support. She desperately hoped she wouldn't let him down.

Even entering the spacious reception area proved a daunting experience of opulent extravagance. Crystal-glass chandeliers sparkled with light against a backdrop of royal red panelling, while a central fountain sent a continuous fine spray over the elegant nearby palms. Amongst all this imposing grandeur, the stylish and fashionable mingled with an easy confidence that Jill knew she could never hope to emulate, and it began to make her feel very inadequate. Sensing her hesitancy, Greg leaned over and whispered simply:

"There's no one here that can touch you." She looked up at him and smiled in gratitude as he added, "I'm the most fortunate man here."

The timely remark helped to restore Jill's confidence, and more importantly, it reflected his level of understanding and she loved him for it. She was also proud to be in the company of, probably, the most eligible and socially erudite man at the event. A suspicion quickly confirmed when they suddenly became interrupted by a chiming and cultured voice.

"Ah, Mr Frederick, dear boy. Good to see you. Though, I must say, I'm surprised with you not being a hunting man and all that."

Greg turned with a smile to face the portly speaker who was sporting the most outlandish ginger side-hair Jill had ever seen, which possibly, she thought wickedly, was a compensation for its total absence elsewhere. Furthermore, the man's obviously buoyant personality seemed somehow enhanced by his glowing cheeks, which, she suspected, was a direct result of excessive alcoholic intake.

"Jill," interjected Greg quickly, obviously anxious to include her, "please let me introduce you to our new mayor."

"How do you do?" she smiled with the customary curtsey while, at the same time, observing his look of appreciation.

"My pleasure indeed," he insisted, taking her hand for perhaps a trifle too long before turning back to Greg. "It's a pity you know, Frederick, that we don't see more of you on these social occasions. You always seem to find time for various welfare committees and such while it's common knowledge you work too hard."

"There's been a lot to do," replied Greg defensively. "The past two years have been extremely demanding. I just hope we're through the worst of it."

"Well, be that as it may," replied the newcomer, "but, frankly, I think it's time you started to live a bit and have some fun; none of us are here forever, you know."

At this, Greg nodded.

"I think you might well be right. In fact, I'm sure of it. And," he added nodding towards Jill, "what's more, I've now got every good reason to take your advice – but, if you'll excuse us, it's time I introduced this lovely young lady to the dance floor."

It had been a brief exchange but enough to confirm Jill's increasing awareness of what future life might be like with a man of Greg's status.

The ballroom itself was situated at the rear of the hotel. Its scale and elegance provided a sumptuous setting for the stylish couples already weaving their way round the floor. Designed as a single-storey extension, its late Victorian-style Gothic glass canopy soared high into the night sky. Being constructed of slim wrought-iron columns, its vaulted ceiling afforded spectacular views of the night sky. In addition, there were numerous tables placed at regular intervals round the edge of the floor for those not wishing to dance.

After the magic of the first waltz, Jill and Greg took their seats at an allotted table, whereupon they were immediately presented with a wine list.

"This makes me realise, Jill," he observed, "that I've so much to learn about you. In fact, apart from your love of tea, I seem to know very little about your tastes in drink or, indeed, anything else for that matter. Please tell me," he said, offering her the list, "is there a particular wine you would prefer?"

In itself, and set in such a luxurious and intimate atmosphere, it was an innocent enough question, but she realised its potential to expose her inexperience of the finer things of life and, ultimately, to the problems associated with her working-class origins. Greg, she knew, had taken her at face value as an attractive young woman residing with a middle-class minister and his wife. She was acutely conscious he neither realised who she really was nor, indeed, anything about her background. She was also aware that the constant suppression of her true identity would, in the long term, prove both stressful and unsustainable. So, even at the risk of losing Greg, she knew the time was coming when she would have to tell him the truth. These agitated thoughts flashed through her mind as she smiled to cover her uncertainty.

"Well, it depends, Greg. What's actually on offer?"

Fortunately, the deliberately evasive reply went unnoticed by her companion.

"It's certainly an extensive choice," he admitted. "But, if I may offer some advice, I suggest we both try a glass of 1841 French Chardonnay from the La Loire Valley. Apparently, it was an excellent year for light, dry, wine and I think it would make an ideal drink between dances."

However, before she could reply, her attention became diverted by a light-hearted voice.

"I trust this young man's not helping you choose the right wine, because he's absolutely no idea what he's talking about when it comes to the vintage nectar." It had obviously been said in fun and, glancing up to trace the banter, she found herself looking at an extremely attractive older man. A man who obviously liked what he saw. "I'll guarantee," he smiled, "that Greg will have recommended some watery rubbish instead of a full-bodied and aromatic sensory drink."

Greg glanced knowingly at his companion.

"This," he exclaimed with a touch of exasperation "is none other than Martin; Mr Martin, that is, of Martin & Sons – a brewers' association based in the City. He's also a wine importer and, therefore, thinks himself as something of a connoisseur on the subject." Then, addressing the interloper, he added, "Well, Martin, may I ask what brings you down to the coast? Haven't you got enough to keep you amused in town? I'm sure your London set must be frantic for any such advice you can offer."

Despite the hint of sarcasm, the businessman took it in good humour.

"Well, Greg – what can I say? Except that I do suppose you realise this is a hunt ball, which begs the question, what on earth are you doing here? And more to the point, how did *you*, as a non-hunting man, manage to persuade such a lovely young lady to accompany you?"

"I'm well aware of the nature of the occasion," countered Greg. "But it's obviously escaped your attention that not everyone is as besotted with the sport as you obviously seem to be. What's more, this young lady disapproves of the cruelty involved as much as I do."

"Touché," smiled the intruder with a slight bow. As he turned to leave, he took Jill's hand in a parting gesture of admiration. "It's been my pleasure young lady, and perhaps later in the evening, with Greg's approval, we might share a dance?"

"I should tell you," exclaimed Greg, as his associate disappeared into the crowd, "that gallant was none other than Master of the Southdown Hunt. Although, I must admit, he's a nice enough chap for all that. But I feel it my duty to warn you, if you decide to take up his offer your feet will suffer. He might be 'all hell on hooves', but he's an absolute menace on the dance floor."

By this time their wine had arrived, duly encased

in an ice bucket. After setting it down at their table, the waiter offered Greg a small sample for his approval. Then, and only after receiving his nod of satisfaction, did the waiter proceed to fill both their glasses. The whole process had been enacted with a graciousness far removed from Jill's memory of the offhand service she had experienced at the Regent Ballroom; but that was a different time and a different world.

"Well?" enquired Greg as she took her first sip. "What do you think?"

Any reply she might have made, however, became lost as the master of ceremonies invited the gentlemen to take their partners for the next dance. Greg immediately reached for her hand before leading the way onto the floor. And so the magic began, as he whirled her away among the swaying crinolines and practice moves of the other couples. It quickly became obvious that Greg was very light on his feet and Jill found herself effortlessly following his every move while the rhythmic music and low-hanging lights combined to provide a compelling and romantic atmosphere.

"For someone who spends their whole life working, Greg," she observed, "I must say you seem remarkably good."

"Oh, I shouldn't read too much into that," he replied. "It's my sister you have to thank for the safety of your feet. She might be fairly frail but she still insists on dragging me into the ballroom at home on every available occasion. What's more," he grinned, "she's not above telling me if I make a wrong move."

As the evening wore on, Greg's popularity and standing in the community became ever more apparent. Indeed, Jill couldn't help feeling slightly resentful when various young ladies, with whom he was obviously acquainted, approached him for a dance – although she certainly couldn't argue with the consummate way he always declined their invitations.

Yet, despite all this gentility, she found it strange how his embrace never once ventured beyond the formal dance posture and, somehow, it didn't feel quite natural. As the evening wore on and the lights grew dim, various couples on the floor began to draw closer in demonstrations of affection which only served to make Greg's behaviour seem all the more unusual. It even made her wonder if there wasn't more to it than just mere reserve. Admittedly, she realised their time together had been limited. But she also knew if there was some underlying problem, any feelings she might have for him could only be doomed to a very uncertain future. Although, of course, what future she could expect in her enigmatic circumstances was, at best, questionable.

True, he'd made the first move in their relationship. But, for whatever reason, he now seemed either unable or unwilling to take their relationship any further.

Feeling confused, she allowed her mind to concentrate on the hotel's elaborate surroundings.

The panoramic view of the night sky above, unquestionably added to the charm of the event. But, even as she gazed up in admiration, the romantic idyll suddenly became overshadowed by a heavy dark cloud formation, which slowly began to obscure the bright crescent-shaped moon. Almost at once, vicious jagged streaks of lightning threatened to rend the gathering darkness while a rolling crash of thunder added to the increasingly threatening atmosphere.

Slowly, the couples stopped dancing to gaze up at the unfolding drama, but for Jill it represented a horror out of all proportion, and overwhelmed with fear, she froze in the middle of the floor with her fingers digging deep into Greg's upper right arm. Mystified by this sudden strange behaviour, he glanced down in time to see her eyes dilated and the same fixed expression he had first encountered on their ride to the Dyke. Following the direction of her terrified stare, he asked urgently:

"What is it, Jill? What's the matter? It's only another thunderstorm." But for a brief moment, she had become inarticulate. And seeing her stricken condition, he guided her back to their table where he gently placed a hand on her shoulder. "Tell me, Jill," he urged anxiously. "What's the matter? What's upsetting you so? Is it the thunder that's bothering you again?"

By now, however, Jill was slowly beginning to recover.

"Oh, it's just me being silly again, Greg," she finally managed. "That's all. Please. I'm sorry. Take no notice."

But Greg was not to be so easily deterred.

"No," he insisted. "There's more to it than you just being silly, isn't there? I don't know why, but for some reason you're terrified of heavy storms. I mean, what is it? What is it about them that terrifies you so?" Her pale and shaken appearance caused him to beckon a nearby waiter. "A double whisky for the young lady – the best in the house. And make it fast." It sounded abrupt – and it was. Then, turning back to his companion, he said gently, "It really troubles me to see you like this. Are you sure there's nothing I can do? You know I'm always here and ready to listen if you think it would help."

However, embarrassed by her own behaviour, Jill realised that continued prevarication was becoming useless.

"You're absolutely right, Greg," she admitted reluctantly. "It's true, I do have certain irrational fears, but it's with good reason and I promise to tell you why when the time's right. But, please, not just now." Taking a sip of the newly arrived whisky, Jill coughed on the potency of its sting. "You're always so considerate and caring Greg, and," she added guardedly, "that is why I'm very fond of you." But then, in her impetuous way, she added, "No. It's more than that..."

She dropped her gaze as he hesitantly took her hand.

315

"Do you think for a moment that I didn't already know?" he replied affectionately.

The moment was a precious but fleeting one, for his demeanour was about to undergo a sudden and dramatic change.

"But what about you, Greg?" she asked in a barely audible voice. "You talk about me as being the only one, so what's holding you back?" Then, in a reflection of her true temperament, she suddenly looked up with a new assertiveness. "If I'm that important to you, why aren't you more demonstrative? Why is it that you don't show a little more of how you feel?"

Until now, she had only ever experienced him as an absolute gentleman. However, in the face of her direct challenge, she saw him almost physically recoil and a different, unexpected facet of his character begin to emerge. In fact, she could hardly recognise how unsure and embarrassed he suddenly became.

"I find some things difficult," he finally managed while studiously avoiding eye contact. "More to the point – I find them almost impossible to discuss."

"But why, Greg?" she pleaded. "What's the problem?"

"Why?" he repeated. "Why? I'm not sure. But the reality is you are the first woman with whom I've ever risked becoming involved." He lifted his gaze to stare across the ballroom. "You'll probably find that difficult to believe but I assure you it's the truth – oh, I've known a lot of young ladies over the years and many of them have been lovely people and yet," he shrugged, "I've never made that first move, because if I'm honest, I'm afraid to."

"But, afraid of what, Greg?" she entreated.

However, he was either unable or unwilling to discuss it further. Seeing his embarrassed resentment, she wondered if she hadn't already pushed her own uncertainties too far. However, by now, the strains of the last waltz were fast fading with various couples drifting towards the exits. As the Master of Ceremonies wished them goodnight and a safe journey, many waved and acknowledged Greg but he made little sign of even seeing them.

Moreover, during the return journey he was noticeably quiet. Sitting opposite Jill, he kept his gaze firmly averted towards the window as the carriage glided smoothly back through the darkened streets. Gently rolling in her seat to the vehicle's rhythm, she sighed resignedly and did the same thing – although there was precious little to see, because by this time, all the gas-lamps had long since been extinguished. Covertly, she glanced across at her companion and the fixed expression on his handsome features, struggling, she suspected, with some inner turmoil, which made her wonder if she'd got too involved with style rather than substance. He was obviously a man of great complexity and she realised any future with him would require a lot of understanding.

Arriving at the Vicarage, he nevertheless dutifully helped her alight before escorting her to the front door. After reservedly expressing his gratitude for her company, he bestowed the customary kiss to the back of her hand. Then, without a further word, he turned and made for the waiting carriage. It all seemed such an anti-climax to an otherwise wonderful evening.

Once inside the house, she leaned back on the door with a heavy sigh. Shrugging her shoulders, Jill made her way down the hall towards the kitchen with the fervent hope that Rose would have already retired for the night. What she didn't know, was that as Greg approached the gate he had hesitated and turned back with a lingering look at the closed front door. She was also unaware of his devastated expression and how he remained there for so long that, finally, poor Albert's patience ran out.

"Home is it then, sir?" he enquired.

"Yes, Albert," he nodded quietly. "Home."

But it was said with such an unmistakable finality and sadness, that Greg's right-hand man deemed it better to refrain from comment.

Chapter 15

JILL FELT MORE than a little grateful the previous evening to discover that Rose had, in fact, gone to bed, because it avoided any well-meaning inquisition. But she also knew the following morning would offer no such reprieve. Therefore, she awoke determined to get it over with as quickly as possible and, dragging on her dressing gown, hurried downstairs where she found her friend busy at the stove.

"Good morning," she said brightly. "I thought you'd have been in the drawing room with your piano."

In response to this overture, Rose turned from her chores in mock surprise.

"Well, I was this morning," she replied with a certain feeling. "But as it's now well past midday, we call it afternoon in this part of the world; which begs the question, what time did you eventually get in last night, young lady?"

"Oh," replied Jill vaguely. "Late. Very late."

"And?" quizzed Rose, passing her the almost sacramental cup of tea.

"And," shrugged Jill. "And, nothing – I just don't understand it Rose. I mean, I knew Greg was a complex person, but I found out last night that I have to be very careful about what I say."

"But, you must admit," Rose smiled with a touch of envy, "he's very handsome."

"That's all very well," Jill replied listlessly, "but what's the point if you don't know what's going on in his mind? Perhaps it's all for the good that we don't get too close because, as we both know, I could well revert back to my own era at any time and without warning."

"Oh, don't give me that negative rubbish," retorted her friend sharply. "You've got to live in the here and now. You've said so yourself. In any case, none of us have any guarantees you know. I do suppose you realise he's a catch in a million? So, more to the point, how did you leave it with him?"

"You may well ask. He didn't say. He was in such a strange mood by the end of the evening. He just kissed my hand and virtually left without a word I don't know where I am. He's so formal Rose – sometimes it feels that I hardly know him at all. He never does anything, well you know, physical. I don't know. It's either he doesn't find me attractive or he's abnormal in some way." She stopped to take a sip from her cup before adding, "In any case, I can hardly go chasing off up to Merton Hall saying 'Hi. How about taking me out again?,' can I?"

Rose went quiet for a while as she laid out her

laundry before proceeding to iron it with a firm, smooth, action. She was quick and meticulous as she alternated the hot irons from the stove, while paying particular attention to the cuffs and collars of her husband's shirts. Only when the last item had been neatly stacked did she finally sit down.

"I didn't tell you, but Albert came to see me the other day. I think you were out visiting at the time. Anyway, he gave me the distinct impression that Frederick, oh – sorry," she smiled, "I mean Greg, was very serious about you." She paused for a moment while endeavouring to choose her words with care. "You probably don't know – well, you have no means of knowing – that he lost his mother when he was quite young. Actually, it all took place long before my time here. I'm unsure about all the details but I can tell you I've heard they were very close while she was alive, and perhaps significantly, that they used to ride out together quite frequently. Anyway," she mused, tapping the side of her cup, "as I say, she died unexpectedly and it left him inconsolable for years; so much so that Albert seems to think the trauma might have had an adverse effect on his attitude to women in general. There's also something else you should be aware of. Greg's mother's beauty was virtually a byword in the area and I've heard on a number of occasions people commenting on your striking resemblance to her. Which does make you wonder, doesn't it?"

"You mean," observed Jill bluntly, "that I've

become involved with someone who has a perverse attitude towards women and sees me as some sort of replacement for his mother?"

Rose just shrugged without further comment and contented herself with another sip of tea.

Jill was destined to have no further contact with Greg for some time. As the spring of that year gradually gave way to summer, she began to wonder if she would ever see him again. But after the exchange with Rose and Greg's strange behaviour, she faced the possibility with a certain equanimity. In any case, her time was largely taken up with church-related activities and new-found friends as well as Martha's welfare at the Vicarage. However, after one afternoon out visiting, she returned to find Rose bursting with news.

"Oh good, you're back," enthused her friend. "Guess what? Greg's been here to see you. In fact, you only just missed him."

"Really?" she observed with a certain indifference. "He's certainly taken his time."

But Rose was quick to jump to the landowner's defence.

"Despite his seemingly easy manner, Jill, I think he finds relationships difficult. I even sense he struggled to get here today. But, more to the point," she added, "there's something you should know – although I promised not to tell you. You see, apparently, the night he returned home from the Ball, he discovered that his sister, Isobel, had been rushed to the isolation hospital with suspected tuberculosis. Mind you, she's never been very strong. Anyway, it seems she'd been coughing badly for several days which everybody had attributed to a cold, but the night he was with you she started coughing up blood." Rose stopped and looked thoughtful. "You just never know, do you? However, it seems his sister's back home now, although still quite frail and in constant need of attention."

Hearing this, Jill sank slowly onto a chair as she tried to take it in.

"Oh, poor Greg. How awful. I didn't even know. I'll just have to write to him and tell him how sorry I am."

"Well," quipped Rose, "as it happens, that won't be necessary."

"Oh?" queried Jill.

"Well," emphasised her friend with certain relish, "that's because he's coming to pick you up at ten o'clock tomorrow morning. I think he's hoping to show you around one of the estate farms and introduce you to the rural way of life. I tell you, young lady," she added triumphantly, "that man's got his eye on you for the long term. Oh, I should add, I think he's bringing the same grey mare you rode last time."

Despite her initial reservations, the following morning found Jill watching expectantly from the drawing room window. Duly dressed in her riding outfit, she felt surprisingly elated when three horses turned in towards the Vicarage. As Jill watched Greg dismount, she had to admit he possessed a very real panache, but after opening the gate, she saw him pause and gaze uncertainly up at the house. Seeing his difficulties, she hastened to the front door and down the path to greet him and his look of relief and pleasure told Jill it had been the right move.

Ironically, it transpired the farm Greg had in mind lay to the west in an area not far from her old home. It appeared their route would take them back along Church Road, past the very spot where she and John had originally become separated. Poignantly, it would also be the first time Jill had visited the area since that terrifying night now, unbelievably, almost a year ago, and the closer they got, the more her emotions churned.

Finally, she found herself once again gazing down at the road surface where John's car had dematerialised around her. Many had been the nights spent wistfully gazing in this direction from her bedroom window and she dearly wanted to pull on the reins and just linger for a few minutes. But the place held no significance for Greg and to have stopped would only be to invite a lot of unwelcome and difficult questions. None of this, however, failed to prevent her mind drifting back to that terrible occasion when night-time and heavy mist had allowed for little more than a general impression of the area.

Now, in the broad daylight, she could see the whole of Church Road properly for the first time. It came as a shock for, although not overly familiar with this part of Hove, she had, nevertheless, known the road to be a busy urban thoroughfare. Now, as she looked west, the noisy junction John had so desperately tried to find appeared little more than an intersection of dirt tracks among an endless vista of open fields.

As they rode forward towards the crossroads, Jill reined in to stare incredulously at the view ahead. There was no sign of the dense urbanisation she remembered. All she could see now was open farmland stretching far away into the distance. Although she had half expected this sort of thing, the actual experience still came as a shock. While somewhere out there in all that emptiness she knew lay the eventual location of her home district with its narrow streets and little terraced houses. But that had been her world and despite its limitations, she still desperately missed it. Sad, yet fascinated, she determined to see at first-hand the place where, one day, it would all exist.

"Well, shall we camp here?" smiled Greg, puzzled by her delay but then observed, ironically, "By the way you're looking at those fields, you'd think you were in a different world."

She smiled but managed to refrain from comment.

Finally, she asked, "Tell me Greg, does all this land really belong to you?"

"Well, not exactly to me personally," he stressed modestly. "But it does constitute part of the Gregson estate which, in effect, means my father. But," he added with a sweep of his hand, "as I explained to you on our trip to the Dyke, much of this area, particularly around Portslade harbour, will eventually be requisitioned for housing."

"So much land," she murmured. "Yet all belonging to one man."

"Does that really matter?" he replied curiously.

"Oh, I don't know," she responded soulfully. "Some families seem to have so very little. I see a lot of poverty in my work. People with hardly any money and struggling to just exist. Anyway, Greg, changing the subject, I know you planned to show me one of the farms but would you very much mind if I took you somewhere else instead? It's in the same direction."

"Well," he observed, while trying to control the restive Pitch. "I'm out to make amends for my long absence, so I'll be happy to go along with anything you suggest. But, tell me, what have you got in mind?"

"Oh, somewhere familiar – familiar to me, that is. And somewhere we can talk quietly."

"Well," he replied as his horse bucked suddenly, "I'll let you take the lead."

Wanting to locate her home was one thing, but actually finding it in a landscape bereft of any familiar features, was quite another matter. To the south lay an unobstructed view of the coast road and its traumatic memories, while, to the north, ran the east-west railway embankment which, in her own time, had been such a physically and socially divisive barrier. Now, however, it was the only landmark available and, if the Cattle Arch existed in this era, then her problem would be effectively solved.

Nudging their horses forward, they left the intersection behind. Straight ahead, cattle and sheep grazed peacefully or lay basking in the midday sun. The whole area, in fact, seemed so unbelievably tranquil when compared to the vibrant urbanisation she knew would eventually supersede it. Glancing about, Jill could see the poignant sight of a partially used hayrick in one of the fields while, further on, a parked horse-drawn plough stood with its shafts pointing forlornly towards the sky. However, she couldn't help the unavoidable sadness of knowing this centuries-old agricultural idyll was fast approaching its demise. She also realised that this must have been the world of her grandparents, although she had never known them personally for they had died long before her birth.

Further on, the potent and unmistakable aroma of a pigsty filled the air and, as the two horses approached, the inmates fled squealing in all directions. But it was the tiny piglets that really got through to Jill as they scampered frantically to keep up with their parents. However, beyond the pigpens, the landscape seemed to just open up into an endless expanse of empty fields which intrigued Jill and she turned questioningly to her companion.

"I can see you're a town girl," he smiled. "The fact is, these fields have been left fallow for the hay harvest. It's used for cattle fodder during the winter. Normally," he continued to explain, "farmers would expect to get two crops during the course of a year, but as you can see, the grass is still quite sparse although it's now approaching mid-August."

As they rode on through the unfamiliar countryside, Jill began to sense they were nearing the area she had in mind. Sure enough, as she glanced along the railway embankment, she could make out the welcome outline of Portslade station. Situated in a densely built-up area in her day, it somehow felt uncanny to see it standing isolated and alone in the midst of farmland.

"Well," observed Greg as he reined in his horse, "we're now virtually on the Hove-Portslade boundary."

So, finally and after nearly a year, Jill had returned to her own home area and she desperately wondered what it would be like. Unaware of her thoughts, of course, Greg turned in his saddle. "So, young lady," he smiled, "where do we go from here?"

"Oh," she exclaimed, "just keep straight ahead. It's only a short distance beyond the station. I'll know it when I see a footpath that passes under the railway bank."

"I think," he replied, "you're probably talking about the Cattle Arch. It's part of a right of way that runs from the hills down through Old Goacher's place and straight on to the abattoir. Goacher, I might add, is one of our tenant farmers who rents all the land between the railway line and the coast, but if that's the place you've got in mind, I can tell you now there's nothing very special about it."

Again, despite the irony of his remark, Jill managed to refrain from comment. Pointing ahead, Greg then indicated a road which ran due south from the station to the seafront.

"That," he explained, "is known as Drove Street. Although I've heard recently it's to be renamed Boundary Road because of its location."

She could have confirmed the point, but wisely decided to remain silent. However, as she gazed down the road, which was little more than a wide farm track, she found it barely recognisable. Apart from the occasional isolated dwelling, there was no trace of the busy shopping street she remembered so well.

After leaving Drove Street behind, they rode out into the open wasteland beyond, but the track they were following quickly petered out into an increasingly overgrown wilderness. Derelict fencing lay everywhere, while straight ahead stood an ancient Sussex flint barn in a terminal state of decline. Bereft of its doors and most of its tiles, the splintered rafters still remaining stood stark and exposed to the mercies of the elements. Briars and brambles grew abundantly in every direction and were obviously completely out of control. In addition, and partly concealed among the chaos, lay various old rusty and abandoned pieces of agricultural machinery.

"Well," observed Greg as he caught her expression, "I did warn you. The place is nothing more than a neglected disgrace."

Slowly Jill let her eyes wander over the desolation and found it difficult to believe that one day, this would all become a densely populated urban area.

"This," he said with a sweep of his hand as he eased himself in the saddle, "is all that remains of a once thriving farm. The fact is, Old Goacher has been past it for years but won't admit defeat. My father's offered him a place at Merton where he could live out the rest of his days in comfort, but he just doesn't want to know." Her companion paused as he looked about. "Like my father, I haven't got the heart to force the issue, although I know only too well we can't afford to run part of our estate like this. Anyway, the problem of Old Goacher is trivial compared to the wider threat we face. The country's population has expanded beyond recognition during this Queen's reign and more and more land will be needed to meet the housing demand. Instinct tells me that the days of the landowners and their tenant farmers are numbered. Well, certainly in this area."

Suddenly realising how depressing all this must sound, he added brightly, "But we're not here to discuss my problems – you're in charge today, so tell me, have we much further to go?"

"No," she replied, gazing about in an attempt to establish her bearings. "I think we must be quite close."

After urging their horses forward, Jill suddenly spotted the mouth of the underpass and, again, reined in to stare about in disbelief, because like the station, the familiar arch now stood isolated and alone.

"Is this the place?" he asked as he followed her gaze. "Well, at least it's a nice day I suppose and it's quiet – I'll say that – but I'm afraid its attraction completely eludes me."

After tethering their horses, Greg motioned towards a fallen tree lying half concealed in the long grass, and suggested she take a seat.

"Well, here's to this special place of yours," he smiled while pouring her a drink.

It was a light-hearted enough comment, but Jill felt increasingly irritated as she watched him join her at the far end of the log. Suddenly it felt no longer good enough and she determined to have it out with him once and for all – no matter what the consequences might be.

"Why, Greg, are you sitting right over there? Are you afraid to come any closer? You tell me I'm special, but if I am, you have a strange way of showing it. For goodness sake, what's wrong with you? What am I supposed to think? Tell me!" she demanded. "Are you interested in me or not?"

Surprisingly, this time, however, his reaction was both muted and contrite.

"You know, you really don't have to ask that."

"Well," she retorted, "I'd like to point out that I first saw you almost a year ago and in all the time we've known each other, the nearest you've got to any show of affection is kissing the back of my hand."

He'd been put on the spot and he knew it.

"Don't think for a moment," he murmured, "that it hasn't crossed my mind." And so saying, he moved in closer. "Is that better?" he enquired gently.

"Much better. But, for heaven's sake, I can't understand why I have to mention such things – surely you can't be that inhibited? Normally I have trouble fending men off, not having to encourage them."

At this he grinned slightly before responding.

"I know, I know," he admitted. "I do appreciate what you're saying and I'm afraid it's fully justified." He paused. "If you can bear with me, I'll try to explain."

However, before he could continue, Jill gave vent to another concern.

"There's something else as well, Greg. You see, I've heard that some people who knew your mother seem to think I look very much like her. Tell me – is that true?"

He looked surprised.

"Why do you ask? I mean, does it really matter?"

"Oh, just tell me. Is it true?" she insisted with a touch of impatience.

At this he nodded slowly.

"Yes, as a matter of fact, you do. Very much so. In fact, I would go so far as to say you might even be a younger version of her."

His reply did little to calm her misgivings, and although knowing she was on sensitive ground, she nevertheless determined to see it through.

"Greg. I really don't know how to put this any other way. And again I want you to be quite honest with me. Do you really see me as some sort of mother substitute?"

This second outburst resulted in a heavy silence as her companion sighed and leaned forward to vacantly study the long grass between his boots. But finally he looked up.

"It's not like that," he began softly. "I know how it might appear but please believe me – it's nothing like that."

"Well then, Greg. Tell me, what *is* it like and what am I supposed to think?"

At this, his expression changed to one of sadness.

"You see, Jill," he said, "if I'm honest, I have certain fears. Phobias if you like. And it's not entirely without good cause. I try my best to keep it to myself, but when I think my defences are being challenged I become quiet and withdrawn. It's just me I'm afraid and I'm sorry."

He looked out again over the neglected landscape.

"You asked me if you look like my mother. Well, again, the answer's yes. And she was the most beautiful female I've ever seen." At this point, his voice became slightly choked. "She was also an incredibly lively and happy person who played with us for hours when we were children. She had unbelievable patience and never left our side if we were hurt or ill. And, you know, if we were crying she would always cuddle us until we stopped."

As he spoke, the attentive Jill noticed the sparkle of a tear at the corner of his eye. Then, making a visible effort, he added:

"One thing I most remember was her singing. She had the most lovely soprano voice and would play the nursery piano while we all sang along together. But then, one day, and without any warning, it all ended abruptly for, suddenly, it seemed she wasn't there anymore. I was, I suppose, about nine or ten at the time, and when we asked our father where she was he would tell us she had gone away for a rest and that one day she would come back. The sad fact was, of course," he murmured, "she would never come back because, in reality, she had died giving birth to our sister Isobel." He drew a deep breath. "My father, you see, lacked the courage to tell us the truth and every day we were left to wait and hope and then wait again – but that vibrant life, so full of energy and with so much to offer, had gone forever."

"Oh, Greg. How terrible. Rose did mention that you were quite young when you lost your mother, but I had no idea how traumatic it had been for you."

"I'm telling you this, Jill, to help you understand why I'm hesitant over physical contact, because as I've said before, I'm afraid. And the reason I'm afraid is because I know only too well what the consequences can be."

Although now well past midday, the sun seemed hotter than ever as it bore down on the desolate scene. They just sat quietly before Jill finally broke the silence.

"You know, Greg," she said gently, "just because your mother died in childbirth doesn't necessarily mean the same thing would happen to me. Granted there are risks but..."

"I realise that," he nodded. "And I know it's an irrational fear, but that's how it's left me. Everyone was affected in different ways. My brother Alistair tends to drift from woman to woman, fearful, I believe, of making any permanent commitment. Albert, who was just a stable-lad at the time, has chosen to remain single – she really was loved that much."

Again, a silence ensued, but this time it was a reflective one for there was little that could be said to relieve such sadness. With the exception of a single blackbird swooping low overhead, everything seemed very still in the heat-laden air. It was a brief respite that left Jill an opportunity to stare out over the neglected farmland and wonder where her home would eventually stand. Following the period of quiet, Greg spoke with a sudden passion.

"Please believe me, Jill, when I tell you I sought you out for the same reason any man would and certainly not because you happen to resemble my mother – but, I have to admit, had it not been for Alistair and the fact of seeing you for myself then it's almost certain I would have chosen to spend the rest of my life alone."

"Well," she replied demurely, "I've already told you how I feel, but I'm afraid there's a lot you don't know about me." At this Jill drew a deep breath before adding, "You've been very honest with me, Greg, and now it's my turn." However, she knew that what she was about to say could very well shatter any hope of a future together. "To start with," she began, "you must realise we come from very different social backgrounds."

Greg just smiled and shrugged.

"So what? Does any of that really matter? I'm interested in you, not where you came from."

"Well, yes it does matter," she stressed. "It matters very much, because it makes me nervous that I might somehow let you down."

"Absolutely not possible," he retorted. "I always feel very proud to be seen in your company. You're the most beautiful and elegant woman in every respect. More to the point, when I'm with you, in some strange way, I seem to feel complete."

The smile sparkled from her eyes.

"Well, thank you, Greg. That's a lovely thing to say. Even though it's not quite what I'm getting at."

And with that, she momentarily glanced up at the deep blue sky as the blackbird again swooped in low. "You see, Greg," she tried to explain, "there's a far more serious problem that I need to discuss with you, and one I've agonised over for months. But," she insisted, "it's something you must be aware of."

At this his handsome features suddenly paled.

"What else *can* there be? You're not already married, are you?"

"No, no! Nothing like that," she assured him while, at the same time, withdrawing a coin from her riding skirt.

"What's this?" he smiled. "There's no need to give me money. I really have got enough already."

"Yes – I know that, Greg, but this is not just any money and it might help you to believe what I'm about to say."

"You make it all sound very mysterious. So, what's so special about a penny?"

But his light-hearted remark was rewarded with a solemn look.

"It's the date, Greg. Please check the date and the image on the front."

At her request he held the coin carefully between his forefinger and thumb to examine the reverse side.

"1901? That's a bit odd, isn't it?" he exclaimed. "Mind you, irregularities like this do happen from time to time and when they manage to slip through into general circulation they can become quite valuable. I should hang on to it if I were you." He handed the coin back. "Anyway," he then added, "how did you happen to come by it?"

"That's just the point, Greg," she replied earnestly. "I didn't come by it. It came *with* me and I've others like it. Look at this shilling."

"Where did you get these from?" he frowned. "They aren't even valid currency."

At this point Jill drew a deep breath and braced herself for the final exposition from which there might be no return.

"They aren't forgeries, Greg," she insisted. "Where I come from, they're everyday currency."

"I'm afraid," stated the now puzzled Greg, "that you've got me totally mystified."

"Perhaps, Greg," she replied lowering her gaze, "I should have said '*when*' I come from, instead of 'where'."

"*When* you come from?" he protested. "No, I'm sorry. What are you trying to say?"

"Oh, it's impossible," she sighed. "I just don't know how to put this without sounding insane. What I'm trying to tell you Greg," she insisted, "is that I belong to the same era as these coins."

Numbed and speechless, he stared back as if from out of a nightmare as doubts of his own and her mental condition flashed through his mind.

"Please, Greg," she pleaded. "Please don't look at me like that. I want to be truthful but I'm in an impossible situation, because it makes me appear unstable and I'm not, Greg," she insisted. "Honestly

I'm not. Have you ever had any reason to doubt my state of mind before?"

Although his incredulous expression remained, he shook his head.

"No," he murmured. "None whatsoever. It's never even crossed my mind and I know Rose thinks very highly of you, but... I mean, it just can't happen. It's not possible."

She took his hands and added imploringly:

"Please try and believe me. You can't begin to imagine the hell I've been through." And, not wishing to capitalise by crying, she fought to hold back the tears. "You see, that's why I've shown you these coins, Greg. Because there can be no other explanation for my having them – I find myself stranded in late Victorian England and I don't belong here. I belong to the middle of the next century." But, despite all her efforts, the sound of misery had crept into her voice. "Can you begin to imagine what that feels like, Greg? It's like... it's like... starting your life all over again without anything or anyone that's familiar. Worse," she insisted, "you daren't say anything for fear of being shut away in an institution. In fact, had it not been for the understanding and kindness of Rose, I dread to think what would have happened to me."

"Rose knows all about this?"

Jill nodded dumbly.

"Yes, she's been an angel. It's ironic, Greg, that you fear losing me in childbirth whereas, in reality, there is a far greater danger of losing me if I revert back to my own era. It nearly happened the day I met your brother in Hanningtons."

The blackbird finally ceased circling and selected a long thin bramble branch, which swayed perilously under its weight.

"Rose is certainly a wonderful woman," he admitted. "But, I mean, does she really believe you?"

"I think she had severe doubts at first," Jill admitted. "And who could blame her? But after what happened at Hanningtons, she became totally convinced."

"Are you by any chance, talking about the day my brother took her back to the Vicarage? Because I just understood she fainted or had some kind of nasty turn."

"Yes," Jill replied bluntly. "That was because I almost dematerialised in front of her which, incidentally, made me think I was about to be drawn back to my own time. It was an awful experience. Rose told me later how my hand suddenly felt as though it had no substance, and it was the horror of it all that caused her to faint." She shrugged. "And, well, you know the rest."

"I certainly do," he replied, still studying the shilling coin in his hand. Clearly devastated, he shook his head and his voice momentarily trailed off. "Even if what you say is correct, how on earth did you manage it? I mean, how did you even get here in the first place? It's just beyond belief."

"You still think I'm deluded, don't you?" Jill replied dejectedly.

"Well, for heaven's sake, tell me how...?"

"I don't know how, Greg. I only know that it happened. You see," she then added quietly, "in the world where I come from, there had just been the most terrible war. Some twenty-two million people were killed. Every country in the world was involved. I don't know the exact details, but in order to bring the horror to an end, a new and terrible weapon was used, which scientists suspected might cause a chain reaction."

Greg's expression was a study as his eyes became narrowed.

"What sort of weapon are you talking about?"

"I've told you, Greg," she insisted. "I don't know the details. I'm not scientifically minded. All I know is, two cities in Japan were totally destroyed and that, several years later, areas of darkness began to appear in the sky over the Atlantic. I saw one of them moving up the Channel towards Brighton, and my friend and I got caught up in its outer fringes. It was absolutely terrifying. We couldn't even breathe."

After listening to the remainder of her ordeal, Greg just stared fixedly into space.

"Well," he said finally, "at least I know now why you are so afraid of dark-looking clouds. But, as for the rest of it," he added with a taut look around the edges of his mouth, "I don't know what to think... I just don't know."

And with that, and while juggling the coin in the

341

cup of his right hand, Greg got up without another word to move several paces away and gaze blindly at the dark pall of the Cattle Arch as he struggled to come to grips with a fluctuating sense of reality.

Fast approaching forty, he had virtually abandoned any hope of marriage until now, but then only to discover his new chance of happiness had turned out to be a false dawn, for seemingly, he had fallen in love with a madwoman. Sombrely, he focussed on the black opening through which so many animals had unprotestingly passed en-route to their final destruction at the local abattoir. Although well acquainted with the grim portal, it was only now in his present state of torment that he really began to appreciate its malign purpose.

Gradually, however, his mental numbness slowly subsided to be replaced by blazing anger and a bitter resentment. Fate, he felt furiously, had toyed with his emotions and his immediate impulse was to mount his horse and ride away without a word – away from this woman who so reminded him of his beloved mother.

He snatched the riding crop from his boot and headed towards the faithful Pitch. Even as he did so, he heard a slight noise and instinctively glanced back to find himself face-to-face with Jill, who had quietly followed him. Placing a restraining hand on his arm, she looked up pleadingly to meet his gaze. However, sensing his repressed rage, she drew back and allowed him to pass. As he reached his horse and prepared to mount, he heard her gentle voice.

"I do love you, Greg."

Facing the animal's flank and with his left hand on the saddle, he hesitated – torn between a passionate love and bitter disappointment. He listened, but although he heard no more, he knew without looking that she would be standing there, waiting in hope and expectation. Slowly he turned to again face the woman he had come to love. Slim and elegant in her long riding skirt, she had removed her hat to allow clusters of blonde hair to brush across her face, yet somehow, despite her sensual appeal, she appeared lonely and terribly vulnerable amidst the bleak landscape. It was a sight that filled him with guilt and he just bowed his head while allowing his arms to limply and symbolically hang down by his sides.

"Greg," she said quietly, "were you really going to ride off and leave me here all alone?"

"Well," he replied dejectedly, "if it's any consolation, I doubt whether my conscience would have allowed me to get very far. It's no excuse, I know, but I'm absolutely confused and bewildered. I want to believe you but..."

The hot, still air was suddenly disturbed by a gentle breeze.

"You say, Greg, that I will always be the only one. Surely, isn't love about trust?"

He nodded dumbly.

"Ironically," he observed quietly, "I've always

believed that love should be selfless yet, when it comes to the test, I just sulk and run away."

The welcome breeze had passed almost as quickly as it had arrived, and for a moment, Jill thought she could detect the tolling of a distant church bell on the warm static air – although it was so faint she couldn't be sure.

"Don't be too hard on yourself, Greg," she said gently. "After all, who would believe me? But in any case, does it really matter how I got here? The fact is, I am here and surely that's all that really counts, isn't it? But I had to tell you, Greg, didn't I?" she pleaded as much with her eyes as with words. "I mean, if we are to have a future together, we can't build it on something false, can we? Well," she added uncertainly, "that's supposing you want us to have a future."

During the brief exchange, Greg had not looked up once and when he finally responded, it was in subdued tones:

"Believe me, Jill, nothing would make me happier. In fact, I would go so far as to say I feel I was born to spend my life with you. But," he said hesitantly, "I'm not sure if I'm qualified to make you equally happy. I'm far too temperamental. You saw it at the Hunt Ball and what's happened just now." At this point, he looked up slowly. "Am I really worth it?"

She inclined her head.

"I think so. I know you mean well and always make me feel like a lady. In fact, where I come from, you would be considered a true gentleman. Some might even refer to you as a 'toff'," she giggled. "But that's what you are, Greg – a gentleman – well, most of the time anyway. So, yes I think you're worth it – quite a bargain in fact."

"I trust," he replied, "you're not just after my money." Then, patting his horse's neck, he said unexpectedly, "I'm not sure if this is quite the moment I had in mind but, before I left this morning, my father gave me something very special for you." And so saying, he reached into the slip pocket of his waistcoat to withdraw a small gold ring which he gazed at intently for several moments. "This is one of our family's most precious possessions. It was my mother's engagement ring and, if you will, I'd like you to wear it for me."

"Greg!" she cried out. "Are you asking me to...?" But the question became lost as she buried her head against his neck, before finally pulling away to examine the ring. "It's exquisite, Greg. It's absolutely exquisite," she exclaimed breathlessly. Then, dazzled by the ring's entwined heart-shaped rubies, she extended her hand as, for a brief moment, her twin worlds merged into a single ecstatic reality. "Will you please put it on for me, Greg? I promise faithfully it will now be my most precious possession and I will never, ever, take it off."

"A snug fit," he observed, slipping the ring into place. "My father had it specially designed for my mother when he proposed on the eve of her eighteenth birthday. Theirs was a lifelong romance, because he'd known her since childhood and there'd never been anybody else." He looked into her shining eyes. "I said earlier that I'm not seeking a maternal replacement and I meant it, but I do know you will make a most wonderful Mrs Gregson – even if you are on loan from somewhere in the future," he smiled while gathering her close.

"Oh, Greg, I'm so proud and honoured."

But then, even as she spoke, there came the sudden vicious crack of a gunshot and, almost instantly, she stiffened in his arms with a gasp before becoming horribly limp. Gradually her hands slipped away from behind his neck as, numbed with shock, he gently lowered her to the ground where she lay, ashen-faced and unmoving.

"No, no! Dear God," he sobbed. "Not now. Not like this!"

Frantically he tore at her coat to discover a crimson stain spreading slowly across the left side of her white blouse. Casting convention aside, he desperately undid the buttons to finally reveal an ugly dark hole at the junction of her upper arm and collarbone. Relieved that the missile had apparently passed right through, he immediately became anxious to stem the flow of blood and, ripping off his shirt, started to tear it into strips and bind the wound as tightly as he could. It was, however, a temporary measure and his mind raced for the best course of action. Stuck in the middle of virtually nowhere and with no medical assistance available within an hour's hard ride, he realised they were in a dire situation.

Casting about for a solution, he suddenly spotted the cause of his dilemma, for there, approaching him with his gun still at the ready, was the old reprobate farmer himself.

"Goacher!" he heard himself roar. "It's me, Gregson. Get over here at once. Run man, blast you. Run. Do you hear me?" Totally distraught, Greg snatched the gun from the old man's hand before repeatedly smashing its butt against the log. "You bloody maniac," he screamed. "You could have killed us both. What the hell's the matter with you? Shooting at people to frighten them off your land? Which, in any case, belongs to me!"

The sudden shouting and noise had managed to penetrate the mists of Jill's pain and, to Greg's relief, he saw her eyes slowly flicker open but only to reflect alarm as she looked about in fear.

"Greg. What's happened to me?" she asked, weakly wincing in pain. "My shoulder hurts so much. I'm not going to die, am I?"

"No, of course you're not," he hastened to assure her while kneeling down to tenderly cradle her head. "You'll be fine. Some lunatic let off a shot in our direction and you've stopped one of the pellets! It's only a flesh wound and certainly not fatal."

Greg reached for his coat which was lying nearby, and gently placed it over her. "In any case," he continued with the ghost of a smile, "remember you've a long career ahead as my wife and I don't want to hear anything about you ducking out at this stage." Then, in more sombre tones, he endeavoured to explain their predicament. "I know you won't find it easy," he said gently, "but I want you to lie as still as possible while I ride for a doctor."

"Oh, please, Greg," she pleaded, trying to get up. "Please don't leave me here on my own; not like this."

But, easing her back gently, he insisted.

"Jill," he said. "Please try to understand. I simply must get medical help. I've done what I can – I've stopped the bleeding. But you must lie still or it might start again. I'm just not qualified to do any more and I certainly can't attempt to move you. We need proper transport. In any case, I'm not leaving you alone – Mr Goacher will stay here with you." Then, under his breath, he muttered grimly, "His life will depend on it."

"Isn't that the old man that's a bit...? Well, you know... I won't feel very safe with him," she objected feebly.

"Jill," he urged. "I'm wasting valuable time talking when I should be on my way."

During these entreaties, the contrite old farmer tried to express his regret and plied Greg with offers of help, but was abruptly cut short as the distraught landowner took him to one side.

"I don't want to hear it, Goacher – I really don't. It's thanks to you that my future wife is lying badly wounded and bleeding. If I should lose her, I promise you faithfully I will swing for you. Just stay by her side until I return. Don't you dare leave her, even for a second." Then, lowering his voice so that Jill couldn't hear, he added, "Remember, if she dies – you die... One other thing – if her wound starts bleeding again, apply pressure on that pad I've made."

Then, without another word, Greg raced to his horse and, ignoring the stirrups, vaulted straight into the saddle and set off at a furious pace back the way they had come.

Born of an Arabian mare on the Gregson's stud farm, the big black animal carried a high pedigree and knew how to run. Having been Greg's horse from the beginning, the two had forged a strong bond. Sensing his master's urgency, Pitch gave his all as he lowered his head and stretched out his front legs in order to gain maximum speed.

Doctor Clements was, by any definition, a small man, but he was always immaculately dressed in a black frock coat, pinstriped trousers and spotless white spats. His habitual Gladstone bag and pince-nez glasses, completed a clinical portrait. But Greg knew him as a classical example of fine medical practice.

So, while urging Pitch to ever-greater effort, Greg desperately wondered if he'd find the doctor at home. However, upon arrival he was relieved to see him just about to climb into his horse-drawn buggy.

"Why, Greg!" exclaimed the medic, turning to ascertain the sudden clatter of hooves. "What on earth's the hurry? It's not more trouble with your poor Isobel I hope?"

"No, Jim. Fortunately not," Greg assured him as he breathlessly leapt to the ground. "But there's been a shooting accident further west on Old Goacher's spread. My fiancée is lying out there with a bullet-wound high on the left side of her chest. I've managed to stop the bleeding but she needs your urgent attention."

"I didn't know you were even engaged, Greg..." began the doctor but was quickly cut short by an agitated Greg who stressed there was no time for explanations.

"You see, I've had to leave her with Old Goacher so you'll understand why I'm anxious to get back as soon as possible. So, look," he then added urgently, "couldn't you put your instruments in my saddlebag and take Pitch? He's fast and willing and I'll follow in your buggy."

At first the doctor hesitated at the prospect of mounting such a large horse, and sensing his reluctance, the anxious Greg, hastened to reassure him.

"You can ride, can't you, Jim? He won't play up. He'll just take you straight there. He's probably a bit bigger than you're used to, but he's perfectly safe. Here," he offered, "let me help you up."

Indeed, once in the saddle, the doctor seemed to become more confident.

"Some time since I've been on a horse, Greg, but I'll be fine."

Doctor Clements then urged the big animal into a headlong gallop towards the derelict farm while Greg had to be content with the much slower pace of the doctor's pony, who was only accustomed to a gentle plod around his master's practice. Desperately frustrated, Greg could only hope that the doctor had understood his directions for, by now, Pitch was completely out of sight. However, if Greg had known what lay ahead, it's doubtful that he would have been in quite such a hurry.

The intense heat of that summer day in 1888 had finally given way to an evening cool as Greg once again crossed Drove Street and out onto Old Goacher's farm. With the blinding sun in his eyes as it dipped towards the western horizon, he could just make out Jill who was by now, thankfully, sitting on the log with her arm in a sling. At the same time, he noticed that Cloud had strayed some distance from where he'd tethered her. At first, she appeared to be grazing, but then, to Greg's horror, he noticed she was nuzzling at a dark-looking mound in the long grass, which he suddenly realised was his beloved Pitch.

Mortified and sick beyond belief, he leapt from the buggy. Torn between concerns for his horse and Jill, he approached the doctor who sympathetically reached to place a hand on his shoulder.

"The young lady will be fine," he stressed reassuringly. "It's a clean wound, so with plenty of rest and barring any infection, it should be completely healed within a couple of weeks or so. We've a lot to be grateful for to Joseph Lister and his carbolic acid. But what can I say about your poor horse, Greg? He gave his best." The doctor shook his head sadly.

"He got me here but, before I could dismount, he just gave a sigh and slowly collapsed from under me. In fact, I believe he was already dead when he hit the ground. Mind you, he was in a pretty good lather when you reached my surgery, and I think the strain of an immediate return was just too much for his heart." He paused reflectively.

"In some strange way he seemed to sense the urgency. And even though I tried to slow him down, he'd have none of it. You know," he observed philosophically, "animals can often possess a greater sensitivity than some of us humans." He sighed briefly. "Anyway, Greg. I'm terribly sorry. It's been a bad day for you."

The doctor patted him on the shoulder.

"You know, I've been associated with your family for nearly half a century. Your father and I saw military service together in Africa – these days, however, it seems we only ever meet on sad occasions. But that, I suppose, is often the doctor's lot. Your mother was a fine woman, Greg," he observed with a slightly bowed head. "I did my best to save her, you know..."

"We never doubted it for a moment, Jim, and it goes without saying the whole family hold you in the highest esteem." Then, changing the subject, he added urgently, "However, I'm sure you'll understand that, at the moment, I'm just anxious to get my fiancée back to Merton as quickly as possible. The question is, do you feel she's strong enough to be driven back in your buggy?"

The doctor nodded while, despite her pain and weakness, Jill had managed to struggle to her feet – although, before she could take a step, Greg scooped her up in his arms and gently placed her in the medic's little carriage.

"Oh, Greg," she whispered. "I saw your poor horse go down. I'm so sorry. I know how much he meant to you." She would have said more, but was prevented from doing so by a loving kiss. "Well, at least that's an improvement," she observed with a wry smile.

"Jill," he replied, clutching her hand, "you're going to be fine and remember you're my future now and that's what really counts. True – I thought the world of Pitch but he died in the best of causes. Now, much more to the point, I want you to keep my coat on and buttoned, while the doctor takes you back to Merton. It's going to be your new home anyway – and I'll follow on Cloud after I've said my goodbyes to Pitch."

"Tell him goodbye from me as well, Greg – and tell him I'm grateful," she whispered.

"I will, I promise. Now off you go," he insisted.

Then, as Jill and the doctor pulled away, Greg turned with a heavy heart to his beloved horse. The huge black animal lay on its side just where he had fallen, with his head and neck stretched out in the long grass as if asleep. It reminded Greg of the many times he'd caught him at first light in the paddocks behind Merton Hall where often, just before sunrise, he would find him slumbering on the ground in just such a position. When approached, the animal would gently raise his head and call out a greeting before heaving himself up by his front legs and enjoying a good shake.

Now, sinking down on his knees beside his stricken Pitch, and with a choking sob, Greg knew he'd raised his head for the last time.

Reaching to stroke the still glossy, but now flaccid neck, he murmured:

"And I never even gave you a proper name, did I? But I promise you this – I won't leave you here. We'll take you back home to rest in your paddock, where you'll never be disturbed and where you will always have Cloud close by." And, with these words, he reached to gently unbuckle the throat lash and noseband before easing the bit from his pet's mouth. "There, old friend. You were never very fond of that, were you? Well now, at least, you'll never have to wear it again."

By now the sun had all but disappeared in the west and was causing the lengthening shadows to merge into a general darkness. Greg, still in his vest, was starting to feel the chill, and climbing regretfully to his feet, he bid his friend farewell.

"I gained a wife today, old fellow," he murmured.

"But I lost you in the process. I'll have to go now, but I promise I'll be back for you in the morning. I promise."

All this time, Cloud had stood pitifully to one side as if aware of the tragedy that had befallen her companion. Stroking her muzzle in sympathy, Greg reached to tighten the girth before mounting. Then, turning their backs on the darkening scene, they headed sadly north-east towards the Cattle Arch and from there in the direction of Merton Hall.

Chapter 16

A WEEK LATER found Jill sitting alone in the vastness of the Gregson drawing room and, while her arm was still supported by a sling, she nevertheless felt grateful to finally be free of pain. It was early morning and very quiet except for the rhythm of heavy rain beating against the huge west windows. Strange, she reflected, how the weather had changed so abruptly – almost, as it were, to the very day of her accident. She wondered briefly if it could be some sort of omen or just coincidence for, as far as she knew, it was the first serious rainfall in nearly a year.

The Vicarage had been an impressive experience, but was nothing compared to the sheer scale and impact of Greg's home. The high-backed wings of her chair obscured much of the room but by leaning forward she found it easy to become overwhelmed by the immensity of her surroundings. Soaring wooden vaulting, combined with windows that reached from floor to ceiling, made the place seem more like a hall than a room. Even the mantelpiece towered above her head, which with its two intricately carved wooden lions standing either side of the huge fireplace, only served to increase her sense of awe. Then there was the massive and heavily ornate dark oak furniture, which added to an already overall sense of bleakness; a bleakness which caused Jill an inner chill.

However, one disturbing exception to this essentially cold, male preserve was a full-length, life-size portrait of a lady, which enjoyed a commanding position in the centre of the far north wall. The powerful composition made Jill somehow feel that nothing escaped its subject's majestic gaze. Suspecting the woman's identity, she had initially kept her distance, but now, feeling slightly bored and more than a little curious, she finally got up to examine it more closely, but then only to recoil at the woman's eerie resemblance to herself. However, it was a resemblance that ended with mere physical similarity for, although about her own age, here was someone of inimitable poise and charm who projected a presence Jill found quite intimidating.

Eternally confined within its heavy frame, the image smiled out at the world with a tangible warmth, which somehow seemed to transcend any mere skill of an artist's brush. At variance with prevailing Victorian styles, the subject's honey-blonde hair had been allowed to fall in thick tresses against the pallor of her neck, while her flawless skin was further enhanced by a dazzling off-the-shoulder, deep-green ball gown. Obviously cut from the finest silk, the dress had been delicately matched by a folded parasol, which she carried in her right hand. This, together with her left arm resting gracefully along a low classical balustrade, combined to render a timeless symphony of poise and beauty.

Perhaps most compelling were the woman's sparkling blue eyes, and several minutes elapsed before Jill managed to wrench her gaze from their hypnotic effect. Finally, as she glanced down at the base of the ornate frame, she saw the simple inscription:

'THE BELOVED LADY HELEN'.

And that was it.

There was no indication as to why the portrait had been displayed in such a prominent position or, indeed, anything to signify who the subject really was. However, Jill instinctively knew the lady was Greg's mother, which caused a sharp resurgence of all her earlier misgivings. Feeling depressed, she wretchedly recalled Rose's description of the woman's beauty as being a byword in the area. Now, looking at this facsimile, she realised even *that* had been an understatement. Moreover, there was the question of her being a titled lady – Rose had never mentioned anything about that. Momentarily she glanced at her gleaming engagement ring and, suddenly feeling totally inadequate, almost wrenched it from her finger. How, she asked bitterly, could she – a mere Miss Nothing from the working class – hope to hold her own when compared to a titled lady? It all felt so impossible, for she knew the gulf existing between herself and the beautiful creature portrayed in the frame was all but unbridgeable.

Longing for the comfort of her familiar surroundings with John, she suddenly felt an aching need to be back with him – just plain, ordinary John, whose dad delivered milk and whose mum ran the corner shop. That was her world. That, she knew, was really where she belonged, not here. Not out of her depth among all this grandeur. For a moment, she wondered guiltily how they were and whether they still missed her. She also wondered if John had moved on and found someone else, although, she doubted it, knowing what she had meant to him. But even thinking about it made her feel a traitor for wearing another man's ring.

Overcome with homesickness, Jill desperately wished she could just leave Merton Hall and make her way south across the Downs to the Cattle Arch, beyond which lay the safety of her own world. But then, even in the midst of this self-pity, yet another disturbing thought flashed through her mind. As she again glanced down at her beautiful ring, sure enough and just discernible on the lady's left hand, was the same piece of jewellery. Knowing the ring had belonged to Greg's mother was one thing, but to effectively see her wearing it somehow felt grotesque and she slowly backed away towards her seat.

Situated opposite where she had been sitting stood an imposing organ with pipes that rose high up towards the lofty timbered ceiling. Moving closer, she noticed that the keyboard lid had been left rolled back to reveal three manuals of ivory and black keys. The music rest still displayed a score entitled 'Greensleeves', which she knew to be a famous Tudor folk song. Eerily, it seemed as though the instrument had been deliberately left waiting for someone to occupy the stool and begin to play. Jill felt a slight shiver as her gaze reverted back to the portrait, for she remembered Greg's description of his mother playing their nursery piano. Was this then, she wondered, where the multi-talented woman had played to entertain the family and their guests? Was this, in fact, the last piece of music she'd ever played? The macabre thoughts fuelled her imagination and she began to wonder, perhaps, whether the whole room was a kind of memorial.

Feeling trapped in the oppressive atmosphere, Jill decided to move down to one of the morning rooms. On the way, she paused by the spacious windows, which normally afforded panoramic views right across the rolling downland – although today's persistent rain had caused thin rivulets to chase each other across the glass and reduce visibility to a minimum. Even so, it was still possible to make out the sad and freshly dug mound of earth in a nearby paddock. Glancing in the opposite direction, she could just see the near end of the mile-long drive that ran directly to the distant gatehouse.

Greg was away for long periods and time was beginning to hang. Moreover, even before her encounter with the portrait, she had begun to feel uncomfortable in the huge household. There was also the difficulty with her injured shoulder, which meant there was little she could do to occupy herself. Greg had kindly insisted she remain until fully recovered, but boredom was now becoming a persistent problem. Even to gain access to a cup of tea entailed summoning a maid via the internal bell system. Unlike home or at the Vicarage, the kitchen here seemed to be the sole province of the head chef and to venture there was to invite a courteous:

"May I help you, Madam?"

On the surface it all seemed very genteel, but Jill had sensed an underlying hostility, which made her feel like an intruder. Ignorance of the social conventions governing Merton had left her vulnerable to embarrassment and without the necessary experience she found it difficult to assert herself without actually resorting to rudeness. Destined one day to be mistress of this complex community, it made her seriously wonder how she would ever manage.

However, of one thing she was certain: Lady Helen would never have had such a problem; a thought which, yet again, drew her attention to the magnetic portrait.

"Well, what do you think of it, my dear?" came a sudden and deeply resounding male voice. Startled and thinking herself to be alone, she spun round clutching at her throat to find a tall silver-haired gentleman standing just inside the main doorway. "Oh, I'm sorry," apologised the newcomer as he advanced into the room. "I didn't mean to frighten you."

Watching him approach, Jill detected something familiar and guessed she was probably looking at Greg's father. Although facially similar, he was even taller than his son and conveyed a quiet air of authority. In the Gregson mode, he bowed to kiss the back of her hand.

"I'm afraid I've not had the pleasure," he smiled with admiration. "But you can only be Jill who I've heard so much about and, if I may say so, I can see why." Here, she thought, was a consummate performer with a charm capable of eclipsing even that of Greg. "I'm away on business a great deal of the time," he continued, "so I'm afraid I missed out on your first visit." His gaze drifted to the commanding portrait.

"I don't find much to keep me in the old place now my wife is no longer with us. But please," he insisted, "I'm being selfish and we have so much to talk about." Whereupon he indicated the chair she had recently vacated and, while inviting her to take a seat, he remained standing with his back to the imposing fireplace. "Now, the first thing I need to ask," he exclaimed, "is how is that poor arm of yours? And what a terrible thing to happen on the very day you became engaged." Then, without waiting for a reply, he quickly added, "I can promise you one thing. That's the last time Old Goacher will ever have any access to firearms. I've long had doubts about the old fool and should have evicted him years ago for the disgraceful way he's neglected that farm. Now, unfortunately, you've had to pay the price for my ineptitude. So, please, do accept my apologies." He paused to straighten up and clasp his hands behind his back. "Oh, and by the way," he smiled, "in case you hadn't already suspected it, I'm Frederick's father, Thomas." He coughed briefly. "Late, that is, of Her Majesty's Light Horse. Although, sadly, too late for the Crimean campaign, I might add." He looked down at her with a smile. "My close friends all call me Tom, so I do hope you will feel able to do the same."

His diatribe seemed endless.

"And of course," he continued without even a pause, "congratulations on your engagement; and welcome to the family. Which makes it all the more imperative that you receive the very best of attention; which, I trust, has been the case?"

Finally, Jill managed to break the monologue.

"Well, it's lovely to meet you, Tom, and thank you, yes, my arm is much better. In fact, I'm beginning to feel a bit of a fraud really because I just sit around all day doing nothing." She paused for a moment to let her gaze rest on the portrait. "Tell me, Tom," she asked cautiously, "was that lovely lady your wife and was she really that beautiful?"

At this his eyes suddenly saddened.

"Yes," he admitted finally in a subdued voice. "She was my wife and that painting is all I have left of her memory. Was she that beautiful? If *anything*, the portrait fails to do her justice, but I'm eternally grateful to the artist for his skill and patience. You have to understand, she was not an easy subject to paint. In fact, she hated posing and the inactivity it demanded."

Watching his expression, Jill suddenly realised that he had momentarily slipped away to an earlier time.

"You see," he continued sadly, "she was so considerate and full of fun. Everyone loved her."

Somehow, it seemed that he shrank a little as he moved to the chair opposite. He sat silently for a moment before leaning forward to clasp his hands between his knees. Even after all this time, his sense of desolation was plain to see and, filled with sympathy, Jill instinctively reached to take his hand. Briefly he responded to her grasp as something indefinable passed between them, which made Jill suspect this was probably the first physical contact he had experienced with a woman since his wife's death.

"You seem to have loved her very dearly, Tom."

But the look in his eyes precluded any necessity of a reply.

"Jill," he said finally, "perhaps I shouldn't say this but, when I first arrived, I saw you standing by the window and when you moved, the light caught your face and it made me think that, for a split second..."

"You mean," she answered, "you thought I was your wife?"

"I'm sorry," he apologised. "But you must realise that I'd only just got back and had no idea you were even in the house, so yes, momentarily it seemed... But you must have seen how you and Helen bear an uncanny resemblance."

His words left her with an eerie feeling. She was also unsure whether to feel affronted or honoured. Either way, it reinforced all her uncertainties, which on the spur of the moment, she decided to share.

"Tom. I'm sorry if I opened up old wounds."

"Oh please. Don't be sorry for a magical moment, my dear."

"But Tom," she insisted, "what you've just said shows the problem I'm up against. When I look at your wife's portrait, I know I should feel flattered to be mistaken for such a beautiful woman and, please believe me, I do. But," she insisted almost desperately, "I'm not her and never can be. We're totally different people and it makes me worry that I might be seen as some sort of poor substitute." She hesitated and lowered her head before adding quietly, "In fact, I even wonder sometimes if Greg only wants me because I remind him of his mother. Oh, I know," she stressed apologetically, "it sounds dreadful put like that and, in all probability, it's quite unfair. But sometimes that's how I honestly feel." She looked up pleadingly. "I tell you this in confidence, Tom, and I hope it's something we can keep between ourselves."

Even before he answered, she could see from his kindly eyes that she had nothing to fear.

"Jill," he assured her. "You absolutely have my word. Nothing will go beyond this room and, please believe me, I do appreciate how you must feel but, if I may indulge in a little flattery, I'm confident that your beauty and poise will more than carry the day." He smiled his sad smile. "You know, once the two of you are married you can depend on my full support, because I shall make a point of being about the old place a lot more. And, as regards Greg, I can assure you his feelings are based entirely on you for your own sake. I ought to know because every time he sees me he talks about nothing else. What's more, it's common knowledge he's never had much time for the fair sex so he must see you as something very special."

"Tom...!" she murmured feeling slightly embarrassed.

Momentarily, the sadness faded from his eyes.

"However," he continued, "I must admit you probably will remind me of my Helen from time to time. But would that really be such a bad thing, if you rekindled a few happy memories for an old man?"

"You're not that old, Tom!" she objected with a

certain warmth. "In fact, I think you look pretty good to me, and no, of course I wouldn't mind."

For a brief moment, he even looked slightly mischievous.

"You know, if I were thirty years younger, your Greg wouldn't even come into the equation."

"Tom. That's dreadful!" she exclaimed. "But, seriously though, you must understand I'm no 'titled lady' and that I come from a quite humble background, which makes me fearful that I may not be able to hold my own in a place like this. I mean, after your wife, do you think the staff could ever really come to accept me?"

"Believe you me, Jill, when I say if I accept you they certainly will or be answerable to me. And, with regards to you not being a titled lady, I can see you've read the portrait's inscription. Well, don't let that worry you because Helen was never any part of the aristocracy, and even if she had been, she would have kept it very much to herself because she was that kind of person. The fact is, everybody referred to her as Lady Helen out of love and respect." At this point, he glanced away for a brief moment towards the great west window, which was still awash with rain. "You see, she had an endearing quality that made everybody feel they really mattered. In fact, she was a bit like... humph... I can't think of the woman's name. Anyway, she's married to that Reverend Hewish fellow."

"Oh!" exclaimed Jill. "You mean my dear friend

Rose. Yes, she's a lovely person and I'm lucky to know her."

Thomas swivelled round to gaze once again at his wife's portrait.

"Originally, I was going to put 'My Beloved Wife Helen', but then I thought, no, because in a special way she belonged to everyone who knew her."

Turning his attention to the imposing mantelpiece, he stared reflectively at the fire grate. "The home became just a house the day she left us. It was as though its soul had gone. Which, of course," he stressed, "sadly it had. Oh, I know the servants are very good, particularly Albert." He shook his head. "But it's not the same. It's just not the same anymore."

Finally, he looked up and managed a smile.

"I'm sorry, but I'm being an absolute bore again which is quite unforgiveable and particularly in the presence of such a lovely lady. But in any case," he added with a sudden upbeat note creeping into his voice, "when you join us, the whole place will become alive again. Although," he emphasised, "please don't think I'm looking to relive the past, because that's all it is, the past. No, I'm hoping for a complete change of direction which, I believe, you and Greg will provide with your youthful vitality and fresh ideas. Certainly I know Helen would have wished you to be very much your own person.

"Who knows? I might even yet become a grandfather. I'd like that because it gives one the opportunity to relive the joys of childhood when there are youngsters about. I'm afraid Alistair's numerous affiliations will never come to anything and Isobel's health precludes any thoughts of children. So, Greg really is my only hope for keeping the family name alive. You see," he explained, "my great-grandfather moved south with the fortune he'd made in the cotton industry and acquired vast tracts of land across the south-east but, as yet, there's no heir to carry on the traditions he started." He indicated the room. "All this and Merton Hall itself was his design, so you'll understand, I'm sure, that I need a grandson." Thomas then strolled across to an ornate oak bureau to withdraw a long slim cigar. "You know, Jill, there's one very definite change I'd like to see and that's the licence to smoke the occasional Havana. In the old days, I was always banished to the smoking-room. So," he smiled, "do you mind?"

She shook her head with a smile and he proceeded to light up with a certain relish.

"Wonderful!" he exclaimed, inhaling appreciatively before returning to the bureau and extracting a wine decanter together with two glasses. "Best Burgundy!" he enthused amidst a haze of smoke while pouring her a generous measure. Then, raising his glass, he proposed a toast. "Jill. Here's to your future happiness and the beginning of a new era at Merton Hall."

As Jill basked in the afterglow of Tom's encouragement, her earlier forebodings gradually began to fade, although a lingering curiosity persisted and she turned to the open organ with its music sheet.

"Tell me, Tom. Who plays the organ?"

"Ah," he replied, putting down his drink. "I have to plead guilty to that one, although if the truth be told I've never been very good. So, I've always had to choose my times quite carefully before sneaking in here for a crafty play. My wife was brilliant on the piano," he continued, "but always believed I was tone-deaf. Anyway, I enjoy it because I find organ music quite uplifting."

All that day, Greg had become increasingly conspicuous by his absence. Even after 9pm when dinner had been served and cleared away, there was still no sign of him. Therefore, feeling bored and slightly neglected, Jill decided to while away the remainder of the evening by playing cards with Thomas, who obviously enjoyed her company. However, as 10.30pm came and went without Greg putting in an appearance, she made the appropriate excuses and retired to her bedroom.

At the Vicarage, it had been necessary to carry an oil lamp, but here at Merton the place was always ablaze with lights, which made it totally unnecessary. Regularly serviced by a member of the staff, the numerous lamps burned continuously with no apparent concern for time or cost. Jill had come to realise that money at this social economic level was of little consequence.

Once comfortably settled in bed, she thought back over the day's events and her unexpected encounter with the likeable Tom. It made her wonder, though, if being stuck in this sprawling mansion with an ever-absent fiancé was an indication of future married life. Laying back in the silken luxury, she allowed her gaze to wander over the high, ornate ceiling and pondered on what Greg's father had said concerning grandchildren. Strangely, this was the first time she had considered the possibility of having any children with Greg in what was, after all, a questionable reality.

However, such thoughts acted to focus her mind on an apparent glaring discrepancy. Despite being born in 1920 and having spent her entire life in this very part of the county, she had never once heard of this prominent family, and 1888 wasn't really that long ago. It was conceivable that Greg might even have survived into her early years, albeit as a very old man. Moreover, there was now also the issue of any possible children who would have, almost certainly, survived well into the 1940s. Increasingly perplexed, she wondered desperately what could have gone wrong. Of course, it might be that Greg succumbed to one of the rampant diseases of late Victorian England while any children could also have suffered a similar fate.

It was an interesting conundrum until she was

suddenly struck by a blood-chilling alternative which brought her bolt upright in bed. For she knew only too well, that in twenty-seven years' time, the horrors of World War One would burst upon the world stage. Therefore, any sons she might have would almost certainly become eligible for military service and face death along with a whole generation of other young men.

Sickened by this possibility, she pushed back the covers to sit miserably on the side of the bed while, at the same time, realising that Tom's dream of a future family was just not going to happen.

Finally, although feeling completely unsettled, she managed to drift off into an uneasy sleep, while determining to keep all such thoughts strictly to herself.

It seemed as though she had hardly closed her eyes before a knock at the door brought her wide awake to find it was broad daylight. Beckoned to enter, the early morning maid, complete with a silver salver, crossed the room to place tea and biscuits by her bed. She was a slim, severe-faced woman, immaculately dressed in traditional black and with a white apron and cap. Altogether the essential Victorian housemaid: formal, rather unapproachable and a very different proposition from the affable Josie.

"Good morning, Madam. Your bath will be ready in fifteen minutes."

And that was it – correct and to the point with no smile and precious little warmth. Just a bare statement which made Jill dread the thought of even being a moment late for the wretched bath because she could well envisage the woman's resultant look of disapproval.

Later, and feeling fully refreshed, Jill finally arrived at the dining room for breakfast; a place that, even after a week, she found breathtaking, for its scale seemed so disproportionate to its function. Purposely situated in the east wing, its vast window network allowed early morning sunlight to stream in and herald the freshness of each new day. Possibly its most impressive feature was the head-and-shoulders portrait of a young army officer, whom she now recognised as Greg's father. Situated above the fireplace, it depicted him in his prime and amply demonstrated just how handsome he had once been.

Turning to the table, Jill could only guess its length; probably, she imagined, somewhere in the region of twenty feet. Hewn from a single slab of English oak, its mellow, rich colour blended well with the high wooden panelling of the surrounding walls. Flanked on either side by twelve ornately carved oak chairs, it was ready laid for morning breakfast. Normally Greg would have been there to greet her in a way that always made her feel so special. However, today there was no sign of him, even though it was now well past 9am and his continued absence began to seriously worry her.

Finally, with 10am approaching and feeling hungry, Jill decided to wait no longer and dutifully rang the bell for service. She was then politely informed it was not policy to serve breakfast without the Master of the house being present. Therefore, when Greg finally put in an appearance, Jill was not feeling in the best of moods.

"I hate to say this, Greg," she observed sharply, "but these servants of yours can be downright rude. They act as though they're in charge instead of it being the other way round. If you ask me, I think it's time they were put in their place. I'm prepared to respect *them* but at the moment I feel it's a one-way process."

However, despite her discontent, she couldn't help noticing his drawn and pale appearance as he slowly sank down on to one of the chairs with a heavy sigh. Immediately forgetting her own irritation, she reached out to take his hand.

"Greg? Are you all right? I've been so worried about you. Did you even manage to get home last night?"

He looked up with a wane smile.

"I did," he replied slowly and wearily. "If you could call it last night, because it was almost light before I finally got in."

"Well, what kept you out so late?" she asked with a look of uncertainty. "As it was, I spent virtually the whole day with your father, which I don't mind... but you weren't out...?"

But Greg immediately retorted angrily to the innuendo.

"Certainly not. Surely you know me better than that? Even to think such a thing!"

"I'm sorry, Greg. No. You didn't deserve that, but you must realise I've had some extremely unpleasant experiences with men."

"Well, not with this man," he asserted with an edge to his voice.

"I know and I'm sorry," she repeated humbly.

But, rising without a word, he crossed to the window and just stood gazing out over the rolling downland. Then, after what seemed an age, he finally spoke:

"What have the servants done to upset you so much?"

"Oh, it doesn't matter. It's not important," she murmured.

"But it does matter," he stressed emphatically. "It matters to me, so tell me. What's wrong?"

After listening carefully, he pressed the service bell.

"Yesterday," he explained suddenly, "I toured the nearest farms to see the most recent effects of the drought. At my last stop I stayed on to help deliver a calf, but it was a difficult birth because the labour went on too long." The corners of his mouth tightened and he sighed briefly. "We struggled to save the mother but in the end her heart gave out. Then, shortly afterwards, the calf died as well so, you see, I couldn't just leave. She was the farmer's prize animal and I felt duty-bound to stay and help."

Hardly had Greg finished speaking, however, when the door opened to admit a footman.

"You rang, sir?"

"Yes," he answered abruptly. "Please have breakfast served immediately and, while you're at it, tell the butler to report to me at once."

"Very good, sir," he replied stiffly and withdrew.

"Oh Greg!" exclaimed Jill. "There's no need to make a fuss." And looking embarrassed she added, "I'm beginning to wish I hadn't said anything now."

But Greg's expression remained adament.

"One day," he exclaimed, "this house will be your home, Jill, and, more to the point, you'll be mistress of all you survey. You will be my wife and it is my responsibility to ensure your comfort and happiness, which I fully intend to do. Although, having said that, I think you need to realise the servants often hide their feelings behind an outward professionalism, which can sometimes appear curt. In a way, it's a form of compensation, because in reality they have no family life; no life at all, beyond the confines of these walls. And their future?" He shrugged. "In all probability, the workhouse."

Any response Jill might have made was cut short by the arrival of the butler: a man, she had to acknowledge, who looked every inch a professional. Immaculately dressed in a tailored black suit complemented by a spotless white shirt and waistcoat, he conveyed an air of absolute confidence.

"I understand you sent for me, sir," he stated politely.

"Ah, yes, Barton. Indeed, I did," replied Greg shortly. "And it's because I want to reiterate my express wishes that all guests at Merton should be treated with the utmost civility and," he emphasised, "that means complete compliance with their wishes. Now, you do know that, don't you?"

"Absolutely, sir."

"You also know," added Greg in the same unmistakable tone, "this young lady is staying with us until her arm is completely well and that she is to be shown every consideration. Therefore, can you please explain to me," he asked whilst glancing toward the ornate grandfather clock, "why it's now approaching 11am and she has yet to be served any breakfast?"

"Sir," he responded stiffly, "I'm sure you are aware that, in most big houses, protocol dictates that meals should not be served until the Master is present."

The tension between the two men was tangible. However, as they were both gentlemen in their respective social spheres, etiquette demanded that they were scrupulously polite. Although Jill could see from Greg's expression that he found it difficult to restrain himself.

Yet, despite the apparent immediacy of the drama, for a fleeting second Jill realised she was but witnessing a trivial and long-past event.

"You may not be aware, Barton," emphasised Greg, "that this young lady is not only a guest but also my future wife and, as such, the eventual Mistress of Merton. Therefore, her wishes are to be treated as mine."

Upon hearing this, the Butler turned to Jill with a professional bow of recognition.

"My apologies, madam," he said formally. "I'm afraid this fact had not been drawn to my attention. Therefore, may I congratulate you and also say how sorry I am if any of the staff have caused you distress."

"That's all right," she smiled. "I do understand."

"Thank you, madam," he answered graciously. Then, turning to Greg, he asked, "Will that be all, sir?"

"Not quite, Barton. I want the entire staff assembled and reminded of the protocol governing Merton."

"Very good, Sir. I will see to it immediately."

As he withdrew, Jill could detect his repressed resentment and she pulled a face as he closed the door.

"Oh, Greg. I don't think that went down very well, but I am grateful for your support. I was beginning to feel almost invisible." Greg, however, had sunk back into his chair, noticeably more tired than ever. "Are you sure you're all right?" she enquired earnestly; to which he leaned forward and folded his forearms on the table.

"Yes, I'm fine," he managed. "I'm just not very

good without sleep. But there is something on my mind which I need to discuss because it's been worrying me for some time."

While speaking, Greg held up a restraining hand as their breakfast trolley was finally wheeled in by the austere-faced housemaid. However, still obviously irritated, Greg quickly dismissed her with a wave of his hand saying they could manage for themselves. After pouring Jill her coffee, Greg observed quietly:

"You know, I've been thinking about what you said just before the Goacher episode. Quite apart from any contravention of known physics, it made me wonder about the people you must have left behind. If," he added with a slight smile, "that's quite the right way to put it. I mean, what about your family and friends? Surely they must be wondering what's become of you?"

Jill looked at him and saw the pain in his eyes.

"It's caused me more sorrow than you can imagine, Greg, and it's a sense of loss that never entirely leaves me."

"I'm sorry," he said gently. "I didn't mean to upset you, but I can see for myself that what you've told me is only too true. I just wish I could make it right for you." He shook his head. "But I can't, can I? And, even if I could, it would mean losing you."

She nodded.

"I'm afraid so, yes. But, as I've said before, I'm here now and, really, that's all that matters, isn't it? And," she added, "I know you really need me."

He took her hand.

"Please believe me, I do." He paused to drink his coffee, but then added tentatively as he put down his cup, "There's also something else that concerns me and it's what you said on our first ride together when you mentioned the men you have known. I think you said there was someone, but they weren't here now and never could be; well, something along those lines anyway. I thought it strange at the time but in the light of what you've told me, it now begins to make a kind of sense." He reached out and took her hand. "Tell me, Jill, honestly. Have you left anyone behind that's still special? Someone you would really prefer to be with if you were given the choice?"

She lowered her eyes for a moment before replying quietly:

"I would not lie to you, Greg." And, lifting her head to meet his gaze, she added, "Yes. There was someone, although we got separated on the night I slipped into this timeframe. But," she emphasised, "that was nearly a year ago and, to all intents and purposes, he might as well be dead."

For several moments it went very quiet in the vast dining room before Greg finally spoke.

"I see. So, effectively, you're telling me there are two men in your life separated only by time." Again, silence prevailed and stayed that way until Greg spoke in a voice barely above a whisper. "I hope you will understand, Jill, when I say I feel compelled to ask that, if you were given the choice, would you stay here or want to return home?"

"I hope, Greg," she whispered, "I never have to face that decision, because you see..."

But Greg was destined never to hear her answer, for at that very moment his father entered the room and greeted them in his usual upbeat way. Stopping to drop a kiss on Jill's cheek he asked:

"Is everything all right, young lady? You haven't touched your breakfast and it's gone 11.30am."

"Yes, I'm fine, Tom. Really," she replied guardedly. "It's just that Greg and I got carried away with a lot of talk, that's all."

However, Greg's father was a perceptive man who had immediately sensed an atmosphere and he wasted no time in pointing it out.

"No," he objected, taking his place at the head of the table. "There's more to it than that. So, come on... tell me what's been going on."

Although unable to be precise, Greg did his best to deflect the old man's curiosity.

"There's no problem, father, but if you must know, Jill and I have been discussing previous relationships. I don't know how we got on to the subject, but one thing just seemed to lead to another."

Tom just grunted before starting to unfold a copy of *The Times*. Then, after only a cursory glance at the headlines, he peered round the edge of the paper to express his opinion.

"Forgive me for saying so, Frederick, but is that really the sort of thing to be discussing with this beautiful young lady? Especially when she's been hurt so recently. I think, my boy," he added with a touch of acid in his voice, "that you've a lot to learn when it comes to the fair sex. What's more, I can tell you this, if I were thirty years younger...!"

Greg cut him short.

"Well, you're not thirty years younger and, while I'm at it, I might point out that you seem to have forgotten how mother always hated you reading the newspaper at the table."

Thomas ignored the barb and instead turned to Jill.

"Tell me, young lady. Have you any objection to my little indulgence?"

"None, Tom," she smiled. "Absolutely none whatsoever."

"That's your answer then, Frederick. Things are going to be different around here in the future."

The banter served to lift the mood and conversation veered round to the forthcoming events of the day. However, despite the grandeur and luxury of Merton Hall, Jill was beginning to miss the close relationship of Rose and her involvement with vicarage life.

"Greg," she said quietly, "I wondered if it would be possible to take me home sometime today? I'm really much better now and there's not a lot I can do just sitting about all day. I don't think I can ride but if we could take one of the smaller carriages then it might be nice to stop off for lunch at the Dyke Hotel on the way."

If Greg felt any disappointment, he didn't show it.

"If that's what you would like, Jill," he agreed, "then that's what we'll do."

However, none of this exchange had escaped the ears behind the newspaper.

"You're off today then, Jill?" exclaimed Tom with a noticeable tinge of disappointment in his voice. "I suppose it's not that you're afraid I might get my own back with the cards by any chance, is it?"

"No, of course not, Tom," she smiled. "In any case, I'll be back before you know it so you won't miss the chance."

In a relatively short time Jill had undoubtedly grown quite fond of her future father-in-law. She also sensed that, come the day, he would make for a wonderfully supportive friend. So with this in mind, she rushed to the end of the table to give him a parting hug.

As the long driveway approached the house, it opened out into a vast circular reception area, which allowed for visiting carriages to draw up with their new arrivals. Surfaced with gravel chippings, the whole forecourt was enclosed by elegant and lofty pines. Dominating the centre, was a wide ornamental fishpond surrounding the pedestal of two life-size bronze horses poised in head-on confrontation.

As Jill descended the curved stone stairway that led down from the house, she caught sight of Greg approaching at the reins of a twin-seater trap. However, while preparing to climb up beside him, she unexpectedly heard the crunch of footsteps immediately behind her and, turning, came once again face-to-face with Tom.

"I'm sorry," he apologised, "but I just had to come and say goodbye." And, with that, he placed his hands gently on both her forearms. For a moment his pale, sad brown eyes gazed down at her with such a poignancy that it prompted her to reach up and kiss him briefly on the cheek. Yet still he stood there, softly holding her arms. "You will come back?"

He made it sound almost like a plea.

"I promise, Tom," she replied earnestly.

Even then, he didn't immediately let go but continued gazing into her eyes until Jill almost began to feel uncomfortable. But then, suddenly, she realised it was not her he was looking at and, impulsively, reached up with her arms to kiss him full on the lips.

"I only wish I could be Helen for you, Tom," she whispered.

But then, as her arms slowly slipped away, Tom murmured:

"For a brief moment there, Jill, you were. And I'll always be eternally grateful."

And, with that, he took her hand to assist her

aboard the trap where, once beside Greg, she waved and smiled as he urged the magnificent bay horse into a fast trot.

"Goodbye, Tom."

The last memory Jill had as they pulled away was seeing him standing in front of the family mansion. Somehow dwarfed by its huge facade and curving balustrade entrance, he seemed to cut an isolated and lonely figure as he waved until they were quite out of sight. Behind the great house, dark storm clouds were beginning to gather and in the distance, Jill thought she could detect a slight rumble of thunder. Feeling oddly bereft, she settled back against the upholstery whilst strangely sensing perhaps that she might never see Tom again.

"Well," observed Greg, "dare I ask what all that was about?"

"I won't go into details," she assured him. "But it was not what it appeared." Surrounded by a protective hood on three sides, their vehicle was ideal for casual summer travel, and as it was another lovely day, Jill prepared to enjoy the ride. "You know, Greg," she said finally, "it's ironic, isn't it? Because, at first, I was wary of becoming a mother substitute and that people might compare me with Helen, whereas, for a moment back there, I voluntarily stepped right into her shoes."

"For a brief moment you became Helen for my father," he replied.

By now they were within sight of the gatehouse

and, at the sound of their approach, the keeper dutifully appeared to swing back the massive wrought-iron gates.

He nodded his appreciation.

"Is that all he does, Greg?" she asked curiously. "Just open and close the gates all day?"

"Well, no!" he exclaimed. "There's a bit more to it than that. He is in charge of overall security and his wife is virtually the head gardener. She's responsible for these flower beds either side of the drive which, I think you'll agree, are absolutely beautiful."

Finally reaching the Vicarage, Jill noticed a slight mist starting to creep in from the sea, which after the earlier warmth of the day seemed to impart a distinct chill. However, while they were still seated in the trap, Greg gently took her hand with an anxious expression.

"I do hope you enjoyed your stay with us because, I must admit, I was a bit surprised when you wanted to leave so early. It's just..." And he faltered as he stroked her hand. "I hope the servants didn't upset you or put you off our future there together. In fact, I even wondered, perhaps, if my father had offended you in some way."

"Oh, it's nothing like that," she quickly assured him. "Although, if I'm honest, I did get a bit lonely when you were away for such long periods. I mean, the servants run everything, don't they? Which left me with very little to do until your father arrived and *he* was certainly no problem, because we got on famously."

"I know," he grinned. "I could see that back there."

"You must also realise, Greg," she continued, "that I miss Rose. She's been a very close and supportive friend from the moment I arrived and, even after we are married, I shall still want to keep in touch with her."

"You mean I'll have to share you?"

"No of course not," she smiled. "But you must realise I shall need some sort of extra interests if you're going to be away a lot of the time."

"When we are married," he stressed emphatically, "and you're quite well, I shan't let you out of my sight, so that difficulty will never arise. But I am concerned about your problem with the servants. You know I would dismiss them all if I thought it would make you happy."

Jill knew by his tone that he meant every word and it showed what she meant to him.

"Greg," she insisted. "That would be quite unnecessary. I'm sure when I become the official mistress of the house, there will be no problem. It's just that, at the moment, I have no real status there or experience of dealing with the servants and their ways. But," she stressed adamantly, "I fully intend to learn."

Jill's reception at the Vicarage was little short of rapturous. However, this was only after a long and tender embrace with Greg. When he finally relinquished her hand, he backed slowly away down the garden path as if anxious not to lose sight of her until the last possible moment.

"Remember I love you, Greg," she called out. "See you tomorrow."

Then, with Greg still lingering outside the gate, Jill slowly but reluctantly closed the front door. Finally inside, she leaned against it with a heavy sigh and closed her eyes as, once again, she experienced the sudden surge of an indefinable something. Unable to contain her emotions, Jill threw back the door and raced down the path straight into Greg's arms. In the deepening mist, she whispered urgently:

"Hold me, Greg. Please just hold me."

"Hey, what's all this? What's brought this on?" he exclaimed as he gently stroked the back of her head. "What's upset you so suddenly and why are you shivering?"

"Oh, Greg, you just don't understand us women, do you?"

"I must admit, that's a lamentable fact," he admitted before adding assertively, "But, in any case, there's only one woman I want to understand."

At this she looked up at him and whispered tenderly:

"Do you mean that? I mean, truly mean it?"

Gazing at each other in the ever-gathering gloom and with their hands entwined, it was an eternal moment as Greg finally murmured:

"Absolutely and completely."

Chapter 17

AS JILL CLOSED the door for the second time, Rose instantly pounced.

"Oh, you're back!" she exclaimed excitedly. "I thought I'd heard the door but wasn't quite sure. It's so lovely to see you."

Then, grabbing Jill by her good arm, she steered her down the hallway towards the kitchen.

"We've so much to catch up on," her friend enthused. "I just couldn't believe it when Albert dropped in to tell me you'd been shot. I was horrified. I mean, things like that just don't happen in conservative Hove. Oh, but I forgot – it was in the Portslade area, wasn't it? That place has always had an unsavoury reputation so, in a way, I'm not really surprised, but I'm just so glad you're all right. Anyway," she beamed, "I do declare it's time for a celebratory cup of tea."

Vicarage rituals, it appeared, never changed. Whether the occasion be a funeral, parish difficulties or just plain family problems, the situation always seemed that bit easier when accompanied by the soothing fluid that flowed so liberally from Rose's Wedgewood teapot. And Jill still found it very reassuring, while Rose's vicarious enthusiasm for other people's romance, had obviously also remained as strong as ever. The kitchen itself was just how Jill remembered it on that first fateful night. There was the great wooden table with its top scrubbed virtually white and there, too, were the gleaming copper pans still hanging in their orderly rows above the kitchen range. Yet, despite how everything appeared, she nevertheless felt an intangible air of unreality about it all, rather like the final scene of a dream just before daybreak.

Angry at herself, Jill quickly dismissed the sensation as imagination and turned her attention back to her friend, who was still in full swing.

"Albert was also saying," Rose continued excitedly, "how Greg proposed on the very day you were hurt. But, tell me, did you get the ring first or afterwards?" Once assured of the correct sequence, Rose ploughed on. "But what a day! Because I heard that poor Greg also lost his horse. I'd noticed, on the few occasions he attended church, he always seemed to ride the same big black gelding. Was that the animal that died?"

"Yes," Jill admitted sadly. "He was called Pitch. I know it sounds a funny name, but he was Greg's favourite and he died trying to save me. Apparently, he over extended himself while racing to get medical aid and now I feel absolutely awful about it."

"Oh, how distressing," sympathised her friend. "But you mustn't blame yourself and it could have all ended so differently you know. Anyway, leaving that to one side, I'm just dying to see your engagement ring." And there, even in the absence of sunlight, the precious stones flashed their vivid message as Jill extended the third finger of her left hand. "Oh, double red hearts!" gasped Rose excitedly. "They're rubies, aren't they? How terribly romantic. I don't think I've ever seen such a lovely ring. Mind you, I'm not surprised," she added while taking a sip from her cup. "I told you how I got the impression from Albert that Greg was very serious about you." She then leaned forward and lowered her voice. "But do tell me, did it originally belong to his mother?"

Had it not been Rose, Jill would have told her to mind her own business, but instead, contented herself with a smile and a nod. Rose stared thoughtfully at her cup.

"Mind you, Jill, once you become mistress of Merton Hall you'll want for nothing and be the envy of every woman in the area. That's not to mention a handsome new husband." Her voice trailed off as she rose to collect the cups before placing them by the sink. "It's funny, you know," she observed poignantly, "but the place hasn't seemed quite the same while you've been away. It's not just me; everyone's missed you. Especially Martha. And now it looks as though we'll be losing you altogether."

"But Rose, it won't be like that," insisted Jill as she rushed across the kitchen to put an affectionate arm round her friend. "You're the best companion I've ever had. In any case, no firm date has been set for the wedding, so nothing's going to change overnight."

However, before Rose could reply, Josie entered the kitchen and the tempo of questions and answers started all over again. Consequently, by the end of the evening Jill felt quite emotionally drained and was only too glad to drag herself off to bed.

Once inside the now-familiar bedroom, she paused to gaze about nostalgically. Firstly at the washstand and then at the four-poster comfortable bed with its silken sheets. It had seemed so quaint on her first night. Finally, her attention turned to the window from where she had so often gazed in the direction of St Andrew's Church and all its emotional connotations. Yet, somehow, those traumatic events now seemed so distant and long ago. Even until quite recently she had managed to keep a clear image of John in her mind, but the passage of time and subsequent events seemed to have made it increasingly difficult.

Moving towards the window Jill hoped that it might be possible to reconnect with him in some way. Sadly she was disappointed as she found herself faced with an almost impenetrable mist. However, the occasional clip of horse hooves was still audible, and turning away, she dimly caught sight of a rider passing beneath one of the street gas-lights. Jill briefly recalled having seen the him before; always at about the same time and always headed towards the centre of Brighton. For a moment, she wondered idly who he might be and why he seemed destined to continually repeat the same late-night ride.

Finally climbing into bed, she laid back to gaze

at the opposite wall now dimly illuminated by the street lights from below. She pondered on the possible purpose of the man's journeys but just before drifting off to sleep, she realised she had yet to determine the purpose of her own strange destiny.

The following morning, Jill was dragged back to an already wakened world by two familiar sounds and she was grateful to hear them both. First, there was Josie busily pouring out hot water into the wash-hand basin. The second, she recognised as Rose playing the drawing room piano immediately below.

Sensing her to be awake, Josie hurriedly put down the jug and turned with a smile.

"Good morning, Miss Jill. I do hope I didn't disturb you, but as it's now past 10.30am, Rose sent me up to see if you were quite all right. Which," she added with an ever-widening smile, "I'm happy to say you are." After her frosty experience at Merton, Jill felt only too glad to be back in the homely atmosphere of the Vicarage. "I know I said it yesterday," stressed Josie as she busied herself about the room and drawing back the curtains, "but I'm going to say it all again anyway, because it's that good to have you back. People, you know," she added earnestly, "can very easily become part of your life and when they're suddenly not there, they tend to leave an awful gap."

It was a pleasant and familiar start to the weekend and despite the persistently dense mist, Jill thoroughly enjoyed a late lunch with Greg at the Castle Inn. Situated on the north side of Castle Square in Brighton, she recognised it as a public house from her own time and marvelled how little the interior had changed during the ensuing years. However, in this era, it had obviously been the haunt of the privileged and, as such, boasted an adjacent dance floor. A facility which allowed them to spend a leisurely afternoon gently swaying to the waltz and other relaxing rhythms. Finally, Greg dropped her off at the Vicarage about 4.30pm.

Then, back in the kitchen and duly equipped with a hot cup of tea, Jill sank down to bask in the afterglow of a very pleasant day, although she had only been settled for a few minutes before being joined by the frail and white-haired Martha. Martha had now been reduced to walking with the aid of two sticks. But, as they sat chatting while Josie busied herself with the evening meal, they were suddenly startled by the sound of Rose's hysterical voice coming from the drawing room.

"Jill! Jill!" they heard her almost screaming. "Come and look at this! Please, please, hurry!"

Alarmed by the urgency of her friend's voice, Jill raced from the kitchen to discover Rose leaning against her piano and mesmerised by something she could see through the drawing room window.

"What is it Rose? What's the matter?"

But her friend could only mutely point out something beyond the glass.

"Look! Look! Out there in Church Road," she managed in a strangled voice. "What on earth is it?" Then, clutching her hands to her face, she added in a terrified voice, "It's like something out of a nightmare."

Moving to the window to follow Rose's distraught gaze, Jill could scarcely believe her eyes as she recognised the outline of a double-decker red bus from her own era. The huge vehicle was looming slowly and menacingly out of the mist with its powerful headlights piercing the gloom, so she could well appreciate her friend's terror. The sight, however, held no such dread for her even though, for a split second, her mind struggled to cope with the impossibility of it all. But she then slowly began to realise that this vehicle was probably her long-awaited means of returning home. For there, emblazoned on its front display panel were the familiar words: 'Portslade Station'.

Almost at the same time, some instinct seemed to have warned Rose of the vision's portent and she turned to her friend with a stricken expression.

"It's your bus, isn't it?"

Jill could only nod dumbly.

Momentarily immobilised by the magnitude and emotion of the situation, they just stood looking at each other in abject silence before embracing in a mutual display of affection as the full implications sank in. Finally, with the tears streaming down her face, Rose pulled away to look up at her friend.

"The time's arrived, hasn't it, Jill?" she said sadly in her richest Welsh accent. "It's something I've dreaded for so long. What are you going to do? If you intend to catch it you'll have to hurry because this may be the only chance you'll ever have."

An agonising split-second of indecision followed. But finally, in the way of an answer, Jill reached for her treasured engagement ring and slowly slipped it from her finger before handing it to her friend.

"Oh, Jill," Rose protested passionately. "Are you sure? Are you quite sure you know what you're doing?"

"I'm sure, Rose," she whispered very, very quietly.

"But what on earth am I going to say to poor Greg? He'll be devastated when he finds you're gone."

"I hope and believe, Rose, he will understand. Because, you see," she explained brokenly, "I've never told him about my little daughter. I wonder, perhaps, if you could do that for me please, because then I feel sure he will know that I've not rejected him for someone else. And, above all, please tell him... tell him that I love him and I always will."

By this stage, the bus had ominously pulled to a halt with a characteristic hiss of air brakes. A sound that reminded Jill her moment of opportunity was passing.

"Oh Jill," urged her friend. "If you're going, you must go now or it will be too late. Oh, and take your little handbag," she added, retrieving it from the bureau drawer. "You'll need it when you get back home." She paused and then said finally, "Goodbye, my dear friend, God bless you and give my love to your little Anna – you know I really do believe that one day we will all meet again."

And so, the two friends parted for the last time as Jill raced down the Vicarage path and out into a mist-bound Church Road.

Approaching the bus, Jill glanced back at the Vicarage for one final look, but it was already too late because the swirling mist had obscured it from sight and it was now lost to her forever, along with her best friend. She felt herself desperately torn between unbearable separation and the hope of seeing her little daughter again. Despite these doubts, the bus still beckoned with its bright lights and throbbing engine that emitted the familiar yet somehow comforting smell of diesel.

Once on board she felt sure that all her uncertainties and emotional turmoil would finally seep away. The vehicle revved threateningly, as she hastened towards its apparent sanctuary. But the gremlins of time had yet to run their course for, to her horror, when she reached for the handrail, there was nothing tangible to grasp while her foot also passed straight through the running board. Panic-stricken, she desperately tried again, but with the same result and then, as if to add to her terror, the bus slowly started to move forward.

For a split-second her mind froze as she envisaged

an eternity spent marooned in a timeless mist-bound limbo. Hemmed in on all sides by a sea of grey, she was about to surrender to the seemingly inevitable when, suddenly, the rail firmed under her hand and, breathless with fear and exertion, she finally managed to scramble aboard.

"Nice outfit if I may say so," the driver observed cheerfully. "But not much good for climbing on buses I would imagine. Fancy-dress do, was it?"

In her agitated state, however, Jill could barely muster a reply.

"Yes, yes, something like that," she muttered incoherently, for things had happened so fast that there'd been little chance to think about clothes and how conspicuous she might look.

"Are you sure you're quite all right, miss? I couldn't fail to notice the difficulty you had getting on board."

"Yes, I'm fine, really. I just lost my balance for a moment that's all. Now if I could have a ticket for Portslade Station, please."

"That'll be just two pounds, then," he replied as he turned it out on his machine.

Despite being flustered, she couldn't help but notice the whole procedure seemed a bit strange, while the fare itself appeared absolutely absurd.

"I don't understand," she protested feebly. "It's usually only about tuppence. So why has it suddenly become so expensive?"

"Well," the driver retorted, "times have moved

on a bit, you know." Then, in complete ignorance of any irony he added, "That might have been the fare when your dress was in fashion but it's certainly not now, I'm afraid."

With her emotions at breaking point and less than a pound in her bag, Jill felt overwhelmed and the tears began to prick at her eyes.

"Oh, I don't know what to do," she replied desperately. "I haven't even got that much money on me. I can't understand why it's so much. I'll just have to get off and walk."

"You'll do absolutely no such thing," came a sudden interruption. "It's no place out there for a young lady on her own, especially on a night like this."

Turning, Jill noticed a kindly-faced middle-aged man who had apparently watched the entire exchange from the rear of the bus and who had moved forward to her rescue.

"Here's the young lady's fare," he offered handing over the correct money. "Now if you'll be kind enough to give her the ticket, the problem's solved."

Jill felt a wave of relief; a relief that was obvious.

"Oh, that's very kind of you," she breathed gratefully. "I can't tell you how much that's helped me."

"I sensed you were in a bit of a flap," he observed sympathetically. "Please think nothing of it."

Then, with a boyish smile and a dismissive wave he returned to his seat wishing, perhaps, he were some forty years younger.

Exhausted and weary, Jill collapsed thankfully onto the nearest seat where she released a long pent-up sigh of gratitude. Glancing around the virtually empty bus, she hungrily soaked up its comforting familiarity. The patterned upholstery and the welcome warmth of its interior seemed to confirm a return to normality. However, it felt a little strange to have boarded the bus at the front and pay the driver instead of the conductor who, she remembered, would normally have dispensed the tickets. But she quickly dismissed these apparent anomalies in the relief of the moment as she elatedly turned her thoughts to a reunion with John.

She tried to envisage his reaction at seeing her after nearly a year, although she'd long realised it possible that he might now be in another relationship. Leaning back Jill closed her eyes and tried to brace herself from such an eventuality. Looking down at her left hand now devoid of its precious ring, she knew only too well the gamble she'd taken, for, despite his eccentricities, no one could have been more devoted to her than Greg. Miserably, she wondered how he would cope with the news of her decision. A thought that made her feel wretchedly guilty knowing how she had toyed with his life and emotions. Incredible as it seemed, Jill really believed she had been the only woman he'd ever taken seriously. Bitterly she recalled her words the day he gave her his mother's ring: *'I promise you faithfully it will now be my most precious possession and I will never, ever, take it off.'* So much for her word, she thought sadly.

However, her recriminations were suddenly cut short by the driver:

"Portslade Station. This is as far as we go."

It had now been dark for some time and as Jill tried to peer out of the window there was little to be seen except the reflection of the bus's lighted interior. However, this did nothing to detract from her overwhelming excitement at the prospect of being so close to home, for it all seemed so unbelievable as she finally stepped from the bus. For a brief moment she just stood to soak up the familiarity of her surroundings. Even the normally dreary-looking grey pavement slabs seemed to have assumed a certain magic. She had no idea of the time, but imagined it to be late evening, because despite a prevailing mist, most of the shop window lights along the busy Boundary Road high street were still visible. She remembered poignantly how Greg had referred to this road as Drove Street but that, she thought nostalgically, had been his world.

Yet, despite the reduced visibility, everything looked just how she remembered it with, perhaps, the exception of numerous cars picking their way through the gloom. However, this was a detail that barely registered for all she could think of was closing her front door on everything she'd been through and resuming her normal life.

Unable to contain herself, she raised her long

skirt and broke into an ungainly run down the mist-filled streets that had once been the domain of Old Goacher's farm and where Greg had so tragically lost his beloved horse. She glanced briefly in the direction of the railway embankment and the Cattle Arch but they were completely obscured by the all-prevailing fog.

Turning at last into Norway Street, she finally found herself outside number 62 and, briefly leaning on one of the garden pillars to catch her breath, she reached into her shoulder bag for the keys. A light shone from the front door glass panels and she was overjoyed to realise someone was in and that the long-awaited moment of reunion had arrived.

Frantically she inserted the key in the lock, but to her utter disbelief, found it failed to turn and subsequent attempts proved equally futile. Exasperated to breaking point, she banged furiously on the door.

"Mum! Anna! It's me, Jill. I'm home!" However, it seemed interminable before there was any response and she heard herself mutter impatiently, "Come on. Hurry up, hurry up."

It required a further determined assault on the door before she heard a movement from deep within the house and the appearance of someone's silhouette on the glass panel. Filled with anticipation, she prepared to go in, but then only to recoil as the door swung back to reveal a complete stranger. Totally nonplussed, she could only take in the most general impression of a young man somewhere in his early twenties: of medium height and wearing thick pebble-type lenses he looked every inch the typical student.

"Good evening," he greeted her affably. "Is there something I can do for you?"

For a brief moment she found herself unable to speak although, finally, managed a rather incoherent:

"Who the hell are you?"

"Well, for what it's worth," he answered in the same friendly manner, "I'm Mr Johnson; Ben Johnson that is."

A million questions flooded her mind while, once again, the horrific and familiar sensation of losing her grip on reality began to take hold. Finally, she struggled to formulate a more coherent response:

"Look. I'm Jill Bower and *this* is *my* home, so may I ask what the devil you're doing here and, more to the point, where are my mother and my daughter?"

The conundrum was absolute for they were on entirely different wavelengths. From Ben's perspective it was late evening and he was faced with a completely strange and apparently deranged woman. A woman whose bizarre appearance alone was disconcerting enough for, with her long blonde hair and full-length costume, she presented an eerie if enticing proposition.

"Are you sure," he ventured cautiously, "that you have the right address?"

"Yes," she snapped irritably. "Of course I'm sure. This is number 62 and I've lived here all my life, so I ought to know."

Taken aback, the poor man seemed at a loss but was suddenly rescued from within the house by the sound of an elderly woman's voice enquiring irritably what was going on.

"That's my grandmother," he informed her with an obvious sense of relief. "She's lived in the area all her life so perhaps she might be able to help you. But please, do come in. It's such an unpleasant night out there."

Bewildered and now utterly dejected, Jill followed the young man inside where she immediately realised it was no longer the cosy little home she remembered. Gone was the narrow hallway with its separate doors leading off to the 'best' front room, and the small, cramped living room at the rear. Now the staircase led down into one large open space, which was illuminated by spotlights set high in the ceiling. Aghast at the change and standing transfixed she vainly cast about for something, anything in fact, that was familiar. Desperately, she looked, but there was nothing. Absolutely nothing.

Feeling numbed, her attention was drawn to what appeared to be a small cinema screen on the rear wall. Situated not far from the window that had once witnessed the horrific fight between her father and her mother's lover, it seemed to be showing a film, although its clarity and vivid colour far exceeded anything she'd experienced at the local movies. Very few homes in 1947 possessed a television set and she'd never actually seen one, but she did know their tiny screens were, at best, only capable of a very indifferent monochrome picture. Therefore, the sight of this marvel only served to reinforce her earlier unease that something was desperately wrong. Even while struggling with a reeling mind, Jill found herself being introduced to the grandmother. A frail old lady who had been peering at the screen with obvious difficulty, and who certainly seemed far from pleased by the interruption of her viewing.

"Gran," shouted the young man. "This young lady has a problem." He turned to Jill and explained in a more moderated voice, "Sorry – she's ninety-six and can't hear very well. That's why I have to shout." At this, he again raised his voice, "Can you tell us if you've ever heard of a Mrs Bower?"

Obviously still unable to hear, the old woman shook her head impatiently as she fiddled unsteadily with her hearing aid.

"I can't hear a word you're saying, Ben," she protested. "You'll just have to shout louder or write it down."

Patience, it appeared, was not one of the old girl's virtues and her grandson responded with a deep sigh.

"This is very remiss of me. Please, do take a seat while I try to make her understand. And, sorry, I didn't catch your first name."

"Oh, just call me, Jill." she replied vacantly.

"Right then, Jill. I'm afraid this won't be easy, but I'll do my best."

Finally, with the question written in large capitals and placed in the old lady's hand, they waited tentatively for a response. When it came, it only confirmed Jill's worst fears for, as the grandmother looked over the top of her glasses she again shook her head.

"Yes," she faltered eventually. "I've certainly heard of this lady, if that's what you'd call her. In fact," she continued, "she used to live in this very house, but she's been dead for some forty years or more. Well before your time, of course, young Ben."

Now completely stunned, all Jill could do was stare at the old woman in absolute disbelief while Ben, who was about Jill's own age, also looked at odds with this revelation – although for entirely different reasons.

"I'm sorry," he said turning to his unexpected visitor, "but I just don't understand. How can your mother have been dead for forty years? I mean... well, you're too young."

Devastating as it was, this latest revelation barely pierced the fog of Jill's already beleaguered brain. Yet, despite the mental turmoil, she vaguely realised that the time disruption she had experienced had now placed her somewhere in the future. And, while struggling to cope with its various implications, she, nevertheless, instinctively sought to conceal her true predicament.

"Oh," she hastened to explain. "She's obviously talking about my grandmother."

But, even as Jill spoke, there again came the quivering sound of the old lady's voice.

"Anyway, why does this young woman want to know about Mrs Bower? She was a disgrace to the neighbourhood." Then, with a senile impertinence, possibly only excusable in the very old, she asked, "And why on earth is she parading around in that funny costume?"

Angered and sensing the futility of the situation, Jill prepared to leave, but not before trying to find out the fate of her little girl, so she again turned to the young man.

"Could you please ask your grandmother if she knows anything about a little girl called Anna. She used to live here and would only have been about three in 1947."

After scrutinising this second question, the old lady seemed to tire, and closing her eyes, she leaned back in her chair with a sigh.

"What I remember of it," she said finally in rather slow and definitive tones, "is that Mrs Bower... or Rita as she preferred to be called... had an illegitimate girl with a Canadian soldier and," she added spitefully, "a thoroughly grubby affair it was. But that's the only child I know of and I certainly can't recall her name."

Listening to the old woman's vindictive tirade, took Jill back once again to that fateful day when her father unexpectedly returned home from the war. She remembered the terrifying fight and the inquisitive crowd of self-righteous neighbours who were gathered outside as the badly beaten Canadian was stretchered out to the waiting ambulance. Suddenly, in a flash, she recognised the grandmother as being one of that vociferous crowd; although she had obviously been a great deal younger in those days. However, the old woman had apparently remained the same prejudicial, caustic busybody she'd been then. And she was far from finished as her memories began to flow back.

"Now I come to think of it," the old girl muttered, "I believe she had a much older daughter as well. In fact, I seem to remember she looked a lot like her mother. They used to think of themselves as the local glamour girls, that was it; the local glamour girls. Certainly they flaunted themselves round the local men. I'm just trying to recall the elder daughter's name... it was something like Jane or Jean... No!" she suddenly exclaimed triumphantly. "It was Jill! That was the name."

Again her grandson looked perplexed.

"But that's your name, isn't it?" he queried turning to his guest. "She can't be referring to you, it's just not possible."

"No, she's not," retorted Jill with a touch of exasperation. "She's getting confused again and talking about my mother. We both have the same first names." It was, of course, all lies but with no desire to become bogged down in any further inane exchanges, she determined to leave. "Thank you for your help, Ben. I appreciate it, but I've been here long enough already. I'm just sorry to have troubled you."

She made for the door, but her host was not so easily dismissed and knowing he could not be overheard, obviously felt free to speak openly.

"Look – I'm sorry about my grandmother's uncharitable remarks. But that's the way she is. Even at her age she still just ups and speaks her mind."

"I noticed," Jill responded acidly. "You'd think she'd have learned better."

He shrugged and looked awkward.

"I don't pretend to understand what's gone on here tonight. None of it makes any sense that I can see. So I really don't know how to help, much as I'd like to." He paused as if uncertain quite what to say. "Well, I mean, you obviously think, for whatever reason, that this is your home so, where will you go from here? I can't just turn you out onto the streets – especially on a night like this."

Jill's mind was frozen by confusion and disappointment. She found it difficult to make any immediate reply, but finally she insisted:

"Please don't worry. It's not your problem – I'll be fine."

Despite Jill's protests, her distraught and shattered appearance prompted Ben to persist.

"Look. We have a spare room. At least I could put you up for the night and then, in the morning, perhaps we could contact the Social Services. I'm sure they would be able to help you." Jill had barely heard of such an organisation but, in any case, had no desire to be brought to the authorities' attention – no matter what title they might labour under – and, opening the front door, stepped resolutely out into the night. However, as she retreated down the garden path, Ben called out after her, "Please, at least let me give you a coat or you'll freeze out there in that dress."

For a moment Jill hesitated, but it was enough and allowed him to grab an overcoat from the hallstand before draping it loosely around her shoulders. It was a kind gesture and she showed her appreciation.

"Thank you and goodnight."

But her tone was resolute and echoed a finality that forbade any further discussion as she moved out onto the pavement and became engulfed by the all-prevailing mist.

Now wrapped in the heavy overcoat, she again leaned back on one of the familiar pillars of her old home and breathed a sigh of relief as she heard the front door of 62 finally close. Even a deep gulp of the foggy air felt refreshing after the stifling atmosphere of the old woman's vindictiveness. At least the working-class bigotry in the area had remained unchanged.

She thought longingly of Rose and wondered briefly how two people could be so different. But it was a nostalgia quickly superseded by the starkness of her predicament, for she felt utterly cold inside and desperately isolated. Standing on the darkened pavement, she squinted up at the street lights as they vainly endeavoured to penetrate the persistent gloom. Suddenly, she realised how they differed from the ones she remembered. In fact, in some bizarre way, this didn't even feel like *her* Norway Street at all.

She recalled the exorbitant bus fare and the endless rows of shadowy parked cars, which now began to make some sort of sense. Sinking down onto the kerb in despair, she again experienced the abject mental vacuum that had accompanied her separation from John. But then Rose had been there, a veritable angel who had stooped down in the hour of her desperate need. But now there was no Rose. This time she was completely alone.

As Jill squated wretchedly on the edge of the pavement, she bitterly regretted how hastily she had abandoned her dear friend and longed for her reassuring presence. However, Rose, like the rest of her recent experiences, had now become little more than a fast-fading dream. Furthermore, it was all too obvious that any hope she might have entertained of a return to normality was now nothing more than wishful thinking. In her desolate state, it seemed impossible to imagine how she was, in fact, probably only a matter of yards from the spot where Greg had proposed on that beautiful hot afternoon. A lovely day, when a blackbird had swooped down from a clear blue sky.

Now all she could see were the once familiar but ghostly outlines of suburbia and endless banks of swirling mist, which were so thick she could actually taste the damp. She turned her thoughts to John and bitterly recalled how she had envisaged their reunion, but now she had no means of knowing whether he was even still alive. Depressed beyond measure, her mind turned to the aspirins in her shoulder bag, but just as quickly, she dismissed any such idea, and, levering herself up, determined on one final port of call. John's old home was just round the corner and she briefly wondered if, perhaps, just if... She knew, under normal circumstances, his parents' shop stayed open late in order to catch any last-minute customers and, in her mind's eye, she could still see the lights from its windows streaming out in welcome.

However, as Jill turned the bend in Gordon Road, any such hopes she might have entertained were immediately dashed, for the reliable beacon had long since been extinguished by the passage of time. She stared in dismay at the bricked-up shop doorway and then at the domestic windows which now replaced their larger counterparts. Manifestly this was also not *her* Gordon Road either and, for a moment, she faltered, being uncertain quite what to do. It was already late; probably, she estimated, somewhere in the region of 10pm, which made her realise that if she were to make any move it would have to be at once.

Conscious of her weird appearance, Jill slowly approached the once familiar side-entrance. However, one thing remained unchanged and that was the lack of either a doorbell or knocker. So, reluctantly, she gently tapped on the front door glass panel. After a brief wait, it was again answered by a complete stranger who peered nervously out into the gloomy night. Jill was quick to recognise the apprehension of an elderly person who she estimated to be somewhere in his early eighties.

"I'm sorry to disturb you at such a late hour," she apologised gently. "But it's vital that I contact a Mr John Harper who used to live here. I wondered if, perhaps, you might know anything of his whereabouts?"

Visibly relieved to discover that his late-night caller was nothing more threatening than a woman, the householder leaned back against the doorframe while cupping his hand reflectively over his chin.

"I've certainly heard the name," he admitted slowly. "I'm trying to think. I seem to believe he was caught up in some sort of unsavoury business with a local girl and moved away. I don't know all the details. But, as to his whereabouts now, I'm afraid I can't help you; although, come to think of it, the people next door might know something because they've lived in the area for many years. Anyway, I wish you luck."

The man slowly closed the door to again leave Jill in the gloom and none the wiser.

Even just looking at the adjacent house made Jill hesitate for there was no sign of any lights and she wondered if the occupants hadn't already gone to bed. However, with nothing to lose, she walked cautiously up the garden path and gently knocked on the front door. To her surprise and relief, it was answered relatively quickly by two people whom she took to be husband and wife. At first, they both tried to speak at the same time although it was the gentleman who was the first to give way.

"Good evening," the woman smiled warmly. "This is an unexpected pleasure. We don't seem to get so many visitors these days. So, can we help you in any way?"

She was a diminutive person who spoke with a strong northern accent and, although quite elderly, exuded a warmth reminiscent of Rose. To the emotionally exhausted Jill, this came as very welcome.

"I'm sorry to trouble you," she apologised. "But the gentleman next door suggested that you might be able to help me." Although acutely conscious of her bizarre appearance, she continued tentatively, "You see, I'm trying to contact a Mr John Harper who used to live there when it was a shop and I wondered, perhaps, if you remember him or might know where he can be contacted."

It could have been her imagination, but Jill thought the man suddenly caught his breath at the mention of John's name, although his response was amicable enough.

"Yes. I certainly remember him. Although he hasn't been seen in these parts for years. But, please," he invited, "do come in. It's such a foul night and we can talk more comfortably inside."

Once in the brighter light of their living room, Jill was shocked to recognise the woman as being a much older version of someone she had occasionally encountered in Jack's little shop and hoped fervently that neither of them would remember her. She tried to keep her face slightly bowed and away from their direct gaze.

"I'm sorry," apologised her host. "I'm afraid I didn't catch your name, but in any case, could I perhaps offer you a cup of tea or something?"

Desperate to conceal her identity, Jill had no option but to lie.

"Oh, just call me Susan. And yes, thank you. It's been a long day. I'd love a cup."

Finally, with the three of them grouped around the small living room table, the sequence of events during Jill's absence slowly became clearer by the minute.

"Yes," repeated the man. "I remember John Harper. Well, we both do, don't we?" he added nodding towards his wife. He paused briefly to take a sip from his cup. "In fact, John and I used to attend the same school: Windlesham Elementary School for Boys, to be exact. No eleven plus and grammar schools in those days." He sighed wistfully."But, of course, we were a lot younger then. Although John was a bit older than me. Let me see. He'd be in his late seventies by now; well, that's supposing he's still alive."

"Jim," interrupted his wife. "None of that is of any help to this young lady. She simply wants to know John's whereabouts and, the fact is..."

But Jim was a northerner in full flow and someone who obviously enjoyed the sound of his own voice.

"We used to be regular customers in the little shop you know. It was very handy and quite a social centre in its way. John's mother served behind the counter and was always willing to spare time for a chat. Then, of course, there was Mrs Grimshaw from number 11 who helped out occasionally. No little corner shops now, only massive supermarkets on the outskirts of town with no sense of community spirit at all. But, be that as it may, the Harpers were good neighbours and, you know, sometimes in my mind I can still hear Jack rattling along on his old trades bike. It was all very sad. Very sad."

"Why?" asked an increasingly frustrated Jill. "What was so sad?"

"Sad," interjected the woman, "because it was John's liaison with a local girl that we believe led, indirectly, to his mother's premature death."

At this point, the husband again took up the story.

"While I don't want to condemn anyone, it's my honest belief that the Harpers were as closely knit and honourable a family as you could wish to find.

416

Well, until that is, the mysterious disappearance of this girl my wife's just mentioned. You see, she'd already had an illegitimate child which, in those days... well, you can imagine." He shrugged expressively. "Anyway, as far as I understand it, the last time anyone saw this girl was in his car on their way to college. But, from that day on, she was never seen again. He always maintained they'd stopped along Church Road for her to get out and buy some cigarettes and that she had never returned. But I don't think anyone really believed him."

"Jim!" protested his wife again. "None of all that is of help to this young lady."

"No, no, that's fine," insisted their visitor for, though anxious to establish John's whereabouts, she was nevertheless fascinated to find out what had been happening while she was away.

Undeterred, the husband pulled a face before pressing on.

"Certainly the police had severe doubts about his account because they hauled him back to the station on numerous occasions. It was all a bit macabre really. There were massive searches for the girl but she was nowhere to be found. They even excavated a fresh grave in St Andrew's churchyard in case he'd buried her in the loose soil. But, as my wife just mentioned, it was his mother I felt sorry for. She was a lovely woman and it must have been a terrible shock for her. All the local and national newspapers had a field day. Everybody around

417

here was sure he'd murdered her. They ostracised the whole family and avoided the little shop like the plague." At this point he suddenly slapped his hand on the table and turned to his wife. "Do you remember that terrible Christmas Eve shortly after it had all happened?"

"Strictly speaking," she objected, "what you're thinking about happened in the early hours of Christmas Day." Then, addressing Jill, she added, "You see, Jim and I sleep in the top front room and on that particular night I was violently shaken awake by the sound of smashing glass. Mind you, *he*..." she smiled, indicating her elderly husband, "could sleep through an earthquake and would have done had I not roused him. Let me see, it must have been around 1am I think. Anyway, we both heard a lot of loud voices and more glass being smashed, so it soon became obvious that the shop next door was being attacked. We both rushed to the window to see what was going on, but the street lights around here go off at midnight which made it impossible to see anything. It was only the next day we realised the full extent of the damage. The shop front was completely boarded up, and in the deep snow the whole place looked like a disaster area."

"In fact," stressed her husband, "I believe Violet died that very night. You see, she'd already had a stroke. I remember because we'd not seen her in the shop for weeks. Obviously, all the trauma was the final straw and, you know, she was comparatively young." He looked at his wife. "What would you say she was? Fifty? Something like that."

She nodded sadly.

"But what really got me was that Violet never lived to realise her dream of a little place in the country. She often used to talk to me about her plans to live in a small village somewhere – but, of course, that was destined never to happen."

Patiently, Jill again raised the question concerning John's whereabouts.

"Well," answered his wife, "all we know is that John's father died shortly after his wife, and the shop was sold. Then, both their son and his sister, Margaret, moved away almost immediately. There was just nothing left to keep them here. You see, John was completely shunned by almost everyone; nobody trusted him. Do you know? I've even heard how some people would cross the road to avoid him. It must have been a living hell – especially if he was innocent. But, of course, you can never be sure because only *he* knew the truth."

Jill felt an unbearable sadness well up as the details continued to unfold. "I don't know how true this is," the woman added, "but I heard from somewhere that he repeatedly returned to the scene of her disappearance." She shrugged. "Whether, of course, you can place any credence on that is another matter. In any case, it might have been just a ploy."

Jill knew only too well it was the very sort of thing she would have expected of him. Nevertheless, she asked yet again, "And you've no idea where John might have gone?"

The husband shook his head.

"I'm afraid not. I did hear he'd been killed in a road accident. But again, that might only have been a rumour."

So, Jill had finally come to a dead end and, although feeling utterly deflated, she ventured a final question.

"You mentioned this young woman had a child. I don't suppose either of you know what became of her?"

The wife sat quietly for a moment.

"I think her family lived in Norway Street but, really, we didn't know much about what went on round there. Do you happen to recall anything about a child, Jim?"

Her husband shook his head while again mentioning the time factor which, in turn, caused Jill to ask desperately:

"But how long ago? Just how long ago are we talking about?"

"Hmm..." he muttered uncertainly. "It must be all of some fifty years. Let me see, the young woman disappeared around 1947. So, yes, it must be about some fifty years plus."

At last, Jill had a clear picture of the situation. She was half a century ahead of her time which, she suddenly realised in horror, would make her close to eighty years old. Although, as she glanced down at the backs of her hands, they gave no hint of such an age.

"But, in answer to your earlier question," her host continued, "now I come to think of it, I believe there were two small children involved. One of them – I'm not sure which – eventually married young Mr Baker. I remember that because his father ran the local tobacconist company, and when he relocated to the States it caused a lot of local unemployment. But what happened to the other child, I'm afraid I've no idea."

For a short time, the little trio sat in silence, a silence which was eventually broken by the mantelpiece clock chiming 11pm. Finally, as Jill rose to leave, she inadvertently allowed her face to catch the full glare of the main light and for an awful moment, feared that she might be recognised.

"You know," observed the husband, "when I come to look at you, it's almost as though I were looking at that poor girl all over again. Strange coincidence. Anyway," he apologised, "I'm just sorry we can't be of more help." Then, on the way to the front door, he stopped briefly. "Just out of curiosity, may I ask if any of these people were relatives. I know tracing ancestors has become quite a popular pastime lately."

At this she replied with a wan smile.

"Yes, I suppose in a sort of way, they were." With that, she held out her hand in a parting gesture. "Well, thank you both for your time. It was especially kind of you at this late hour and it's been more informative than you can know."

The husband took her hand and nodded as he opened the front door.

"It's still very unpleasant out there – have you got far to go?"

"No, not too far," she smiled. "And, in any case, I've got this heavy coat."

It was, of course, a direct lie which obscured the stark reality that Jill had absolutely nowhere to go. As the front door closed with a ring of finality, she found herself once again alone in the mist-impregnated darkness. Standing on the corner of Gordon Road, she became engulfed in an unbelievable sense of despair and pulled the overcoat ever tighter round her shoulders as she wondered what on earth to do next.

At this late hour, the once familiar urban area was deathly silent and deserted. The only hint of movement came from the mist as it swirled about the street lights, and as if to add to this melancholy atmosphere, it slowly began to drizzle. And there, in the gently falling rain, Jill tried to draw strength from the memory of her friend Rose, but it did not come easily in this void of hope. She glanced towards the indistinct outline of John's old home and numerous memories of the busy life that once flowed round it flooded back. Now, there was only this utterly unbearable quiet. Everything it seemed was dead as, she suspected, were the people themselves.

Longingly, she thought of John and all they had meant to each other.

'And when we are apart we'll remember this place.'

Suddenly she knew exactly where she was going although, at the same time, realised it would entail braving the interior of the forbidding Cattle Arch.

The underpass itself lay directly opposite Jack's old business premises, but she was well aware that it was a place to be avoided in daylight let alone in the dead of the night. Above all, there was the total quiet capable of generating mental horrors even where none existed. Nevertheless, to reach her objective, she knew there was no other option, and steadying herself, she crossed the road and gradually edged her way down the narrow lane which led to the black opening. But, when she finally faced the brooding entrance, an acute sense of vulnerability caused her to hesitate. The blackness was made worse, by a curve in the tunnel's structure. She could see no sign of an exit and it gave the whole thing an almost cave-like quality.

However, even with the continued rain and darkness, she steeled herself to again inch her way forward. Although, once inside, she instinctively shrank back against the moss-covered walls and desperately clung to the ancient brickwork in order to maintain any sense of direction. Apart from an unsavoury reputation, the cavern itself was a filthy place with an air of damp that mingled freely with the smell of dog urine and their faeces; a stench that made her feel physically sick. Nevertheless, gradually but gradually, she persisted ever deeper into the abyss while, despite the velvet-like layer of moss, she still managed to cut her finger quite badly on a sharp protruding piece of masonry. In her agitated state, however, the pain almost went unnoticed. Suddenly the oppressive quiet unexpectedly became rent by a far-off cry of an animal in dire distress which was, probably, the last anguish of a chicken as it succumbed to the predatory activities of a local fox. Nevertheless, it was a sound that sent a shiver right through her.

However, as Jill reached the bend it became just possible to make out the oval-topped exit. But even as she breathed a sigh of relief, there came a slight tremor in the walls; a tremor that gradually grew in intensity until the whole edifice began to shake. But, after a fleeting moment of terror, she heard the reassuring whistle of a steam train and a rushing sound overhead that heralded the midnight express to Portsmouth.

Once the vibrations slowly died away, Jill couldn't help comparing her lot with the passengers in their comfortable seats, all of whom were, undoubtedly, on their way to familiar and secure destinations. Finally, emerging from the cavernous ordeal, Jill was still conscious of unspoken horrors flickering around her shoulders, and even glanced back fearfully in case some real or imaginary terror had followed out after her.

Straight ahead lay a steep incline which led to the main east-west bound Victoria Road. But, as gusts of rain swept into her face, Jill felt little enthusiasm for what she knew lay ahead. The road itself, which was almost completely obscured by mist and rain, ran north of and parallel to the railway embankment. Perhaps more significantly, it marked the boundary between Portslade recreation ground and the local cemetery. Therefore, as Jill peered over the park wall, she couldn't help feeling aware of the numerous fog-enshrouded graves that lay immediately behind her.

Although effectively retracing the footsteps of her first date with John, Jill was now facing a very different and daunting proposition, for the normally inviting recreation ground with its little tea house and rose gardens appeared nothing more than a pitch-dark misty expanse. Even the street lamps marking its boundary had been reduced to mere pinpricks of light in the prevailing gloom. It all combined to make any thoughts of spending the night out there a terrifying prospect. But she had a stark choice between lying down on the wet street pavement for the rest of the night or braving the unknown in favour of a park bench. However, it was not just any bench she had in mind but the one she had first shared with John.

Still uncertain what to do, she gazed back at the totally deserted Victoria Road awash with fog and rain. Again her mind turned to John. She so desperately wished he could be with her now.

Finally, however, with no alternative she reached the entrance and pushed back the wrought-iron gate, which screeched deafeningly in the utter silence. For a moment it seemed that the drizzle had eased, but the inky blackness made it virtually impossible to remain on the path, let alone locate a specific bench. Frustrated and weary, she eventually became reduced to groping about like a blind person.

Finally but finally, her ankle came into painful contact with something solid, while further groping confirmed the discovery of her objective. By this time, however, she was beyond caring which bench it was and, utterly spent, just sank down thankfully on to its unfogiving, saturated surface.

For several moments she could only sit in the miserable damp gloom feeling breathless and drained from all the emotional tension and physical effort. Gradually, the night chill began to bite, and without even attempting to get up, she struggled to push her arms through the sleeves of the long overcoat. It was far too large and she had to roll back the cuffs in order to free her hands. Nevertheless, she was extremely grateful to even have it and for the neighbour's kindness at number 62.

For without it, she would have been in for a night of exposure and extreme cold.

After securing the buttons to her neck and stretching out on the hard bench, she attempted to switch off her frantically overactive mind and shelve the imponderables until the following day. But the deadly hush of the park gave her the horrors while an overriding sense of loneliness was so strong that it felt almost like a physical presence. A feeling which made her all too aware of how vulnerable she was so late at night and in such a public place.

She found herself straining to catch the slightest sound that might indicate a threat, while at the same time trying to take comfort from the improbability of there being any prowlers during the one night she happened to be there. Imagination, however, can be very powerful and that, more than anything else, provided the real hell, although she also strove to reassure herself that her silence and the very darkness itself would afford sufficient protection.

Turning onto her back, she again experienced the chill of fine drizzle on her face, and staring up into the blackness she found it difficult not to compare her predicament with the quality of life that had been on offer at Merton Hall. A life she had voluntarily exchanged, it now seemed, for one of vagrancy. To avoid the rain, she turned back on her side to face the direction of the fog-bound Victoria Road. Now fluctuating on the borders of sleep, she wondered vaguely if it was the same mist that had engulfed the Vicarage during her last hours with Rose or whether it had any connection with the fog she and John had first encountered along Church Road. But a hundred years ago...? So, how...? Lucidity, however, was slowly slipping away as she gradually sank into the merciful oblivion of sleep.

* * *

The following morning, awareness returned to the mellow chime of church bells, but at first, being only partly awake, she found it difficult to identify their source. Slowly, it dawned on her that the sound was not coming from St John's Church near the Vicarage but rather the Parish Church of Portslade and the brutal reality of her situation stormed back. In spite of the overcoat, a night spent in the open on an uncomfortable bench had left her feeling cold and stiff. Worse, as she gradually levered herself up, she found the pain in her shoulder had also returned. Gazing blearily around the park, she could see that what little mist remained now hung in a thin veil just above the grass while the dew still on the ground sparkled in a late autumn sun.

By the pealing of the bells and the freshness of the air, she took it to be a Sunday morning and probably in the region of 10am. Apart from a couple walking their dog in the distance, the park seemed completely deserted. This came as a relief knowing how strange and dishevelled she must appear.

Swinging her feet to the ground, Jill realised just how hungry and thirsty she had become. A condition, she suspected, not uncommon to the vagrant way of life. Sitting miserably hunched up in the overcoat, she so longed for a hot cup of tea and remembered only too well the many she had enjoyed at the Vicarage. Now there was no access to even a glass of water. It reminded her of the tea room at the far side of the park. She was surprised to see it was still there looking very much as it did the day she had enjoyed a coffee there with John. She wondered idly if it was open, but being mindful of the bus fare incident, doubted very much whether the little money she had would be either valid or sufficient to buy anything. However, such thoughts helped her focus on a serious appraisal of her prospects. Were her circumstances really any different from those of poor Martha she asked herself? Martha who had faced the possibility of life on the streets.

The night had been cold and it made her wonder what January and February might be like out in the open. That was without taking into account the need for food. She had abandoned Martha with no thought for her welfare. She had almost certainly broken Greg's heart and willingly left behind the best friend she was ever likely to have. Was this then her just desserts, she thought miserably. Bereft of any means of support, the idea of homelessness seemed unbearable. But, without being able to establish her identity and with no valid credentials, she knew it would be impossible to find employment.

Also belonging to the mid-1940s made 2001, or there abouts, seem inconceivably far in the future, and by all dictates she should now be a very old woman while John, if he was still alive, would also be a similar age. Effectively it meant that her immediate relatives were, in all probability, long since dead, and even little

Anna would now be well into late middle age and, apparently, living somewhere in America. Bitterly, Jill was forced to accept the inevitable conclusion that all those dear to her were once again forever beyond her reach.

With her emotional and mental reserves exhausted, she had little or nothing left with which to combat this final roll of fate's dice. All she could envisage was a slow and lonely death brought on by exposure and starvation. The thought of which drained away what little will she had to continue living.

Now dangerously depressed, she briefly considered the possibility of turning to the social welfare services, which she remembered was some kind of new local government agency. However, she dismissed the idea, feeling quite unable to contend with the inevitable barrage of questions and outright disbelief she knew would ensue. The reality was that, no matter how often or carefully she considered her circumstances, they all resulted in the same dead end.

Slowly and with a feeling of finality, Jill lifted her shoulder bag from the path and reached inside for the small bottle of aspirins her mother had so thoughtfully insisted she take on the morning of that last fateful car journey. Sitting there in the autumn chill and having made up her mind, she gazed sadly around the recreation ground for one last time.

By now, all remaining trace of the early morning mist had lifted and the church bells seemed to have assumed an ever-greater clamour of urgency. There were also more people about. In the distance, she could hear the delighted cries of children playing on the swings and a small group of boys had become busily engaged in a game of football not far from where she was sitting. This, she knew, was their world; a world in which she had no place and to which she did not belong.

However, it couldn't help but remind her of the many happy times spent as a child in this very park, which made the sadness almost more than she could endure. And so she emptied the bottle into the palm of her hand. Desperately hoping there would be sufficient, she put the first aspirin in her mouth, but before there was time to consume any more, a slight movement at the edge of her vision distracted her attention. Glancing sideways, she spotted a tiny robin perched on the metal armrest of the bench and beadily watching her every move. Poised on the brink, she hesitated for a second to watch the little creature's sharp movements as it agitatedly hopped about in an apparent concern over her activities. But, as she studied the antics of her little visitor, she was violently startled by a familiar voice.

"Nice dress. Though I'm not sure about the coat."

Thunderstruck and thinking herself to be completely alone, she looked up with eyes that widened in total disbelief.

"John!"

Incredibly, there he was. Just how she remembered

him. Sloppily dressed, unkempt, thick dark blond hair and a loosely buttoned shirt that had so obviously seen better days. Before she could speak or even think, he had reached to gather her up in his arms.

Then, with a mind barely able to cope, she finally managed to gasp breathlessly, "John! I don't understand! I mean, you're still young. But how can you be...?"

"Is there any good reason why I shouldn't be?" he insisted with his familiar boyish grin. But, after that, he only seemed able to repeat:

"I've got you back. I've got you back," as he pulled her ever closer.

Laughing and crying simultaneously, Jill felt the tears of relief well up as they stood tightly embraced in the morning sunshine, oblivious to what anybody might think. Then, quite suddenly, Jill's overwhelming pent-up emotions gave way and her initial tears of joy turned to an uncontrollable torrent of weeping.

"I'm so confused, John," she sobbed. "I'm so confused. I heard from one of the neighbours that your mother was dead and the shop no longer existed and that you..." she managed brokenly, "... and that you had also probably died."

At this outburst, his euphoria turned to alarm.

"That I'd done what?" he protested. "Who on earth gave you that idea? Because, as far as my mother's concerned, I know she's always been a bit on the anxious side, but she's still very much alive."

Jill's tears had helped to assuage much of the recent emotional turmoil that had brought her to the edge of suicide. However, even so, his words made no sense although, slowly, a new suspicion began to creep into her mind.

"John?" she asked in desperation. "Tell me, how long has it been since we lost contact in Church Road?"

Obviously surprised by the question, he was nevertheless quick to reply.

"Well. Let me see. I think it must be about a week. It's Sunday today, the 19th if I've got it right. So yes, it's just over a week. Why do you ask?"

"But the 19th of what?" she persisted urgently while ignoring his question.

"Well, October of course," he replied looking puzzled, but then added playfully, "1947 in case you're in any doubt."

Jill was too confused to appreciate his humour.

"John! Do you realise," she exclaimed frenziedly, "that I've been away for almost a year?" She sank uncomprehendingly onto the bench adding miserably, "How on earth can it have been only a week... unless...?"

Totally mystified by her behaviour, John immediately sat down and again took her in his arms just at the moment when the strident bells suddenly fell silent to leave an empty, almost eerie, calm.

"Well, it might have seemed like a year," he said

gently. "It certainly felt like it to me, but honestly, you've only been gone for about a week."

Everything he said totally contradicted what she'd been through since the time of their separation. It made the neighbours' descriptions of events seem little more than fiction. However, despite the blatant inconsistencies, nothing could detract from the sheer joy of their reunion for it symbolised a return to normality; a normality desperately yearned for, yet which had seemed so completely elusive. And, with the warmth of relief flooding over her, she determined to thrust all the imponderables to one side and bask in the sheer radiance of the moment. Mindful, perhaps, of the many lonely vigils spent at the Vicarage bedroom window.

Only later would she come to realise that her midnight ordeal through the Cattle Arch had, in some way, acted to compact the flow of time, thereby cancelling out the tragic events that would have occurred had she not returned, and which had been so graphically described by John's elderly neighbours. But, she agonised, if that were the case it raised serious and emotional questions about the duration of her stay at the Vicarage, which had included so many deep and lasting experiences. Now, however, there seemed a distinct possibility that the whole episode had been little more than a delusion probably brought on by her exposure to the Channel threat.

Jill often thought of the sad yet loveable Tom

and her dear friend Rose. Could they also have been only a product of some dream-like state? Above all, she tormented herself over her tenuous relationship with Greg. Was it possible even that could have been part of the same delusory process? Somehow she doubted it. Especially when remembering how she woke up on the park bench still clad in her long Victorian costume. Although, of course, the outsize overcoat presented difficulties of a different order. However, she reasoned, if proof were ever needed, surely it belonged to the scar on her shoulder.

Nevertheless, of one thing Jill was certain, she would never find any rest without knowing the final truth about the handsome, yet so unpredictable, stranger – Frederick Oliver Gregson.

The End